Some Place South of Perfect

ANDREW BYRNE

First published in Great Britain by Dockrell Books in 2012

ISBN: 978-0-9573059-0-8

TO JANET, ALWAYS.......

ACKNOWLEDGMENTS

There's no agent for me to acknowledge in this brave new publishing world so my heartfelt thanks to the people who encouraged me and kept a straight face when I said I was going to write a novel. You know who you are but special thanks to :

My family and extended family.

My ex-colleagues and eternal friends from the banking world, many of whom encouraged me to try my hand at words rather than numbers; especially Janet Heckman, Stewart Allen, Bridget Kennedy, Alan Skene and Barbara Mullaney.

Sonia Ribeiro at The Institute in East Finchley for allaying apprehensions about sharing my writing with an audience.

Stewart Permutt and everybody from the Muswell Hill WEA *Writing For Pleasure* group whose erudite opinions and joy in creative writing have been (and continue to be) inspiring and where a one-word prompt set this novel in motion.

Sasha Harker, my collaborator on an abandoned screenplay. As an environmentalist, I'm sure Sasha will approve of the couple of passages from the screenplay which I've recycled in this novel.

My friends and colleagues at Oxfam Books, Muswell Hill where I hope this book will add to the work-load. A special mention to Michael Freeman for alerting me to flaws in an earlier version.

Doug Heatherly for assistance with the cover design.

And most of all to my wife, Janet. This book is for you.

I wander thro' each charter'd street,
Near where the charter'd Thames does flow,
And mark in every face I meet
Marks of weakness, marks of woe.

William Blake, *Songs of Experience*

1 - WEDNESDAY

Later, Philip Anderson would remember the day as a series of increasingly unlikely occurrences, the first of which was a glimpse of a neighbour's leg. He stood among a small group of people, most of whom were on jury service, outside an Islington courthouse on a cold February morning awaiting admittance to the building. A man in a liveried suit solemnly announced a delay as the disgruntled group blew on their hands and stamped their feet against the chill. The man, confirmed by a name tag as Mr. Price, spoke to a young colleague, one who Philip thought was surely too young to work in the courthouse. The youth edged away from Mr. Price to escape an expletive-laden reprimand and rushed off as the stream of vitriol ended.

'Pillock,' Mr. Price muttered as he turned to face the group with a sanctimonious smile. 'My apologies everybody, one of my colleagues has mislaid a key but we should be furnished with a replacement within minutes. I'm afraid we have to wait here until then.'

There was a chorus of exasperated sighs as wrist watches and mobile phones were examined with exaggerated interest but Philip's attention was diverted by a new arrival. A taxi pulled up across the road and he watched as a shapely leg emerged from the cab and planted itself on the kerb. It belonged to a woman wearing a knee-length black coat, a woman Philip recognised as Elizabeth Harris, who lived only a few houses away from him.

She paid the driver and asked Mr. Price for directions to Court No. 5 - the same court to which Philip had been summoned for jury service. Well, this was a coincidence. His previous encounters with Elizabeth were mostly chance meetings in the street or at the local newsagent's where their conversations had been perfunctory. He knew little about her; her husband worked in banking and Philip guessed her age as early-30s, a couple of years younger than him. He walked towards her, smiling, but she turned on her heel, walked away and embraced a formally-dressed man who'd also just arrived. Philip attempted to nonchalantly retrace his steps but the delay and the cold had darkened the mood among the group on the pavement and he heard giggles as people registered his discomfort.

Elizabeth disappeared from view along with the formally-dressed man and Philip racked his brain as he tried to remember her profession. Lawyer or barrister? No, definitely not. Newspaper reporter? No, not that either. Maybe she worked for the administration staff at the courthouse? Again, no; had that been the case, she wouldn't need directions from Mr. Price. So, why was she here? His mind ran to fanciful conjecture. Had she been assigned to photograph the drabbest buildings in North London? Or was she an actress researching a court drama? Or a serial courtroom visitor with a morbid interest in winding up orders, petty offenders and applications for late-night bar extensions? Or even the courtroom equivalent of a trainspotter who trekked from one municipal building to another and jotted down details in a notebook?

Philip, amused by this, smiled and then realised he had been addressed by a ruddy-cheeked man who awaited his response. Making a show of being distracted, Philip stared at the man who frowned. 'I said we're finally being allowed inside,' he said and walked away from Philip shaking his head.

The chastened young man had returned, brandishing a key which Mr. Price snapped from his grasp. Everyone went inside to a briefing room where the jurors were addressed by a court official about their duties. Friends of Philip who had been on jury service described it variously as everything from days of stultifying boredom to a week of intrigue, either a welcome week off work or an imposition which would leave a backlog of tasks waiting their return. Philip smiled again as he remembered a particularly work-shy colleague who extended his jury service to two weeks having asked for extra time off to recover from the trauma of sitting in on a murder case. Philip realised that the ruddy-cheeked man was speaking to him again, this time in an infuriated tone.

'I said are you OK with that?'

Philip glanced around the group hoping for a clue but was met with blank expressions.

'Er, yeah,' he stammered, irked that the man seemed pleased with this reply.

'Fine, I'll be the foreman then,' the man said.

       ***

'Just here will be fine, thanks.' Elizabeth Harris spoke through the half-open window connecting the front and back of the taxi. The taxi halted, she climbed out, paid the driver and groaned when she saw the small group waiting outside the courthouse in the icy conditions. Would be just my luck to have some newsworthy case scheduled for today, she thought. A court official confirmed this was Court No. 5 and apologised for the temporary lack of access to the building. She exhaled with relief and then noticed one of her neighbours, Philip Anderson, among the disgruntled bunch. Elizabeth groaned again and this time it was mingled with real dread. A neighbour was the last person she wanted to see as a juror and being a juror had to be the reason for Philip's presence; this news would be all over Russell Road by the end of the week. Jesus Christ, Libby, you really have screwed up here.

When she saw Philip approach her, she stopped, turned away and saw Marcus, alighting from a taxi. She rushed to him and startled the circumspect Marcus when she greeted him warmly and acceded to his suggestion that they use a designated room for some final strategic discussions. She glanced back to see Philip trudging towards the courthouse. Was she compelled to disclose the presence of an acquaintance on the jury to her lawyer? Why had she ever got into this mess? A piece of recklessness was now developing awkward ramifications.

She could deal with her husband, Geoff, whose disapproval had been expressed without any attempt to understand why she had acted so uncharacteristically. His curt refusal to attend the court session, however, had angered her but a lot of things which Geoff did these days angered her. Still, this was her own fault; she had to stop thinking of herself as a victim. Show remorse, accept whatever fine was given – surely it wouldn't be more than a fine - and leave as soon as possible, she admonished herself. She listened to Marcus's advice and divulged that she knew one of the jurors.

'There's no obligation to disclose this but my advice is to not engage with him in conversation,' Marcus said in the dry, impartial tone he used for legal matters. He added that he'd find out the running order and left the room.

Elizabeth paced the floor, first in the room and then the corridor outside, glad to escape the confines of the airless room. A door opened in front of her and a group of people trooped through it. She saw Philip in their midst and froze as she registered the smile of recognition on his face. Once more, she blanked him, re-entered the stuffy room and waited for Marcus's return. Where was he? Was there a complication? She spotted a mirror in the corner of the room and peered at her image. A two-piece suit, subdued make-up, ear-rings and necklace reflected a woman of understated elegance, not somebody one expected to see in such surroundings. Her anxiety increased; she could be made an example of justice being blind. Unable to settle in the room, she again walked out into the corridor and saw Philip alone walking towards the exit, an unlit cigarette in his hand. At last, a chance to explain.

'Phi...,' she began before seeing Marcus turn a corner and walk towards her in the company of a man wearing a long black robe. Philip stopped as he heard her truncated greeting and turned to see Elizabeth disappearing through an open doorway. Oh God, she thought, this was entering the realm of slapstick. If she opened another door, she'd probably find a barrister and a judge writhing around, naked, on the floor. Marcus returned to the room, smiling.

'I've got good news and bad news,' he said. 'There won't be a jury for your case which probably means a small fine as long as you seem suitably contrite but it does mean you'll have to wait for a few hours before your case is heard. It'll be in Court No. 6.'

Elizabeth arranged to meet Marcus closer to the scheduled time for the case and resolved to seek out Philip as soon as she could to apologise for her erratic behaviour. In the meantime, she sat in the public gallery while the early cases in Court No.6 were heard.

***

Philip Anderson realised that a few days of tedium lay ahead. The North London courthouse's location accorded it a catchment area ranging from leafy streets with multi-million pound houses and residents with exalted social aspirations to over-crowded, often lawless, estates and tower blocks. The case he'd been assigned to involved a litany of thefts, assaults and intimidation perpetrated by a group of mixed-race teenagers. The defendant in the dock that morning was an 18-year old petty criminal with designs on becoming a major criminal. His swaggering posture and sullen insularity when addressed by the bench resulted in his lawyer whispering instructions to him to modify his demeanour.

Philip - whose preference was to hand the youth a stiff sentence - sat with his fellow jurors while they discussed the case and his mind returned to Elizabeth Harris. Why had she been so rude to him? It didn't square with his impression of her. Perhaps it was best to put her out of his mind if that was her reaction to him but he couldn't help feeling disappointed – she was attractive and he was single although she wasn't. Oh, somebody's speaking to me again.

'Mr. Anderson, in your own time, please.'

The sarcastic tone of the jury foreman grated with Philip but, unable to guess the question, he had no suitable retort.

'Well, I'm giving it some thought right now,' Philip improvised. 'Perhaps you'd like to ask somebody else and come back to me.'

'Everybody else has spoken, as you'd be aware had you been attentive,' the foreman sighed.

'Oh hang the little toerag and have done with it,' Philip snapped, impatiently.

4

Two people, one of whom winked at Philip, laughed; more assumed an outraged silence and others addressed the foreman in hushed, urgent whispers. Philip heard the words 'contempt of court'. This was becoming ridiculous.

'Look, I'm only thinking aloud. I don't condone capital punishment but this guy needs locking away for a while, for his own good too.' Philip noticed nods of agreement around the room. Warming to the task, he embarked on a long monologue explaining his rationale.

***

Elizabeth left Court Room No. 6, head bowed, until she reached the corridor outside where she clenched her fist and smiled. The judge had given her an £80 fine, warned her about her future conduct and praised her candour. In the corridor, she shook hands with Marcus and then rang her husband from her mobile.

'Geoff, it went OK. A gentle slap on the wrist and a small fine,' she said. Geoff's response was one of relief before he frostily added that he would be in a meeting until late in the evening. Aw, to hell with him, she thought and paused outside Court No. 5 where a notice indicated the day's session was due to finish at 3:30pm, ten minutes from now. She felt weightless, light-headed and decided to wait until Philip emerged. Soon, a door opened and Philip was one of the first to emerge, smiling.

'Philip,' Elizabeth called out.

Philip turned, saw Elizabeth and awaited another humiliating encounter.

'Oh, hello Elizabeth.'

'Look, I'm sorry about earlier, long story, well not so long but...,' she gushed. 'Er, fancy a coffee?'

Philip nodded, intrigued by this woman's strange mood swings. They found a table in a nearby café and ordered coffees.

'So?' Philip asked.

'Oh, it was just something frivolous which I did. Something and nothing,' she shrugged.

'Didn't look like that to me earlier. Er, you were avoiding me, weren't you?'

'Yes but I had a reason, honest. Look, I'd like something stronger than coffee, how about you?'

Minutes later, Elizabeth's feeling of weightlessness had extended to ordering two glasses of champagne in a wine bar across the road. As Philip waited for her to continue her tale, she waved a hand dismissively.

'Just a stupid mistake on my part.'

'You may as well tell me, Elizabeth. I'll keep schtum.'

'OK,' she sighed. 'I was having, y'know, one of those days...wandering around Sainsbury's picking up groceries and things. I thought "sod it" and walked out without paying.'

'You're kidding.'

'No. I tried to fob off some jobsworth with £100 when he stopped me but they insisted on pressing charges. Stupid of me, stupid of him but it's only resulted in a fine and a ticking off. Anyway, enough of that,' Elizabeth said, staring at her empty glass. 'I'm feeling extravagant. Another one?'

***

Elizabeth woke to the sonorous sound of snoring. Odd, Geoff doesn't normally snore. She saw from the bedside digital clock that it was 02:14...but she didn't have a bedside digital clock. Her woozy champagne-clouded brain unscrambled itself as the last 24 hours came back to her...starting with an early morning row with Geoff and ending up here, Jesus, how did that happen, why was Geoff so obstinate when he knew I was worried about the court case, ah well that's behind me now, the court case at least, along with what else I wonder, crossed the Rubicon here haven't I, Christ what a bizarre day, first all that avoidance of Philip at the courthouse, then seeking him out after my hearing, guess I shouldn't have worried about the case after all but that's easy in hindsight, judge was decent though, suppose I was a change after that sorry procession of losers with their petty crimes, well so was mine but I guess at least it looked like an aberration, I won't be as stupid again, well I say that but what I'm doing here isn't my normal behaviour either, I've never done this before Philip, cheated on Geoff that is, glad I told him that lest he think I'm well whatever, I've never questioned Geoff but *he* may have strayed at some stage, that Hannah at work with her smirk whenever I meet her, this is my invaluable assistant Hannah, OK whatever, God the feeling of weightlessness after I got that snotty response when I called Geoff, providence wasn't it to pass the court room and realise Philip's session was just ending, the look on Philip's face when I called him, funny, he didn't know what to expect from me by that stage, funny, that weightlessness, champagne enhanced it, made me feel reckless, what was it...one bottle, two and a couple of glasses, whatever, Philip's a good listener, I'm not used to such an attentive ear any longer I guess, so different to Geoff, Geoff has his mind made up before you're half way through a sentence whereas Philip seems generous with his advice, God, I'm comparing them already, at what stage did he see what was coming I wonder, inviting me in for a brandy to finish off the evening, must've been on his mind during the taxi journey, before that probably, definitely, God we were like awkward teenagers in the taxi, never did have that brandy, maybe I should wake him and ask where's the brandy, he'd find that funny, like his sense of humour, droll, and I like the way he glances at you over the top of his glasses, I get the impression that's worked for him before, well it worked with me anyway, probably should go home now, leave him a note, what'll I say to Geoff, he'll assume I've stayed at Rachel's again, best to play along with that for now, wonder if he texted me, my phone is downstairs, I think, not even sure where all my clothes are, yes what to say to Geoff, does he even care, do I care, yes I'll leave Philip a note and if Geoff wants to talk when I get home fine although he'll probably just tell me I'm drunk, sleep it off, got that weightless feeling again, maybe I should've done this a long time ago but we were happy then, maybe not the case now, him with his bloody deals and meetings, and I thought it was work which was making me unhappy or was it Geoff that was doing so, shouldn't have given up work, maybe time to return, need to sort out the whole Geoff thing first, crossed the Rubicon, God my mind's racing, need some rest, OK I'll leave a note, talk to Philip tomorrow, talk to Geoff tomorrow, Christ what a day, should get some sleep first maybe, yes, tired, tired and happy, apprehensive too, a bit anyway, Christ what a day.....

***

Philip was awoken by a leg encroaching into his half of the bed and the sound of somebody sighing languorously. His view of the bedside clock was obscured by a shoulder and tousled hair silhouetted against the faint streetlight which penetrated the curtains...Crikey, what a day that was, freezing my nuts off outside the courthouse, it's bloody cold still, guess I'm used to having the duvet all to myself these days, small price to pay, ah she's moved, just gone half-two, strange woman, strange in a good way, couldn't figure out what she was doing at first by ignoring me, other jurors picked up on it, could see the sly smiles, guess they were frozen and looking for any sort of diversion, can't blame them really, then that smarmy foreman, deliberately trying to catch me out I'd bet, was thinking about Elizabeth at the time too, well she has that effect, waiting outside the courtroom to apologise, nice touch that, wonder if she had any inkling at that stage, doubt it, likes the good things in life, Moet Chandon and more Moet Chandon, husband sounds a bit of a creep, why do women stick with bastards, could never understand that, not as if she seems the retiring type, proper firebrand on politics, champagne socialist, well not a socialist but definitely left-leaning, hmmm leaning in against me now, mmm, like that, Christ what a day, think it was half-way through the first bottle when I had that moment of absolute clarity, she's coming home with me tonight, why was I so certain, intuition, wasn't as if she said anything but I just knew, want to come in for a brandy, pretty corny line I guess, no hesitation mind you and none once I closed the door either, wonder why she nicked those things in Sainsbury's, will never see the tinned tomatoes aisle in the same light again, Elizabeth, ha, Elizabeth and Philip, the royals of Russell Road, slow down mate, let's not get ahead of ourselves here, I would though, would she, wow I've fallen for her already, certainly sounded like she was considering writing Geoff out of her life, I've never done this before Philip cheated I mean, cheated...odd way of putting it, seemed pretty true to me, Christ what a day and people say jury service is boring, ha, not in my case, better get some sleep I suppose, will she just stroll home first thing as if nothing's happened, what's it seven no eight doors away, God who'd have thought, don't remember her ringing the creepy hubby or him calling her either, can't be a regular occurrence, I've never done this before Philip, believe her too, Christ what a night......

***

Geoff Harris woke as normal about 5:30 and noticed that Elizabeth hadn't returned...must be at Rachel's again, always her bolthole, refuge at Rachel's, available for celebrations and soul-searching sessions both, reliable Rachel not just there for the bad times and *I* should know, I guess it was likely Elizabeth wouldn't return home last night, never seen her as angry as yesterday morning, silly really, how could I take a day off work just to be there for that ridiculous court case, yesterday of all days, presentation scheduled for 10, went well too, besides she was jeopardising my chance to advance with her silly acts of rebellion, doesn't look good when your wife's in court for theft, Geoff I did something silly today, thought it might involve a scratch on the car but no, stealing from Sainsbury's, Jesus Christ, Elizabeth you're 32, what the hell are you doing this for, you're not an angst-ridden 14 year old looking for attention, and I got a barrel of abuse from her in return, clearly unhinged that day, not just that day mind you, I know she doesn't appreciate what I do but she could at least acknowledge what it provides for us, us, is there an us still, not sure after this morning, always thought it was me who was unhappy, unhappy not the right word really, more unappreciated, it's my income which allowed her to quit work, much good that did her, complaints increased if anything, it's not money with her though, she's above that of course, time to get up soon, can't go on like this though, maybe time to confront Elizabeth, I know she's unhappy for whatever reasons but there's no way she'll do anything, it's in my hands as normal, if I even mentioned splitting up she'd freak, tough love is what's needed, I'll broach the subject, yeah, look Elizabeth neither of us are happy at the moment so let's talk about it, God what a response that'll get, tears, tantrums, the whole works, she's holding me back, I'm that much away from stepping up at work and I end up shopping and going to the cinema at weekends, if I put in those extra hours I could have an unanswerable case for promotion, the things I sacrifice for her and she doesn't even seem to notice, oh that's the front door, she's home, funny, I didn't hear a taxi pull up, Rachel's house is a good 25 minutes walk and there's no way she'd do that, bus maybe, no, they're unreliable and Elizabeth wouldn't be in a fit state to bus it after a night's drinking with Rachel, hmmm curious, time for me to get up anyway, got lots on today, I'll do the decent thing and offer her a cup of tea and some Panadol, God what a martyr I am, most blokes would bollock her to the high heavens, well maybe later, let her stew on whatever grievance she has before she sees the error of her ways, anyway I've got more important things to worry about, blue suit and red tie today methinks, sets the right tone and usually gets an appreciative nod from Hannah too, odd, she's still downstairs and it's gone quiet, OK I'll wander down, I'll be gracious, she did have a rough time yesterday after all, OK here goes......

***

2 - THURSDAY

Just before 9am, Philip Anderson, wearing a charcoal grey suit under his black cashmere coat, walked into the jury room at the courthouse. He was greeted by smiles from other jurors among whom his stock had evidently risen. His opinions were now eagerly sought on a variety of subjects.

'Did you see that courtroom drama on TV last night, Philip?' asked Grace, a woman in her early forties with a playful smile. Grace had established herself during the previous day as somebody who strove to find a positive angle to everybody's actions and utterances.

'No, I was er, out last night. Bit of a busman's holiday watching something like that, isn't it?'

'Well, it's interesting to watch it with some insider knowledge,' Grace replied.

'The defendant in that programme was guilty as hell, I reckon.' Roger joined the conversation. 'I ended up shouting "hang the little toerag and have done with it" at the TV.'

Philip and Grace laughed and glanced surreptitiously at the jury foreman. Colin, an irrepressibly cheerful juror, arrived and patted Philip's shoulder in an exaggerated show of *bonhomie*.

'What's the recipe today, Jim?' Colin asked in a high-pitched voice.

Grace, puzzled, turned to Colin. 'But his name is Philip, not Jim.'

'It's a catchphrase from an old radio show, my dear,' Colin responded, winking at Philip and smirking, 'But a young lady like you would never have heard it, years before your time, dear.'

Philip winced; he really didn't have much time for Colin.

***

Elizabeth Harris stared out of the café window. She wasn't due to meet her friend, Rachel, for another 15 minutes but she was already in place, eager to leave the house and do something to occupy herself. *God, what a tangled web we weave. I think ill of Geoff and then he's all kind, considerate and charming.* For once Elizabeth had wanted him to act surly and make it easier for her. *Easier? Make what easier?* She didn't know. Disillusionment with Geoff led her, first, to a silly theft and then last night. *Last night! Likeable, considerate guy listens to her, provides some advice and wham, bam, thank you ma'am, she's in bed with him and thinking about leaving Geoff.* In the cold light of day, things seemed different. *Of course they did.*

Should she confide in Rachel? She often sought Rachel's advice when things went wrong but it was usually something less wrong than this. Elizabeth pondered the likely course which a conversation with Rachel would take. They were such long-standing friends that each found it difficult to conceal anything from the other but could she listen to Rachel providing rational advice when her own brain was in turmoil? She decided she was better served by not mentioning anything about the previous night...and now here was Rachel, standing outside the café waving to her.

***

Geoff Harris stared out of his office window. He had meetings scheduled but lethargy washed over him, sending his mind elsewhere. 28, Russell Road, to be precise. Elizabeth had acted strangely earlier when he walked downstairs and found her standing by the kitchen sink, a glass of water in her hand. He hugged her, asked about the court case and she turned away, mumbling a reply. He told her to forget about the case - it was over – as he made tea and toast and chatted but she remained remote. At least that was better than yesterday morning's raging row; he decided to leave well enough alone.

A 'ping' noise from his computer screen alerted him to the arrival of an e-mail. Geoff smiled when he saw it was from Tom Brady, the droll Irishman in charge of communications for Alpha Venture. Part of Brady's role was to prepare and distribute the company's bland press releases and anodyne internal memos which he would sometimes enliven by playing linguistic games - acronyms and acrostics being his favoured devices.

His most audacious effort occurred at a time when two senior directors at Alpha Venture (AV), Mark Llewellyn and Deborah Jarvis were involved in a clandestine affair. Brady composed a short, run-of-the-mill press release concerning AV and the purchase of another company which contained the acrostic 'Mark and Deborah who knew.' His hidden message was undetected until Deborah Jarvis herself noticed it when a glitch in her e-mail format displayed the press release in discrete sentences rather than paragraph form. She confronted Brady about it, citing unprofessional behaviour and infringement of her privacy. Tom's response was 'Deborah, I have no idea what you're referring to'. Deborah, unsure whether or not to believe him, realised she would merely draw attention to her affair by pursuing the matter and walked away. Llewellyn never asked Tom about it and Deborah left AV soon after, ending her liaison with Llewellyn by which time the acrostic had entered AV folklore.

The e-mail which Geoff now read was an update from Tom on AV's work in the local community, a campaign titled Outreach. In 2008, AV held a sizeable stake in a beleaguered high street bank, Supranational Bank. AV sold the stake, precipitating a market stampede to offload Supranational shares. The treasury intervened and provided funding which prevented Supranational from going under. When the share price appeared to bottom out, AV repurchased the shares at 40% of the cost at which they had sold them. It was viewed as a cynical, calculating piece of opportunism at the taxpayer's expense and AV was sufficiently shaken by the outcry to embark on a charm offensive. They provided financial backing for a number of community projects and ordered senior directors to waive 50% of their scheduled bonuses for the year. The community projects didn't achieve much but the favourable publicity was all that mattered to AV.

Brady's *communiqué* concerned a new phase of the Outreach project and Geoff soon identified the latest instance of Brady's mischievous wordplay. The e-mail stated that visits by AV staff to local schools had been well-received and a notorious secondary school, St. Ambrose's, was next to be so favoured. Geoff remembered that a young man who briefly worked for him on a work experience placement had been a student at St. Ambrose's. Well, that particular placement hadn't been a success and Geoff didn't hold out much hope for a visit to the school either.

Brady provided the details under the heading 'Outreach Initiative: Alpha Venture's External Interests Thriving.' Geoff recognised the title as an acronym of "Oi, 'ave it," the catchphrase from a television advertisement for a lowbrow tabloid newspaper in which the words were recited by an aggressive, guttural voice. This was, presumably, Brady's wry comment on the intellectual boundaries of the school's students.

Reading this didn't lighten Geoff's mood for long as he continued to stare vacantly at his screen and think about Elizabeth; there really had been something odd about her this morning. Geoff considered himself an expert at recognising nuances – such expertise was, after all, how they'd first connected. His mind wandered back eight years to 2002.

***

Elizabeth Davenport sighed. Only two days in, this skiing holiday - such a good idea when suggested by her friend, Helen - wasn't turning out as planned. Her last group holiday had been during her university years when it seemed natural to do things en masse. Post-graduation, she found a job as a teacher and started a relationship with an academic, John Hooper, and the hitherto prevalent group dynamic faded.

Engaging socially with John could be hard work for the uninitiated; his aloof demeanour doing little to put them at ease. He was, in truth, a witty and engaging person but this emerged only when commonality was established. Their relationship was showing signs of strain when Elizabeth first mentioned the holiday. At first, John hadn't shown much interest but he acquiesced in the face of Elizabeth's enthusiasm.

'It'll be fun, John,' she gushed over drinks at a Christmas party. 'Helen, over there, is going; you already know Patrick, Michelle and Colin. The others are all friends of theirs.'

John warmed to the idea and a grey, austere spell of weather made the idea of blue skies, crisp Alpine mornings and outdoor activity seem attractive. By the time February arrived, he'd thrown himself into the planning and shared Elizabeth's anticipation. Upon arrival, the beauty of Combloux in the French Alps captivated them and their companions as the first night passed in a hedonistic blur, fortified by the local Pinot Noir and bottles of champagne. But Elizabeth worried that John would retreat into insularity - it had happened before...meet my boyfriend, yep, the one who views you disdainfully because he's intellectually superior to you. After the first two days of skiing, she asked him whether he was sure about the evening ahead in a resort bar.

'It may not be entirely to your taste, John but let's join in, OK?'

'Sure. I'm not a complete snob, you know.'

She had cause to remember this later that evening when she glanced across the bar to see John engrossed in conversation with Laura, a striking, auburn-haired, opinionated banker in her mid-20s. John had only ever displayed contempt for banks and Elizabeth tensed, aware of the possibility of a confrontation. On the contrary, the two were laughing companionably...this wasn't the John Hooper she knew. She sat, drink in hand, feeling abandoned, distracted to the extent that she didn't notice somebody sliding into a seat alongside her.

'Mind if I join?' Geoff Harris asked.

'No, sure, er, fine, yeah sure,' Elizabeth replied.

'Just that you're on your own and look a bit fazed. Are you OK?'

'Yes, fine. Fine.'

'Yours?' Geoff asked, glancing to where John and Laura sat.

'Sorry?'

'The guy talking to Laura Holmes, he's your boyfriend or husband or whatever, yes?'

'Oh, you mean John. Yes, he's my, er, my other half. He's probably boring the poor girl to death wittering on about cinematic genres and the sub-text of some Japanese art-house film. Sometimes, his opening line of conversation is to ask a person the last five films they've watched and if the first few aren't to his liking, he's been known to yawn ostentatiously or even walk away. She may need rescuing. You work with her, don't you?'

'Yes, Laura's a colleague of mine. Films, you say? Well, they probably have more in common than you think. She's an investment analyst specialising in media outlets, film companies in particular. It's probably

13

an interesting conversation if John's such an art-movie connoisseur as Laura knows the film industry inside out, more from the money side – very much opposite perspectives.'

'She doesn't sound like his type.'

'His type? Your other half has "types"? Wow, you academics really go in for open relationships.'

Elizabeth bristled, an indignant response ready until she saw his teasing smile.

'Ah. I fell for that,' she said with a smile. Moving her chair so that her back was turned to John, she topped up her wine glass and tilted the bottle towards Geoff.

'Oh, why not,' he replied, examining the label. 'Hmmm, you've got good taste or is this one a random selection?' Again, the teasing smile.

'I see. The little lady can't be trusted to get these things right, it's something best left to the gentleman, eh? So, it's true that you financiers are fuelled by adrenalin and testosterone?'

'And would that explain why Laura earns about half-as-much again as I do? Admittedly, she knows how to use her feminine charms but there's more to it than that.' Geoff noticed Elizabeth's frown and surreptitious glance towards John and Laura. 'I didn't mean it like that. Anyway, tell me about you. Are you a regular skier?'

'Do I come here often, you mean?' she replied, smiling again.

From there, the holiday improved for Elizabeth and John and a tacit agreement seemed to have been reached where they allowed each other as much social latitude as was desired. A sub-group composed of Elizabeth, John, Laura and Geoff formed in which, to an outsider, the demarcation lines between who was with who blurred. Alone, Elizabeth and John made neutral comments about Laura and Geoff with no acknowledgement that there could be a role for either in their lives beyond this holiday.

On the last night, the entire group joined for a raucous night at a restaurant. Phone numbers and addresses were exchanged and Elizabeth discreetly picked up Geoff's French phrase book from the table and put it in her bag. Back home in London as John and Elizabeth unpacked their cases, she feigned surprise when she found the book and ostentatiously checked the fly-leaf where she found the initials G.H.

'GH,' she mused aloud and clicked her fingers. 'Oh it must belong to Geoff Harris, I used it in the restaurant last night and it ended up in my bag. I'd better return it, lucky we all exchanged numbers.'

'He probably doesn't need it straight away, Elizabeth.'

'Probably not, I'll post it to him although I'm sure he lives near my

14

school.' Elizabeth ran her finger along the list of names and numbers which she'd jotted down the previous evening. 'Yes, here it is, 28, Russell Road, it's only about 10 minutes from the school. I'll drop it through the letter box one evening on my way home.'

The next day was Sunday; John decided that he would spend the day at his office on the university campus, Elizabeth said that she'd go for a walk as it was such a bright early spring day. When John left, she changed, put the phrase book in her bag and walked to Russell Road but hesitated as she approached Geoff's house. She knew he was single but wondered whether she was being hasty in renewing their friendship. Would the wine-fuelled conversations remain a happier memory if consigned to a holiday flirtation rather than find that the magic had evaporated somewhere between London and the French Alps? Oh to hell with it, she thought, strode up to no. 28 and rang the bell.

'Elizabeth, what a surprise,' Geoff exclaimed.

'I just wanted to return your phrase book. I er, picked it up at the restaurant on Friday night and wanted to return it in case you.....'

'In case I needed it urgently today?' he asked with that now-familiar teasing grin. 'Yes, I was about to rush out to get a new one but since you're here, why don't you come in? We may find a use for it.'

She dropped the book on the hallway table, kicked the door shut behind her and threw her arms around Geoff. 'We won't need it just yet,' she said, unbuttoning her coat.

'I've never done this before, Geoff. Cheated on John, that is. I wanted you to know that,' Elizabeth said as she leaned across him, picking up a packet of cigarettes from the bedside table. 'Do you mind if I smoke?'

'The post-coital cigarette, eh? I'll join you,' Geoff replied. 'I'm glad you took the initiative, er, with the phrase book, I mean. Since returning, I've tried to devise scenarios where I could meet you. They were becoming more and more unlikely so you've saved me by taking the first step.'

'Oh yeah?' She leaned back against the headboard, stretching her arms in a languid movement. 'And here's me thinking you alpha-male bankers were more the make-the-running type.'

'Oh, I'm too chivalrous for that though I did hope it was you who picked up the phrase book. I guess I won't have to look up the meaning of "cherchez la femme" after all now.'

Elizabeth laughed, left down her cigarette and nestled against Geoff.
***

And that was how it all started, thought Geoff. When Elizabeth returned home that evening in 2002, she heard that John's day at the university had been truncated when he 'bumped into' Laura as she went for a jog around the campus grounds. Elizabeth and John acknowledged their futures were likely to be separate and two months later, she moved in with Geoff. They married in August 2003 and the years since had been good but Geoff knew their marriage had entered a new phase. Elizabeth's oscillating moods – incandescent rage yesterday, distance bordering on indifference this morning – were baffling. Geoff was aware that he could appear cold and preoccupied with work at times but they'd muddled through so far...no, that was unfair on both of them, they'd not just muddled through, they'd been very happy but recently, less so. They discussed having children but without real conviction. Then, two years previously, Geoff's father died and he felt that he had shirked a responsibility.

It didn't seem a logical reaction but people's lives were rarely purely governed by logic. He struggled to gather all the divergent thoughts swirling around in his head into a coherent narrative. Worryingly, this was impinging on his role as a portfolio analyst, a well remunerated job which required a level of attention to detail which was, at times, punitive.

Today, he was distracted. Memories of the start of his relationship with Elizabeth had summoned John Hooper from the recesses of Geoff's memory. Geoff held a benevolent memory of John and, for a while, they maintained the tenuous friendship forged during that strange week in the French Alps. Elizabeth, on the other hand, made little effort to stay in touch with John and whatever updates on him she received from mutual friends were treated mostly with indifference.

Geoff also remained in contact with Laura Holmes who had turned John's head so much that he left academia for a job in the City before leaving that to create a successful *zeitgeist* website. In a curious *volte face*, Laura left Alpha Venture deeming her job "shallow and inconsequential", enrolled for a degree in film studies and became a film critic for an avant-garde arts magazine. She split up with John claiming that they'd changed beyond recognition, effectively swapping personalities in a modern-day Faustian pact. For Geoff, the two of them were frozen in his memory in a happier time. He wondered what John and Laura were doing now.

***

John Hooper motioned to the other occupant of the room for quiet. The television was tuned to an American business channel where a man wearing a striped blue shirt with a white collar and sporting red braces shouted into an out-sized microphone.

'Phenomenal, this is phenomenal! Wall Street shows love for British irony. What's going on? They come over here stealing our dollars, inflating stock prices and all through that,' here the presenter adopted a Dick Van

16

Dyke-type English accent, 'uniquely British irony. More now from Morton Fenelstein. Morton?'

The screen image changed and a young man with slicked-back hair wearing a luminous yellow shirt leaned towards the camera and spoke in a grave voice.

'Say, thanks Howard. Yeah, Wall's gone big on Monochromus, the newly quoted stock. We're hoping for more details on this, what our trans-Atlantic cousins would call, quintessentially English firm. More soon.'

John pointed to the screen and laughed.

'We've done it, Chris. They've no idea what we're about, it's unnerved them, we'll make a killing here. It was one of their own, H.L. Mencken, who said to never underestimate the stupidity of the American people. He was right and not just about Americans. People everywhere, they're stupid.'

John rocked his chair back, his jowelled cheeks trembling as he guffawed. Chris Williamson smiled indulgently. They'd first met when they worked for a London finance house, Foden Barnes. Chris was mesmerised by John and saw him as a polymath. John had come late to Big Business and threw himself into it with abandon, labelling academics as 'up-their-own-arse flat-earthers inhabiting a petty, jealous Hades', a world which he claimed he was glad to have left behind.

Meeting Laura Holmes during a 2002 skiing holiday was the catalyst for this change of perspective. When he began a relationship with Laura, they embraced each other's interests. Laura became enthralled by non-mainstream cinema; previously her main interest in this field was confined to the finances behind it. John, meanwhile, was captivated by the financing of films and soon displayed an unsuspected aptitude for understanding the machinations of financial markets.

He left his university post, started work in the back office of an American bank, Foden Barnes (FB), and was soon trading derivatives at FB. Within two years, he found the restrictions of this environment suffocating and left to trade modest amounts of his own money. The profits were small but it excited him more than working within confines. Laura was aghast at the transformation she witnessed in the austere, thoughtful man she'd met in France who now often lapsed into a brash, hectoring bully. She ended the relationship and John didn't seem perturbed; he viewed her departure from banking to start a degree in film studies a hostile usurping of his position as the intellectual in their relationship.

John's academic interests survived and he became obsessed with what the media referred to as the 'dumbing-down of modern society.' He started a website which railed against this trend and posted links on his site, *Ironic Times*, to articles or features which exemplified stupidity or philistinism.

He was amazed when his website received comments betraying how people viewed the on-line postings or newspaper columns, those which John mocked, as well-reasoned opinions.

At this point, John adopted a post-modern approach to the subject and started another website, *The Bleedin' Obvious*, where he posted long, ostensibly meticulously-researched treatises about subjects which to him were self-evident truths; *'China and Japan....maybe they just don't get on?'* and *'Democracy and its origins in equality'* were just two examples. The response was beyond John's comprehension - once again, a significant number of people failed to see the inherent irony. John negotiated a deal with a publisher to produce a book containing some of his articles and the replies they elicited. The book, published with an eye to the Christmas market, was a hit with merchandising spin-offs from *The Bleedin' Obvious* equally successful.

John recruited Chris Williamson, friends from their time together at Foden Barnes and set up a fledgling organisation, Monochrome – the name an allusion to the origins of its owners; John, the non-more-English Mancunian with a lineage back through generations of Anglo-Saxons and Chris, the son of West Indian immigrants. Chris' easy-going charm made him a good foil for John as he reined in some of John's more fanciful ideas. Even some of their more preposterous ideas proved popular and they floated the company on the stock exchange. They then added a trans-Atlantic arm, Monochromus, which now floated on the US stock market.

Chris shook his head in disbelief as all three phones in their cramped office rang. John answered one, laughed at the caller's greeting and replied: 'I can hardly believe it either. Oh, I'm sure there'll be a little celebration ...That's bleedin' obvious, I would think...Yeah, cheers, I'll let you know when and where.'

They answered more calls of a similar vein. Chris took one where the caller asked if they could speak to John.

'He's on another line now...Ok, shouldn't be too long if you want to...Can I ask who's calling?'

Chris knew there was something familiar about the caller's name – Laura Armitage – but couldn't place it. John ended a call, already his phone was ringing again.

'Don't answer it, John. I've got someone for you...Laura Armitage.'

'No idea who she is. Ask her what she wants.'

The caller heard this exchange and said to Chris, 'He'll know me better as Laura Holmes.'

Recognition dawned on Chris; he covered the mouthpiece and said, 'Laura Holmes, John. It's Laura.'

John arched his eyebrows and took the phone from Chris.

'Laura, crikey, it's been a while. To what do I owe the pleasure?'

'Hi John, it has been a while, yes. I got a call from an old colleague at Alpha Venture who said there was something on that American TV business channel which might interest me and I've been watching it. So, world domination beckons for you guys then? Well done.'

'Laura, oh Laura, you created a monster. I'm telling you, Mary Shelley had nothing on you, kid. I probably still wouldn't know the first thing about business were it not for your tutelage.'

'Come, come John. You didn't need much nurturing before you were dazzling the traders at FB. Do you miss that or the academic life at all?'

'Not when I meet my accountant, I don't although I haven't renounced the arts world: I still subscribe to *Sight & Sound* and buy *Rosebud* each month. I see you've got your own byline there now.'

'Actually, I've been working with a colleague on something you'll find interesting. I assume you still like Fraser Guthrie?'

'Of course. Don't tell me he's moving into film scores?'

'Well, in the scale of things Fraser Guthrie-related, it's pretty earth-shattering news. I won't tell you more now but it's due for publication very soon. I thought about you when I was writing it.'

'Laura, you tease. You can't leave it like that. Let's meet for a drink, you can tell me more.'

'It'll be out next week. Besides, going for a drink isn't a good idea.'

'Afraid you won't be able to keep your hands off me now I'm a master of the universe, eh?'

'Don't flatter yourself, John. God, I did create a monster,' she laughed. 'In any case, don't forget I'm *Mrs.* Armitage now. Gotta go, John. Good to talk again, I'll be in touch.'

John replaced the receiver, frowned, ignored a ringing telephone, picked up his jacket, told Chris he was going out for a few minutes and left the room.

***

Laura Armitage flicked her mobile phone closed and smiled. That's piqued his curiosity for sure, he won't spend the day wallowing in a haze of self-congratulation and I bet he digs out his Fraser Guthrie albums when he goes home. She shrugged, shook her head and turned back to her computer screen but couldn't concentrate on her work. She had, genuinely, contacted John to congratulate him but sub-consciously also wanted to remind him how obsessed he had once been by cinema and music. Was it petty to denigrate his new wealth and status? No, not entirely but it was dispiriting to think how easy it had been for sudden wealth to turn his head.

Having herself renounced the relentless pursuit of money in favour of what she saw as a more elevated calling, it pained Laura to see her former boyfriend abandon his more rarefied interests. He had opened her eyes to the power of visual images and narrative as portrayed on screen and she felt little remorse at leaving a lucrative job and a potentially even more lucrative future to learn about herself and the world through the medium of cinema. She envisaged them encouraging each other to expand their minds ever further and was amazed when John headed in what she saw as the opposite direction. She recalled the precise moment when she realised their destinies might, after all, diverge.

When John moved in with Laura, her newsagent delivery order absorbed his reading preferences. One Saturday, hearing the sound of the newspapers dropping on the doormat, John padded downstairs and returned with the *Independent*, his monthly *Sight & Sound* and her weekend *Financial Times*. John left the bundle on the bed, climbed back in and instinctively reached for the FT while she picked up *Sight & Sound*. They paused, looked at each other and laughed. A bridge had been crossed and Laura was surprised to find they were on opposing sides rather than together. How unpredictable life could be!

When John started work in the City, Laura knew their relationship was damned. She'd escaped once and had no wish to return through osmosis. She missed the generous salary – who wouldn't – but was happier within herself. The persistence and self-belief which she'd acquired in the competitive financial world served her well in landing a staff role at *Rosebud*, a monthly arts magazine titled as homage to the opening word of *Citizen Kane*.

She thrived in this environment to the extent that she was often contacted by other publications and newspapers for a reaction to events in the arts world in general and cinema in particular. Her style of writing was deliberately oblique, one which strived to find new perspectives on her subject or to critique an artiste's output from a less exalted viewpoint than her peers. It granted her credibility; one commentator described her writing as that of 'a benign iconoclast.' Laura agonised over whether this was a clever insult, a backhanded compliment, a glowing testimony, all or none of the above. She decided to ignore such analysis and pursue her new calling without dwelling on other's opinions.

She'd grown up in Suffolk where the US Army deployed her American father as an *attaché*. It was a perfect posting for her Anglophile parents and allowed Laura to explore the cultures of the two countries. Summers spent at her grandparents in Massachusetts surrounded by cousins and family friends heightened her competitive instincts whereas rural Suffolk gave her a sense of history and permanence. Now that she was recognised as a journalist of substance, Laura was often sought out by colleagues to add heft and credence to their own work. She met a young freelance music writer, Nick Ellis, at a *Rosebud* party. They discussed at length their mutual interests in music, including the enigmatic American singer/songwriter, Fraser Guthrie.

Guthrie had emerged during the late 1980s as lead guitarist in a critically-lauded but commercially unviable band called the Fast Propellers. He left the Fast Propellers to form his own three-piece band, Facts Machine. In 1994, Facts Machine, on the cusp of breaking into the mainstream having released two well-received albums, was disbanded as Guthrie again jumped ship without warning. He released a solo album *From Here to Nowhere* which was, again, favourably reviewed. Guthrie's neurotic aversion to popular acclaim meant that few people were surprised when he then disappeared from view.

It had never been established what happened to him during that period although it was the subject of fevered speculation; he'd been jailed, he'd had a breakdown, drugs had gotten the better of him, he'd simply had enough of people hanging on his every word – each theory had its advocates and each a certain plausibility. In 1997, without fanfare, he released an album *A Good Education (And See Where It Got Me)* which divided both critics and fans. It seemed to describe the end of a relationship using ornate floral and nature-related metaphors backed by lush, pastoral music at odds with his hitherto distinctive guitar-based sound.

It was lauded by sections of the music press as a ground-breaking soundtrack for the impending millennium whereas others viewed it in less laudatory terms. Among its detractors, the most-quoted comment was from an eminent English critic who dismissed it as sounding like the 'semi-coherent fanciful ramblings of a man sitting in a deck chair at his allotment on a summer's evening having over-imbibed on home-made dandelion and burdock wine.'

Guthrie, ever reluctant to grant interviews, refused to cast further light on this album – something which only fuelled the heartbreaking exorcism / throwaway whimsy debate. He released three more albums of which the last two, in 2000 and 2002, were the ones which Laura really liked whereas John held the view that '*Education*' was a work of uncompromising genius.

The album highlighted the obsessive nature of some Guthrie enthusiasts; one American academic spent 18 months writing a book which compared the language Guthrie used to Keats, Shelley and Byron, finally extending his allusions to passages from the bible. The book was ready for publication when the publishers' lawyers ran it past Guthrie himself who identified 24 factual errors in the first chapter alone. The mortified writer demanded that the book be pulped, quit his lecturing post and was last heard of working, appositely, as a florist.

Laura always carried a torch for enigmatic Americans – dating back to her teenage years spent shuttling between US air bases where dozens of chisel-jawed pilots resembled the young Guthrie and holidays spent near Providence endlessly discussing music with her cousins – and was intrigued by Guthrie's career and unexplained disappearance. Soon after the *Rosebud* party, Nick Ellis rang her to ask advice on something he'd discovered about Guthrie. They met and Ellis told her he'd spent an evening in the company of a revered music critic, Laurence Tolliver, who made knowing references to the story behind Guthrie's disappearance. Tolliver was a famously priapic individual and Ellis alluded to a possibility that Laura's looks and charm could coax more detail from him.

'It's not how it sounds, Laura,' Ellis pleaded as she gave him a withering look. 'I'm supposed to meet Tolliver at the Lead Pencils' concert tomorrow night and you could just happen to be there too, get the conversation around to Fraser Guthrie, bat your eyelashes a few times and the old soak might elaborate on whatever it is that he knows.'

'Exactly what do you take me for?' Laura asked and smiled as she saw Nick's hurt expression. 'I'm just teasing you, Nick. Yes, count me in. I'm intrigued by this and, for all Tolliver's sleaziness, he's a good writer and has been known to give young hacks a leg-up through some juicy leads...and it isn't necessarily in return for some leg-over, either. Though he won't be interested in that from you, Tolly is very much a ladies' man.'

'So I hear. Let's meet at the Grapes of Wrath tomorrow at 7. I'll ensure Laurence is there.'

'God, the Lead Pencils have fallen from grace. What a dive!' Laura wrinkled her nose in distaste as she surveyed the Grapes of Wrath pub where she sat with Nick. 'Ah, speaking of seeing better days, here he is.'

Laurence Tolliver, raffish and dressed in trademark dandy fashion – the image he strove to portray was that of a Parisian boulevardier, an image he augmented by ordering absinthe in any bar which looked likely to sell it - sauntered towards them nodding to people en route, a wolfish smile spreading across his face when he noticed Laura.

'Young Ellis, good to see you again,' he drawled, shaking Nick's proffered hand before turning to Laura. 'And who do we have here? Had I known we were expecting company, I could've brought roses, chocolates, bubbly. Time for that still, perhaps.'

'Hello, Mr. Tolliver. I'm Laura Armitage, a colleague of Nick's. He mentioned seeing the Lead Pencils this evening and, well, I've always been interested in antiques and relics.'

'Not just looks but caustic wit too,' Tolliver smiled. 'Well, this calls for something better than fizzy, tepid lager in a plastic glass. Let me have a nose around and see if I can't find something and somewhere more salubrious. Don't move, darlings.'

Tolliver ambled to an office door from which, minutes later, a woman emerged to ask Laura and Nick whether they could join Mr. Tolliver in the backstage bar. The backstage bar was no more than a small room with a trestle table set up at one end but it did, at least, contain comfortable chairs and a carpet to which their shoes didn't stick. Tolliver had also acquired a bottle of bordeaux which he uncorked. Laura, aware of the bands Tolliver held in esteem, ensured that the conversation referred to them without making it seem too deliberate. When he asked about her music preferences, she didn't mention Guthrie's name, instead listing a number of groups including his first band, the Fast Propellers.

'Ah, the much-missed Propellers. I'm sure they would've gone on to great things had Fraser Guthrie remained. Still, he wasn't one to linger.'

'But what a talent, don't you think?' Nick asked.

'Didn't we discuss Guthrie before?' Tolliver frowned. 'Odd, you don't hear of him for ages and now, he's ubiquitous. What do you make of the elusive Fraser, Laura?'

'I don't know, there's something phoney about him. Great guitarist and I like some of the solo stuff but he sort of tried too hard to make a mystery of himself. That's my opinion, anyway.'

Tolliver stared at her and nodded his head slowly.

'There's more to him than you think. I've met him a good few times, spiky at first but if you steer the conversation away from music, he's quite engaging. He has an inherent mistrust of the fourth estate and, Christ knows, we can't blame him for that,' Tolliver grinned. 'Johnny Journalist isn't a friend to rock music's more sensitive souls.'

Laura warmed to Tolliver as the conversation continued; he was self-deprecating about his writing, genuinely interested in Nick and Laura and an entertaining raconteur. Aware that Tolliver's career took off when as an eager 20-year-old, he was given access to a story by a benevolent colleague, Laura casually asked:

'And what was your first break? Was it persistence or one story?'

'The latter; a lucky break did it for me. Look, forgive me saying this but you two are still on the lower rungs of the ladder. *Rosebud*, for all its earnestness, probably won't get you the recognition you may be entitled to,' he said to Laura before turning to Nick. 'And, right now, you're only aspiring to that level, young man. I can put you in touch with somebody who has a real story to tell about Fraser Guthrie. Both of you seem *simpatico* to Fraser and I know for a fact that he despairs of some of the wilder speculation about his life. In the right hands, he might be happy to have some of that speculation quashed.'

Nick nudged Laura's knee and she, in turn, granted Tolliver her most coquettish smile.

Soon after the evening in the Grapes of Wrath, Nick and Laura knocked on the door of a house in Clapham. Joan Hudson, a sprightly, sharp-witted academic in her late-50s, had invited them there and all three sat in a room surrounded by book-laden shelves, chatting during what Laura interpreted as a preliminary interview. Before long, Joan seemed to approve of her new acquaintances.

'Laurence said both of you are interested in Fraser Guthrie and asked me to have a chat. He was complimentary; no reason why he wouldn't be in your case, Mrs. Armitage but let's leave that aside. I'm aware of your innovative approach to writing about the arts,' Joan said to Laura, smiling as she nodded to a copy of *Rosebud*. 'Or so it says here anyway.'

Laura and Nick laughed politely and waited for Joan to continue.

'I've also read some of your output, Mr. Ellis and I think you're worthy recipients of what I'm about to tell and show you. Yes, you can use that recording device, dear. I assume you know the song *Hardly a Perennial*?'

They nodded and Nick replied, 'Oh yes, you almost feel like you're intruding on Guthrie's anguish, all that stuff about the closed gate and the flowers, the archway leading nowhere and the view from a window. Everything seems tangible but still tantalisingly beyond reach. Why?'

'Let me show you something,' Joan said. All three walked towards a window which overlooked the herbs, shrubs and lawn in the garden. Joan pointed to a distant corner. Laura and Nick followed her gaze, laughed and turned back towards Joan.

'So, you're a Guthrie fan?' Nick asked. 'It's all there, the gate with a "closed" sign, the archway, roses, everything. Crikey, that's homage.'

'No, that's not it. The garden design wasn't my idea.'

'Oh, you bought the house from a Guthrie fan then?'

'No, that's not it either. Try again.'

'I suppose you'll tell us he spent time here and the garden inspired him to write the song?' Laura snorted.

'You're getting closer,' Joan laughed. 'During the 1990s, I was an English Literature lecturer and I gave tutorials to students here in this house. One of my students, Liz Raymonde, visited and we spoke about the garden which was an over-grown mess. I had no time to tend to it what with work and looking after two children. Liz said that her boyfriend was a gardener who was looking for work and he could drop by to discuss what could be done.'

'A few days later, a tall scraggly-bearded American called Frank arrived. He didn't say much but seemed to know what he was doing. My husband, Paul, and I had a vague idea of how we wanted the garden to look and we shared that with Frank who added some more ideas. We employed him and he worked steadily without engaging much in conversation. He interested me, there was something familiar about him but I couldn't work out what it was. I knew Fraser Guthrie's music and liked the album with that *No Clutter in the Gutter* track. You know it?'

'Yes,' Laura replied, 'it's the track on *From Here to Nowhere*.'

'Yes, that one. A couple of days after Frank started his work here, I watched a programme on TV about contemporary American music which featured Fraser Guthrie and showed that famous interview where he explains what he meant by the phrase "no clutter in the gutter." Even though the gardener looked like an inverted version of Fraser - he'd cropped his hair and had an unkempt beard - there was no mistaking the Southern drawl however hard he tried to modify it.'

'Good God, you mean it was him,' Nick gasped. 'I need to sit down.'

'In that TV interview when Fraser explained that "no clutter in the gutter" meant starting again and shedding all baggage, it made sense to me. "Frank" was here the next day so I put one of Fraser's albums on the stereo and invited him in for a coffee. It was a cold day and he was glad of a break. He walked in to the room we're in now, heard the music, froze and mumbled something about "needing the bathroom."

'I turned up the volume a bit, he returned, laughed and said, "People tell me I look like that Guthrie guy, thing is I'm way better looking." He sat down and glanced at me surreptitiously. I said, "You are Fraser Guthrie, aren't you?" He nodded. I assured him neither my husband nor I were obsessive fans and I wouldn't tell anyone if that was how he wanted it.'

'So, it really was him?' Laura interjected. 'Wow...wow.'

'Yes, it was him. He'd been serious about the sentiments expressed in *No Clutter in the Gutter*, wanted to get away from people hanging on his every utterance and was on the verge of quitting music when he met Liz who was on holiday in New York. She liked Fraser's music but was unfazed by his cult status. She was, he said, exactly who he needed to meet at that particular time. He did a crash course in horticulture and took a flight to London to see Liz. They had a pretty stormy relationship by all accounts –

she's a feisty lady – but the *'Good Education'* album is not about them. Sorry to shatter any preconceptions you may harbour but the album is about appreciating nature, nothing more.'

Nick slumped back in his seat. 'I feel like the Archbishop of Canterbury finding out there's no God,' he mumbled.

'I'd imagine it's worse than that for you. Isn't it pretty much mandatory for a Church of England or Anglican bishop to question the existence of God these days?' Laura said with a smile.

'Are you the Joanna mentioned in the album's credits?' Nick asked.

'You even remember the people acknowledged on the liner notes! Yes, that's me. Fraser wanted to protect people's privacy so he used my proper name, one I don't use.'

'People have spent hours, no, *days*, trying to decipher who's credited in those notes,' Nick said, smiling. 'Are they all South Londoners who had a garden make-over twelve or so years ago?'

'I don't know. Fraser was never as forthcoming as that although judging by the names...' Joan frowned, remembering '...Terry, Margaret, Geoffrey and whoever else, it's quite possible.'

'Er, can we use this story?' Laura asked. 'Not being funny but I'd hate to see this published and have your house bombarded by intense men with bad haircuts and a lack of social skills asking whether they could, y'know, have a look around the garden.'

'Well, I wouldn't want you to be specific about my address but I have no objection to being quoted. As for Fraser, we've kept in touch on a superficial level over the years. Laurence said Fraser would like some of the mystique and speculation about his 'disappearance' and the *Good Education* album dispelled.'

Laura and Nick exchanged a glance, barely able to believe their luck.

'Are you still in touch with Liz Raymonde?' Laura asked.

'Yes, I am. We're friends and she'll be pleased to verify the story but only up to a point,' Joan answered with a smile. 'Let's not get prurient about all this. I'm sure that Laurence and I can get some sort of tacit approval from Fraser too.'

Nick and Laura smiled at each other.

***

Philip Anderson lapsed back into reverie as the next defendant's case was heard. Michael Benson, from a Jamaican-English background, had a different demeanour to the defendant from the previous day. Behind a muscular physique, he was apologetic and downcast, his voice barely rising above a murmur as he answered the charges. He already seemed resigned to a custodial sentence and became animated only when the judge asked whether he had anything to say in his defence. Benson whispered to his lawyer who shuffled some papers and then addressed the judge.

'Mr. Benson wishes to mention some salient facts in his defence, Your Honour. In 2009, he spent three months on secondment to a finance company and, only when this ended, did he became embroiled in the unfortunate events described earlier. My client's involvement in these events was peripheral and he is cognisant of his misdemeanours for which he expresses remorse. He contacted his former employers to request a testimony for this case and is upset at not being favoured with a response.'

Philip yawned, then stifled the involuntary action. He noticed the bored expressions on the faces of his jury colleagues and only half-listened to the ongoing legal discussion but was jolted awake when the prosecution lawyer requested and was granted the chance to speak.

'Your Honour, I took the opportunity to contact Mr. Benson's former employers at Alpha Venture. The defendant worked under the mentorship of a Mr. Geoffrey Harris. I requested of Mr. Harris why he allowed the defendant's contract to be terminated. He replied as follows:

"'I can confirm that Michael Benson was in the employ of Alpha Venture from June to August 2009 as part of our Community Outreach programme which offers young people a brief tenure with an option to continue the arrangement should the candidate so merit. Initially, he showed promise but, regrettably, this soon disappeared. Mr. Benson was error-prone, truculent and displayed little willingness to learn. His period of employment coincided with the theft of a watch and mobile phone from the floor on which he worked. I am not asserting that he was responsible for the theft but it has been the only such occurrence during my time at Alpha Venture. I sanctioned the decision to discontinue his contract beyond the three month trial period and did so with regret as it was an opportunity which may not be extended to him in the future. I wish him well in his future endeavours. Geoffrey Harris, Portfolio Analyst, Alpha Venture Ltd."'

Philip was quietly indignant. The letter was surely from Elizabeth's husband – she said he worked for Alpha Venture - and the sanctimonious, snide, insinuating tone squared with the impression of Geoff which Philip formulated in the wine-bar. Michael Benson looked distraught and his lawyer altered his strategy to one of damage limitation. When the jury met to discuss the latest evidence, most agreed that Benson seemed as culpable as the first defendant. Philip, nonetheless, tried to argue his case.

'I'm not so sure. It seems to me that his confidence was shattered when that bank let him go. I think he deserves some leniency; he's more a victim of circumstance and peer-group pressure.'

27

The jurors exchanged puzzled glances. Ever the voice of reason, Grace spoke. 'Philip, I hear what you're saying but it doesn't make him less guilty, does it?'

The jury foreman, Andrew Butler, peered at Philip. 'Yesterday, you were all for hanging one of the accused; today, you side with an accomplice. That's not very consistent, Mr. Anderson. Why the change of heart?'

Philip paused before replying. A few jurors nodded in agreement with Butler and Philip needed to be careful not to give the pompous man any grounds to further pursue this line of thinking.

'Well, look at him - Benson's whole demeanour is different to his co-defendants. They strut around the courthouse giving the impression they're enjoying the attention; Benson doesn't.'

Simon, a quietly-spoken juror scoffed. 'What about the fact that he's admitted guilt? Come on, Philip, admittedly he's not as unsavoury as that...toerag yesterday but he's still culpable.'

Philip raised his hands and spoke in a tone which indicated this was his final word on the matter.

'Just my feeling, that's all. I think he's more unlucky than culpable.'

***

Philip walked away from the court berating himself for allowing emotions to impinge upon his judgement. The reason for his dislike of Geoff Harris was pretty obvious but the proximity of the courthouse left the maxim 'innocent until proven guilty' ringing in his brain. Elizabeth's diatribe against her husband yesterday and Geoff's supercilious letter supporting the prosecution's case had coloured Philip's judgement. The latter might have been justified; as for the former, he'd only heard Elizabeth's side. She was on an adrenalin rush after her reprieve in court and copious amounts of champagne but had seemed genuine. Besides, his tryst with her last night was enough to influence anybody's judgement.

Ahead, Philip saw the five young men whose trial he was attending, Michael Benson among them. He seemed remote from the others despite an attempt to participate in their raucous conversation. Perhaps he thought his immediate future was inextricably linked with his co-defendants and he may as well make the best of it. Philip wanted to speak with Benson but it wasn't judicious to approach him directly. Again, he examined his motives. Was it a desire to gather more ammunition for his personal vendetta against Harris or a desire to persuade Benson of better opportunities away from his low-life friends? Mostly the former, he knew.

Benson bade farewell to the rest of the group and turned left at the corner of the road as the others continued straight ahead. Philip followed him until they'd walked about 20 yards.

'Michael?' Philip called. 'Michael Benson?'

Benson swivelled around and stared at Philip, defiance evident.

'Who are you?' he asked.

'I'm Philip Anderson, I'm sitting in on your court case,' Philip replied, thinking it best not to disclose his jury member status; the conversation might not be convivial, he could legally compromise himself. 'I thought you were pretty roughly dealt with, what with being ditched by that bank and er, you don't seem like the rest of your gang. I just wanted to get your side of the story.'

'Why? You a batty boy or somefink? What's your game?'

'Like I said, I just feel uncomfortable with the way people are sometimes treated in court.'

'Well, there ain't much me or you can do about that.' Benson's tone modified. 'Not when you're from round here, there ain't. You a do-gooder?'

'I work for a newspaper, one committed to highlighting injustice. If you deserve a fairer hearing than you're receiving here, maybe I can help. For instance, that bank guy more or less accused you of theft. If that's not the case, it's slander. Did you steal anything while working there?'

'No, I took home bits and pieces of stationery for my kid sister but I didn't have nuffink to do with someone's mobile getting nicked. Nuffink.'

'Well, there you go. That, what's his name, Harris bloke implied you did and that's a nasty thing to do. Was it typical of your experience there?'

Benson looked at Philip with renewed interest. Having spent his youth learning the rudiments of self-preservation on what was often referred to as "a problem housing estate", he was adept at recognising potential opportunities.

'Mr. Harris was no better nor worse than any of 'em. He wanted to get me interested in the work but all I wanted was somefink to put on application forms for a proper job. I was happy running errands and didn't really care about anything else. Best bits were when his missus came in and Mr. Harris wasn't there.'

'Why's...' Philip voice's faded and he cleared his throat, attempting to sound indifferent to this information. 'Why's that? Bit of all right, was she?'

'Yeah mate, proper piece of ass. I thought she had a thing for me at one stage, teasing me about girlfriends and that. She'd do me fine for a girlfriend, know what I'm saying?' Michael leered.

Philip smiled hesitantly. He wasn't enjoying the conversation now.

'Well, Michael, you should tell your legal guy that the insinuation of theft is untrue and see what he thinks. You should think about what you're doing with your life too. You don't want to hang around that bunch of losers getting into trouble. I've got to go but take care, OK?'

Philip made a clumsy attempt at a fist bump.

'Stay safe, bruv,' Benson said, struggling to keep a straight face. He waited until Philip turned to leave. 'Hey, put a good word in for me with the rest of the jury.'

Well, that didn't go as planned, Philip thought. The crafty bugger knew all along that I was on the jury and strung me along to see what I wanted. What were the chances of him bringing Elizabeth into the conversation? And what's all that about her flirting with him? No, that didn't go at all as planned. I'd better tread carefully with young Benson; he could put me in an awkward position. I'd better take my mind off Elizabeth for a while too. Yes, that would be best.

He heard the trilling sound of his mobile phone, fished it out of his pocket, saw Elizabeth's name, sighed, then smiled and answered it.

***

Michael Benson watched the receding figure of Philip Anderson. So, what was all that about then? Concerned about injustice? Yeah, right. He's a juror but what possible interest could he have in me and what's his interest in that Harris geezer? Harris stitched me up good and proper. No wonder he didn't answer the letter my legal aid guy sent to him. Bastard. But why is Anderson interested in him or is it his wife? He near choked when I mentioned her. Harris might like to know that, might even help me out if I told him. Hmmm, I'll have a think about this, there has to be something in it for me, there *has* to be. Maybe I should tell my brief or bump fists with Anderson tomorrow morning in front of the other jury geezers, it might scare him into saying what he's up to. What's it called? Contempt in court or something like that.

At home, Michael told his mother, Dorothy Benson, that the court case wasn't going well but he had an idea which could work in his favour.

'And what's that? You don't do nothing else wrong, Michael, you hear me? You be setting an example in this family, boy. No more trouble.'

'Don't worry, Mum. It's all good.'

His mother reached out and hugged him.

'You a good boy, just fell in with the wrong crowd. OK, get changed and tell Clyde dinner's soon.'

Michael went to his room, lay on his bed and tried to make sense of things. His mother had nailed it - he was a bright boy with good grades at school but he'd fallen under the influence of a group of youths who terrorised his estate. Once this happened, Michael could either run with them or live his life in fear of incurring their displeasure. He was an unconvincing gang member and the more hard-nosed members only called on him when they needed an alibi or help with whichever nefarious scheme they'd hatched up - Michael was articulate and could talk them out of trouble through the simple virtue of sounding polite and reasonable.

He didn't enjoy the company of his so-called friends but he had little choice; growing up on this estate, his horizons were restricted. His mother, Dot Benson – a conscientious, hard-working woman who adored her children and exemplified the matriarchal church-going Caribbean lady - possessed an aptitude for choosing her partners badly. Her three children were the progeny of two different fathers, both of them feckless individuals who maintained minimum contact with their offspring or their ex-wife, and she had now thrown in her lot with a new man.

Dot's engaging personality and tireless endeavours on behalf of her family made her the recipient of much goodwill around the Shillingtree Estate, a sprawling amalgamation of high-rise flats and small houses. Unfortunately, this presented a problem for Michael who received the taunts of the more recalcitrant youths on the estate. He hated Mondays in school when he would run the gauntlet of a barrage of sneering remarks such as 'Benson, yo mama tek you to Sunday school yesterday?', 'Still saving souls, Benson?', 'Your Dad still your Dad, Michael?' all delivered in a parody of the rich Jamaican patois used by Dot Benson.

As a consequence, Michael developed an aversion to acknowledging his roots. This tormented him, contributed to his rejection of school and led him to associate with the reprobates on the estate, landing him in trouble with the law. He knew, however, that this wasn't a fully valid excuse.

When his school, St. Ambrose's, announced that they had been invited to participate with Alpha Venture on a part-time "Working within the Community" scheme, Michael applied for one of the two available positions. His early academic promise and the fact that he was Dot Benson's son made his selection a formality and for all his bravado in dismissing the initiative when talking to Philip Anderson, he'd hoped it would be an opportunity for self-improvement. Michael abhorred the mentality of his associates who enjoyed notoriety and grudging deference around Shillingtree. Alpha Venture might be his means of escape.

Such optimism was misplaced. True, Geoff Harris had hoped that his young protégé would be imbued with a desire to build a career for himself but Michael didn't share that hope. Conscious of his gauche vocabulary and preference for MacDonalds' burgers over the elaborate sandwiches ordered by Geoff and his colleagues, he resented the efforts of the AV staff to include him in their conversation and office banter.

Michael knew such chippiness was self-defeating but years of Shillingtree ridicule over his righteous upbringing gave him the idea that he was being patronised within Alpha Venture. When told that he would not be offered an extension to his contract, he was indifferent, only later realising the opportunity he had spurned. Resuming contact with the young hoodlums on the estate, he became embroiled in petty crime.

Hearing the clatter of saucepans and dishes in the kitchen, tears rolled down his cheek, tears born of polar opposites: self-pity and self-disgust. He'd let his mother down, he'd let himself down; it was time to change. Tomorrow, he'd speak to his brief about Anderson's suggestion. He wiped his cheek with the sleeve of his shirt and strode to his brother's room to tell him dinner was ready.

***

'You never!' exclaimed Rachel Appleby, coffee cup half-raised to her lips. 'Good God, it *is* always the quiet ones. How on earth did this happen?'

Elizabeth shrugged, immediately regretting her mention of Philip. She hadn't intended doing so but the weightless feeling manifested itself again as their conversation meandered along and she blurted out that she'd slept with somebody she barely knew.

Rachel replaced her coffee cup on the table, sat back in her chair and gazed at Elizabeth, awaiting more. Elizabeth remained silent, staring down at the table willing the words back into her mouth.

'I shouldn't have said that, Rachel,' she mumbled.

'Probably not but you have and you can't leave it there,' Rachel replied. 'C'mon, you're my dearest friend, you can tell me these things. Who? Why? Er, further details aren't essential but.......'

Elizabeth smiled; Rachel wasn't easily shocked - her patrician serenity usually withstood even the most surprising news. Now, that porcelain-like complexion was flushed with excitement and her eyes twinkled with a curiosity which Elizabeth was thrilled to be responsible for.

They first met at university. Rachel's aura of sophistication and maturity was equally admired and envied by fellow students and great things were expected of her. She attained a first in Art History and her PhD on Renaissance sculpture was lauded as "visionary". Then, she surprised everybody by dating Gerry Appleby, an East End building contractor and trumped this when she announced their engagement on her 24th birthday. Rachel hoped to escape her background of entitlement and privilege; furthermore, she was smitten by Gerry's gregariousness and ambition.

Rachel's instincts had been right, Gerry prospered and they revelled in a mutual introduction to a social circle removed from their upbringing. Their two children, Bradley and Elaine, were precociously at ease with their extended family and provided the final flourish to a relationship which Elizabeth felt fortunate to proximate.

'Well, I don't know how to explain it really,' Elizabeth replied with a shrug. 'After that court case, I met a neighbour of mine. Two things here; one, I felt lightheaded at the outcome of the case and two; Geoff has been annoying of late. Besides, the guy in question is handsome and amusing.'

'That's three things. Is there anything else to add?'

'A lady doesn't kiss and tell, Rachel. I can still hardly believe what happened and I've no idea what'll happen next.'

'Geoff? Where does he fit in now?'

'I don't know. We're going through a ropey patch and I don't know, he's still....look, I know you don't like Geoff though I've never understood why you took against him so much,' Elizabeth replied. Rachel looked away, sipped her coffee and then resumed eye contact with Elizabeth.

'Just one of those things, I guess. I'm sure he's not very enamoured of me either. But *who is* the guy?' Rachel asked.

'Just a neighbour, look Rachel, can we leave it at that? Like I said, I shouldn't have mentioned it.'

A hush fell over the two friends. Elizabeth thought Rachel was holding something back but couldn't even begin to guess what that might be; Rachel saw her position as Elizabeth's confidante threatened by the arrival of somebody new, however presumptuous it was to assume she would always retain that role. The uneasy silence lingered until they looked at each other, laughed and cordiality was restored. When they left the café an hour later, Elizabeth sensed the return of that light-headed feeling and reached into her bag for her mobile phone.

***

Tom Brady smiled as he read another reply to the internal memo he'd sent to Alpha Venture's staff. 'Probably one of your better ones, Tom, and that's saying something,' it said. He was alerted to another incoming message, this one from Mark Llewellyn, the Chief Executive of Alpha Venture. Llewellyn had never discussed the press release/Deborah Jarvis incident with Tom and two years on, it rarely crossed Tom's mind when he communicated with his boss.

Llewellyn's message was also a response to Tom's announcement of the latest Outreach initiative; something which Llewellyn wished to discuss with Tom. Tom's finely attuned antennae were alerted by the tone of the e-mail even though it was standard practice for him to discuss such ideas with Llewellyn and to select the participants. He rang Llewellyn, asked to see him and tried to clear his mind of negativity en route. Llewellyn was somebody respected for his business acumen rather than any personal characteristics - like many others in such a position, Tom mused. He arrived at Llewellyn's office and was beckoned in through the open door.

33

'Tom, come in, take a pew. Oh, close the door behind you, please. I'm sure you've seen references to the Outreach programme in the press, things like Martin Glover's snidey remark in his column last week. As an expert in press statements...' a pause for effect, '...you'll be aware of Glover's implication that this initiative is all style and no substance?'

Tom nodded.

'Well, I was thinking we should maybe go for something bolder, something the media would acknowledge as substantial. What I'm proposing is that the seniors lead from the front, so to speak. I think it would send out a strong message if you delivered the speech, presentation, whatever at St. Ambrose's. What do you think?'

So, Tom thought with grudging admiration, this was how Llewellyn would get his revenge for the infamous press release. How subtly he'd managed it! St. Ambrose's was colloquially known as St. Asbo's in recognition of the school's unruly reputation; many of its students had received a court-issued ASBO (Anti-Social Behaviour Order). The school's very notoriety was the reason Tom suggested AV pay a visit there and he'd hoped a few career-minded employees would volunteer for this visit to curry favour with senior management. Llewellyn had neatly turned the tables on Tom cognisant that Tom could hardly refuse the suggestion.

'I had in mind a small group making a presentation but I can er, see the value of this idea,' he replied.

'Good man, Tom, I knew I could rely on you. Can I leave you to put it all together? Anything you need from me, just call.'

'Thanks for your support, Mark,' Tom said with a pained smile as he walked towards the door.

'OK, I'll tell the head at St. Ambrose's that he'll see you next Tuesday.'

Tom, hearing the last four words, bit his lip to prevent himself from replying and left the room. Was Llewellyn really adding insult to injury? Tom was grateful that nobody was present to witness his humiliation.

***

Mark Llewellyn saw the door close and leaned back, smiling as he heard Tom's footsteps recede down the corridor. Revenge was, indeed, a dish best served cold. That would teach the smug bastard to play his silly little game.

Llewellyn had been a peer of Brady's at the time of the press release but had since moved to the most senior position in the firm. The embarrassment inflicted on him and Deborah Jarvis by Brady was never publicly spoken about within earshot of Mark who, nonetheless, realised his colleagues were aware of it. He hadn't necessarily waited for a chance of retribution but Brady needed to be reined in. It had been enjoyable reminding him who called the shots around here.

Knowing the workings of Tom's mind, Mark was aware that the communications man could still make it sound like his own initiative and probably turn the visit into a success but it would require considerable ingenuity to do so and leave him with an awkward few days ahead. Yes, that had indeed been an entertaining few minutes.

***

Jeremy Mead winced as he heard the door slam in the office next to his. It wasn't like Tom Brady to betray emotion but that sounded like a tantrum finding some release. Jeremy returned to his work but curiosity got the better of him and he visited Tom's office.

'Oi, 'ave it,' he roared in a coarse accent as he walked into Tom's office. 'Got to hand it to you on that one, Tom. I take it you don't see St. Asbo's as one of London's great seats of learning, then?'

Jeremy had been a friend ever since they joined Alpha Venture within a few months of each other and their respective career paths had followed a similar upward trajectory. Tom frowned, removed his glasses and squeezed the bridge of his nose.

'Don't mention that bloody place to me. Llewellyn's dumped me with addressing those thugs - not at all what I had in mind. A banker and one with an Irish accent too, they'll have a field day.'

'Ah. Sooner you than me,' Jeremy said with a grimace.

'Tell me, J, have you ever picked up any hints from our esteemed leader that he dislikes me?'

'Mark's far too shrewd for that, Tom. Come on, you of all people should know that. If you didn't quite write the book on never showing your hand, you probably penned the introduction. You think this dates back to that press release? He's bided his time, if so.'

'I'm sure that makes it all the more enjoyable for him,' Tom shrugged. 'Oh well, I guess I'll have to spend a few hours getting down with the kids or hanging or whatever idiom they use these days.'

'For Christ's sake, don't try that approach. Think back to when you were at school and one of your teachers tried sounding cool. No, no, no, last thing you should do.'

'I'm Christian Brothers-educated,' Tom said in an exaggerated Irish accent. 'They just beat seven bells out of us, I wouldn't know about that.'

'You know, I wouldn't be at all surprised if you turn this into one of your PR successes. Mind you, it'll take something to sow the seeds of self-improvement in the minds of St. Asbo's finest. Good luck with that one.'

It was already past 6pm; Tom had spent the afternoon doodling on an A4 pad as he tried to think of a hook around which to draft his speech for the

35

St. Ambrose's visit. Jeremy was right, trying to communicate on their level would leave him open to ridicule - something in which those kids no doubt excelled. He checked the e-mail from St. Ambrose's headmaster. A Year 10 class had been selected which the e-mail described as '30 or so of our 14-15 year old students whose teacher, Mr. Murtagh, will be present. We expect the allotted hour to consist of a presentation followed by a Q&A session. We very much look forward to the visit.'

Q&A! Sweet Jesus, that should be fun. Tom consoled himself with the thought that a teacher would keep things under control but noticed on the A4 pad that his distracted doodling had produced a simplified depiction of a hangman's noose. For God's sake pull yourself together, he chastised himself as he twiddled the keyboard mouse to re-activate his computer terminal and typed the words 'St. Ambrose's London', into Google. The search returned 'about 420,000 results'. Tom added the word, 'success' to his search and the results were reduced to 'about 800.'

He noticed that the name Darren Peters appeared on many of the links. Darren Peters was a famous footballer who even Tom, whose interest in football rarely stretched beyond watching the more important games on television, knew of. Peters had been the subject of a series of lurid tabloid newspaper stories which gleefully detailed his complicated love life and multiple infidelities. The hounding of Peters became so intense that some newspapers referred to it as a witch-hunt. Public censure eased when he gave an interview which hinted at contrition. From the Google results, Tom gleaned that Peters had once been a pupil at St. Ambrose's.

What was the likelihood of getting Peters to help with the St. Ambrose's visit? He saw the possibilities – ring Peters' agent and candidly outline the benefits for both parties; Peters could join the visit which would receive no advance publicity to enhance the degree of self-effacement on his part; from Tom's perspective, the exercise could be turned into a success. He opened another window on his PC, clicked on a link to Darren Peters' website and recoiled from a torrent of garish images and advertisements for merchandise...and a contact number for his agent, Jack Watson. Tom dialled the number.

'Jack Watson speaking.'

'Hello, Mr. Watson. My name is Tom Brady, head of communications at Alpha Venture. I'm sorry for calling you outside what could be termed office hours but I'm guessing you're a man who doesn't conform to normal work parameters. I'd like to talk about your client, Darren Peters.'

'Alpha Venture? Dazzle's already got deals although some are, er, under review so pitch me.'

Tom reclined in his chair and smiled. This would be a breeze.

'I don't have what you'd perceive as a pitch, Mr. Watson, but I can propose something of greater value to your client.'

'How much and what's involved? Oh and call me Jack.'

'Jack, let's drop the act here. I've worked in the media business for about 20 years so I know what I'm talking about. Darren has an image problem right now and, to be frank, so does Alpha Venture. Now, I'm visiting St. Ambrose's school on Tuesday and you'll probably be aware that (a) St. Ambrose's also has an image problem and (b) it's the school where Darren spent some no-doubt happy years immersed in his studies. It strikes me that there's an opportunity here for Darren, us and St. Ambrose's to garner some favourable publicity.' Tom paused.

'Go on,' was Watson's response.

'You mentioned a pitch so how about Darren joins me on Tuesday? No prior announcement or publicity but a local press reporter can just happen to be there, his jaw drops as he realises Darren Peters, yes *the* Darren Peters is passing through to say hello, local paper gets a scoop, Darren looks bashful and says he's just dropping by, never lose touch with my roots me, also glad to help this community-minded unfairly-maligned financial organisation to share their largesse with the less-privileged, a kick-about in the playground, pupils lap it all up, Alpha Venture seen as good guys, Darren seen as a good guy, we all walk off into the sunset.'

'Hey Tom, you're a player, that's impressive. Short notice and I wouldn't normally entertain the idea of Dazzle doing anything for free other than having a dump or attending some newsworthy charity event but you've put forward a good case for waiving his fee. So, what's next?'

'Can you speak to Darren and get the green light? I'll call St. Asb...sorry, St. Ambrose's, let them know that the arrangement is contingent upon secrecy but I'll ensure someone from the local paper is in attendance and that's about it. The pupils would normally be a concern but I'm sure they'll be awestruck by an A-list celebrity footballer.'

'Dazzle's already ok with this,' Jack laughed. 'He relies on me to handle stuff like this and I'm sure he'll enjoy it. He's genuinely a nice guy, you know. Just been portrayed unfairly recently.'

'Just one thing, do I have to call him Dazzle? I'd struggle with addressing another adult as Dazzle.'

Tom held the phone away from his ear to evade the loud guffaw.

'That's priceless. Darren it is, then. Bell you first thing tomorrow. Cheers, mate.'

Tom exited Peters' website and the computer screen returned to his original search on the school. He noticed a link to a local newspaper with details of a court case in situ where a St. Ambrose's student, Michael

Benson – the name sounded familiar – was among the accused in the trial of a gang of youths.

Then, Tom remembered Geoff Harris referring to him letters from two lawyers asking for an opinion on Benson's tenure at AV. Geoff said that the boy had been unproductive and his stay coincided with the disappearance of a watch and mobile phone. They decided that their response would subtly imply that Benson was unworthy of the trust invested in him. Tom replied to the request which seemed to favour a negative assessment and received a note of thanks from the lawyer.

So, young Benson ended up in court after all. Tom re-read the story which stated that the case was continuing with the defendants due back in court again tomorrow, Friday. Tom gazed out at the now-darkened sky as various scenarios formed in his mind. He would sleep on it. He left a note for Hilary and Calvin, his assistants, saying he wasn't sure but he could be late in tomorrow and left.

***

John Hooper returned to his office building after a stroll around the block. If Laura's intention was to rain on his parade, she'd succeeded but that wasn't Laura's style and her opening words had been congratulatory. During his walk, he thought back to various turning points in his life. Born into a comfortable middle-class background in Manchester, John had achieved good A-levels, a 2:1 in Classics at Cambridge and moved inexorably to an academic role at the same college he'd attended there. During a weekend in London, he attended a screening of the Kieslowski *Three Colours* trilogy at the National Film Theatre and a latent passion for arthouse cinema was activated. He became obsessed with *cinema vérité*, *nouvelle vague*, neo-realism, American independent films, any cinematic genre which tended towards the left-field.

He moved to a university post as a lecturer in Film Studies in London, met and fell for Elizabeth Davenport at a film club screening. A year later, Elizabeth suggested a skiing holiday which both of them silently hoped would rejuvenate a floundering relationship. During that holiday, John met Laura Holmes, Elizabeth met Geoff Harris and within days, they were an ex-couple. There followed John's epiphany and within a year of meeting Laura, he was working on the trading floor of Foden Barnes. When anybody mentioned the dichotomy inherent in John's conversion to capitalism, he argued that his wasn't a mindless pursuit of money, rather an endorsement of democracy.

'On the trading floor of any bank, you'll find Oxbridge graduates, barrow boys, French, Germans, science graduates, guys who quit school at 16 – all at ease with each other. *That* is the epitome of democracy.'

Even armed with this mantra, John was surprised by the prevalent ethos of the trading floor at Foden Barnes where people continually reinvented themselves. This was best exemplified by two new traders and even John, aware of his own propensity for changing careers and girlfriends, was astonished by their transformation.

Gareth Holman and Gavin Hamilton-Jones, Cambridge graduates both, soon made it clear they wished to distance themselves from that city's rarefied culture of learning. Gavin insisted on being called Gav, Gareth refused to answer to anything other than Gaz; their elegant Saville Row shirts and neckwear were abandoned for striped shirts and loud, garish ties which depicted cartoon characters in sexual congress. Strangest of all, their clipped, cut-glass accents morphed into the harsh *lingua franca* of a street market or football club dressing-room. John remembered one typical Monday morning exchange:

'All right, Gav? Fuck, you look a bit rough this morning. Larging it, was ya?'

'Too right, Gaz. Got any Red Bull in your desk, mate?'

'Yeah. Here, catch. So, what did you do? Still seeing that Marion bird?'

'Yeah, met her on Saturday night.'

'Smash it?'

'Nah, too pissed, innit. You, mate? Go down the football Saturday?'

'Nah, missus wanted to go to a bleedin' art gallery but I wasn't having none of that. Told her to behave; Saturday I either go down the football or the pub. She goes off in a huff and I went to the boozer to watch the football on telly. Nice pie, bit of banter, enough lager to float a ship and watched Dazzle score the winner for the Reds. Sweet.'

'On fire at the minute, the Dazzler is. I stuck a ton on him to get the first goal on Saturday at sixes, so that's me beer money for the weekend...get in there! Took Marion down that new curry house in the High Street, then on to the pub, met up with a few others and really went for it. Ended up slaughtered, hence the spot of difficulty with Marion. She wasn't best pleased.'

'I'm sure you'll make up for it, mate.'

'Too right, mate.'

John doubted the Ga-Ga twins, as they became known, saw this act as convincing but, to the bemusement of colleagues from genuine Cockney backgrounds, they persisted. A foreign exchange trader, Frank Garfield, who grew up in a down-at-heel part of East London invited the pair to what he termed 'a proper East End Friday night out.' Gavin and Gareth, thrilled, saw this as acceptance into a circle to which they craved inclusion. John, along with four colleagues, was invited along to witness the entertainment.

The evening started at a pub called the Pied Bull Tavern, known colloquially as the Pitbull & Tattoo, located in a dimly-lit street next to a stretch of lock-up garages. Gavin and Gareth looked around uneasily as a succession of thick-set men with scarred faces arrived and worked their way through pints of lager. Before long, Frank Garfield, who greeted many of the new arrivals by name, announced that it was time to move on.

'Why, where we going, mate?' Gavin asked, 'I er, quite like this place.'

'Yeah, the Pitbull is legendary around here but this is just a few warm-up pints before the main event. Lots of these guys,' Garfield gestured towards the thick-set men, 'are going there too.'

'The main event?' Gareth leered. 'Strip-joint, yeah?'

'Maybe later, Gaz. First we're going to see the best bare-knuckle fighting in London.' Frank pointed to a muscular man sipping a pint of water. 'See that bloke? He was unbeaten for years before he had to spend a bit of time away. He's out again and is taking on a geezer who's also just finished a stretch. It should be a cracker. Aha, our transport's arrived.'

Outside, a battered Transit van pulled up at the kerbside and the group from FB climbed in along with others from the bar. Frank sat at the front of the van with Gareth and Gavin. At the back, one of the scarred men chatted amiably with John and his colleagues.

'The two geezers with Frank, they're the two we're to sort out, yeah?' he asked. 'Nothing nasty, mind... just Frank said they was taking the piss.'

The van stopped in a quiet street and during the short walk to the hall, a man called Colin who wore a chunky gold chain and sported sovereign rings on both hands fell into stride with Gareth and Gavin within earshot of the rest of the FB group.

'You carrying?' Colin asked Gavin.

'Carrying? Carrying what?' Gavin replied.

'Shooters, blades, anything. Anyone the management don't recognise may get searched and they take a dim view of blokes carrying.'

Gavin and Gareth glanced at each other, alarmed, and Gavin assured Colin that they had no weapons, either on them or anywhere else.

'Good for you, mate,' said Colin. 'Nice to know we're in civilised company. Course if you ever want any, Frank can put us in touch and I'll sort you out. Do a good deal, I do, no questions asked.'

'Er, yeah, thanks,' Gareth mumbled.

At the hall, they were ushered in when Colin vouched for them. Inside a large room with crepuscular lighting designed to detract attention from passers-by, everybody was warned to keep the noise level down. A makeshift bar at one end of the hall seemed to sell cans of beer only.

'Not a good idea to sell bottled beers at something like this,' Frank said and no further explanation was deemed necessary. When their eyes adjusted to the enveloping murk, they saw that the audience was exclusively male and, predominantly, white. Conversations were conducted with minimal eye contact as the participants stared straight ahead. A tangible air of menace prevailed and even though he was part of Colin's entourage, John didn't feel comfortable. Gavin and Gareth looked ill at ease as they were provided a potted history of the contestants about to begin the first bout.

'Stacey there, bloke with the tattoos on his neck, is pretty new to this. Tried his hand as an amateur boxer but couldn't be doing with the regulations, never was one for sticking to laws, Stacey. The other bloke's a pikey, a lot of the bare-knuckle boys are. On the move a lot, you see, have that surprise element about them,' was the pre-fight preamble from one of Colin's friends.

Gavin gulped when a man issued a bellow of encouragement and was immediately hushed. The two boxers, both of wiry build, moved towards the centre of the hall where an obese man introduced them to the crowd as being in the middleweight category and succinctly outlined the rules: 'No kicking, no gouging, no biting, anything else goes. OK, fight.'

There followed a sickening exchange of blows as the two contestants soon drew blood from each other. John glanced towards Frank who clearly had no appetite for this. Frank caught his glance, shrugged and inclined his head towards the bar where they were joined by Chris Williamson.

'Maybe I've overdone this a bit but those two needed something to steer them away from that geezer act of theirs,' Frank said.

'Agree on both counts. Jesus, this is pretty brutal,' Chris said with a shudder as the sound of another punch finding its target reverberated around the hall. 'I take it this isn't your normal idea of an evening's entertainment, Frank?

'God, no. Last night, for instance, I was at a Tate members' private view.'

'Mind you, I guess there was just as much blood and bruised flesh on show there,' John said with a smile. 'Isn't it a Francis Bacon exhibition at the moment? I didn't have you down as an art connoisseur, Frank.'

'I don't think anybody on the trading floor is as they seem. The Ga-Ga twins had the sort of education I'd kill for but here they are trying to come across as the blokiest blokes imaginable.'

Frank, Chris and John winced at the sound of bone cracking against wood and turned to see one of the fighters spread-eagled on the wooden floor, blood trickling from his nose.

'That probably constitutes a knock-out,' Frank drawled. 'I think our work here is done. Let's round up the others and slip away while the guy's being revived.'

The rest of their group were grateful to leave and John saw Frank flash a thumbs-up gesture in response to Colin's enquiring gaze. Henceforth, Gavin and Gareth's laddish banter dwindled and their accents reverted to their normal refined tone.

John recalled Frank Garfield's words...how accurate they were! Everyone at FB seemed to be involved in an act, one which John soon tired of. And now he was tiring of his nascent career as the co-owner of....of what exactly? A website which poked fun at modern-day mores but which only seemed to reflect those self-same attitudes back at him. And people were interested in this? Good God, the layers of inherent irony would frazzle anybody's brain. All it took was one phone call from Laura and her implicit disapproval to make him question what he was doing. Not disapproval, more like disappointment. If one call from Laura could shatter the idyll of his current chosen career, it clearly wasn't based on much.

And then there was Laura. How had he been so indifferent to her years earlier? He'd lucked out when she'd fallen for him, why hadn't he been more aware of that? Well, that was then and now she was Laura Armitage. John walked into the men's toilet at his office, saw his reflection in the mirror and recoiled. He was a picture of an unhealthy lifestyle - too much drinking and takeaway meals. It was time for a change.

'Hey, John, stock's still heading north,' Chris said when he returned to the office. 'Where have you been? The phones have hardly stopped.'

'Just out for a walk, I needed some fresh air. I'm going to call it a day.'

'Are you OK?' Chris asked, concerned. 'You look pale, too much excitement for one day, eh?'

'Yeah, something like that. I'll see you tomorrow, Chris. You should head home as well; we've been doing silly hours recently,' John replied as he left the office again.

***

The front door closed and the click-clack of high-heeled shoes receded into the distance. Philip saw from his bedside clock that it was 19:20, rose from the bed, pulled on his clothes and noticed that Elizabeth had left her scarf on a chair. He held it to his nose, breathed in the scent of her perfume and dropped the scarf on the bed. His earlier resolve to put Elizabeth out of his mind disappeared when she called and suggested meeting for a drink. They met in a bar close to Russell Road and were soon back at Philip's house where there was little time for conversation as they tumbled into bed. Later, they lay together, content, before Elizabeth sighed wistfully and said she had to leave. 'I don't want to bump into Geoff as he walks past.'

The spell was broken when she mentioned Geoff's name and a desultory silence settled over the room while she dressed, lightened only when Philip offered to drive her home. Elizabeth paused, sat down on the edge of the bed and laid her hand on Philip's shoulder.

'It doesn't have to be like this, Philip. Y'know, an hour or two grabbed here and there followed by me running off. But let's not rush things, OK?'

'Sure,' Philip replied breezily. 'Thirty-six hours ago, I barely knew you. I still barely know you but I'd like to find out more.'

'I really better go,' she said, smiling as she squeezed his shoulder. 'Don't get up, I'll let myself out and call you tomorrow.'

He heard her walk downstairs, heard the sound of curtains being opened in his living room, then hurried footsteps through his hallway followed by the front door being closed. All that remained of her was the lingering smell of her perfume on the scarf. Picking it up again, he went downstairs and left the scarf on the table in the hallway; he'd return it when he met her again, it could even be the excuse to call around to her house. Philip poured himself a small glass of Scotch, sat at his kitchen table and tried to piece together the whirlwind events of the last two days. His last romantic attachment – more of a fling – had been with a woman in the art department of *The Chronicle*, the newspaper where he worked as a sub-editor. It started at an office party, continued for a few weeks and then died out, much to the unspoken relief of both parties.

Philip couldn't be classified as commitment-phobic: he hadn't terminated enough relationships to qualify for this title, he just seemed to pick the wrong women. There was the Argentine heiress who took offence when Philip went to work on a weekend which she'd set aside to be with him; the aspiring actress who took exception to his defence of a TV critic with an unfavourable opinion of her minor role in a TV drama, the nurse he met while recuperating from a knee operation but who struggled with what she termed Philip's flippancy. And then there were the relationships which Philip himself had ended. It seemed as if he had a penchant for relationships which were doomed almost from the outset and since the fiasco with the art department woman, he had been more cautious in his pursuits. Now, the intriguing, mercurial Elizabeth dominated his thoughts less than two days after his first proper meeting with her.

He topped up his glass and walked upstairs to his study. Philip was the chief sub-editor at *The Chronicle,* a liberal newspaper proud of its political impartiality and championing of minority causes. Newspapers were in Philip's blood; his father had been a compositor for a national daily in the heyday of Fleet Street but lost his job in the early-90s when the industry embraced digital technology.

Philip, never one of life's natural delegators, immersed himself in the same minutiae as his supposed subordinates. In addition to a reluctance to delegate, he was skilled and meticulous. Journalists knew they could hand in lazily punctuated, ungrammatical copy to Philip and the resulting article would be buffed and polished to perfection without losing the signature style of the writer. In moments of loftier rhetoric, Philip would refer to his job as a noble calling and summarise it as 'applying gloss to dross.'

Philip knew he could pen better prose than many of the paper's regular columnists and held a comprehensive knowledge of the specialist fields of other correspondents. However, he lacked the conviction to articulate his thoughts with enough force for inclusion in *The Chronicle*. In discussions with journalists, Philip would envy the belligerence with which they expressed their views; his own world was less black and white.

One chastening experience came to mind when he conveyed his admiration for a rock band to a music critic who responded by dismissing the band's entire *oeuvre* in a manner which, to Philip, betrayed jealousy.

'Well, you know what they say; those who can, do; those who can't, criticise,' Philip said.

'And you know what else they say?' the rock critic spluttered, glaring at Philip. 'Those who can, write; those who can't, sub-edit. So you get back to inserting commas and full stops for people who *are* capable of articulating their views, you twat.'

At *The Chronicle*, it was acknowledged that certain sub-editors excelled at knocking pieces on the arts into shape, others were more adept at political news while others specialised in sport. One day, Philip suggested to the editor that the sub-editing staff be rotated for a few days. The editor, ever open to innovation, agreed and some of the resulting articles became minor *cause célèbres* in the newspaper world.

A report on a football match by Sam McNabb, the grizzled, forthright football correspondent was sub-edited by a woman more familiar with art reviews and the report abounded in florid language:

'...*the inherent beauty of Morgan's free-kick which described an arc over United's goalkeeper, evocative of a swallow diving in the evening twilight...Antonelli, Rovers' new Italian signing from Venezia, added a delicateness of touch which turned the midfield battle into a chiaroscuro of subtlety and brutishness...the winning goal was a serenely majestic sweeping move of Canalettoesque expansiveness, appropriately finished off by Antonelli, the new doge of Rovers' midfield. It was time for United to summon the gondoliers and head home, a sunken team.*'

McNabb was delighted with the piece and henceforth added baroque flourishes to his gritty reports. Less pleased was the political commentator,

Adam Haynes, whose *exposé* of parliamentary expense abuse was sub-edited by a man normally confined to the sports page. Haynes was aghast to read passages of the printed article:

'...*MacKenzie, the new MP, is viewed to have taken a punt and backed the three-legged nag rather than the hot favourite...Tom Nicholson, shadow Treasury minister, professed himself gutted when falling at the last fence of parliamentary privilege after a strong run on uncertain ground...Melanie Barrett, lauded as a pioneering filly holding her own among the male front-runners for a cabinet role will now be carrying extra weight as a penalty for her excessive use of the party whip.*'

One of *The Chronicle*'s financial journalists, Brian Curtis, writer of an influential weekly commentary was subbed by a woman whose normal post was on the lifestyle section of the Saturday edition:

'...*Clearly unaware of the current fashion for brown, the company's preference for blue in their annual report casts doubts on their levels of awareness...wearing an uncoordinated black and green combination, the CEO's speech lacked conviction...a* hors d'oeuvres *of plausible authenticity was followed by a financially ruining second course, a* smörgåsbord *of derivatives and other esoteric products which left one too sated for more.*'

Philip smiled in memory of the ensuing recriminations – both from irate journalists and Melanie Barrett, who felt ridiculed. The furore soon died and Philip's idea was lauded by one media commentator as 'a welcome piece of blue-sky thinking, a refreshing exercise in journalistic democracy.' It was, however, not repeated.

He sat in his study and sipped his drink but the computer remained switched off, work could wait for another day. Before long, he dozed off into an improbable dream where Elizabeth Harris and Michael Benson clinked champagne glasses together as they watched Canaletto, clutching an artist's palette and brush, score a goal from a difficult angle for a Premiership football team.

***

Elizabeth paused outside Philip's house, looked around before striding on to the pavement, crossed the road and noticed lights glowing from her house...typical, the one evening she wanted Geoff to work late. She wanted to shower and change before his return – a symbolic gesture of which only she would be aware. When she unlocked the door, a fragrant smell filled the air. She walked through to the kitchen where Geoff was arranging lilies in a vase.

'Elizabeth, darling, I was just about to call you.'

'You're home early Geoff, earlier than recently anyway.'

'Yes. Where were you?'

'I met Rachel.'

'Rachel? Again? I guess you've been putting the world to right?'

'You could say that, I love the flowers. Always my favourites, lilies.'

'I just wanted to say sorry for being a bit distant. Well, distant and a bit of a jerk, really. I spent ages at work today just staring out of the window and thinking. I know things haven't been perfect and I want you to know that I know that. I was thinking about when we first met...'

'Geoff,' Elizabeth stepped forward and placed her hand on his arm. 'Can I just freshen up a bit first? I went to an Italian café with Rachel; my breath must reek of garlic. Back in a minute.'

She raced upstairs to the bathroom, closed the door and leaned back against it...Jesus Christ, half-an-hour ago I was in bed with a man I only met yesterday; now my husband is all sweetness and light just when I have doubts about him and my head feels like it'll explode.

What was she doing? She liked Philip but hardly knew him. Exhilarated by their trysts, she didn't feel much remorse but what sort of person did that make her? She wasn't being entirely fair to Geoff. Sure, he wasn't always attentive to her but was she to him? Was her need of attention so all-encompassing? She towelled herself dry after her shower, her mind cleared and she knew what to do. She sent a text from her mobile and waited for the reply. It came within a minute and contained just three words – 'yes, of course.' She walked downstairs aware that this was the second staircase she'd descended within the last hour. In the kitchen, Geoff hugged her and murmured.

'Hmmm, you smell nice; I'm not getting garlic at all. As I said, I was sitting at work today thinking about Combloux when it occurred to me that it was eight years ago yesterday we first met. Let's get back to where we were then. I've been too remote, too tied up in work. I want to change that.'

'Geoff, I've got something to tell you.'

***

The street lights cast their vapour glow on the Thames and reflected back woozily from the river's oily surface. This was Tom Brady's favourite walk, one he shared with his Scottish terrier, Twigs. On a cold, clear February evening with the lights of Albert Bridge ahead and the giant chimneys of Battersea Power Station silhouetted in the distance, Tom paused to take in the view from Battersea Bridge. Twigs looked back, impatient to resume and Tom waved apologetically. Hang on, I'm apologising to a dog! It had been an evening of apologies; he'd arrived home from work just as his wife, Catherine, and their daughters, Angela and Jennifer, finished dinner.

'Sorry, Tom. The girls like a routine, we couldn't wait.'

'My fault, love, I got sidetracked at work.'

Tom ate his dinner and decided to take Twigs for a walk. Twigs, reluctant at first as he'd already been for a walk, acquiesced and soon realised it would be that nice riverside walk, it was night time and that would probably mean a visit to the pub where Tom often stopped on such occasions. The pub with the tasty crisps!

Tom was glad of the chance for a walk and as he buttoned up his coat in the hallway, his gaze drifted to the framed photograph of his parents hanging on the wall. Tom was from Cavan, on the southern side of the border with Northern Ireland. Some of his family made no attempt to hide their Republican sympathies and a cousin had served a prison sentence for terrorist offences. His father, Tom senior - a combative but fair-minded, tolerant man - favoured a united Ireland but held no truck with pursuing this through recourse to weapons and explosives.

Tom, third eldest of six, was the only Brady to attend university but his subsequent career path received a muted reaction at home. He had grown up in the shadow of his eldest brother, Michael, a renowned sportsman, whose collection of gaelic football medals were on prominent display in the Brady home. Tom Brady senior seemed to think that young Tom had 'gotten above his station' in his choice of career and relocation to England to pursue it and Tom was unable to mollify this opinion. When Tom returned to Cavan on holiday, he joined the forays to the pub and showed enthusiastic support for the local gaelic football team but this merely seemed to antagonise his father.

'Now wouldn't you be more at home cheering on Chelsea or Arsenal, Tom?' his father would ask him or question whether 'Guinness tastes as good to you as the English ales, Tom?'

The barbs hit home. During visits to Ireland, Tom would answer queries about work and London with the air of somebody avoiding snares even though he knew his father's thought process was a method of keeping in check any ideas of self-importance on Tom's part. In truth, Tom senior was proud of his son but Tom's wariness absorbed itself into his spiky persona and, in turn, made him adept at identifying weaknesses in others.

Tom's thoughts digressed towards Michael Benson. He remembered the sly, insinuating tone of that wretched letter he'd written which undermined young Benson's efforts during his time at AV. Geoff Harris said that the boy wasn't up to scratch but where was the crime in that? A kid from an estate who attended a school with a bad reputation wouldn't immediately shine in the high-achieving environment of Alpha Venture. Moreover, it was possible that Benson's descent into a downward spiral of crime was triggered by his summary dismissal from AV. Tom shuddered as he considered how his father would view Tom's testimony, how it might deprive Benson a chance of redemption. But what could he now do? And wasn't he jumping to conclusions anyway? Maybe Benson merited whatever punishment was coming to him.

And yet, he thought of Jennifer and Angela. He remembered how he and Catherine tried to make them appreciate the advantages bestowed upon them and to treat everybody with equanimity. It was time he, for once, showed altruism. He would turn up at the courthouse next morning and talk to Benson. It could be futile but he would, at least, feel better next time he walked past his father's assessing gaze. He was yanked out of his reverie as Twigs halted and whimpered. They'd reached a pub called the Jolly Butcher which Twigs recognised as a regular stop during their strolls. Pleased with his plan for the next day, Tom felt he deserved a drink.... and Twigs could munch some of those crisps which he liked so much.

**

'You change with the seasons,
You're less than celestial,
You'll wilt and then die,
You're hardly a perennial.'

John Hooper sang along to *Hardly A Perennial*, the Fraser Guthrie song playing on his stereo. Upon arriving home, he rifled through his alphabetically-filed record collection and retrieved his copy of *A Good Education (And See Where It Got Me)* because only vinyl would suffice on this occasion. He put on the album, poured himself a glass of red wine as the twinkling light on his answering machine caught his eye. The number 14 was on the small digital display. John frowned, played the messages - mostly congratulatory – and jotted down two names on a notepad before deleting all the calls.

He settled down on the sofa, played the first side of the album and remained motionless for a full minute when it finished. Picking up his wine glass and the two-thirds full bottle, he walked upstairs to his study where he used a search engine on his computer to locate recent internet references to Fraser Guthrie. One written a few days earlier by Laurence Tolliver caught his eye and he followed the link to Tolliver's website and a blog - *Tolliver's Travails* - which contained the music writer's musings.

One is reminded of the old cliché about London buses – yes, that one, dear reader, none for ages, three at once – when having heard diddledy-squat of Fraser Guthrie, erstwhile guitarist to the gods (how thrilling does the Fast Propellers' first album sound in these days of land-fill indie garbage?) in such a long time; one finds his name dropped in the hippest circles. The Lilliputians who keep the wheels of Tolliver's Travails oiled are a-quiver upon hearing that two of Her Majesty's Press' finest are about to unveil news which will cast a new light on Guthrie's magnum opus. Ah but where, I hear you cry? I'm saying nothing more but keep your eyes peeled for this story of stories. Think Orson Welles and Randolph Hearst, Fraser fans.'

'That'll be Laura,' John thought as he read the blog. Among the clumsy allusions to *Gulliver's Travels* and *Citizen Kane*, Tolliver was surely hinting at an article about Guthrie in a forthcoming issue of *Rosebud* which meant Laura was likely to be the author. She had mentioned something along those lines earlier. He picked up his mobile and rang her number.

'Laura Holm...er, Laura Armitage.'

'Never did envy you ladies that name-change business when you tie the knot. Hi, it's John here.'

'John, gosh, twice in one day. I am fortunate.'

'Oh, it used to take a lot more than twice in one day before you considered yourself fortunate, Laura, but we'll gloss over that.'

'Can't have been your sense of humour which attracted me to you, John, but we'll gloss over that too. What's up? Do you want me to write something for your website? A thousand words from a proper film critic on how *Titanic* is a movie about a boat based on, you know, a true story perhaps? I have to admit that piece on your website about North and South Korea having distinguishing characteristics other than being two halves of the same country was funny. I laughed...out loud.'

'Thanks for picking one of the pieces which I didn't write. Chris and I have a new contributor and that was his first piece for us. On another day, I might hold you to that *Titanic* idea but it's something else in print that I'm calling about. Are you now a friend of Laurence Tolliver?'

'Why do you ask?'

'Don't get all mysterious. In his blog, he's referring to the *Rosebud* article you said you'd written about Guthrie...am I right?'

'Me and another, actually. I had a collaborator who could out-geek even you about Fraser Guthrie.'

'So, what's the revelation? I'm going to keep asking you, you do realise that? I'd tell you.'

'Like hell you would. You'd pass cryptic comments and drop hints until I was left no choice but to batter his brains out, Your Honour.'

'How I miss these conversations, Laura. At least tell me when the world will find out.'

'You mean the few thousand who'll actually give one? It'll be next week and please don't join the pathetic debate on that Guthrie forum. You're better than that. So, are you happy with today's market activity?'

'You won't believe me but it's hardly crossed my mind since your phone call today. No, I tell a lie – it has crossed my mind but only in a not-sure-whether-I-care-a-lot sense.'

'I believe you, John. Yours is too lively a mind to be held captive by something as sordid as money for long. I always hoped you'd rejoin the pursuit of higher things. Will you?'

'I don't know. It's been an odd day. I came home today to find 14 messages on my phone and the only two I was really interested in were quotations from decorating firms to do some work on the bathroom.'

'Gold-plated tiles, eh? You're right to shop around for quotations; it's a competitive corner of the market. It's good talking to you again. Despite what I said earlier, I *would* like to meet for a drink.'

'That's better. Let me know when you're free.'

'I will. Bye.'

John reached for the wine bottle and decanted the remainder into his glass. He scrolled through the messages on his mobile until he found the one he wanted and read it again.

Ya hit m oudda the ballpark dude. Way 2 go. Guess u'll nvr listen to my offer now but it stands...yr 40%, name the price. Doug

Maybe he'd call Doug tomorrow after all.

    ***

3 - FRIDAY

Geoff Harris awoke, heard toiletries being gathered together in the en-suite bathroom and saw a small suitcase open on the bedroom floor: Elizabeth was already up. She walked in as he climbed out of bed.

'So, you're off then?'

'Well, it makes sense, doesn't it? No point in lingering now that I've decided.'

'I suppose not. Want a hand with anything?'

'No. It's OK, Geoff.'

A silence settled over the room as she closed the clasp on the case.

'I'll be off then. I'll call you later and er, thanks for being so.....'

'That's all right, best you get going. Talk to you later.'

'Yes. Bye Geoff.'

They embraced awkwardly as she pushed the case in front of her, descended the stairs, picked up her coat and bag from the hall table, searched for her scarf, frowned, shrugged her shoulders and left the house, eyes fixed straight ahead, determination personified.

***

'Wake up, Tom. Tom.' Catherine Brady shook her husband's shoulder.

Tom opened his eyes; at 6:45, it was later than normal for him to rise. Two things came to mind immediately; he'd spent longer in the pub last night than intended and he didn't need to rise so early, anyway. He went down to breakfast and his daughters giggled at his dishevelled appearance.

'Did you and Twigs go to the pub last night, Daddy?' asked Jennifer, the youngest.

'Did Twigs say so, sweetheart?'

Angela, 10 years old a week earlier, walked gravely to the door leading to the living room where Twigs sat, head resting on his front paws. She folded her arms and addressed the dog.

'Mr. Twigs, did you lead Daddy astray last night?' she asked. She then turned back towards Tom and Jennifer and nodded. 'You were right, Jen, Twigs admits it. Daddy, are you hanging over?'

Tom laughed, his heart ablaze with affection.

'It's "have you got a hangover", darling. Yes, a bit, not much though.'

'As much as Grandad when he goes out?'

Catherine entered the kitchen, heard this exchange and smiled.

'Grandad's older, Angela. When he has drinks, it has more effect.'

'Did Daddy start singing those songs about Ireland last night, Mum? The ones Grandad sings.'

Sensing the conversation was headed for more contentious waters, Catherine reminded the girls that they were running late for school and bustled around preparing lunches. The girls left and Tom remained at the table gazing out of the window. Catherine returned, wrapped an arm around Tom and ruffled his hair.

'You're not suffering this morning, are you? That dog is a bad influence, he leads you astray.'

'No, I was just thinking about Dad and how he must seem to the girls.'

'As he should do, Tom, he's a doting grandfather. Don't read much into it, he saves the more bloodthirsty rebel songs 'til none of the grandchildren are around. I should know; I'm pretty much word perfect on songs like *Skibereen* by now.'

'You're about the only English person he has regular conversations with and he thinks the world of you. I won't be so presumptuous as to say you should consider that an honour but, you know. Besides, *Skibbereen* is a great song.'

'Granted. But not in a pub in rural Cavan at one in the morning when you're trying to tone down your English accent.'

'Hmmm, you're right, love. OK, I'll be off. I'm not going to the office first thing. I'll tell you about it later, it's a new departure for me – Tom the good Samaritan.'

'Never saw you as anything else, Tom. Don't forget, you promised the girls that we'd all watch the DVD Angela got for her birthday tonight.'

'Sure. I can have a drink with Twigs during it. It is Friday after all.'

'Booze hounds, the pair of ye,' she said in a mock-Irish accent.

Tom left and walked to the underground station singing the courtroom lines from Bob Dylan's *The Lonesome Death of Hattie Carroll*. Christ, he thought, I feel virtuous.

***

The alarm clock shrilled in Philip Anderson's bedroom, loud enough to wake Philip, asleep in the study. He shakily stood up and rushed to the bedroom to switch off the alarm clock. Philip had woken at his desk just after 2 am, stumbled over to the comfortable armchair, pulled a blanket over himself and fell asleep. Alarm clock switched off, he opened the curtain eager for further confirmation that the mornings were starting to brighten earlier and gasped as he saw Elizabeth Harris striding down the road towards his house, wheeling a suitcase.

'Jesus Christ, she's left Geoff. Bloody hell,' he said aloud and ran to the study to clear away the blanket and whisky bottle. He returned to the bedroom, tousled the bedclothes and waited for the doorbell to ring. Ten seconds went past, 20 seconds, 30 seconds; silence prevailed. He edged towards the window and peered out to see Elizabeth reach the bottom of the road and turn the corner. A woman of mystery, no mistake about that. Did I imagine all that? What is she doing?

He remained at the window and noticed that his neighbour who lived directly opposite was also standing at the window of her house looking out, staring at Philip. Not quite sure what to do, he waved a greeting towards her. To Philip's amazement, Geraldine Simpson – Mrs. Geraldine Simpson – opened her dressing gown and smiled at Philip as she stood semi-naked by the window. Philip remained rooted to the spot.

What in God's name is happening in this road, he wondered. Geraldine was married to Howard Simpson, owner of a local café, one where Philip often had breakfast. He knew the Simpsons' well enough to receive an invitation to their annual summer barbecue, an event which usually ended in bacchanalian excess but this dawn striptease was a new departure. It was shaping up to be an odd day.

***

The sound of squeaking leather on the polished wood floor outside her office made Michelle Holley look up in surprise. She'd called Jan Netherby about 30 seconds earlier to ask him if he could come to Mark Llewellyn's office. After a knock on the door, Netherby entered the office, flashing what he considered his open, friendly smile.

'I await the day when you assume control from Mark, Michelle. Board meetings will be more interesting *and* more pleasing on the eye.'

Michelle rummaged on her desk for a sheet of paper which she pushed towards Netherby.

'Mr. Llewellyn can't make it in today. He told me to ask you to, in his words, keep an eye on things for him, Mr. Netherby. Here's a list of meetings which he was scheduled to attend. I've cancelled them all but I thought I'd let you know.'

Netherby's smile disappeared as he glanced at the list.

'Ah, I'm sure I could've muddled through these but never mind. Oh and no need for the Mr. Netherby. Call me Ned,' he said, smiling.

'I'll let you know if there's anything else, Mr. Netherby.'

'Bloody impertinence,' Netherby fumed to himself as he left. 'Acts as if she runs the place. Those looks will fade one day, then see what happens.'

Jan Netherby joined Alpha Venture a year earlier from the London office of Banca Argento where he was seen as a specialist in 'streamlining', a euphemism for periodic rounds of job cuts. His method, when appointed department head, was to attempt to endear himself to staff by assuming an air of conviviality and *bonhomie*. When the time arrived for him to announce the job cuts, he would sigh and inform staff in a wracked voice that he was truly sorry and would understand if he was held to blame.

Enough people were convinced by this act for Netherby to use it with subtle variations. His preference for matey familiarity and a dislike of the gender ambiguity of Jan led him to ask people to address him as Ned. Lacking formal qualifications, he insisted that 'the school of hard knocks gave me the skill-set needed for business.' Netherby's meteoric rise within Banca Argento was due to his willingness to repeat the job-cutter role allied to a feral instinct to ingratiate himself with senior management. When attending a work function, he would mentally sketch an organisation chart of those present and ensure his time was spent with those at the pinnacle of that chart. The 'Netherby nod' entered Banca Argento vernacular indicating the moment he noticed the arrival of somebody of greater importance than whoever he was speaking to. The nod was his own recognition that the conversation be terminated so he could engage with the new arrival.

Jeremy Mead's wife worked at Banca Argento and Netherby's grim reaper reputation preceded him to Alpha Venture when he was appointed to a senior role. It caused a ripple of consternation – AV was known as a retainer of staff - and he was viewed with suspicion. Within the narrower confines of AV (500 employees against Banca Argento's staff of 3,600), Netherby's trusted *modus operandi* for self-advancement was stymied and his joshing conversation and pleas to be addressed as Ned were met with disdain. His ego, however, refused to entertain the idea that he wasn't either liked, respected or feared and he made himself more unpopular by inveigling himself into Llewellyn's trust. It was Tom who first referred to Netherby's office as 'the nether regions'...a phrase soon widely used.

Michelle Holley, regularly exposed to Netherby's oleaginous attempts to curry favour with Llewellyn, smiled. Having raised his hope of assuming Mark's role for the day, she'd quashed it by cancelling all Mark's meetings. Guyana-born and aware of her exotic appearance, she took particular exception to Netherby's condescending flirtatious remarks. She tossed back her dreadlocks (today's choice of hairstyle) and wondered whether she could have some more fun in Mark's absence.

***

The short walk to the bus stop brought Philip Anderson into contact with both Howard Simpson and Geoff Harris. During the last twelve or so hours, he had been in bed with the wife of one and accorded a full-frontal view of the wife of the other. Howard greeted him warmly and Geoff nodded to him at the bus stop.

En route to the courthouse, Philip decided against any further contact with Michael Benson. When he arrived, Benson was talking to a tall, bespectacled man dressed in a suit, tie and expensive-looking overcoat. As Philip passed, he heard Geoff Harris' name mentioned. Benson beckoned his lawyer across and the three chatted before the newcomer shook hands with them and departed. Philip walked towards the man in the overcoat.

'Excuse me, do you have a minute? My name is Philip Anderson.'

'Tom Brady. What can I do for you?'

'I'm a juror in Michael Benson's case. I couldn't help over-hearing you mention Geoff Harris to Michael just now. I'm curious to know why.'

'Just clarifying something with Mr. Benson. I'm a colleague of Mr. Harris and I wanted to ensure...sorry, did you say you're one of the jurors?'

'Yes, I thought Michael was treated harshly yesterday. He's accused of crimes but is, I think, more a victim of circumstance rather than the instigator. Your firm's statement hasn't helped him.'

'You may well be right about Mr. Benson's innocence but I'm not privy to the details. I have, however, clarified something which should work to his advantage. I'm sure you'll hear about it. Nice speaking with you, I hope it works out for Michael. It sounds like you'll help him anyway.'

'I'll try.'

Tom left and Philip walked towards the courthouse for the resumption of the case. He was puzzled by Tom Brady's presence and, although eager to find out more about the conversation between Benson, Brady and the lawyer, he knew it was unwise to ask. Brady's intimation that more details would be revealed in court was correct as Benson's lawyer requested he be allowed to add more detail to the previous day's proceedings; a request accepted by the presiding judge.

'Mr. Benson wishes it known that the letter sent to the prosecution lawyer concerning his time at Alpha Venture will either be retracted or materially altered. Any inference that Mr. Benson was responsible for the theft of valuables is erroneous. An amended letter will be provided within the next two hours. It has recently been determined that the valuables in question – a mobile phone and watch – were mislaid rather than stolen and Alpha Venture wish to amend their testimony lest it prejudice my client's hearing. A laudable gesture, in my opinion, Your Honour.'

'Quite. You can read out the revised testimony upon receipt, Mr. Fowler,' the judge said. Philip noticed that some of his fellow jurors glanced in his direction and nodded in approval. There was bound to be an ulterior motive, he thought, but fair play to Harris and Brady for, at least, making the effort.

***

The morning sun shone above Tower Bridge to the east of London Bridge station on this clear, crisp spring day; a day to gladden the heart after a recent spell of snow and storms. Tom Brady sauntered along the street towards Alpha House, the building which housed Alpha Venture's offices, feeling virtuous by dint of helping young Benson. Furthermore, he'd done so without a secondary motive.

His mood improved further when he reached the office and read Jack Watson's e-mail which confirmed that he and Darren Peters would join Tom during the St. Ambrose's visit. Tom replied saying that he needed the approval of the Alpha Venture chief executive, a formality given the worthy nature of the venture. One, Tom added wryly, to which the organisation was enthusiastically committed.

Tom left for Llewellyn's office to deliver the news and get the requisite consent in person. He wanted to witness Llewellyn's response which would, presumably, be pleasure at the favourable publicity for the company tempered by disappointment that Tom was likely to emerge triumphant from an exercise assigned to him as punishment. For Llewellyn, AV's enhanced standing would hold sway – he wasn't a vindictive man, his professional probity would triumph.

'Morning, Michelle,' Tom said to Michelle Holley. He pointed towards her hair. 'Looks like it's dread-down Friday.'

'That's almost original, Tom...almost. Work on it, you may get the hang of communications yet.' Michelle smiled. 'What can I do for you?'

'Is the boss free? Oh, looks like he's not here at the moment.'

'Mark's not here at all today.'

'He's hardly ever in on a Friday any more, I think he's got a new lady.'

Llewellyn had divorced two years earlier, everybody assumed that the Deborah Jarvis affair was a contributing factor but his domestic arrangements were off-limits in his conversations with colleagues.

'Actually, he rang in ill and asked not to be contacted unless absolutely necessary.' Michelle said in a harsher tone. 'Anything I can help with?

'No. I need his sign-off on an Outreach thingy for Tuesday."

'The school visit? You got the short straw there.'

'Well, it looks better now which is why I wanted to see Mark. I don't suppose this constitutes a good enough reason to call him, does it?'

'Hmmm, I wouldn't say it does, Tom. There is an alternative, though.'

'Oh yeah?' Tom's expression brightened. 'And that would be?'

'Mr. Netherby is acting as Mark's deputy. I'm sure he'd like to help.'

'Oh God, so much as speaking to that man makes my skin crawl but I guess it'll speed things up. I take it he's lurking in the hope that his say-so will be required by somebody.'

Michelle nodded and dialled the number.

'Mr. Netherby, Miss Holley here...Er, yes, I do actually...Tom Brady wanted to run something past Mark which can't wait until Monday...Yes, he is...Just needs a signature, nothing of major importance or I'd advise him to wait for Mark...Yes, I'll let him know...Thank you, Mr. Netherby.'

'Congratulations,' she said to Tom. 'You've been granted an audience. He'll see you now.'

'Jesus, I dislike him more than most but I couldn't convey half as much contempt in my voice as you managed. That was worth hearing, Michelle. I'll be off to the nether regions then. Thanks.'

Tom made the short walk to Netherby's office.

'Tom. Good to see you, Michelle says you need something approved?'

'It's the Outreach programme, Jan. I've been asked to visit St. Ambrose's on Tuesday and I...'

'Can't be something you're looking forward to,' Netherby interrupted. 'But I guess a man with your communication skills relishes the opportunity to speak to a diverse audience.'

The bastard is enjoying this, Tom thought.

'Oh, I don't know, Jan. We operate an inclusive creed here at AV, even a relative newcomer like you must realise that. Anyway, I wanted Mark's approval to invite an ex-pupil of St. Ambrose's along on my visit. It's a formality really, hence my reluctance to call him when he's ill.'

'An ex-pupil? Do you think that's a good idea?' Netherby replied while Tom remained impassive. 'Well, if you say so, I suppose. I hope you'll brief him about AV's work in the community if he's addressing the students as well but I don't need to tell you your job, do I? Where do I sign?'

'There and there, beside my name and the other visitor's name. You may have heard of him.'

'Darren Peters? *The* Darren Peters?'

'The footballer, yes. St. Ambrose's is his alma mater and I've arranged this through his agent.'

'Good God, what a coup. I assume you'll arrange media coverage too?'

'As you said, you don't need to tell me how to do my job, Jan. As a matter of fact, I haven't. This is low-key in keeping with Mr. Peters' wishes. Someone from the local paper may well be present but we don't want a media scrum interrupting school schedules.'

'You know best, Tom. If you need my involvement in any part of this, er, commendable scheme, just give me a call. Don't you think I should call Mark and let him know?'

'I don't but you don't need me to tell you your job. Thanks for your help, have a good weekend.'

'Er, I was thinking of going for a drink after work if you're free.'

'I can't. Family stuff but thanks anyway.'

'OK, maybe another time. Ned here is always up for a beer or two.'

'I'll bear that in mind, Jan.'

Tom returned to his office and mimed vomiting into his dustbin.

***

John Hooper was awoken by a mobile phone which vibrated inches away from his ear. He fumbled for the phone and saw it was already 9am.

'John, Chris here. Where are you? The phones are buzzing and the FT wants a comment about the flotation.'

John's head slumped back on to the pillow.

'Chris, I don't feel well. Any chance you could cover for a bit? I'll see how I feel in an hour.'

'Not being funny, John, but I fielded all the calls yesterday afternoon. This needs both of us. Sorry you're not tickety-boo but y'know, a hangover shouldn't keep you away today of all days.'

'It's not a hangover. Well, it is sort of but I genuinely don't feel up to dealing with this right now.'

'Glad you think we have the luxury of being so selective. I'll deal with as much as I can but we're missing out here by being at half-strength.'

'Appreciated. I'll call you back, Chris. Give me an hour or so.'

John walked gingerly to the bathroom, showered and went downstairs. He put an empty wine bottle in the recycling box and retrieved another one, half-full, and an ashtray from the study. It had been a night of wine, cigarettes, music, introspection – all triggered by Laura's call. Something snagged at his mind. Yes, that was it: her reference to the Fraser Guthrie forum. He logged on and was transported back to a time when this forum was something he checked and contributed to.

Along with the music fans who engaged in open-minded dialogue about Guthrie and other artists, the cranks were still there: the Bob Dylan obsessive who insisted every song which Guthrie wrote was a lesser version of a Dylan song; the guy who claimed Dylan was a poor man's Guthrie; the ex-roadie who claimed to have compromising stories about Guthrie which he was willing to reveal if offered enough money; the lexicologist who maintained that Guthrie's output was based on rhythms and cadences from Chaucer; the woman who interpreted Guthrie's lyrics as originating in the Qur'an; the man who sourced Guthrie's themes back to the bible and then there were the ones who seemed really deranged.

John noticed a posting from the previous night under the pseudonym, *NoShitSherlock,* a non-de-plume which he remembered Laura using in reference to her surname: Holmes.

Much talk about imminent news which will cast Fraser's output in a new light, surely it's time for the definitive tome on Mr. Guthrie to be written. Someone who once contributed here could write it with erudition and detachment. Over to you, JH. Re your phone call earlier, yes I'd like to meet. Saturday night? That place we used to go to? 7? Text me.

God, she knows me so well, John thought. She guessed I'd log on to the forum, intrigued by her impending piece on Fraser Guthrie. The teasing reference to their shared past-life ('that place' was an Italian restaurant in Soho) was also interesting. Was she hinting that...no, she couldn't be. She had married just 18 months earlier. Still, this was titillating.

He sent a text to Laura saying *'Saturday? 7? That place? I'll be there. You know me well. JH.'*

Minutes later, he received a reply.

'Ha, good to see you haven't changed much. See you Saturday. Lx'.

John grinned. He'd find out more about the Guthrie story but far more interesting was the Laura angle. Suitably cheered, he rang Chris to say he'd be at the office within 10 minutes.

***

The train rushed through suburban stations and Elizabeth sank back into the head-rest, grateful to Harry for rescuing her although the gesture had been more than reciprocated on other occasions. Elizabeth had been a mainstay in the life of her younger brother, Harry, who'd suffered traumas involving relationships, drugs, work and money. At crucial junctures, Elizabeth helped him out, both emotionally and financially. When she sent him a text on the previous evening asking whether she could stay with him for the weekend, he was happy to comply.

Harry, three years younger than Elizabeth and her only sibling, lived in Sussex on the South Downs. He had been a carefree child and their mutual support and friendship were the envy of many parents. Their own parents, however, had marital problems and split up when Elizabeth was 18. She coped well with the upheaval, less so Harry. He became withdrawn, volatile and prone to aggressive outbursts – a condition exacerbated by his discovery of drugs. Elizabeth nursed him through the worst of these times acting as an emotional crutch and steering him clear of his less palatable friends. Harry stabilised and was weaned off a destructive, expensive heroin habit. He travelled for a year to assert his independence, returned a transformed man and started work as a graphic designer. A relationship with a girl he'd met in Norway ended and he displayed worrying signs of lapsing back to previous dependencies but again, Elizabeth stepped in and cajoled him back to an even keel.

Harry was now in a relationship and enjoying his work but people still showed concern at signs of introspection but Elizabeth recognised this as his sensitive nature manifesting itself. When he invited her to visit him, she knew he needed some succour but such requests were infrequent now - the most recent visit had been initiated by Elizabeth. As was this one; she told Geoff that Harry had called and Geoff accepted her departure without question. Her guilt at Geoff's remembering the anniversary of their first meeting increased exponentially at the realisation of how she'd spent that particular anniversary.

She had to escape for a couple of days, confide in Harry, go for walks along the Downs and work things out in her mind. Geoff had been the Geoff of old for the last day invoking in her a wish to, as he'd said, return to where they'd been. But there was also Philip - attentive, amusing and the catalyst for that exhilarating weightlessness she'd experienced. The train pulled into Brighton station and her spirits soared. She would spend the morning wandering around The Laines and along the sea front before meeting Harry in the afternoon. It was a measure of Harry's status at work that he could leave early and Elizabeth felt proud of her younger brother. She hoped she'd feel the same about herself in, say, a month's time.

***

'You what?' spluttered Darren Peters. 'Fuck's sake, Jack. I spent years there even though I tried to get chucked out. Only reason they didn't was they wanted me for their football team. Why would I want to go back?'

'Dazzle, I've explained to you before,' Jack Watson replied. 'You need to keep your nose clean for a while - no scrapes, no bimbos flogging stories to the tabs. And you did say that we'd see a new Darren Peters.'

'Yeah but, to be fair, hanging around Ambrose's ain't my idea of a new Darren Peters. It's not on, Jack. Sort it out, mate.'

'Dazzle, your boot sponsors and your newspaper column ghost writer have expressed discomfort about the tabloids' stories. That's getting on for ten grand a week you're in danger of losing. Go to Ambrose's for half-an-hour, an hour tops, sign a few autographs, nod when this banker bloke says hard work is the key, say that you're reconnecting with your roots and you're Golden Boy again. We may even be able to up your current deals. It's a no-brainer, Daz.'

There was an outburst of laughter from Peters.

'Dazzle, you still there?'

'Yeah, I just received a link from a mate on my Twitter feed. I'll forward it to you. It's good.'

'Daz, don't. Is it something dodgy? Delete it straight away, tell your friend to delete it, too. I've warned you about Twitter; it's public domain.'

'Oh hell, yeah. OK, give me a minute.' Jack heard mumbled swearing from the other end and soon, Peters was back on the line.

'OK, sorted. Now, what was you saying? Going to Ambrose's could be worth half a mil a year and it's just an hour. Why didn't you say so at the start? Sometimes I wonder about you, Jack.'

'That's more like it, son. There's a few areas of modern technology which you need to familiarise yourself with but let's deal with that another time. I'll see you after the game tomorrow; your TV appearance is scheduled for 8. OK?'

'Sweet, mate. Cheers.'

***

'Come in, Geoff. How's tricks?'

'OK, Tom, OK. I just wanted to see if everything's all right with that letter to the lawyer guy. I feel better now that we've retracted the bit about Christine's watch and mobile being stolen. You know what, she's paid too much if she can lose a thousand quid's worth of accessories down the back of the sofa and not worry unduly about them.'

'Must've been traumatic for her though, a few days with only her spare mobile and no designer watch.' Tom shook his head. 'I thought it would be best if we did the decent thing by young Benson. OK, he wasn't AV-standard but that's hardly his fault. I think he fell in with a bad crowd after leaving here.'

'Hmmm, maybe. Is there anything else for me to do?'

'No, it's all done and dusted. I signed it on your behalf and biked it over to the court house. A funny thing happened while I was there this morning. A juror overheard me mention your name and quizzed me about it. He seemed OK, concerned about Benson's portrayal in court. Good to know that jurors are so concerned about justice being upheld, I'd be happy to have people like him on a jury if I was on trial.'

'Assuming you deserved his concern, Tom. Why did he ask about me?'

'I guess your name was mentioned during Benson's hearing and then he overheard me...unless you know a man called Philip Johnson, no, Anderson, Phil or Philip Anderson.'

'We've got a neighbour called Philip Anderson, bit of a coincidence if it was him. Journalist chappie, I don't really know him though.'

'He didn't look like a journalist; no egg stains on his tie, no grubby raincoat or trilby hat either.'

'It's reassuring to know our press guru holds the fourth estate in such high regard,' Geoff laughed. 'Anyway, thanks for sorting it out. I'm leaving soon, not much happening today. Doing anything this weekend?'

'A quiet one. I'll do some work for an assignment on Tuesday...I got

61

landed with the St. Asbo's gig but I may have turned it to my, er, to AV's advantage. How about you? Have you got anything planned?'

'No. Elizabeth's at her brother's place so I might take some work home as well and wallow in being able to smoke a cigar after dinner. Smoking is banned *chez* Harris, these days.'

'No harm if you ask me, never took to it myself. If you're after some company this evening, our good friend Mr. Netherby is at a loose end.'

'I'll pass on that one, thanks. Pretty unbearable, isn't he?'

'That's what I'd call a generous assessment, Geoff. Have a good one, see you on Monday.'

***

A knot of people gathered on the steps outside the court house as Philip received plaudits. Even Andrew Butler was magnanimous.

'Your intuition about young Benson seems well-founded,' he said.

'Well, he just seemed different to the others, especially that first guy. Anyway, we all agreed on the verdict, that's the main thing,' Philip replied.

'Well said, Philip,' Grace added. 'It makes me happier to know we live in a proper democracy.'

'OK, I'm off. It's been nice to meet you people,' Philip said and turned to walk to the bus stop.

'Fancy a drink, Philip?' asked Colin, arching his eyebrows. 'The wine bar you were in with your lady friend the other day looks quite nice.'

'Love to, Colin, but I really have to go,' Philip replied, eager to escape Colin's company. Michael Benson was sitting on a low wall ahead of Philip. The young man extended a hand as Philip approached.

'Just wanted to say thanks, Mr. Anderson,' Benson said. 'This worked out better than I expected.'

'I was just a part of it, Michael. Those guys from Alpha Venture helped by modifying that letter and all the jurors agreed you were far from being a ring-leader. I hope you've learned a lesson.'

'Not easy when you live on Shillingtree Estate but I'll keep my nose out of trouble from now on.'

'Look, I said yesterday that I work for *The Chronicle*. We're doing a feature on Britain's underbel...er, stuff about the living conditions experienced by young people in British cities. I could give your name to the features' desk, they may get in touch for an opinion.'

'What? Me in the paper? Yeah, cool. I'll give you my number. Cheers.'

They exchanged phone numbers and Philip handed Michael his business card, shook hands and they went their separate ways. After the meandering pace of the first two days, the hearings for the remaining defendants had concluded quickly. It was evident to the jurors that the swaggering youth from the first day, Simeon, initiated the crimes and coerced the other four into joining him. The jury's verdicts chimed with the case presented by the prosecution lawyer and even the defence lawyer seemed to agree with the verdict; Simeon was sent to a remand home with suspended sentences given to the others.

Philip slumped into a seat on the bus, glad to return home for a quiet evening. Alighting from the bus, he saw Geoff Harris step off another bus, a slim manila folder and a newspaper under his arm. Geoff fell into step alongside Philip.

'Hello. It's Philip, yes?'

'Yes. Funny, we live just a few houses apart yet barely know each other. You're Geoff, right?'

'Yes, Geoff Harris.' They shook hands and Geoff continued, 'That's London for you, you don't always get the chance to get to know your neighbours. I'm home a bit earlier than normal, quiet day today. Quiet weekend ahead too, I guess. The wife's away.'

'Right.' Philip feigned indifference. 'Damn, I intended getting a bottle of wine, I'll just pop back to the off-licence. Er, enjoy the weekend.'

'You're at a loose end too, then? Fancy a drink in the Joiners?' Geoff asked. 'Go on, Elizabeth – my wife – is always saying I should get to know more of the neighbours.'

Philip hesitated until curiosity and mischievousness kicked in so they retraced the short journey back to the Joiners Arms, the local hostelry. As they entered the pub, Philip's mobile rang and he checked the display.

'I have to take this. I'll be with you in a minute, Geoff.'

'OK, what are you having?'

'A glass of red wine, please. Thanks.'

Geoff pushed open the door and entered the pub; outside, Philip answered his call.

'Jesus, Elizabeth, your timing is something else. I'm just about to have a drink with Geoff.'

'Geoff? My Geoff? Why? He doesn't know you, what's up?'

'We bumped into each other and he suggested a drink. He said you'd gone away.'

'I just needed to get away for the weekend, Philip...to clear my head. It's all been a bit much over the last few days, you do understand?'

'Yes. I don't want to pressure you. I hope *you* understand that?'

'Yes. It's bizarre Geoff going for a drink with you, not bizarre because it's you, just bizarre. Oh Christ, I'm not making sense, am I?'

'Lots of things aren't making sense right now. I'd best be off, have a good weekend.'

'I will. Have a nice evening.' She giggled and added, 'I suppose you'll be talking about me. How exciting. You won't, you know, let anything slip.'

'Of course not. Bye. Er, see you soon.'

'Bye.'

***

The cork was eased from the bottle, two glasses held up against the kitchen light and some miniscule motes of dust wiped away with a towel. Red wine gushed forth from the bottle, a glugging sound issued as air filled the space vacated by the wine. The purplish liquid swirled around the glasses and the bottle was placed on a table. Both glasses were picked up and carried from the kitchen until the carrier halted, walked backwards a few paces, picked up the bottle and resumed his short journey.

As he opened the door to his sitting room, Harry Davenport saw Elizabeth smile as she said 'Bye' and flipped shut her mobile phone. 'Lover boy or hubby?' he asked.

'They're not mutually exclusive, Harry.'

'Libby, Libby, take that cross look off your face, it doesn't become you. Now sit down and tell little brother all about it.'

Elizabeth sat back on the sofa, kicked off her shoes and curled her legs beneath her. Her face was still flushed from two bracing walks; first a solitary one along the sea-front in Brighton followed by a slog up the hill from the train station at Hassocks to Harry's cottage in nearby Ditchling, tucked away against the sweeping backdrop of the Sussex South Downs. A heady mix of smells wafted from the kitchen as a pasta sauce of garlic, tomato, onion and *pancetta* bubbled in a saucepan and mingled with the warm, comforting aroma of *ciabatta* from the oven. Elizabeth peered through the large window frame in the fading light and marvelled at the expanse of fields and sky around them. She unfurled her legs, sat up, flicked away a speck of mud from her jeans and examined the sofa.

'Oh sorry. I forget how muddy these country lanes can be. I'll get changed.'

'Don't worry about it. Chin-chin,' Harry said as they clinked glasses. 'It's good to see you, whatever the circumstances.'

Elizabeth had said 'I just needed to get away for a couple of days' as justification for her hastily arranged visit. Harry's intuitive guess at what was meant by this irritated her. It pre-empted her disclosure and, as with Rachel, she'd savoured the prospect of shocking her younger brother.

'It's good here, London gets claustrophobic. I could stare out at this view for hours...during daylight, anyway.' Harry remained silent; his sister would soon get around to whatever she wished to tell him. 'It must be magical during a full moon too. Are the stars visible from that window?'

'On clear nights, they are. If you walk a mile or so north, the halogen glow fades even more and it is pretty impressive. Hmmm, this is decent wine but you've always had good taste; I bet you've stolen the thunder of loads of wine-bores over the years – the little lady isn't supposed to have expertise on such matters.'

Elizabeth picked up the implicit reference to Geoff, an allusion to the oft-repeated story of their first ever meeting in the French Alps and how they bonded over a bottle of red wine.

'Very clever, you've got a good memory for stories. You're right...the flight from the capital is linked to Geoff.' She gave an abridged account of arguments with Geoff, the court case, relief at her acquittal and resentment at Geoff's detached response. 'Then, to cut a long story short, I ended up in bed with a neighbour. It was spontaneous. I felt reckless, weightless and I wanted to hurt Geoff...without him even knowing, I guess.'

'And?'

'And, well that's it. I did the deed, then guilt kicked in and here I am.'

'So this is recent?'

'Wednesday. What really threw me was arriving home yesterday to be met by Geoff at his most charming, saying nice things and mentioning the anniversary of our first ever meeting.'

'And that was when? The anniversary, I mean.'

'Wednesday, the day I slept with Philip. Philip is the neighbour.'

'Wow, what a sense of occasion you have, Libby. I guess the fact that the date didn't register with you says something.'

'But it didn't register with Geoff either until the next day. It wasn't as if he was waiting for me with flowers and champagne while I was, you know, eight or so doors away.'

'That close? And you both know the guy?'

'No. Well, only to say hello. It gets weirder. I've just rang Lover Boy as you call him and he's going for a drink with Geoff. Honest, they don't even know each other.'

'Who'd have thought it?' Harry laughed. 'My fragrant, radiant sister getting it on with the man from across the fence, someone she hardly even knows and now this guy is having cosy chats with the cuckolded husband. It's like something from Graham Greene. Priceless.'

'Shut up, Harry. It's not funny. Oh hell, I wish I hadn't told you. First Rachel and now you – both of you mocking me, making me feel like a ... Harry, it's not funny, OK?'

Harry leaned forward and laid his hand on her knee.

'I know it's not. But you're here to put things in perspective, right?'

She nodded.

'Well, allow somebody who's remote from it to help you do that. I owe you a lot, a hell of a lot. You can tap into my first-hand experience on how to screw things up and, take it from me, you're hardly any distance down that road right now. OK, the sauce and pasta are ready. Bring that bottle and get another one from the rack in the kitchen. You choose.'

They went through to the kitchen and when they'd eaten their meal and opened another bottle of wine, Elizabeth sensed the return of that light-headed feeling.

'I'm going to call Geoff,' she said as Harry topped up her glass.

***

The bottle of carbonated soft drink was opened and a hissing sound punctured the excited shrill voices in the adjoining room. The bubbling black liquid cascaded into two glasses which were adorned with depictions of dinosaurs. Glasses filled, the plastic bottle was placed on the table. Another bottle was selected from a cabinet and uncorked, emitting a quiet pop and from it a small quantity of amber liquid decanted into a squat tumbler. A third bottle was taken from the refrigerator, the top unscrewed and a third of its straw-coloured contents poured into a tall, stemmed glass. Both bottles were placed alongside the four glasses on a small tray which was picked up as the carrier nudged the door open on to a scene of happy domesticity.

Friday night *chez* Brady and Tom, having cleared away the dishes after dinner, was acting as drinks waiter to his wife and daughters.

'Daddy, you've been ages. The DVD's all set up, we skipped the trailers. Can we start it now?'

'Of course, sweetie. Here's your drinks and pass the glass of wine to your mother. Is Sauvignon Blanc OK, Catherine?'

'Whatever's open, Tom.'

When everybody settled, the film began and Tom's mind drifted back to the phone call an hour earlier from his cousin, Kieran, in Ireland. Kieran Bradley – 40, six years younger than Tom - was the youngest son of Tom Brady senior's sister, Deirdre. According to family legend, Tom senior and Deirdre, were inseparable as children, one covering for the other if implicated in youthful scrapes or pranks. Deirdre revealed a rebellious streak as she left her childhood behind and became involved in the Civil Rights movement around Derry in the late 1960s. She cited it as a political awakening and argued passionately about the campaign to eradicate religious discrimination and inequality in Northern Ireland.

Her family were concerned by her firebrand nature and the ease with which she lapsed into the rhetoric of the nascent paramilitary organisations and her involvement with Martin Bradley. Bradley had been a moderate member of the Civil Rights group but his views hardened as the Troubles escalated. Deirdre was smitten by him, they married and had two sons – Michael and Kieran. Tom's brother, Liam, played for the same gaelic football team as the Bradley brothers and the families were in regular contact. Tom, aware that he lacked the sporting prowess of his brother, remained distant from the Bradley boys. Desperate to prove himself, he left home to attend university and then moved to London where a job in advertising led him into media consultancy.

Communication with the Bradleys lost its immediacy and Tom was surprised when Michael Bradley invited him to join Kieran and himself on a driving holiday in Northern England and Scotland in the autumn of 1989. With a burgeoning career and his friendship with a colleague, Catherine Gill, developing into romance, Tom viewed the invitation as a sign that he'd usurped his brother's position as the high-achiever of the family. He accepted the invitation; his cousins were lively company and Tom relished being the urbane guide around the country which was his new home.

They met in Birmingham and meandered around the Lake District and the Borders, lodging in bed and breakfasts, their evenings in rural pubs interspersed with forays to Newcastle and Sheffield in search of a racier night life. Tom demurred while his cousins' ribald charm attracted girls with Kieran's irrepressible devil-may-care attitude establishing him as the centre of attention. Though the nightclubs were fun, Tom was enamoured by Catherine back in London and had no desire to jeopardise this.

The Bradley brothers suggested spending the last few days in Glasgow where they had friends and tickets for a Glasgow Celtic v. Glasgow Rangers game, famously – or notoriously – the epitome of sectarian tribalism with a game of football thrown in. The Bradleys' friends in Glasgow were a mix of Irish emigrants and native Glaswegians who met in small, shabby clubs where Irish paraphernalia adorned the walls and bands played raucous rebel songs. Tom grew less comfortable in the presence of his cousins and tried to avoid speculation on the precise nature of the 'wee jobs' and 'deliveries' which peppered their conversation.

The day of the game was also the final day of the holiday and Kieran and Michael reached a frenzy of excitement which they cajoled Tom into sharing as they entered Glasgow Celtic's stadium.

'Breathe this in, Tom. It's as good as seeing Cavan in an All-Ireland final at Croke Park. To be honest, I'd prefer this; Mikey there is the same,' Kieran gushed as he joined in a deafening rendition of an Irish rebel song.

The noise increased, the air crackled as bloodthirsty taunts were traded between the two sets of rival fans and the stadium became a sea of green, white and orange broken by one corner bedecked in blue and Union flags. It was a thrilling, visceral spectacle but the undercurrents of sectarian bigotry and hatred unsettled Tom. That evening, the Bradleys' opted for yet another small club, one patrolled by burly bouncers where it seemed the entire clientele sported Celtic scarves or replica shirts.

The conversation revolved around the sporadic outbreaks of fighting between rival fans after the game. The pub hushed when a local news report on television told of a Rangers supporter who was hospitalised, still unconscious, after one ruckus. The bar erupted in cheering and a chant of 'one-nil to the Fenian boys' rang out. Tom withdrew into himself away from the noisy chatter and was joined by Michael Bradley.

'What about ye, Tom? Something else today, so it was. There's nothing like an Old Firm game to set the pulse racing,' he shouted above the din.

'Yes, it was pretty amazing but it's not really about football, is it? That poor kid who was beaten up after the game, what's all that about? '

'Oh, come on, Tom. Next time, it'll be one of our lads. I know one lot is as bad as the other but we have history on our side. Think of what we've been through for centuries.'

'I know, I know – it's just, oh I don't know.'

'So, sounds like you're well settled in yon London. A lively place, so it is. Do ye drink in many Irish bars at all? I've been to a few good places.'

'Of course I do but I don't limit myself to Irish pubs alone.'

'A man of the world is what you are, Tom Brady. Me and Kieran will be in London soon, we could meet up again, have a bit of craic.'

'Er, sure, that'd be good.' Tom assumed a request for accommodation would follow but Michael's next question surprised him.

'Would you be able to distribute a few things for us? Leaflets about Irish language meetings, ballad sessions in pubs, that sort of thing.'

'I have a lot of catching up to do when I get back to work. I'd like to meet you one night but I'm not really into distributing propaganda.'

Michael looked at him, sighed and held out his hand.

'Fair enough, Tom. I was just putting out some feelers to see if you'd be willing to help the cause. No harm done. I respect your honesty.'

Tom excused himself and pushed his way through the throng to the toilets where he vomited.

Now, Tom sipped his whiskey as his daughters sang the chorus of a song from the soundtrack of the film. He shuddered as he remembered the months after his holiday with the Bradleys. Years later, it could still make him break into a cold sweat. He returned to London amid a torrent of conflicting emotions, paramount among them a revulsion at what had been euphemistically referred to as 'wee jobs' and 'deliveries'. He was angry at being sounded out to participate in the Irish language meetings and ballad sessions. Even if they were genuine attempts to keep areas of Irish culture alive in a foreign land, Tom knew that acquiescence on his part would lead to requests of a less innocent nature.

Yet still, despite the exoneration of Michael Bradley's handshake in that grubby club, he felt that he'd somehow failed the Bradleys. Tom grew sullen and insular whenever a conversation broached the conflict in Northern Ireland. Ironically, his silence during such discourses gained him a reputation among work colleagues as a republican sympathiser. His coping mechanism was alcohol and he drank to quell loneliness and isolation. He read about psychiatric problems among emigrants resulting from displacement and fretted, recognising such symptoms in himself.

Catherine Gill intervened. She was alarmed by his listless drinking bouts and recognised the signs of depression. She cajoled him back into animation, restored his feeling of self-worth and alleviated the fears and doubts gnawing at his psyche. They grew ever closer and married in 1993. Their two children were born around the millennium and Tom's life continued its upward curve.

He maintained contact with the Bradleys but the holiday was rarely mentioned. Now, his phone conversation with Kieran took Tom back to a period he was glad to forget. Kieran was due to visit London, would like to catch up 'for old time's sake' and asked Tom to suggest a meeting place. Tom suggested MacQuilters – an ersatz Irish bar which he disliked - because it was bustling, popular with tourists and far removed from Glaswegian drinking dens, once the stuff of nightmares for Tom. They arranged to meet there on the following Tuesday evening.

***

The gold foil was removed, the small wire mesh underneath loosened and discarded. A dark bottle was held in one hand, the cork firmly grasped by the other and twisted until a soft 'pop' escaped as the cork was freed. The bubbling pale-coloured liquid was poured into two small plastic cups which were picked up and brushed against each other.

'Cheers, Chris.'

'Cheers, John. So what brought all this on? Anything to do with a certain phone call yesterday?'

John Hooper sat back and rested his feet on the desk. It was 7pm and they were toasting their good fortune with a half-bottle of champagne which John bought in an off-licence, a few doors away. Earlier, John sent a text to Doug Greenlees in Chicago. He'd met Doug months earlier on a trip to the US with Chris to launch Monochromus and they became friends after spending hours at a dinner arguing about everything from politics to pet food. Doug, the archetype hawkish, monetarist Republican who abhorred liberals – 'goddamn pinko ass-wipes' – was amazed by John's knowledge of financial markets.

'You love literature, movies with no car-chases, peace-mongers and other faggy shit, you don't get an instant hard-on when money walks towards you naked. Why the hell are you even talking to me?' Doug asked him one evening.

Doug was fascinated by John's erudite, considered opinions; John revelled in Doug's combative, earthy discourse. When John found himself in accord with Doug, he often played devil's advocate just to prolong the discussion. Doug's gimlet eye for financial opportunities led him to surmise that Monochromus' stock would appreciate and he hounded John to sell his share in the company to him. When Monochromus was set up, Frank Garfield, their former colleague at Foden Barnes, contributed funding in return for a 20% stake; Chris and John held 40% each. Frank's intrinsic trust in their acumen meant that he had minimal involvement.

'Maybe we can talk turkey after all. I'll contact you' was the text sent to Greenlees and the response arrived within a minute: *'What I wanna hear, Johnny babe. Call me 2morrow. D'*

John swallowed some champagne and frowned at the plastic cup.

'Christ, it's not the same. Just popping out, back in a minute.'

John returned with two champagne flutes, a bag of ice-cubes and two bottles of champagne. He tipped the ice-cubes into a dustbin, wedged the bottles among the ice, filled the two flutes, sipped his drink and smiled.

'That's more like it. Now, where were we? Ah yes, my vacillation or as our American friend would no doubt say, my goddamn dicking around. Yes, Laura's call planted seeds of doubt in my mind on the worthiness of all this. It might not have been her intention but she did.'

'And now, you want out?'

'That depends on you as well, Chris. If you're happy with me selling to Doug, yes. If not, let's find a way around it.' John pointed to the champagne. 'We've got all evening.'

'It's up to you, John. To be honest, I never expected you to be a part of er, whatever this is for too long. Maybe I'm the same; I need to think it through. What would you do next?'

'Well, that's the thing. I don't really know…dabble in writing or return to lecturing, I don't know. I tend to oscillate wildly, as Morrissey put it.'

'We should let Frank know about this but maybe not on a Friday night. That's his bare-knuckle boxing night.'

John smiled at the memory of their night out with Frank. 'I'm having dinner with Laura tomorrow, by the way. She even suggested an old haunt of ours. You've met Mr. Laura. What's he like?'

'What's the word? Supercilious is how I'd put it.'

'Never was one for commoners, our Laura.'

'Still hold a torch for her then?'

'God, yes. I was too smitten by the world of money to appreciate what I had at the time. Doug was wrong, you know, there was a time when money getting naked did blind me to everything else. Laura's the one that got away, I guess,' John sighed wistfully.

'Never say never, Hoops,' Chris said reaching for a bottle. John held out his glass, shrugged and smiled.

***

The bottle was placed on a table and two glasses positioned, one on either side. Two newspapers were moved from the table and placed on an adjacent stool on top of a manila folder. A packet of crisps was, first, prised open and then placed on the table alongside the bottle. The bottle was picked up and its ruby-red contents poured into the two glasses as two hands reached for the glasses.

'Well, here we are then,' Geoff Harris said, sipping his wine.

'Yes, here we are. Hmmm, nice. Not the house red, I'm guessing?'

'No. This is too auspicious an occasion to settle for the house wine.'

'Auspicious?'

'Well, I know we've never really spoken but we have one significant factor in common.'

Philip raised his glass and sipped the wine. 'Er, we do?'

'Of course we do, we're neighbours. We live in the same road, use the same bus stop, buy papers from the same newsagent and I'm sure there's lots of other things we share.'

'Oh, of course.'

Philip looked around. The Joiners Arms was popular with locals who'd resisted the owner's attempt, a year previously, to turn it into a gastropub. To the management's chagrin, the usual clientele turned up, largely indifferent to the new menu. After a month watching the regulars supping pints and disdainfully ignoring the *focaccia* and artichokes before asking for crisps and peanuts, the new emphasis on food was reined in.

Philip was an occasional visitor, Geoff less so. This evening, a number of people were dotted around the bar and some had settled in for the evening, coats and jackets discarded. Music played unobtrusively through speakers positioned just below the ceiling.

'So, you're all on your lonesome this weekend, then?'

'Yes, Elizabeth's at her brother's place. He sometimes needs the loving attention of his big sister. She cuffs him around the ear, imparts words of wisdom, they go for walks in the countryside and life carries on.'

'That's noble of her. Blood's thicker than water, I guess.'

'Suppose so. I'm happy not to get dragged into the Samaritan thing. I'm not insensitive but some of her brother's problems are, to my mind, self-inflicted. But I'm a crusty old banker so I would say that.'

'I guess you bankers get it from all sides these days?'

'Duck, water, back are the words which come to mind. A certain amount of the criticism is merited, a certain amount is jealousy and the remainder is ignorance. But, hey, I'm a crusty old blah-blah-blah.'

'And Mrs. Harris, er Elizabeth, does she work in the City?'

'Christ, no. Libby, er, Elizabeth's a teacher and a very good one too but she decided a while back that it wasn't her true calling. She's still searching for that particular grail. You're a journalist, right?'

'Not, strictly speaking, a journalist but I work for *The Chronicle*.'

'Ah. Not a newspaper with a favourable view of my profession.'

'Doesn't mean everyone there believes you guys should be dressed in sackcloth. Some of your harshest critics on our editorial staff would probably give their typing arm for a crack at what you do or, more accurately, earn.'

'People have a distorted view of the money bankers earn. It's disproportionate: hard to justify the salaries and bonuses at the top but lower down, it's not hugely different from other professions. Forgive me for saying but I don't see you as a suit and tie man. Any special occasion?'

Philip glanced furtively at Geoff and grinned.

'We have dress-*up* Fridays at *The Chronicle*. We defy convention at our brave, innovative newspaper.'

'And what do you do on your brave, innovative newspaper?'

'I'm a sub-editor. Using spell-check is as much as some journalists manage before handing in their copy. Others, the majority, to be honest, are more rigorous but we have to tweak things, make corrections and cut out some of the more fanciful stuff.'

'Sounds interesting ... no it does,' Geoff said as Philip's eyes narrowed.

'Other folk's jobs always sound more interesting. Do you enjoy whatever it is you do in the City?'

'Yes. I'm a portfolio manager – a zero or two short of funds managers' earnings – but I enjoy the work. You need to be pretty clued up on the markets and stay ahead of, or at least keep pace with, the competition.'

As Geoff topped up both glasses, his mobile rang.

'Oh, hello, you got there OK?...Good. And Harry is OK?... Yes, I'm fine. I'm in the Joiners with Philip from a few doors down...Yes, that's him. We met on the way home and I thought I'd be sociable...Well, yes, of course...No, don't be silly...I'm with him right now...Good idea...Me too, darling. Give my regards to Harry...Of course I do...I'll see you on Sunday. Bye for now.'

Philip's mobile vibrated, it was a text from Elizabeth....*You two getting on well then?* Philip glanced at Geoff as he ended his call and sent a reply: *Pack it in Elizabeth...this is too risky.*

Geoff flicked his mobile closed and shrugged.

'Sorry, that was Elizabeth. She was surprised to hear where I am and well, I guess she doesn't know you. Maybe you can come round to our place for dinner one night?'

'Thanks,' Philip said. 'Best check with your missus first. Is she the cook and social organiser?'

'She is. Would it be just you or is there a significant other?'

'Well, I've met somebody but it's awkward. She's married but I think she's not entirely sure about her marriage. She's an intriguing woman.'

'You're not seeing her tonight then?'

'Er, no, not this weekend, she's away.'

'Does her husband have any inkling about this?'

'No. I get the feeling he'd be pretty shocked if he knew.'

'Do you feel any guilt on his part?'

'I hadn't considered that, to be honest.'

'No, I don't suppose you would. Not a situation I've been in although there was one...er, nothing.'

Philip finished his drink and pointed towards the bottle. 'Same again?'

'Yes, please,' Geoff nodded.

Philip walked to the bar, his mind in over-drive. Geoff was on the verge of admitting something and another glass of wine might bring it out. Unsure why he wanted to know, Philip assumed it was because Geoff seemed like a decent guy and he wanted a reason to dislike him. This was becoming complicated.

Philip returned with a bottle of wine and refilled their glasses.

'So, you were saying about relationships?'

'Well, I did find myself in an odd situation once. Elizabeth has a close friend and confidante, someone she meets regularly and ...'

'That'll be Rachel,' Philip mumbled, remembering her name from his conversation with Elizabeth. Drawn into Geoff's story, Philip inadvertently repeated her name. Geoff peered inquisitively at him.

'Did you say Rachel? How come you know her name?'

'Rachel? No, I said Ray Charles, sorry, thinking aloud. The first few notes of the song playing at the moment sounded like Ray Charles but, now I hear more, it's not really like Ray Charles at all. Ignore me, Geoff, carry on. Rachel's got a friend, sorry I mean Elizabeth's got a friend and......'

'Anyway, Rachel, years back, was at a party with us in a hotel. Elizabeth left early as she was going to her brother's place...just like today. Rachel had a bit to drink and threw herself at me. Told me she'd always fancied me, had a room booked in the hotel, Elizabeth was away and, well, you know ...' Geoff sipped his drink and shook his head. 'Rachel behaving like that is a pretty singular event and believe me, she's a looker. Things went a bit further than they should've done, not too far though. I told her thanks, I'm flattered and all that but it was best if I headed home. She's never liked me since. God, here I am telling you all this, the wine's gone to my head, no lunch today. Mum's the word although I doubt you'll ever have reason to discuss Rachel's indiscretions with Elizabeth.'

Philip nodded and smiled.

***

The tab on a can of Heineken was depressed with a quiet hiss and the pale-coloured beer poured into a tall glass. The process was repeated with a second can and glass, the glasses were picked up and clinked together.

'You're a lucky boy, Michael. I hope you pay heed.'

'You know I will, Mum. You'll be proud of me, I promise.'

Michael Benson sat at the kitchen table with his mother. He'd arrived home that evening, told his mother about the court verdict and produced a bag with six cans of lager. Dot Benson drank moderately but recognised this as an occasion to show solidarity with her son; besides, her relief at the outcome needed an outlet.

'This be God's warning, son. You stay on the path now. That Simeon is locked away so you won't come under his influence.'

'I know, Mum. People on the jury and someone from the place where I worked last year, they all helped, they see a good side to me. You too, Mum. I ain't gonna miss classes at school and I can get placements with companies and stuff. I met a bloke who works on a newspaper today and he may be able to help me too. I've learned my lesson, honest.'

Dot wiped away a tear with an outsize handkerchief and patted Michael on the shoulder. 'You pray to God too, Michael. He looks after those who believe.'

Michael nodded and clasped his mother's hand.

***

4 – SATURDAY

The smell of frying bacon activated Philip's appetite as he sat in Howard Simpson's café scrutinising the horse racing pages of *The Chronicle*. Horse racing first interested Philip when he spent a holiday in Ireland in 2000. He had ended a relationship, this time the dumpee rather than dumper and needed an escape. For no obvious reason, he booked a flight to Shannon Airport, hired a car and drove south-east with no destination in mind. He booked into a bed and breakfast in a village near Cashel in Tipperary, dined in a pub and conversed with the locals.

The pub was bedecked in horse racing paraphernalia and Philip's new well-informed acquaintances invited him to a race meeting in nearby Clonmel. Intrigued by the speculation and horse racing gossip, he accepted. At the race meeting, he was thrilled by the thoroughbred horses, exciting finishes, colour, noise and conviviality of the occasion and even managed to back two winners. Since then, he held an affinity with horse racing and Simpson's café on Saturday mornings was the venue where he would select a couple of horses to bet on.

'Morning, Philip.'

It was Geraldine Simpson; she often worked at the café on Saturdays. Geraldine, always a stylish dresser, wore a blue dress which accentuated her curvaceous figure and the image of Geraldine from the previous morning flashed across Philip's mind. He mumbled a reply.

'See anything you fancy?' Geraldine asked, a smile playing on her lips.

'Well there is one in the first race which I might put a few quid on. Do you take an interest in the gee-gees?'

'Not really, just the races which get a lot of coverage - the Grand National, Derby, that sort of thing. The normal housewife fare.'

Geraldine didn't conform to his idea of a normal housewife and Philip, knowing she knew this, opted not to participate in whatever game she was playing. He liked Howard and thought Geraldine should be above acting as a flirtatious tease. If, however, she had any designs on Philip...well, he'd cross that bridge when he arrived at it.

'Taking tips on horses from me won't make you a wealthy housewife, Geraldine. It's quiet today, Saturdays tend to be busier than this.'

'Tough times we live in, belts being tightened everywhere. OK, must keep on the move. Give me a shout if there's anything else you want.' She winked at Philip and walked away.

Philip returned to his newspaper, chose the two horses which would comprise his betting for the day and smiled when he saw that a horse called Neighbour's Secret was among the runners in one race. He thought back to his pub conversation with Geoff – increasingly loquacious as the evening progressed – who'd said that he had something to ask Philip.

'Were you, by any chance, involved in a court case today?'

Philip guessed the source of Geoff's information and replied that he'd quizzed Tom Brady when he heard Geoff's name mentioned, his interest relating only to Michael Benson's case.

'To be honest, I was prepared to think the worst of you when that letter was read out on Thursday but it made a real difference to young Benson's case when it was retracted - some of the jurors were sceptical about Michael until then. I talked to him afterwards, he seems OK.'

'Yes, nothing wrong with him but he just wasn't cut out for our place. That's neither his fault nor a judgement on him. I hope things work out for him.'

They chatted until Geoff, inebriated by now, decided that it was time to go. Only when Philip arrived home did he notice Geoff's manila folder enclosed with his own newspapers. Here was a dilemma: Alpha Venture were frequently criticised by *The Chronicle* for their opportunism; did he not have a duty to his employers to check for anything newsworthy? Just as he was about to do so, he paused. No: that was an unacceptable intrusion. Before he could reconsider, he picked up the folder and walked to Geoff's house. Geoff gasped when he saw the folder in Philip's hand.

'Christ. Did I leave that behind me? I shouldn't get pissed when I've got work with me. It probably wouldn't mean much to most people but, in the wrong hands...' Geoff made a who-knows gesture. 'I doubt there's anything important here but still...Thanks for returning it. I owe you.'

Philip had returned home basking in a self-righteous glow. I've slept with his wife but I'm not a complete bastard, he thought. He finished breakfast and walked to the till to pay Howard who told him Geraldine had mentioned inviting him around for dinner. Another dinner invitation! Another strange set of circumstances.

Bill settled, he left. Saturday was usually leisurely as Philip wasn't involved with the Sunday edition of *The Chronicle* but he still intended catching up on some work at home. With a general election imminent, the features' team at *The Chronicle* had prepared vox pops around the country on the electorate's expectations and Philip had some copy to read through...but there was also horse racing on television.

***

A buzzing sound announced the opening of the wrought-iron gates and the black sports car passed through before they were fully extended. Darren Peters sat back and pushed the accelerator pedal. Wallington Rovers were playing at home and he liked to reach the stadium before the supporters who congregated early in the hope of seeing the players arrive. 'Saddos' was how Darren viewed these people; not an opinion he could voice publicly as he subscribed to the footballer's mantra that it was the supporters who made his chosen career so special. He loved playing football but believed that doing so in bygone years was probably more fun.

'You wasn't letting anybody down no matter how many birds you shagged,' cackled Charlie Dobson, Rovers' star striker from the early 1970s when he met Darren at a club function. 'And nobody cared much about the ale and the fags either.'

Charlie broke off into a hacking cough as evidence of his predilection for the latter while his puffy eyes and florid face betrayed a lifelong devotion to beer and vodka. 'All that stuff about you in the paper, Daz? None of that bollocks back in my day. Granted, I'd loved to have been on even a fraction what you're getting, son.'

And that, ultimately, was the reason Darren knew he was lucky. His salary and commercial endorsements made him a wealthy man and, to top it all, a seemingly unending stream of young women were willing to be seduced by him. It was regrettable that some showed an eagerness to share the details with the more salacious newspapers, allowing the complexity and duplicity of Darren's sex life to become public knowledge. That Peters had a very young daughter whose mother was enraged by the revelations granted him pariah status to the casual moralists in some of the dailies.

To alleviate this, on Jack Watson's advice, Darren expressed remorse in a newspaper interview carefully orchestrated by Watson and Darren's ghost writer. Peters was sure he hadn't actually said some of the comments attributed to him – he didn't even understand what was meant by 'it would be disingenuous on my part' or 'a predicament of my own volition' – but it seemed to help his case.

Kelly Spencer, his girlfriend, needed more persuasion that he was worthy of her forgiveness but she held a pragmatic view on how best to protect the interests of herself and their young daughter, Krystal. She warned Darren that she wouldn't tolerate any more philandering and his acceptance of the ultimatum seemed to appease her...or, more precisely:

'Daz, you screw around again, me and Krystal are off. You've been a proper scumbag and we deserve more respect. Hear what I'm saying?'

'Yeah, Kel. Give me a chance, I'll change.'

'You better and all. Now, piss off outta the room, I'm watching telly.'

Darren meekly departed and decided it would be a judicious move to contact the PR girl from his kit sponsors and postpone their scheduled assignation until a time when he felt a little less under scrutiny. Kelly was a model whose unique selling point involved topless photo shoots. They first met during a 2006 World Cup promotion and theirs was a tempestuous relationship; both would admit their daughter was probably the glue holding it together. Darren felt entitled to a degree of latitude when it came to other women – he did, after all, provide about 90% of the household's income – and was aggrieved that this leeway wasn't granted. He was prudent enough, however, to refrain from airing this view to Kelly. It would not, he felt, be granted a fair hearing.

Darren arrived at the stadium, mentioned his appearance that evening on a TV show to a representative from his boot sponsors before employing a well-used line about having some work to do. He joined his Rovers' team-mates as the team manager, Larry Downing - a garrulous man whose weather-beaten complexion owed much to a lifetime spent on football pitches, training grounds and sunny beaches - barked instructions to each player before addressing the entire team.

'You know what to do, lads, give it your all, nobody come off the pitch feeling they ain't given their all. Remember Tuesday night, you've gone there, you've gone out, you've got stuck in, you've let them know you're there, you've come in, heads held high, you've done it, you've come away with a win. Heads held high. That's what I want, 110%, no shirkers, no fannying about, all in it together. There's no I in team.'

This was accompanied by Downing punching his palm and shouts of 'come on' from some of his players. The French international, Noël Rotane, looked around with disdain as he registered the wild-eyed expressions. He winked at Paul Nevin, Rovers' urbane right-back, who arched his eyebrows acknowledging Rotane's gesture. Nevin's interest in books, art and foreign language films saw him viewed with suspicion by some of his colleagues. At the club's training ground, he would regularly read *The Guardian* or *Independent* and converse earnestly with rank-and-file members of staff.

'Each to their own, I always say,' was club captain, Dave MacKinnon's view on Nevin's interests outside football. 'But sometimes you wonder if he's taking the piss. I don't mind the foreign lads being a bit sniffy about some of the stuff we're into – different culture, innit – but you get the impression that Nevin looks down on us.'

'What is the phrase you English use? Reminds you of Churchill?' Rotane said to Nevin as he nodded towards the manager.

Nevin laughed. 'Yes, Churchillian describes it quite well. Still, if it contributes to a win today, we can't complain.'

Darren heard this, nodded solemnly and joined Nevin and Rotane.

'Yeah, he does fire you up for a game does the gaffer. Makes you think with some of those phrases of his: no I in team...that's a good one. I like the threads, Noël, decent bit of gear there.' Peters appraised the Frenchman's brown three-piece suit hanging from a peg behind him. 'Have to hand it to you foreign geezers, you dress well. Unlike old Nevin here, is that jacket from a charity shop, Paul? You're letting the side down, mate.'

Nevin shrugged. Although he viewed many of the behavioural norms of his fellow footballers as infantile, he was the most superstitious member of the team and clung to the idea of wearing a lucky suit to all home games. He'd first worn it on the day, two years earlier, when he scored the first goal of his career. He continued to wear it since on the basis that Rovers usually won when he did so even though it was pointed out to him that a team of Rovers' standing were expected to win home games.

'Ah, you British...with your lucky charms and your superstitions. You don't understand logic and reason,' Rotane said. 'OK, let's go. You first, Darren *mon ami*, I like being last out into the tunnel.'

Peters laughed and slapped Rotane on the back.

'You know what, mate, you're all right for a frog.'

***

The small barbershop resonated with buzzing razors, cheery chat and running water as Fredo, the owner, lathered John Hooper's face. A proper shave from a barber was one of John's occasional indulgences and today was a day fraught with possibilities. It called for top quality grooming.

'Got anything special lined up for the weekend, John?' Fredo asked in his lilting voice, a curious hybrid of Sicilian and London.

Frederico Bottini was only nine when his parents left their native Sicily in the 1950s and migrated to London. He rapidly picked up English and was often called on to help in the barber shop which his father opened. Fredo was popular with his father's customers and enjoyed his time there more than the hours spent at his studies. It was now his business.

'That remains to be seen. I'm meeting an old flame tonight....someone you know, Fredo. Remember when my girlfriend got her hair cut here?'

'Ah, *la bella* Laura. I never understood why you split up with her.'

'No need to be so polite, Fredo. She ditched me.'

'But you're meeting her again tonight. Hey, you a lucky boy, John.'

Past tense, John thought. I was a lucky boy and didn't appreciate quite how lucky. God, how funny was it when she came to Fredo's for a haircut? It was a forfeit for some bet between us – whoever lost got their next haircut from the other person's hairdresser/barber – and so typical of her that she went through with it. I would've complained and whined until she let me off. Jaws dropped when she walked in and Fredo's two sons begged

79

their father to take his lunch early while Laura just laughed her way through it all. *La bella* Laura indeed.

'Not that lucky, Fredo. Laura got married the year before last.'

'But you're seeing her tonight. Hey, my friend, never say never.'

Chris had said the same thing last night while they drank champagne in the office. John awoke feeling refreshed, visited Fredo and then bought a new jacket in readiness for his dinner with Laura. Arriving back at his house from the shopping and grooming expedition, he played some of the music which would've been the soundtrack to the two years he spent with Laura…Velvet Underground, Fraser Guthrie, Portishead, White Stripes and Mazzy Star. He tried to frame Laura within his memories of listening to these albums but he was too obsessed by music to associate one person with any particular band. Music and film: this was where his real interests resided, not in an ironic website with a transient audience who may or may not comprehend the demeaning component. The afternoon drifted by. Before long, it was time for him to depart to meet Laura.

***

'And why exactly are you meeting him?' Robert Armitage asked Laura.

'I told you why. He's a nice guy, we had fun together and I think he can be rescued from that awful website business of his.'

'And why should it be you who rescues him? Why not himself?'

'Because he's a friend. Look, I'm just meeting him for something to eat. I don't go on about it when you meet your friends for an evening.'

'The friends I meet are guys I play squash with or work colleagues, not an ex-girlfriend who sounds like she still holds a torch for me.'

'My God, you're jealous…and worse, you don't trust me. Robert, you're not serious, are you?'

Even as she asked this, she knew that he was serious. It was in keeping with his possessiveness towards her, the trait she most disliked in her husband. Signs of it were evident from an early stage but it seemed controlled, less all-encompassing. Now, if they were at a party or a dinner, she was aware of Robert's proprietary instincts. Laura explained that she didn't like being monitored and had no intention of modifying her outgoing personality just to placate his insecurities. That outburst had been weeks earlier and she was touched by his attempt to appear more relaxed on social occasions but it proved short-lived. The news that she was meeting John heralded a return of the overt signs of Robert's possessiveness.

They first met at a fund-raising evening for an arts complex threatened by the loss of public authority funding. The evening's main event was a screening of an arthouse film, *The Forgotten Niece*, directed by an acclaimed British director who held a Q&A session afterwards. Robert was the programme scheduler for the venue and over tepid white wine and peanuts, a spark was ignited. Laura admired his commitment to raising the profile of emerging British talent of all artistic disciplines and his attentive personality whereas Robert was smitten by her *joie de vivre*. A relationship developed; within a year, he asked her to marry him, was rebuffed, proposed again months later and this time she accepted. They married in the autumn of 2008.

Laura couldn't say she completely regretted that decision but a side to Robert which she disliked emerged. Aside from his vigilance towards her, he was remote and precious about his work within the arts world. For someone like Laura, a career in cinema and music was still new and exciting but she maintained a balanced perspective on the world; this film and that album were important but more vital things were happening out there. Robert, on the other hand, would rage about any perceived slight on his work or the role of the arts in society. At first, she saw this as laudable but it now seemed devoid of objectivity.

'Yes, I do think it right that lottery money is poured into a new sports centre rather than funding a season of avant-garde arts events. I can be as elitist as anybody, Robert, but let's not lose sight of what's for the greater good,' was a typical comment of hers. Robert would mumble something about 'the barbarians at the gate' and the conversation would fizzle out. The disagreements weren't quite relationship-threatening but they'd grown more frequent. When Laura spent hours with Nick Ellis on their Fraser Guthrie article, Robert made disparaging remarks about Nick's journalistic inexperience and asked why she was working with him; now he questioned her motives for meeting John.

'I'm not jealous, Laura. It's just that I don't really like Hooper.'

'Like him? You've never met him. How can you say you don't like him?'

'A gut feeling. Anyway, you've been critical of that website of his.'

'All the more reason to encourage him now he seems to share my doubts. Look, if there's a rational reason for this or if you object to John so much, I'll cancel meeting him but don't expect any empathy from me.'

There was no good answer to this, he knew.

'No need for that. I was just looking forward to a nice weekend together, we've both spent too much time working recently.'

'And we will have a nice weekend together. Now, let's go out for a sandwich or lunch.'

The afternoon passed with lunch and a stroll in the welcome spring sunshine. Before long, it was time for Laura to depart to meet John.

***

Angela Brady looked at the television and then at her father.

'Daddy, you never watch football. Can't we go to the park?'

'Sorry, sweetie, I have a reason to watch this. It's to do with work, the game will be over around two and we can go then. Is that OK?'

'I suppose so,' Angela grudgingly acceded. 'Oh, look, Dazzle is playing.'

Interested now, she sat next to Tom on the sofa. As his St. Ambrose's visit was only days away, Tom looked at the sports pages of the paper that morning for any news about Darren Peters and saw that Wallington Rovers were playing in a game scheduled for TV coverage. Watching it would give him up-to-date knowledge about Peters to assist in dialogue with him on Tuesday. To Tom's surprise, he became engrossed in the game and Peters' involvement. He was clearly a divisive figure - the opposition supporters barracked him and the commentator made derisive remarks – but one who Tom recognised as talented.

'Do you like Darren Peters, Angela?'

'Oh yeah, he's cool. I love that dance he does when he scores.'

'I didn't realise you liked football.'

'Well I don't really like football, Daddy, but I do like Dazzle.'

From what Tom knew, Peters wasn't the type he would want to see his daughter bring home when she was older but he let that pass. During the game, Peters scored a stylish goal and marked it with a muted celebration, crediting a team-mate's nominal involvement. The commentator expressed surprise at and approval of Peters' response.

'Aw, he hasn't done his dance,' Angela groaned.

'What does he normally do when he scores, Ange?'

Angela ran to the kitchen and returned with a broom. She wrapped her legs around the broom handle against which she mimed vigorous thrusting movements.

'This is what he sometimes does to the flag in the corner.'

Hmmm, Tom thought, definitely somebody I don't want my daughter to bring home.

***

'Come on, Libby, keep up,' Harry Davenport yelled as he cycled along the track snaking through lush greenery below the hills near Ditchling. Elizabeth, on a bicycle borrowed from Harry's girlfriend, Madeleine, trailed him and Harrry waited for his sister, puffing with exertion, to catch up.

'Jesus, this is hard work,' she gasped as she drew level with Harry and dismounted the bike.

'You're not getting enough exercise, sis.....or not enough of this type.'

'Harry!' Elizabeth exclaimed, punching him on the arm. 'You mustn't mock me, I wouldn't you.'

Harry draped an arm around her. 'Of course you wouldn't but indulge me this time.'

'It's good down here,' Elizabeth said, leaning against his shoulder. 'It's exhilarating cycling this route. I hope there's a pub at the end of the path though, I could do with a drink.'

'There is, last one there buys the drinks. I'll give you a 20 second start.'

Elizabeth climbed back on the machine and pedalled furiously along the path. This was reminiscent of their care-free teenage years and she sensed the clutter in her mind clearing. By the time she boarded the train back to London, she would be ready to confront the complications she'd left behind. Turning a corner, she saw the pub ahead and increased her speed, aware of Harry closing the gap behind her. She reached the end of the path seconds ahead and raised her arms aloft.

'Loser,' she taunted, struggling for breath.

'Well done,' he panted. 'But remember, first is worst, second is best...'

'Third the one with the hairy chest,' Elizabeth laughed. 'God, I haven't heard that in years. OK, drinks are on you.'

They entered the cosy pub where most of the clientele either wore walking boots or sat in close proximity to a cycling helmet. Smiles greeted their arrival but the barman glanced at Harry, unable to suppress a quizzical and vaguely hostile gaze in Elizabeth's direction.

'It's all right, Joe. You won't be complicit in any subterfuge, this is my sister, Elizabeth,' Harry said. 'And this, Elizabeth, is the man who runs the best bar on the South Downs.'

Elizabeth and Joe shook hands, Joe visibly relieved that an awkward situation had been averted. Elizabeth, inclining her head towards the seated area, indicated that she didn't want to stand at the bar. Harry bought the drinks while she found the most secluded table in the pub.

'So, it's going well with Madeleine then?' Elizabeth asked.

'Yes, it is. I 'fessed up on day one, well day four or five more like, about the problems I've had and for a while I was alarmed that she saw me as some sort of project. I was wrong and I've never been happier.'

'I like her, you seem a proper couple. Where is she this weekend?'

'When I got your text, I asked her for some space. I wasn't sure why you were bolting down here. It's not that she wouldn't contribute good advice - she would - but you might feel uncomfortable.'

'Oh, Harry, what a wonderful brother you are. Look, why don't I head back home this evening and leave you to carry on as normal?'

'No need for that. You need another day to sort things out in your mind, I can tell. If you want more company, Maddy can come around this evening. It's your choice, no pressure.'

Elizabeth reached over and squeezed his hand. 'Please don't take this wrongly but if you're sure Maddy is OK about it, I'd prefer it as is.'

'Done deal but you have to sing for your supper. This evening, you do the cooking, agreed?'

'Agreed.'

***

Christ, that was close, thought Geoff as he slumped back in his chair, a sheaf of papers from the manila folder in his hand. The papers contained details of transactions between two companies, companies whose shares were part of a portfolio of investments which Geoff managed. The documents had, briefly, been in the hands of a journalist, or somebody working for a newspaper which would enjoy exposing financial malpractice involving, however obliquely, Alpha Venture. Credit then, to Philip for returning the folder.

Two companies – Procter Jones Henderson, a venerable English finance house and Johnston Dudley, an off-shore bank – had subsidiaries which traded a complex financial instrument. The parent companies acted in collusion to manipulate market prices of this instrument until they reached a level acceptable to PJH and JD. The two subsidiaries then opened up the market to other companies and cashed in by selling their holdings. It was a sophisticated sleight-of-hand, one which escaped the attention of regulators and financial authorities. The amounts involved weren't enormous but earned a healthy profit for the two companies.

Geoff had a dilemma - there was no strict obligation on him to disclose the information to financial regulators but it would reflect badly if he was shown to have ignored it. Were the details known, the two companies were likely to receive a hefty fine and barred from trading; one certainty was a dip in their share price. Geoff wanted to disassociate Alpha Venture from the two companies but to do so was tantamount to admitting that AV possessed insider information.

He saw one solution – if this information discreetly entered the public domain, he could ensure AV's dealers were primed to offload their shares in the two companies and he could amend his portfolio without betraying himself or AV. The share prices were trading at a high price now and AV would make a tidy profit from selling them. A thorough investigation would be required to prove complicity on Geoff's part.

But what was the best way to make this information public? Philip Anderson was Geoff's first thought. Beneficial to him, beneficial to us, beneficial to the public...what could go wrong? *The Chronicle* would lap up this story without AV being implicated...perfect. He just needed Philip's collaboration and Mark Llewellyn's approval. If only Anderson had, after all, read the documents before returning them. But there was something scrupulous about Philip which made Geoff think he wouldn't get involved in underhand dealings...although he had mentioned his affair with a married woman so he couldn't be all that squeaky-clean.

Geoff's source was a man paid a retainer by AV for work which was termed consultancy. The information alluded to in the documents were something AV could use but Geoff had to act quickly before the details became more widely known. On Monday, he'd meet Llewellyn, explain the situation and ensure that AV's traders were ready to divest their holdings in PJH and JD. In the meantime, Geoff would find replacement shares for his portfolio. He remembered his dinner invitation to Philip - this was something best done very soon. Would Philip participate? If only Anderson was a hard-nosed journalist in pursuit of a scoop for his newspaper, this would be easier. If only he or Elizabeth knew Philip better. If only.....

***

The sunny spring afternoon became a wet, chilly February evening. Rain-slicked streets reflected the illuminated Soho restaurants, shops and bars as cars swished past John Hooper. The rain forced him to take a taxi rather than enjoy the 20 minute walk from his house near Russell Square. He stood and gazed along the street, so familiar from his time with Laura.

Much was unchanged: the lively bar frequented by dissolute writers and actors; the Chinese restaurant with notoriously rude, impatient staff; the elegant bistro, its façade unaltered over the course of 90-odd years; the bookmakers, reputedly a front for spurious underworld dealings; all still there.

But other things had changed. Soho was now an increasingly sanitised area and John missed the whiff of decadence which once prevailed around the narrow streets. This wasn't unique to the area; society was now an interminable search for acceptance, conformity the new creed, individuality a threat. Yet, even in its modern respectable guise, the sense of promise which John associated with Soho remained, especially tonight.

He pushed open the door of the Italian *trattoria* and instantly felt a sense of belonging. How many evenings had he spent here with Laura talking, arguing, planning, speculating? Loads, 15? 20? It was their ideal Italian restaurant....red and white checked vinyl tablecloths, subtle lighting, candles on each table, attentive yet unobtrusive staff, plain but high-quality food and an amenable owner who joined regulars for a *grappa* after their meal but could intuit precisely when his company wasn't needed.

Ushered towards a corner table which Laura might have requested, he tried to play down the idea that she was evoking an earlier halcyon time but there were too many portents for him to ignore. Having arrived well ahead of the scheduled time, John ordered a glass of the house red which he was sipping when he heard: 'John, oh it's good to see you again.'

He looked up and savoured the sight of his erstwhile girlfriend. She wore a red and black check jacket, light blue jumper, pearl necklace, black jeans and her auburn hair was teased into an elaborate piled-high effect...a typical, casually stylish Laura look. John attempted to cast from his mind how he must appear to her.

'Laura!' he said as they embraced. 'You look wonderful. It's so good to see you too.'

'God, how long has it been? Two years? More maybe, Peter and Alice's wedding, I guess.'

'Yes, that was it. Well, time has been kinder to you than to me, kiddo. Let's see the wedding ring then. Oh, you're not wearing one.'

'I rarely wear it. You must remember my problems with jewellery?'

'Strangest skin allergy I've heard of...I always thought it was a sub-conscious aversion to engagement or marriage but it clearly wasn't. Let me get you a drink. What would you like?'

'The house red was always good here. Shall we get a bottle?'

Paul, the long-standing senior waiter, appeared and performed an elaborate double-take as he took in John and Laura.

'Laura! Joe! No, *ti prego accetta le mie scuse*, it's John. Hey, good to see you two again. What's the occasion? Something good, I hope.'

John and Laura looked at each other and shrugged.

'We're catching up. How are you? Annalisa? How many grandchildren do you have now?'

Paul swelled with pride as he provided an update on his wife and their extended family. Always sensitive to those with lives less linear than his own, he tried to ascertain John and Laura's current circumstances. John, cognisant of Paul's uncertainty, mentioned that they hadn't met since her marriage. This was all the knowledge Paul required, references to them as a couple were dropped and he departed to get the wine.

'So, how are you John?' Laura asked.

'I'm OK,' he replied without conviction. 'I've had an odd few days. I put a lot of time into the website, spin-offs, stock flotation....so much that I lost sight of what I was doing and it took your phone call to snap me out of it. How are *you*? No kidding, Laura, it's great to see you again.'

'Likewise. I don't know why I was so defensive on the phone the other day...I'm glad we've met. I'm fine. Work has been a bit hectic for me too. Robert's OK and well, yeah, I'm fine.'

They looked at each other for a second and laughed together.

'Right, so neither of us are convincing,' John said, smiling. 'Ah, Paul, no it's OK, just pour. The wine has never let you down before.'

Paul poured the wine, gave a half-bow and said he'd give them time to choose from the menu. Again, they looked at each other and laughed. It was a long-standing tradition that John had *spaghetti alla carbonara* while Laura's preference was *trofie al pesto*.

'I assume the menu is still much the same?' Laura asked and Paul nodded. 'Well, I guess it'll be *carbonara* for him and *pesto trofie* for me, a green salad, *ciabatta*, small dish of olives and a bottle of water as well, please. Right?' She looked to John for confirmation.

John smiled, indicating agreement. Paul left and John raised his glass. 'To us...or something,' he said, voice trailing away.

Laura raised her glass, leaned forward and said emphatically, 'Yes, to us. So, why didn't you ask me to be a partner in your enterprise? It sounds like I'd be a wealthy lady by now.'

'Surely that's beneath you, Laura. It's probably even beneath me now, I'm thinking of selling my share to an American guy I know.'

'That's an about-turn...even by your standards. Falling out of love with money now that you've seen her naked without make-up?'

'Funny you should say that. This American guy makes crude references to money's aphrodisiac qualities, implying that seeing money naked should have the opposite effect. I think you're closer to the mark as regards my, er, relationship with money. It's not money, per se, I suppose. It's more the way I've acquired it.'

'A case of that joke isn't funny anymore, right?'

'Always rely on Morrissey for an apt quote; I seem to encounter his words a lot recently. Yes, you're right. It was fun finding out that mankind's capacity for bullshit is nigh on insatiable but you can't spend your life doing that. All it took was your phone call the other day for the cracks to appear and they're now yawning, er, I've lost the thread of this but you get my drift?'

Laura smiled. 'Yes, I do. So what's next?'

'No idea. How about you? You're branching out into music now? You do realise you're not leaving until you tell me about this story of yours.'

'Oh, that'll wait. I want to hear about you. I guess it's safe to assume you're not on Facebook? Thought so,' Laura said as John nodded. 'But if you were, what would your status be?'

'That's a very of-the-moment way of asking me,' John laughed. 'It would be "spending too much time on websites and not engaging enough with human beings" or something like that.'

'Single then?'

'Yes, there hasn't been a significant other for a while. I *have* been spending too much time on websites and no, not those websites, Mrs. Armitage. I really need to get away from geeks and ironists and all the post-modernism which the internet sucks you into.'

'And all it took was a phone call from an old flame?'

'My current job was probably never much more than passing whimsy but yes, your call was the catalyst. Very persuasive powers you have, Laura.'

'Hmmm, well I'm glad if I'm an agent for the betterment of mankind rather than feeding that insatiable appetite you mentioned. Happy to get the credit but it sounds like it would've happened anyway.' Laura glanced towards the kitchen area. 'Ah, stand by for *il proprietario*. Franco, how good to see you again.'

Franco, the Tuscan-born owner of the restaurant walked towards their table, arms outstretched. Dressed in a well-cut blue suit and looking a good 15 years less than his actual age of 67, Franco hugged Laura and shook hands with John, all the while beaming his brilliant smile on them.

'*Come ai vecchi tempi*,' Franco said. 'Sorry, I return to Italian on occasions like this. It's like old times.'

Both John and Laura shrugged uneasily. Franco took his cue and left, saying he'd drop by again later. Their happy chatter continued and John sensed bridges being mended. He could almost hear the sound of cranes and pile drivers hammering into place the bridge supports and felt that they were sufficiently secure for the first tentative steps across them....but it would be best to be a bit more circumspect.

Laura sipped her wine and speared pasta with her fork. She felt the acrimonious weeks of the end of her relationship with John recede in her memory. This was more like the John she'd originally fallen for: witty and self-deprecating. He also had a clearer view on the role of culture and the arts than her husband. She felt comparisons might become a dangerous line of thinking.....it would be best to be a bit more circumspect.

'So what's the Fraser Guthrie story?' John asked.

'I met a music journalist, Nick Ellis, at a party and...I'll give you the short version. Nick knows Laurence Tolliver who inferred that there was an untold story about Guthrie. Nick rang me, we both met Laurence and....'

'Why did Nick contact you?'

'When we met at the party, we discovered a mutual interest in Guthrie and he wanted someone to help coax the story out of Tolliver and...hey, get that grin off your face. It wasn't like that.'

John shrugged.

'Well, it wasn't. Tolly's a decent guy when it comes to.....'

'Tolly?'

'Oh, shut up John. I know he has a reputation and I'm sure it's well-founded. But, with no ulterior motive, he put me and Nick in touch with a woman in Clapham.'

'A woman in Clapham, eh? Curiouser and curiouser.'

Laura recounted the tale of Guthrie's spell as a gardener, his return to the music scene and the source of inspiration for the famous album.

'So, there you have it. It's more to do with suburban London gardens than love-gone-wrong sagas which serve as the yardstick for all soured relationships to be judged against.'

John leaned back in his chair, sipped his wine and exhaled.

'Have you been, er, have you put any of this to Guthrie himself?'

'You mean have we run the risk of him finding loads of factual errors like he did with that poor sod in the States? Tolly put us in contact with Fraser, we've spoken and exchanged e-mails, the most recent of which was yesterday.' Laura smiled teasingly. 'Would you like to see them?'

'What do you think, Laura? Of course I would. I'll get another one of these.' He pointed to the almost empty wine bottle, summoning Paul. Laura fished around in her bag and pulled out a few sheets of A4 paper. She was about to speak but John got there first.

'And yes, you're entitled to demand an assurance from me that I won't memorise his e-mail address. I may well memorise it but I promise I won't do anything stupid. OK?'

She handed over one sheet, retaining the others. 'This is his response to our initial request to write a version of the story.'

John took the sheet, eyes wide with curiosity.

Dear Mrs. Armitage & Mr. Ellis,

I believe you contacted Laurence Tolliver expressing your wish to tell what you describe as "an authentic version" of a period of my life in which, to my mind, a surprising number of people are interested. I have also heard from my friend, Mrs. Hudson, with whom you've conversed.

John peered over the top of the sheet. 'Jesus, he sounds like a local council official replying to a complaint about the bin collections.'

'It gets better,' Laura replied.

I have been reticent to confirm or deny the many speculative accounts of this period but as you have been advised of some facts which are not known to the general public, I am powerless to prevent you from disseminating said details. I do, however, request that you exercise caution and respect the privacy of certain individuals. Should you wish

*my collaboration, I am willing to read your completed article before
publication and advise upon its veracity. Otherwise, I retain the right to
challenge any of your assertions at whatever level is appropriate.*

Yours Sincerely,

Fraser Guthrie III

'Is this a wind-up, Laura?'

'No, that was the first contact. I thanked him, then Nick and I wrote
up our story, sent it to him and we got this back in reply.'

Laura and Nick,

*Thanks for your e-mail. OK, I can drop the legalese bullshit now that
I know you aren't two more of those wackos who spout garbage about me
on the net. I guess you're aware this is approximately the 348th time I've
had people offer their opinions on "The Missing Years". Some of the
speculation has been so patently the product of deranged minds that I've
been tempted to say 'hey, dude, you got it. Hot dang, how did you guess?'
and let them make public assholes of themselves. Instead, a formal
response (like the one you received) tends to discourage enough people to
go no further with their ridiculous witterings.*

*I can confirm that just about everything in your piece is accurate and
the bits which aren't needn't detain us here. I'm real taken by Nick holding
his hands up and admitting that he always saw "Education" as a
profound piece of post-relationship-breakdown angst. It's big of you to
come clean on that, Nick.*

*I laughed when I read the first review way back when which took
this line and felt a bit uneasy when person after person followed suit but,
see, a lot happened during my time in London which I didn't want to come
under scrutiny – relationships and shit – and, yes, I admit that I enjoyed
the mystique a bit too.*

*Before long, I couldn't give a goddamn about that album. People
think I didn't play many of those songs cos they were way too personal to
me. Sorry folks, I didn't play them cos they're not very good and you can
quote me on that if you wish.*

*I hinted to Larry Tolliver that I wanted to come clean on that album
at some stage but couldn't think how to do so without bringing a fresh set
of dumb-ass speculation out of the woodwork. Now, I see a way to do it,
so...it's over to you guys. You can mention that I confirm the essence of the
story and, based on what you've written, I don't think you'll make a whole
hill of beans out of me doing so.*

If there's a God up there – and if he approves of me - something a bit more newsworthy (like a cat being rescued from a tree) will break when you publish this story but I guess it'll occupy the fevered minds of more than a few. Let me know if you want anything else from me and let me know the date of publication so I can arrange a vacation somewhere remote.

Good luck,
Fraser

John threw his head back and laughed. 'That's priceless. I'm surprised that my interpretation of the album is wrong but I like the approach he takes. Well done. Your article must be pretty impressive.'

'Thanks. I am pleased with it but I must admit that Nick is behind some of the better bits. It'll be published on Wednesday in this month's *Rosebud*. We told Fraser and this was the response,' Laura said as she handed John the remaining sheet of paper.

Laura and Nick,

Thanks for the heads-up. I mentioned previously that I'd run for the hills when it was published but I'm being a bit conceited in thinking the world will stop turning on its axis at the news. I guess I'll be the source of a few smartass newspaper articles but I can live with that. Let me know if you get any flak which I can deflect. I plan on being in England before the summer so let's meet up, hey? Course, if you're over here in the meantime, you've got my number.

Fraser

They clinked glasses again as John poured from the new bottle.
'Here's looking at you, kid,' he drawled.

***

'Daz, you're the man!' Larry Downing gushed, slapping Darren Peters on the back. 'That was t'rrific, son, t'riffic. I knew you was going to do it today. You went out, you didn't hide, you showed 'em what you're about, you stuck one in, you're the man.'

Turning away, Larry seized Paul Nevin's arm. 'Nev! Top, top stuff today, son. You've gone out, laid down a marker, shown that winger of theirs what you're about, you've gone up and down that line, you've slung in crosses, you've got your tackles in. Top, top stuff.'

Downing wrapped an arm around Dave MacKinnon. 'Mac! That was super. You're a leader, you've gone out, led the line, put yourself about, a quiet word here and there, let the lads know if they wasn't up to scratch, sorted it out, come back in with a win in the bag. Super stuff, Mac, super.'

'Noël, son, that was the business,' Downing yelled to Noël Rotane. 'People say he's come over here, he's French, he's won't like it on a wet Tuesday night up north, credit to you son, you've gone out, you've put in a shift, you've scored a cracker, son, a cracker, you've come back in, bit of banter, you're one of the lads, son, one of us.'

By now, Downing was hoarse and motioned to one of his coaching staff to get him a drink. He took a lengthy swig from a bottle of water and purple-faced with excitement, watched the players filing away towards the showers.

'Well done lads!' he roared. 'T'riffic.'

'You know what, I think Larry's quite pleased with our efforts today,' Paul Nevin said to Darren.

'Course he is, what else would...oh, I get you. It's you should be on telly tonight, mate, not me.'

'You're on TV? Which programme?'

'That guy's chat show on BBC, the one who wears the stripey jackets.'

'Duncan Moore? I watched him last week and he said this week would be a books, music and film special. You've not been writing a novel on the sly, Darren?'

'It fits in with my new media image, Nev. I'm all responsible now.'

'Well, good luck with that. Did Jack arrange this?'

Peters nodded.

'He usually knows what he's doing. Just nod your head a lot, stroke your chin, look serious.'

'Cheers. Must get to the studio early and check out the talent. Ha, got you there, Nev, it's not just you with the clever comments around here.'

For all that he was never sure whether Nevin was being serious or not, Darren liked him. Decent guy, clever, well-spoken – the sort of footballer Darren would do well to associate himself with as he worked on his media profile. Darren dressed, put on a fresh shirt and went to the players' lounge to meet Jack Watson. Jack was speaking to Duncan Moore's assistant, reminding her that Moore owed Jack a favour. The drive across London to the TV studio seemed interminable but Darren was in high spirits after his efforts that afternoon. En route, Jack briefed Darren.

'Nothing too clever, Darren – I mean no jocular remarks about stories in the papers. Look serious and thoughtful, maybe make a reference to your little girl and Kylie, sorry Kelly, but don't go over the top, OK? And no mention of Tuesday's visit to St. Ambrose's, right?'

'Hey, chill man, it's under control.'

Jack Watson nodded as he gazed out of the car window.

***

Closing the front door, Harry stood in the hallway, sniffed and smiled. Not for the first time, he marvelled at Elizabeth's ability to conjure up a meal from whatever ingredients were on hand. Harry had left only 40 minutes earlier to collect some groceries from the village and Elizabeth's foraging in his kitchen seemed to have resulted in a vegetarian chilli. He dropped his keys on the hall table and pushed open the kitchen door.

'Wow sis, that smells fantastic...hey, what's the matter?'

Elizabeth was sitting with a glass of wine in her hand staring blankly out of the kitchen window. She turned and blinked.

'Oh hi, Harry. Nothing's wrong but I've just had a strange phone call with Geoff. He rang to ask whether we could invite Philip – yes, the guy down the road, him – over for dinner and as soon as possible. There's something he wants to ask Philip and he wants me there as well. "I'd like to clear this up as soon as possible" were his words. I'm baffled.'

'You don't suppose he suspects something?'

'I doubt it, he would've been angrier. He just sounded furtive. It's odd, a few days ago neither Geoff nor I knew Philip and now he's, well, you know.' Elizabeth shook her head. 'What do you make of this, Harry? I don't just mean the latest news, I mean the whole thing?'

Harry poured himself some wine and frowned in concentration.

'I don't know Philip, obviously, so I can't comment about him but my gut feeling is that this er, thing with Philip was some sort of release for you and it's out of your system now. You were right to decamp down here for a couple of days. It gives you time to think things over, clear your head. I think you and Geoff will be OK.' Harry smiled. 'Unless Geoff's fallen for Philip...you did say he sounded furtive. Maybe he'll announce that they don't want to live a lie any longer and wanted to tell you together.'

'That would teach me to get involved with somebody,' she laughed. 'I think you've probably got it right but I have some more thinking to do. First though, I have to sing for my dinner or rather, our dinners. Did you get some mushrooms? Good, I'll add them to this. You OK with chilli?'

        ***

The woozy harmonica, ambling bass guitar and breathy voice of Margo Timmins faded as the Cowboy Junkies' *I Don't Get It* ended. The band was Geoff Harris' musical accompaniment of choice when he worked at home, *The Trinity Session* his favourite album of theirs. The haunting, melancholic sound allowed him to focus on whatever was in front of him. On this occasion, the album had helped Geoff with an inspired piece of thinking. As he researched potential replacements for PJH and JD in his investment portfolio, the Cowboy Junkies' music led him to consider two Canadian banks. After some research, he deemed them to be ideal

93

replacements. Having expected to spend the whole night working, he had serendipitously arrived at a decision and it wasn't even 8:30 yet.

Gesturing a thumbs-up towards the stereo in recognition of the band's guidance, he switched off the player, strolled into the kitchen and selected a bottle of wine. Not a habitual watcher of Saturday evening television, Geoff flicked on the set in the hope of finding something worth watching among the populist, unchallenging fare which seemed to be the limits of what TV schedulers expected their viewers to want on a Saturday evening.

'Coming up in 30 minutes, the Duncan Moore Show with a line-up of guests from the world of arts, books, music and sport,' promised the continuity announcer. Geoff liked the show and a take-away would suffice for dinner accompanied by a bottle of wine, followed by a Cuban cigar. Banned from smoking at home, tonight he could grant himself that little indulgence. He'd called Elizabeth earlier to suggest inviting Philip Anderson over for dinner one evening during the week.

'Yes, Philip, you know, the guy I met in the pub last night. He's a nice guy and besides, there's something I want to ask him and it'd be best if you were there. Just something I'd like to clear up as soon as possible,' he said, savouring the element of mystery.

Geoff thought Elizabeth was probably intrigued by the proposal. Her presence was vital - she did charm better than most and her involvement would add validity and integrity to Geoff's request. Geoff felt guilty thinking of his wife in these terms but she'd understand his reasoning, get on well with Philip and extend their circle of friends into the bargain. Pizza ordered, Geoff positioned a tray on a small table in the sitting room, topped up his wine glass, drew the velvet-lined curtains and searched his wallet for a £20 note: he would tip generously tonight.

***

Surprised at seeing their father watching football earlier, the Brady sisters were amazed when Tom opted to watch television again that evening. Saturday evening programme scheduling was so much to his distaste that it even compromised the prospect of relaxing with his family. A chat show was scheduled which included Darren Peters among the guests and Tom was happy at the chance to glean more information about the footballer. Besides, Duncan Moore's programme was that rarest of beasts...watchable prime-time Saturday night television.

Tom rang his father, a Saturday evening habit since Tom's mother died a year earlier. Tom senior had always spent a few hours in the local pub on a Saturday evening but not since his wife's death. Tom attributed this to his father's dread of returning to an empty house...easier to stay at home than face another reminder of his widower status. Tom asked his father's friends to visit the house on Saturday evenings and this was now a ritual. During his weekly calls, Tom would often hear raucous laughter in the background and detect his father's impatience to rejoin his friends. He was glad that a happy medium had been found - the loneliest evening of the week was now the one his father most looked forward to.

Tom settled on the sofa as the opening credits for the Duncan Moore show rolled. He explained his interest in the programme to Catherine without alerting his daughters to his imminent meeting with Peters. 'He's not somebody they should look up to or admire, Catherine.'

'Hark at you, Mr. All-High-And-Mighty,' was Catherine's amused response. 'And who were your heroes years ago? I bet your father disapproved of Bob Geldof or Johnny Rotten or whoever.'

'Fair point. I'll get a signed football or a shirt or something from him.'

    ***

Duncan Moore acknowledged the studio audience applause and took his seat on the small stage. He wore, as normal, a striped jacket (tonight's was red and black), his customary self-satisfied demeanour also evident.

'Good evening. Tonight, we have a special line-up where we scale the heights of Mount Parnassus to meet some of contemporary culture's more arresting figures and we add a god and goddess from the more populist spectrum of entertainment to the mix. For a brief profile of each, Quentin Shields, literary editor of *The Chronicle* does the honours. Quentin.'

Quentin Shields, early-50s with unruly greying hair, black-rimmed spectacles and an air of amused tolerance, joined Moore.

'Thank you, Duncan. Our first guest tonight is writer, Toby Hawkins, the author of *Why The Long Face?* Hawkins' first book, it was probably the publishing success story of 2008. A droll study of unhappiness, Hawkins wrote it to chronicle his emergence from a period of despondency and described the book as "a light-hearted look at depression". Fazed by the trappings of success, Hawkins has declared himself unhappy with what he calls "the facile world of fame and acclaim". His new book is called *The Painted Smile of Despair* and goes on sale next week.

'Our second guest is no stranger to controversy. Rosalie Berkeley has divided opinions among critics, fans and, we're reliably told, her own family since her emergence as a cultural commentator in the 1980s. A self-proclaimed contrarian, she says that her pronouncements being accepted by more than 50% of any audience leads to revulsion with said opinion and a desire for immediate retraction. An anthology of her newspaper columns, *Well She Would Say That, Wouldn't She* was published last week.

'From the celluloid world, we have William Dalton, director of the bleak, existentialist *The Forgotten Niece*, the 1998 film lauded by *Rosebud* magazine as the best British directing debut since Chris Petit's *Radio On*. It's been a career-defining film and gave multiple-BAFTA awards winner, Freda Cummins, her first major role. Dalton's career has stalled of late due to an ongoing battle with studios, the latest of which has seen him criticise producers for a lack of moral courage in refusing to fund his desire to remake *The Forgotten Niece* in the style of the *Carry On* series.

'Venerable chronicler of the world of contemporary music, Laurence Tolliver has eschewed the temptation, and riches, to accept commissions to write biographies of numerous rock gods. He states that his favourite album of all time changes regularly because "that's how it should be." As of 25 minutes ago in the hospitality suite, it was Nick Cave & the Bad Seeds' melancholic classic *The Boatman's Call* but that may have changed since.

'And so to Darren Peters, Wallington Rovers' England international footballer described by sports writer Sam McNabb as a footballer who "combines the grace and beauty of a Keats' sonnet with the self-destructive hedonism of Shane MacGowan". He comes here fresh from displaying that grace and beauty during Wallington Rovers FA Cup tie earlier today. I can confirm that his Shane MacGowan side – if, indeed, there is one - was kept under wraps in the hospitality room pre-show.

'Finally, somebody accustomed to the word beauty is singer, Susan Pierce. An early Christmas present for music lovers last year was Susan's announcement that she was leaving saccharin-sweet girl band, Dolly Mix to pursue a career as a solo artist. She has revamped her image to portray a raunchier profile and hopes to soon begin recording her debut solo album, provisionally given the intriguing title *Between My Pink Walls*. During tonight's show, she will give us a preview of the title track as well as another song called *Making it Hard for You*. Duncan.'

'Thanks for that, Quentin. We've got a collection of mavericks this evening, you may wish to cover the budgerigar's ears,' said Moore, exaggeratedly checking his watch. 'It's gone nine; the watershed hour is upon us, let's go! Toby, your new book sounds like a bundle of laughs.'

Toby Hawkins, hangdog expression setting off heavy-set features, shrugged.

'It's a cautionary tale, Duncan. One theme is to be careful what you wish for when Dame Fortune beckons. But if my first book hadn't been a success there wouldn't be a second one. I can't complain, mustn't grumble.'

Rosalie Berkeley, eyes gazing out over her spectacles, leaned forward.

'Oh come on, Toby...you wouldn't change a thing. Depression is a horrible affliction but you wrote about it in an engaging and entertaining manner. I loved the book.'

Laurence Tolliver snorted. 'Bob Dylan's quote about people who enjoyed *Blood on the Tracks* being people who enjoyed pain comes to mind, Rosalie.'

'But surely you rate *Blood on the Tracks* as a classic album?'

'Well, of course I do – it's a songwriter at the height of his powers - but I don't get a vicarious thrill from it...likewise Toby's first book. I haven't read the follow up yet but the title tells you a lot.'

William Dalton, a hooded top and baseball hat at odds with his well-cut trousers and polished brown brogues, mumbled something inaudible.

'Sorry, William, we didn't catch that,' Moore said to him.

'I just want to know when it became acceptable to walk around the streets of London wearing wellington boots,' Dalton replied.

'And that's relevant how?' asked Rosalie.

'It's foremost on my mind. I saw three different people on the mean streets of Soho today, all wearing wellingtons. It's wrong, that's all,' Dalton said with a shrug.

The studio guests looked at each other, baffled.

'But surely the whole experience of writing the book has been cathartic, Toby?' Duncan asked Hawkins.

'In many ways it has but one can feel exposed under public scrutiny. I think Darren here will concur with that.'

Darren Peters jolted as all eyes turned towards him.

'As a footballer, you get used to being on telly and that,' he replied and was interrupted by a smiling Rosalie.

'But your recent press coverage hasn't exactly been favourable, Darren. Would you care to comment on that? Do you see yourself as unfairly maligned or was the criticism justified?'

'What? One bad game for England and I have to listen to "he's one-footed, struggles against tight marking" and all that? It's unfair. I've gone out, done my best and people turn on me.'

'That wasn't the press coverage which I'm referring to. I'm talking about....'

She was interrupted by Duncan who resumed his conversation with Hawkins, to Rosalie's visible surprise.

'Toby, your new book, *The Painted Smile of Despair*, begins with the arresting line "Having spent a lifetime becoming an overnight success, I'd like my anonymity back". At another stage, you claim "I was never as happy as when I was depressed". Are those two sentiments genuine or merely good, admittedly very good, sound bites?'

'Questioning a writer's integrity, Duncan?' Hawkins smiled. 'They're not just pretty words – being public property has some unpleasant aspects.'

'Such as?'

'The huge influx of mail...requests for tips on writing, begging letters, requests for advice on overcoming depression, accusations of glamorising depression, accusations of trivialising depression, accusations of over-stating depression, etc. All of these demand attention and a response. It was nearly enough to make me lapse back into depression.'

'Instead, you wrote a book about it. Isn't it all a bit circular, a bit incestuous?' Moore asked.

'I'm a writer, for better or for worse, I can only describe the world as I see it, as I experience it.'

'But your despair at having a public profile doesn't preclude you from making appearances on prime time television, Toby,' Rosalie interjected.

'God, you *are* aggressive,' sighed Hawkins. 'But since you ask, Rosalie, no, it doesn't. I've written the book so I may as well promote it. Besides, it's something I believe in. Unlike some modern day columnists, I don't make my living through engaging in public spats with the nearest target.'

Duncan Moore reclined in his chair, he had lit the blue touch paper and could now preside over a lively debate. The programme was recorded an hour before transmission to ensure that anything too contentious could be edited out but Moore enjoyed hearing discordant views and favoured a laissez faire approach to hosting his show. Writing and writers remained the main topic of conversation and Rosalie addressed Darren.

'Are you a fan of literature, Darren?'

'Eh? Never heard of him...or it could be her, I suppose. What's the name again?'

'Lit-er-a-ture, Darren. You know...books, reading?'

'Not a big fan of books, no. I read the papers, stuff like that. Why?'

'Just curious, I often wonder what footballers do with their spare time. You must have lots of it.'

'Well, I spend some of it helping charities and local community projects but it's not something I like to shout about.'

Rosalie looked chastened as Duncan smiled and turned to Laurence Tolliver.

'Laurence, what's your take on fame and infringements on privacy?'

'Oh, fame has never approached me, Duncan. I see myself as chipping away at the coalface trying to add a few more nuggets to the stockpile of words written about music. Us journalists, we merely serve and are humbled in the presence of those we write about.'

'Very modest of you...' Moore was again interrupted by Rosalie.

'And also complete tosh. You look at any piece penned by a music hack and it'll either make absurd claims of genius for some barely literate youth or it'll be entirely about themselves and their inflated sense of self-worth.'

'Didn't you once try your hand at being a music hack, Rosalie? Don't tell me you weren't successful? Left with a residue of bitterness, perhaps?'

Jerking her thumb in Tolliver's direction, Berkeley leaned towards Susan Pierce. 'That's the sort of smug chauvinism you presumably encounter in that awful world, Susan.'

Susan Pierce cleared her throat.

'I think it's a case of being comfortable with yourself in the music business, Rosalie. I spent years in a band which we'd all outgrown and I want to escape those restrictions. It seems silly to still sing songs about teenage crushes when two members of the band have children of their own. I'm at the stage where I want to explore my own sexuality and see where the journey takes me.'

Tolliver grinned. 'That's an admirable journey you're undertaking, Susan - one where you'll need an experienced guide. Allow me to throw my hat into the ring, so to speak.'

'Don't be disgusting, Tolliver. A wrinkly old degenerate like you is of no interest to a delectable girl like Susan here,' Rosalie sneered.

'Nothing ventured, nothing gained,' Tolliver shrugged. 'But Rosalie has a point, there are a lot of predatory individuals in the music world.'

'Thanks for the warning but don't view me as naïve,' Susan said.

'That's not a mistake I'm likely to make, Susan.'

Laurence was rewarded with a smile from Susan as Duncan Moore announced that she would play the first of her songs.

***

The stark nature of Philip Anderson's house surprised visitors who expected a bachelor with a voracious reading habit to live in untidy surroundings. There were no tables bestrewn by books, magazines and newspapers for Philip had a fastidious side which asserted itself throughout the house. His dinner finished, he rinsed the plate, placed it carefully in the dishwasher and checked for any remnants of food on the work-top. He retained his wine-glass which he topped up from a bottle which he re-corked. It was almost 9pm and his colleague at *The Chronicle*, Quentin Shields, was due to appear on Duncan Moore's TV show. Quentin was a friend, one he valued, affable and devoid of ego.

He chuckled at Quentin's droll profiles as the guests were introduced. Good God, he gasped, when Susan Pierce appeared on the screen, where did she hide that? His abiding memory of her was of a ubiquitous hit single from Dolly Mix when she was one of a group of identikit girls – all legs, hair, shiny smiles and vacuous expressions. No longer, she now had the fringe, cheekbones and sultry demeanour of a young Chrissie Hynde. Philip enjoyed the opening verbal skirmishes between the guests but felt a pang of

99

jealousy towards Laurence Tolliver for his brazen flirtation with Susan. She performed a song with thinly disguised erotic lyrics delivered in a smoky, husky voice far removed from the shrill banalities he remembered from her old group. Philip stared at the screen, oblivious to the ensuing conversation. He was smitten.

***

'I see no reason why not,' Laura said with authority. 'You know more about him than most and you're erudite enough to get your views across. Besides, it's the sort of thing you've always wanted to do – research someone's life, put their work in context, give it a frame of reference. I don't think you'll get too much help from Fraser himself but doesn't that authenticate it even more?'

John stared at Laura, longing to tell her that he would do just about anything she asked him to. The evening was turning out better than he dared hope and an animated Laura was stating the case for John to write a book about Fraser Guthrie and the music world he inhabited. At first, he thought the idea fanciful but Laura was at her most convincing and he warmed to the idea. He had long since harboured a wish to write what would be seen as a learned, authoritative tome but struggled to find a subject not already comprehensively covered. Laura's idea appealed: he was sufficiently remote from the subject for impartiality and hugely knowledgeable on Guthrie.

'Laurence can help too,' Laura continued. 'He's well connected in the music scene without being embroiled in the mutual back-slapping side of it. He'll open doors for you...if that's what you want, of course. And there's Nick as well, again if you need him...and me, it goes without saying.'

'I like the idea, Laura. I really do, I'd like to give it a go. I really appreciate your help.'

'Oh nonsense, you were responsible for me making a life-changing decision which I've never regretted. I'm glad to return the favour, in whatever way possible. Oh, that's my mobile.' She smiled when she saw the display screen. 'It's Nick, I'll take this, excuse me.'

John motioned for her to remain in her seat.

'Hi...Yes, in a restaurant...No, that's OK...Go on...Is he really? How bizarre, I was just talking about him...Hmmm, interesting line-up...Oh, in 15 minutes...Ok, thanks for letting me know...Bye, Nick.'

She snapped closed her mobile and smiled. 'Laurence Tolliver is a guest on the Duncan Moore show this evening. Coincidence that we were just talking about him, isn't it? Thing is, it's on at 9, wish I'd known so I could record it. Ah well, there's always the iPlayer.'

John glanced at his watch: 8:45. He swallowed and tried a casual tone.

100

'Well, we're pretty much finished here. We could cab it to my house in five minutes. Shall we?'

Laura shrugged, picked up her bag and nodded.

'OK, why not? I just need to go to the loo, you get the bill. We'll go halves on this, OK?'

'If you insist,' John replied. He didn't want to press the point but when the bill arrived, he paid it anyway. It was a friendly gesture, one which couldn't be misconstrued by Laura. But why would it? Here they were, two old friends – well, maybe a bit more than that – meeting up after a few years to enjoy a convivial evening together. Together. That word had so much resonance. The thing to do was to act natural and ensure that Laura was comfortable in his company. She returned from the ladies, lipstick re-applied, smiled coquettishly and John's heart melted.

Laura contemplated calling Robert when she visited the ladies but dismissed the idea. He didn't expect her back until late; to ring him would only arouse suspicion. But suspicion of what? Here they were, two old friends – well, maybe a bit more than that – meeting up after a few years to enjoy a convivial evening together. Where was the problem? It was Robert's possessiveness inveigling its way into her subconscious again. All the more reason to savour John's company. It was good to see him, he was fun to be with again and besides, Robert had to get used to Laura living her life as she wanted to. She touched up her lipstick, checked her appearance in the mirror, pouted at her reflection and returned to their table.

'Seeing as you've already paid the bill, shall we go? Next one is on me.'

Paul and Franco watched them leave. Franco smiled and spoke:

'*Come ai vecchi tempi.*'

***

Susan Pierce finished the song and returned to the sofa, smiling. She caught an admiring glance from Laurence who gestured his approval.

'That was *Between My Pink Walls* from Susan Pierce,' Duncan Moore said. 'You're the music critic, Laurence...any comments?'

'Impressed. I can't say Dolly Mix registered on my music radar but it seems they contained one true talent. Maybe the lyrics of that song would benefit from some subtlety but I think Susan will surprise a lot of people.'

'Thank you, Laurence,' Susan said. 'But my lyrics are an important part of repositioning myself in the music world....'

'I hate to step on the toes of my esteemed friend here,' Rosalie interjected, nodding at Tolliver. 'But I think you should write songs which are true to yourself rather than look for a market niche.'

'For once, I agree with Rosalie,' Tolliver said. 'Your voice is evocative of someone like Billie Holliday and you could pick up tips on the craft of song writing from songs like *Strange Fruit*. Less is more should be your mantra, Susan. But I'm not here to snipe, that was impressive.'

'William, are we keeping you awake?' Duncan asked as William Dalton yawned ostentatiously.

'Only just. Mutual congratulations don't interest me. I tend towards confrontation, it engages me, cleanses me.'

'But argument for the sake of argument isn't a great maxim to live by, is it?' Moore responded, glancing towards Rosalie.

'Don't put me in a category with that pretentious man,' she spluttered. 'I, at least, believe in what I'm saying rather than posturing for effect.'

'Isn't that the essence of all art, Rosalie – posturing for effect?' Dalton replied. 'Do you think that Philip Larkin, for instance, poem completed, continued to fret about a tomb in Arundel? Of course not, he probably sighed with relief and sat back to read some saucy magazine.'

'And you place yourself in the same league as Larkin?'

'I do. My films will stand the test of time as much as Larkin's verse.'

'I can't improve on that,' Rosalie sneered, shaking her head. 'Your witness......'

'William, tell us what you would like to discuss...apart from your own undoubted genius?' asked Toby Hawkins.

'Hey, why is everyone picking on me? I'm just trying to get some creative tension going but since you ask, I'd like to talk about...' Dalton paused and looked around. 'I'd like to talk about Darren here. Darren, you must deal with confrontation all the time, the hostility of opposition fans, everybody wanting a slice of you. What's your coping mechanism?'

'I just get on with it,' Peters replied. 'It's a compliment if thousands of people are trying to put me off my game. It means they're worried.'

Dalton opened his hands in a 'there-you-have-it' gesture.

'There speaks a true artist, my friends,' he said. 'What doesn't kill us makes us stronger. Deal with ridicule, throw it back in their faces...' He paused for a second, grinned and turned to Toby Hawkins. 'And then write a best-seller about it.'

A momentary silence ensued, broken by Susan Pierce.

'People read too much into what's said and written about celebrities. Sometimes I wish that I could, as Toby said, have my anonymity back but being invited to meet famous people is something I never thought would happen to me. It's a balancing act and the public should respect that.'

Another lull followed, the studio guests apparently unsure how to respond. Darren Peters spoke.

'Yeah and it affects other people too. There's been a lot in the papers about me - some of it is true and some isn't. I've made mistakes, I hold my hands up but I want to learn from those mistakes. I think I've matured and now that I've got a little girl of my own, I want to look out for her.' A ripple of applause rang through the audience; Darren took encouragement and smiled bashfully. 'These days, I just want to play football, go home to Kelly and Krystal and live as normal a life as possible.'

'Very admirable, Darren,' said the presenter. 'And that's about all we have time for this week, a big thanks to my guests.....Toby, Laurence, Darren, Rosalie, William and Susan. And, now, to see us out, another number from Susan Pierce, *Making It Hard For You*. Goodnight.'

***

The closing credits scrolled down the screen as John Hooper pointed to Laura's glass.

'A top-up?' he asked.

Laura shrugged. 'OK. See, I told you. Tolliver is OK.'

Laura stood up and walked around the room while John went to the kitchen to retrieve the wine bottle. She looked around approvingly and followed John to the kitchen to see more of his terraced, two-storied house on the Camden Town side of Russell Square where they'd arrived back in time to see Duncan Moore's show.

'Yeah, he comes across as likeable,' John shouted back before he realised that Laura was just feet away from him.

'Nice place,' she said holding out her glass for a refill. Gazing around, she spotted a cork notice board festooned with photographs and take-away menus, all kept in place by push-pins. She peered at the photographs and noticed one of her with John.

'What a handsome couple we were,' she said, smiling. 'Cheers. I didn't realise I merited inclusion in the Hooper photo gallery.'

'Why not?' John shrugged. He attempted nonchalance as he wondered how she interpreted the photograph's prominence on the notice board. It was taken one night seven years previously when they attended a Christmas party. In John's memory, it had been a magical night. They remained at the party until about 3am and then walked to Laura's house through streets lightly dusted with snow. The snow continued through the night and the following day, a Saturday. They stayed in bed until the afternoon and then, together, ineptly built a snowman and threw snowballs at each other. How he longed for a weekend such as that again. He gazed at her and tried to read her thoughts.

Laura remembered the photograph being taken by one of her colleagues who joked that John, the academic, seemed perfectly at home among Laura's banker friends. At the time, John was close to quitting his university post and they'd laughed at how prescient her colleague had been.

103

She looked at the photograph again and recalled the blissful weekend in the snow which ensued.

'What a fabulous weekend that was,' she said in a wistful voice and turned away from the board to meet John's gaze.

***

At that moment, in a hospitality suite at the BBC, Jack Watson watched Susan Pierce key a number into her phone. She spoke to Darren Peters and chuckled, gently punching his arm. Jack sighed. Surely Darren wasn't trying it on with her? No, she left the room. As Darren sauntered towards Jack's group, his mobile rang. He answered it, waved to Jack and pointed to a door indicating that he'd take the call outside. Jack returned to his conversation with Quentin Shields, Laurence Tolliver and Duncan Moore.

'Sorry, Duncan, I missed that.'

'It seems like the lovely Susan has caught your eye, Jack. No surprise there, she was quite a revelation tonight. Darren came across well too.'

'He's a good lad is Darren. There's been some rubbish in the papers ....well, there is a certain amount of truth to it but you heard what he said tonight about learning valuable lessons. Besides, most of those liaisons were ages ago, bimbos seizing a chance to get their grubby hands on a few quid. A very sordid business.'

'But you have to presume there were others besides those who sold their stories. It's the sheer scale which is mind-boggling,' Quentin said. 'Christ, I sound like some puritan passing judgement on the town harridan.'

The others laughed. Quentin turned to Duncan.

'I thought you gave Darren a pretty easy ride tonight, Duncan. You're normally more combative than that with your guests. Not a Wallington Rovers' fan, are you?'

'Nothing like that, Quentin. I just thought he deserved a chance to speak without having to go on the defensive,' Duncan replied uneasily and looked to Jack Watson for support.

'Decent of you, Dunc,' Jack said. 'That's the trouble with the media, so quick to condemn – nice to see you take a different approach.'

'Hmm,' mused Quentin. He glanced across the room to where Rosalie Berkeley and William Dalton were chatting animatedly. 'Speaking of being quick to condemn, those two look like the best of friends now.'

'Who'd have thought it?' asked Laurence. 'Sometimes I think the real action takes place off-screen.'

'What?' Duncan asked in mock-horror. 'People put on an act for television? Surely not? Let's wander over and join in.'

They walked across to Dalton and Berkeley, pausing to pick up drinks from a bottle-laden table. Rosalie turned and smiled.

'Ah, here come my chivalrous heroes to rescue me from death by boredom. Hate to disappoint you guys but on-screen hostilities have given way to convivial chat. It was ever thus.'

'What she said,' Dalton shrugged. 'It's disappointing when you want to dislike someone but can't.'

'Still, I have to say that you lot are straight from central casting,' Rosalie sniffed. 'Dishevelled film director, tortured writer, sleazy music hack, smug presenter.......'

'And argumentative harpie,' interjected Tolliver.

Rosalie smiled and the conversation continued. A while later, Quentin Shields left the room in search of the gents' lavatory. Duly relieved, he returned towards the hospitality suite but was unsure of the room. He tried a door, one opening on to a dimly lit room which seemed empty. Empty, apart from the couple in the far corner who, despite the poor light, Quentin could see were engaged in vigorous sex. Quentin quickly retreated and closed the door as he heard Susan Pierce's excited whisper.

'Darren, Darren, I'm going to....'

Quentin paused outside the room and exhaled. Now, there is one fast mover, he thought. No, two fast movers. He continued down the corridor and, at the third attempt, located the correct room. He rejoined the conversation as they discussed Darren's participation in the programme.

'I thought he acquitted himself well, a decent performance,' Laurence said.

'Indeed, he's quite a performer,' Quentin added with a smile.

Before long, Darren returned and apologised for his absence.

'Jack was worried, Darren,' Duncan said. 'He probably thinks you've been talking to another agent.'

'Where's Susan?' Darren asked innocently. 'I was talking to her about media attention; I think she'll receive quite a bit of it.'

'She'll manage,' Quentin said. 'She's a girl who knows what she wants and how to get it.'

Susan returned and the group dispersed. Darren accepted the offer of a driver, requested a lift to Wallington Rovers' ground where he picked up his car and congratulated himself on whatever instinct had made him change before travelling to the TV studio. He donned the shirt he'd worn earlier and disposed of the one which bore the scent of Susan Pierce's perfume. 'A good day, a very good day, you've done good, Darren,' he said aloud as he switched on the ignition.

***

The quiet chatter in The Joiners Arms pleased Geoff Harris – he'd tired of bars where one had to shout to conduct a conversation. This pub was proving to be quite a discovery, or rediscovery...and it was practically on his doorstep. Socialising was not an endemic part of Geoff's persona and he often found himself reliant on Elizabeth's affable charm when attending parties although once she'd eased him into a conversation, he could be as gregarious as anybody.

Tonight, he wanted company and called into the pub when Duncan Moore's TV show ended. He considered asking Philip whether he wished to join him – lights were shining in Philip's house as he walked past – but decided against it. He had a specific reason to speak with Philip and it would be better to do so with Elizabeth present. Maybe he'd issue the dinner invitation as he returned from the pub. At the Joiners Arms, Geoff saw Howard Simpson, another neighbour he was vaguely acquainted with, at the bar and joined him.

'Geoff, we don't see you here often. What's the occasion?'

'Oh, I was here last night and realised that it's a nice place...and Elizabeth is away for the weekend.'

'Same boat as me then, Geraldine's gone to our daughter's place for the night. Mind you, I often come in here of a Saturday evening. So, how are things in the City?'

'So-so, it gets harder all the time to keep ahead of the game. Your café seems to do well but you do work long hours.'

'I like starting early. It's OK when I just stroll down the road to work. I don't envy you your commute.'

'You get used to it, I suppose. Can I get you another one?'

After an hour of amicable conversation, Geoff left. He noticed that the lights were still on at Philip's house and knocked on the door. Philip was clearly surprised to see Geoff on his doorstep.

'Hi Philip. Sorry if I'm disturbing you but I just wanted to ask you something.'

'Sure, Geoff,' Philip answered hesitantly. 'Do you want to come in?'

'No thanks, I won't disrupt your evening. I mentioned last night that you should come over to ours for dinner or a drink some evening soon. Are you free on Monday evening? I know it's short notice but Elizabeth will be back and we thought we'd get the ball rolling, as it were.'

'Er, Monday,' Philip mused, surprised. 'No, I don't have anything arranged. If you're sure that's OK, I'd be delighted to. I er, assume Elizabeth knows?'

'Yes, of course. She's looking forward to it. How about 7:30?'

'That sounds fine with me. Black tie?' Philip asked, smiling.

'But of course,' Geoff laughed. He caught a glimpse of a silk scarf on a table in the hallway. One which was similar, identical even, to one of Elizabeth's favourites. Maybe he's got company, Geoff thought. 'OK, we'll see you then. Is there anything in particular which you don't eat?'

'No, pretty much anything goes with me. Thanks.'

'Elizabeth's the cook. Do you want her to check with you on Monday?'

'I'm sure it'll be OK. Sure you don't want to come in?' Philip asked.

'No, it's late, I'll be off. See you on Monday. Goodnight.'

'Goodnight.'

Philip closed the door, turned and saw Elizabeth's scarf on the table. 'Oh fuck,' he groaned. Had Geoff noticed it? He recalled Geoff glancing briefly over his shoulder into the hallway. There was something odd about this sudden emergence into his life of both Elizabeth and Geoff. Why hadn't Elizabeth texted him about the dinner? Not for the first time, he thought what a strange person she was. She pointedly told him she'd never cheated on Geoff – and he believed her – but she didn't behave in the manner of somebody new to affairs. Curiouser and curiouser.

Geoff walked home. Curiouser and curiouser, he thought. Philip had definitely been alone, evidenced by inviting him in on two occasions. So who did the scarf belong to? Elizabeth had bought her scarf – identical to the one in the hallway - after admiring one which the ever chic Geraldine Simpson had worn at a party. Hang on, Philip said his mystery woman was away this weekend, Howard said Geraldine was away, the scarf clinched it...Geraldine Simpson was having an affair with Philip! Who'd have guessed? Philip had said his lover was an intriguing woman. Well, Geraldine was certainly that. God, what else is going on in Russell Road of which I'm unaware?

***

'Bugger,' Laura muttered as she fumbled with the front door key. This would wake Robert; she'd be accused in a hurt tone of being merry with the implication that she'd enjoyed herself above what was acceptable. Well, she had certainly enjoyed the evening. She leaned against the door, the key turned in the lock and the door opened with a loud clatter as she tumbled over the threshold. Oh Christ, this won't look good at all. From upstairs, she heard the sound of Robert's footsteps on the floorboards of the landing and his head appeared over the banister.

'Laura, are you OK?'

She composed herself and replied in an even tone. 'Yes, course I am. Were you in bed?'

'I was but couldn't sleep until you got back. What time is it?'

'Er, gone midnight. Usual Saturday night chaos on the underground and buses. I waited stages, er, I waited ages for a bus.'

'You should've taken a cab.'

'They're hard to get on a Saturday night,' she answered, raising her voice to drown the sound of a taxi as it turned around outside their house. 'Are you OK? Did you have a nice evening?'

'Oh, it was a quiet one. How about you? How's John?'

'He's fine. I'm just going to get a glass of water. I'll be up in a minute. Do you want anything?'

'No, I'm going back to bed.'

Laura walked into the kitchen and filled a glass of water. Yes, John had been fine. She sat at the table and looked around, thinking back to the cork notice board in John's kitchen and reflected on the emotions which a simple snapshot could unleash. She was aware of something welling up inside her as she thought about how Nick's request to collaborate on a piece of music journalism had led her to.....

'Laura. Are you coming to bed?' The sound of Robert's voice interrupted her reverie and she rose from the table, finished the glass of water and walked towards the stairs.

***

5 - SUNDAY

And Saturday night becomes Sunday morning. The pace of life in London slows. People turn over and go back to sleep, take time over their breakfast, chat at length with each other rather than snatch hurried fragments of conversation before rushing to the next task. Even the weather participates as a pale spring sunshine lazily rises over the city.

Not today are the streets full of cars huffing and groaning in an impotent attempt to traverse the city. Today, it's possible for Tom Brady to drive along Chelsea Embankment and move from one set of traffic lights to the next without frequent stoppages. This particular route involves a detour to reach their destination but Tom deems it worthwhile because his daughters enjoy the view. They sit in the back and sing along to a song playing on the radio as Catherine smiles indulgently. The Brady family are visiting a restaurant in Clapham for Sunday brunch.

It's possible for John Hooper to jog along the pavement near Regents Park without weaving between people rushing towards tube stations or offices. It's the first time in ages that he's been running so he frequently slows to a walk: the generally accepted advice is not to overdo it. The dull pain he feels in his limbs can't detract from his good mood as he sets himself a target to regain an acceptable level of fitness and lose weight before, oh, the end of May.

Russell Road, never the busiest thoroughfare, takes its cue from the rest of London and Geoff Harris is the only visible person as he saunters to the newsagent to collect the papers. He pauses as a black and white cat strolls out to the pavement. The cat's inability to 'miaow' and tendency to make a strange noise which resembles a duck quacking has led to his name, Donald. Geoff scratches Donald's ear and strokes his glossy coat, Donald purrs and saunters away again, mission accomplished.

The tube train moves slowly between Farringdon and Barbican as Philip Anderson drums his fingers impatiently on his briefcase. He enjoys working on Sunday as the streets and his office are quieter than normal. The downside, however, is the cavalier approach adopted by London Underground whereby people working at weekends are deemed less worthy of an efficient service than their weekday counterparts. There are, he knows, logistical reasons for this but they fail to mollify the irritation of those using the service. The train lurches forward and Philip topples against the door.

109

Darren Peters strolls along the pavement to the local shop. Even though the walk is no more than ten minutes, he would normally drive but not today. He enjoys the welcome spring sunshine and waves to an elderly couple who recognise him. Kelly was moved by Darren's on-air comments and his domestic situation has improved....so much so that he decides to contact Susan Pierce to suggest another rendezvous.

Susan Pierce frowns as she sits at a desk in her apartment in the London docklands. A computer screen displays a series of oblong boxes which slowly, sinuously change shape as she chews the top of a pencil. A page of A4 on the desk is covered in doodles and crossed-out sentences. Here we see a song writer attempting to hone her craft, apparently without success. She sits back, sighs, picks up her mobile phone, scrolls through a list of contacts and finds the one she wants.

At the Armitage's house, the relaxed pace is also prevalent. Laura sits at the kitchen table reading a newspaper and drinking coffee while Robert chats on the phone, his conversation punctuated by laughter. She looks up, gazes through an adjacent window into the garden and smiles as a neighbour's cat strolls past. She stands, walks to the cooker, lifts the lid on a saucepan, nods approvingly and returns to her newspaper.

Sunday morning for Rachel Appleby is equally sedate. Her two children are attending various classes leaving Gerry and Rachel on their own. Rachel feels sufficiently emboldened by the pleasant weather to venture into the garden at the back of their Tudor house to check on the plants and happily notes that all seem to have survived winter's ravages unscathed. Inside, Gerry sifts through paperwork from his building business. Rachel returns from the garden and asks whether two o'clock will be OK for lunch. Gerry is happy with this.

A group of sharply-dressed people mingle outside the North London Bible Community Church as Michael Benson emerges into the daylight accompanied by his mother. Michael, a sporadic and reluctant attendee, is happy today to reward his mother's support during his recent brush with the law by walking arm-in-arm with her. Dot Benson beams with pride and strolls magisterially through the throng exchanging *bon mots* with friends. Michael joins the short conversations and his mother beams even more.

A woozy sound fills the air in Laurence Tolliver's living room. The languorous ambience extends to Laurence reclining on a sofa as he listens to a newly released album, one which he will review for a music publication. He exhales wispy puffs of smoke from a cigar. Cigars, two at most, are one of his Sunday indulgences. He salutes a framed photograph of himself and his ex-wife before puffing on his cigar again. They remain friends and Laurence thinks about her as his phone rings.

At Heathrow Airport, the tranquil Sunday air dissipates as harassed staff cater with harassed passengers. Among the passengers, Kieran Bradley looks worried. Still only 40 years old although his thinning hair and gaunt appearance age him, he rushes through the cavernous foyer of Terminal 1 as if he is being pursued. Having just arrived on a flight from Belfast, he checks his mobile phone before descending the escalator into the underground station.

Also in transit is Elizabeth Harris but hers is a leisurely journey. She leans her head back against the soft cushioned headrest as the train rumbles through the Sussex countryside towards Victoria station. Wearing sunglasses to shield her eyes against the unseasonal sunshine, she feels invigorated after the weekend. She has decided to end her brief affair with Philip Anderson but wonders why Geoff has invited him to dinner and wants to know Geoff's motives before speaking to Philip about their relationship. She hopes Philip will accept her decision placidly and further hopes that Geoff's motives for the impromptu dinner won't threaten this. She'd soon find out.

***

'Laurence Tolliver.'

'Hi, Susan Pierce here. Hope I haven't interrupted anything?'

'No, just doing some work but it's work of a pleasant nature. How are you? Have you had any feedback from your TV performance last night?'

'A few calls. Mostly friends who were, like, complimentary and one from my mother asking whether the *Pink Walls* song had what she calls "a second meaning". I didn't quite know what to say.'

'Hmmm, that would be tricky. Y'know, that song really would benefit from some subtlety. Anyway, what can I do for you?'

'Can I pick your brains about song-writing? You said at the studio last night that if I wanted advice or an opinion on my music to let you know. I'm letting you know.'

'OK, do you want to meet? I haven't got too much on this week, just a couple of gigs midweek. When's good? I could do today but that's probably too soon for you.'

'Today would be perfect. Can you spare an hour or two?'

'No problem, always happy to help young talent find its feet. Where do you want to meet?'

'Where do you live?'

'Hackney. You?'

'Docklands, so we're not far apart. Do you want to come over here? It's just that I'll have some material close at hand that way.'

And so, Laurence Tolliver leaves his house with a spring in his step

111

and makes the short walk to Old Street station to catch a train to the Docklands. His reputation in the music world as a Lothario is, he believes, unmerited; he sees himself more an old-fashioned charmer whose enthusiasm for music usually outweighed earthier concerns. Only over the last day has Susan Pierce registered on his music radar; he is intrigued by the idea of helping her and further intrigued that she initiated the process. She has a good voice and, based on a chat at the TV studio, a passable knowledge of various music genres...and, of course, there are those hazel-coloured eyes peering out under that fringe of black hair. Yes, this could be an interesting visit.

Besides, it's a pleasant spring day and he senses winter receding. The snowdrops have begun to droop, daffodils are emerging and will soon open. Laurence buys *The Observer* from the kiosk at the station and descends to the platform noting a photograph of a triumphant Darren Peters on the front page of the sports section. Here was somebody else not previously on Tolliver's radar. Laurence assumed that Peters had been advised by his agent on the need for a charm offensive after recent newspaper stories but he still seemed a reasonable sort.

A glance around the carriage revealed that some newspapers deemed Peters' TV appearance noteworthy. *DAZZLING!* screamed the banner headline on one with the front page given over to a photograph of Peters scoring for Wallington Rovers nestling alongside one of him on the TV programme sporting a sincere expression. The sub-heading read *'NO MORE PLAYING AWAY FOR ME' SAYS PETERS*.

After the short journey to Canary Wharf station, he ascended to the glitzy concourse, checked a map to get his bearings and mapped out the route to Susan's apartment. When he arrived, he was pleased to see that the building was an old warehouse artfully converted into three apartments, each with a balcony overlooking the Thames. Laurence spoke to a security guard who sat in a booth barring entrance to the building and, identity confirmed, was waved through into a marbled lobby. Afflicted by a mild form of claustrophobia, Laurence climbed the stairs rather than use the lift. Breathing heavily as he neared Susan's floor, he paused, reluctant to arrive at her door in a dishevelled state but heard the click of a lock being opened and climbed the last few stairs to see Susan at the door of her apartment.

'Hello. Not quite the athlete I once was,' he gasped.

They exchanged the conventional friends-but-not-really-intimate greeting which involved not so much a kiss as brushing each other's cheeks. Susan was dressed in what Tolliver assumed was supposed to convey an oh-just-put-on-the-first-thing-to-hand style; faded blue jeans, loose-fitting white shirt and a pair of black Dr Marten shoes - very much the antithesis of the black cocktail dress ensemble she'd worn for the TV programme.

'Welcome to my, er, humble abode,' she said.

Laurence glanced around the hallway. With its stripped floors, blond wood and bare whitewashed walls, it possessed an understated elegance, no doubt the work of a handsomely rewarded interior designer. His gaze was drawn to a painting consisting of thin intersecting squiggles which closer scrutiny revealed as human forms. Laurence swivelled around.

'That's a Gary Hume, isn't it?'

She nodded and he whistled in surprise.

'Christ! Singing about teenage crushes and your favourite colour clearly has its rewards...I *am* in the wrong sector of the music business. Was the painting your choice?'

'No. I'd like to claim more knowledge of modern art but it was bought as an investment on the advice of an art dealer. I've come to really like it.'

'I'm glad you're not a collector of young British artists. Hume, I can see the point of but some of it...' Laurence waved his hand vaguely.

Susan ushered Laurence into a spacious room with a sweeping view across the Isle of Dogs, the window framing an aeroplane taking off from the City Airport. The room was sparsely furnished, only a coffee table, three armchairs and a sofa occupying the space. He noted an absence of gold discs on the wall, nor were there any portraits of Susan; instead just a few prints, one original painting and a family photograph which did include Susan, aged about 16. At one end of the room, bookshelves housed novels which appeared well-thumbed, a scan of the spines indicating a number of Penguin classics. Susan smiled as she watched him.

'Ever the journalist, eh? What can I learn from this person's taste in books and furniture?'

Laurence shrugged, mimicked puffing a pipe and adopted a gruff American accent: 'I yam what I yam'.

'Sit down. Can I get you something to drink? Tea? Coffee? Something a bit stronger?'

'The latter, please,' Laurence replied, pleased to see Susan's smile on his response. Red wine was offered, accepted and Susan returned from the kitchen with a bottle of burgundy and two glasses.

'So what can I help you with?' Laurence asked, glancing towards his glass. 'Apart from drinking this very decent wine, that is. Always happy to help you out there.'

'Sorry, Laurence,' Susan said as her mobile rang. 'I need to take this.' Picking up her phone, she moved into the hallway but remained within Laurence's range of hearing.

'Yes, it's me...I'm fine. You?...Yes, well it was a rather strange evening...Me too, yes I would. Not sure when I'm free this week but I'll let you know...Don't you feel a bit, you know, guilty?...Oh, I see, I suppose that's good. I wouldn't like to, er, be the cause of anything...No, of course not. I try not to be at home to regrets...Yes, that's exactly where I am....I have actually. No, that's OK, just something er, work related....Well, I now wish I hadn't sang that one...Ok, good, me too...Bye.'

Susan returned as Laurence stood at the window and looked out over the groups of tourists and families meandering along the walkways beside the Thames. He turned as she spoke.

'OK, back again. Look, I called because I started rewriting some songs this morning, trying out new ideas and well, I came to a bit of a standstill. I guess I'm just looking for some sort of, like, impetus or advice.'

'And why me?'

'I guess I'm aiming for a new audience and I want to know how plausible that is.'

Laurence turned away from the window, placed the wine glass on a nearby table, sat on the sofa and reclined as he considered Susan's words.

'OK, here's my tuppence worth. Don't ostracise your existing audience too much. You'll find that many of them have also outgrown the Dolly Mix stuff and will happily embrace your new material but don't denigrate your old band. You're in an enviable position because of them and the public never likes somebody with ideas above their station. That said, don't sing your old songs and especially not in an ironic way – that's unseemly.'

Susan nodded.

'You said you wanted to write more adult-oriented lyrics but that *Pink Walls* song is too raw. It needs nuances rather than being so, er, in your face. That way, you appeal to the listener's intellect and they're happier for deciphering what you're getting at. But you have to be comfortable with it. Me? I'd cringe if I was up on stage singing about er, you know.'

'So, it's too much too soon is what you're saying?'

'Not necessarily but it must be something you believe in. If that's what you want to share with the world, so be it....but you may find you've tapped into an unsavoury market. I'd stick to everyday experiences; extrapolate, make them humorous. OK, try this. Write a few lines about something which happened recently, the first thing that comes into your head. Spontaneity is good.'

Susan picked up a pencil and the A4 pad festooned with crossed out lines. Laurence smiled at the evidence of her earlier song writing efforts. She frowned, flicked to a new page, jotted down a few lines and paused. He watched as she wrote a few words, crossed them out and wrote some more.

On a wall in Laurence's house was a framed photograph of Bob Dylan sitting by a typewriter with a bottle of wine, cigarettes, ashtray and coffee cup close at hand, a draughtsman's table in the background and Dylan a picture of concentration as he typed. Laurence saw it as the consummate image of a master at work and if the scene in front of him didn't have quite the same resonance, Susan, chewing a pencil with her vivid eyes shining intensely did present a pleasing *tableau*. After five minutes, she leaned back, re-read her words and said:

'OK, it won't change the world but I've only spent a few minutes on it. Here.' She handed Laurence the sheet of paper.

'Lust got the better of me last night,
I should know better but it seemed right,
It's happened before, can't say it won't happen again,
Easy to say it was wrong but I'm only human.

I'm human, I've got desires and I've got needs,
No point denying where this leads,
It may end in tears, it probably will,
But for such moments those tears I'll gladly spill.'

Laurence read and re-read the lines and chose his words carefully.

'Well, not bad for a few minutes work. It sounds natural, genuine. In fact, I'd say it sounds very genuine.' He smiled as she blushed. 'Anyway, much of what anybody writes is based on experience. I'll be honest – on a page, these lines don't read like poetry but not many songs do. I heard your voice last night, you can bring lines to life and I'm impressed that you wrote these off the cuff. Now, what was that you said about struggling with writing lyrics?'

Susan beamed. 'Thanks, that really means something.'

'Well, I mean it. Anyway, have you made much progress with other songs towards completing an album's worth? You referred to it last night on Duncan's show.'

Susan held up the A4 pad containing crossed out lines of writing.

'That much progress. I'm new to this but I don't want to, like, rely on someone else to write my songs.'

'But you're open to a few suggestions?'

Susan sat back, sipped her wine and sighed. Laurence refilled his glass and continued:

'Do you have a manager or are you handling things yourself?'

'A guy who was involved with Dolly Mix is sort of steering me clear of pitfalls although I don't like him much...or trust him much either, to be honest. Is there anybody you'd recommend given that I'm, you know, hoping to move into an area of music which is more your scene?'

***

Catherine Brady opened the door and answered the ringing phone.

'Catherine, how's it going? Kieran Bradley here....again.'

Catherine detected a slight catch in Kieran's voice. Tom had said that he'd meet Kieran soon as he was due to visit London. Without telling her why, Tom was unsettled by his cousins. It was something which went back years and which Catherine implicitly understood as being off-limits for conversation. She treated the Bradleys with a wary politeness.

'Oh, hi Kieran. Everything OK with you and yours?'

'Ach, not too bad, Catherine, not too bad. Tell me, is Tom around?'

'Yes, we've just returned from a drive. He's coming in now.'

She waved the telephone as Tom walked into the hallway, whispered 'Kieran Bradley' and handed the phone to him. There was something ominous about this call and she shuddered as Tom spoke to his cousin. She knew the Bradleys had either been involved in paramilitary activity or were, at least, sympathetic towards it. These were dark forces beyond her comprehension. Visits to the Brady home in Cavan were often punctuated by a terse silence when politics was discussed but, surely, that belonged to a different era and now had less influence on people's lives. Seizing the opportunity to help Angela and Jennifer with their household chores, Catherine walked upstairs. A few minutes later, hearing the phone being replaced, she peered over the banister and saw Tom rub his eyes.

'Everything OK, Tom?' she asked, registering his startled judder.

'Yes. I'll meet Kieran tomorrow rather than Tuesday. He's got here earlier than planned, wanted to meet this evening but I don't fancy that.'

'But he's OK, yes? He sounded a bit frazzled.'

'Probably had a few drinks already, he sounds like that when he's on the sauce,' Tom said without conviction. Catherine walked downstairs, gently clutched his arm and looked into his eyes.

'Tom, you're sure he's OK?'

'Kieran's never OK...not as we'd know it. I expect he's had a row with Fiona and needs a few days away to clear his head. Unfortunately, Kieran's idea of clearing his head involves clouding it with alcohol. I'll meet him tomorrow and try to drum some sense into him.'

'A pretty futile task, I assume.'

'Family, eh? Speaking of which, what are the girls up to?'

'Don't change the subject, Tom. Look, is there anything you're concerned about with Kieran?'

'Catherine, *everything* about him concerns me...he's a loose cannon. I'll meet him out of duty, not because I want to. Can we leave it at that?'

Catherine, not trusting herself to respond in a reasoned manner, strode in to the kitchen, filled the kettle and returned to the hallway.

'Can you make some tea?' she asked in a placatory tone. 'Tom, love, tell me if you're worried. I know he's damaged goods and he's family and all that but I'd like to know.'

'Can I just see what's on his mind tomorrow evening? Sounds like he's been through a lot recently, I'll reserve judgement until I hear him out.'

His weary tone convinced Catherine that there was no more to be said, she nodded in acquiescence and rejoined their daughters upstairs. Tom took off his coat and walked to the kitchen to make tea for Catherine and the girls. For himself, he'd have something stronger.

***

The doorbell rang. Geoff put down his newspaper, walked towards the front door and smiled as he saw Elizabeth silhouetted against the frosted glass. This was a good sign - had the weekend gone badly, she'd let herself in but ringing the bell indicated openness, all was well. He opened the door and Elizabeth buried her face in his shoulder as they embraced.

'Good to be home,' she said softly.

'All OK with Harry?' Geoff asked. 'And with you too, of course?'

'Yes, all's OK.' She stepped back to look directly at Geoff, adding credence to her claim. 'Not sure why he called, to be honest.'

'Maybe he just wanted your company for the weekend. It's reassuring to know that he doesn't just contact you when something's wrong.'

'True. And how's your weekend been? You socialite, you.'

'It's been interesting, very interesting. I'll tell you about it. Shall we have something to eat?'

'OK, I'll unpack and rustle up something....or shall we get a takeaway?'

Twenty minutes later, Geoff returned from a local Turkish restaurant with chicken kebabs to accompany the salad which Elizabeth prepared.

'So, no crisis for Harry this time?' Geoff asked as Elizabeth transferred the food on to two warmed plates.

'No, he's fine. It sounds like he and Maddy are doing really well and the same applies to his work.' She smiled. 'We went on a bike ride and stopped at a pub where the barman was horrified to see Harry with what looked like a new girl in tow. His look of relief when Harry introduced me as his sister was priceless. So, tell me your news. Oh and you haven't got away with smoking cigars in here, there's a lingering smell still.'

Geoff held his hands up in acknowledgement.

'Guilty but I need at least one vice, keeps me sane. Anyway, I bumped into Philip Anderson on Friday and had a few drinks with him. Nice guy, amusing....and there's something mysterious about him too. He told me that he's having an affair with a married woman and I think I've worked out who she is.'

Elizabeth sipped her wine and held the glass in place over her mouth as she grimaced.

'Er, what makes you so sure?'

'I called to his house on Saturday to invite him here – I'll tell you why in a minute – and on a table in the hallway, there was a scarf like the leopard print one you own. I began to...Christ, are you OK?'

Elizabeth coughed uncontrollably, Geoff poured some water which she sipped until her breathing returned to normal. Still red-faced, she exhaled.

'Thanks. That wine went down the wrong channel. Whew.' She exhaled again. 'OK, carry on.'

'Yes, that scarf. You bought yours after admiring Geraldine Simpson's. Philip said his mystery woman was away this weekend and Howard Simpson mentioned that Gerry was away.' He paused, triumphantly. 'Gerry must be the mystery woman. Philip and Geraldine, eh? How about that?'

Elizabeth shook her head, feigning surprise. She was angry with Philip. Did he enjoy playing this dangerous game with the cuckolded husband? It was childish. Then again, she was in no position to get too self-righteous about the issue.

'I always saw something feisty in Geraldine,' Geoff continued. 'She's flirtatious in the café and I can see Philip being popular with women. He has charm and, I guess, he's good-looking. How about, y'know, from a woman's perspective... would you find him attractive?'

Elizabeth averted her eyes and assumed the demeanour of a person considering something for the first time. She returned Geoff's gaze.

'Hmmm, I'd never thought about it but yeah, I guess he is pretty good-looking.' Eager to move the conversation to less hazardous terrain, she added: 'Geraldine...would you find her attractive?'

'Yes, I suppose so. She's stylish and I guess men like the way she seems as if she's listening to you and you alone. It's flattering.'

'Indeed. She does flattery well. So, what's this about inviting Philip here tomorrow night? You're not going to ask him if Gerry is the mystery woman or anything daft like that, are you?'

'No, of course not. It's just that a situation may er, crop up at work and I can see a solution which needs the involvement of a journalist.'

He explained to Elizabeth about Procter Jones Henderson and Johnston Dudley, the potential implications for AV's portfolio and his proposed solution. Relieved to end the speculation about Philip's lover, she now saw other problems: the potential legal ramifications of Geoff's idea, Philip's involvement and the awkward position she might find herself in.

'But isn't your method of disclosure illegal?'

'Strictly speaking, yes...but it's, I know this isn't the best justification, the sort of thing which happens a lot in the City. Loads of transactions in the financial markets are based on fragments of knowledge which really should be passed to the regulators.'

'But you're risking your job and also, it's a bit er, unethical getting Philip to act as whistleblower, don't you think?'

'I'm not entirely comfortable about it either but Philip gets a scoop for his paper, I avert the danger of AV losing a lot of money and I can up my profile at work. Besides, what the two firms are doing really *is* unethical.'

'You were doing so well until the last bit, Geoff. Don't try to claim the moral high ground or if you do, go straight to the regulators yourself without ensuring AV are positioned to benefit.' She raised her hands. 'I know it'd be frowned upon at AV if you did nothing with this information but it just makes me feel uncomfortable, that's all.'

'I've given this a lot of thought and I won't say anything to Philip if you think I shouldn't but, you know, look at it from all angles.'

She shrugged and nodded her head.

'I know, I know. OK, I'll leave the spiel to you, obviously, but I'll make it clear that I concur.' She gasped. 'You're not thinking of hinting about Gerry Simpson if he doesn't play along with your plan, are you?'

'Good God! Who's the scheming individual now?' Geoff said with mild indignation. 'That never crossed my mind, honest. No way I'd try a stunt like that... "Philip, look, I've been reasonable but now I'm going to cut up rough. The thing is, mate, I know who you're sleeping with and I can make it awkward for you"...Your mind works in interesting ways, Elizabeth.'

'I can't imagine his reaction to that. Well, I can't imagine his reaction to anything... I don't know him.'

'I know I'm making assumptions but it must be Gerry Simpson. It's too much of a coincidence - she's married, she's away for the weekend, the scarf in the hallway. It's either Gerry or you,' Geoff said, smiling.

'Wow, that was good,' Elizabeth sighed, looking down at her plate. 'I'm going to have a bath. Can you clear up?'

'Sure. Good to have you home again.'

Elizabeth smiled demurely, ruffled Geoff's hair and walked upstairs. If nothing else, at least she now knew where she'd left her favourite scarf.

***

As Sunday evening moved inexorably towards Monday morning, the pace of life in London slowed still further as people prepared for a new week.

Tom Brady paused outside his house as Twigs tugged on his lead in an attempt to persuade Tom to continue the walk. There was little point in strolling around Battersea unless it included a sojourn at the crisps pub, Twigs seemed to say. Tom patted the little terrier and tried to convey the message that they'd go there another evening. He glanced up as the light was switched off in Angela's room which overlooked the front of the house and opened the front door. He was apprehensive at the prospect of meeting Kieran Bradley but he'd deal with that in due course. Right now, he was content to return to the comfort of his family, a bath and bed.

In John Hooper's house, the pace could hardly be slower. John was suffering after his morning run, his legs already beginning to seize up. There was a certain pleasure in the pain caused by exercise though and this had been a good weekend. He hobbled from his living room towards the kitchen and stopped. No: a new regime was in place, he wouldn't open a bottle of wine...John was imbued with a new resolve.

28, Russell Road was in darkness. Geoff and Elizabeth had retired to bed early where they made love and now lay side-by-side, drowsily content although both were apprehensive about the next day. Elizabeth felt akin to a puppet-master whose inanimate charges were showing signs of independence and rebellion, Geoff felt queasy because his carefully crafted plans could go wrong. Despite these concerns, they snuggled together, all that could wait for another day.

Nearby, a lone figure turned the corner into Russell Road. Philip was returning home from work and paused to mutter a few words to Donald the cat, who, as ever, monitored the street's activities. Donald showed approval of Philip's attention by making one of his quack-like noises as Philip saw a car come to a halt across the road from him. It was Geraldine Simpson who waved as she stepped out of the car. She'd been to visit her daughter, she said before bidding him goodnight and sashaying towards her front door. Philip, with a lingering glance towards the Harris' house, opened his front door and went in.

The sound of a child crying punctuated the air in Darren Peters' house and Kelly dragged herself from bed to attend to Krystal. It was understood that Kelly would be the one to rise if their daughter cried during the night. The toddler's sleeping patterns were becoming regular now that she was leaving early infancy behind and soon, they would have uninterrupted nights. Darren rolled over and reached for his iPhone to check for text messages. One read 'Tues pm? SP'. Darren smiled, erased the text and settled to resume his sleep.

Unable to resist a glance up to the top floor of the building he'd just left, Laurence Tolliver is pleased to see Susan silhouetted against the large window frame watching him cross the road. To their mutual surprise, he has agreed to act as Susan's manager for a trial period although neither of them is entirely certain what this entails. When he suggested ideas for her career, she asked him to act on her behalf and fuelled by a combination of red wine and fanciful plans, he agreed. Susan would now be known, musically, as Lily Pollen – a name prompted by a warning sticker on the cellophane wrapper of a bunch of flowers in her flat. Happy, Laurence hails a passing taxi.

Overseeing this vignette from her apartment window, Susan smiled as Tolliver jauntily hailed a taxi. Earlier, she was faced with navigating her way through the world of rock music weighed down by the liability of her involvement in a band which was anathema in hip music circles. Now, she had the tacit endorsement of one of the country's more respected critics, ideas for songs and a new *nom de guerre* which distanced her from Dolly Mix. Remembering Darren's call, she reflected that last night probably hadn't been such a good idea...but she was only human. She'd see him on Tuesday and take it from there.

The dishwasher chugged into action as Laura Armitage pushed the button on the machine. She slumped into a chair and sighed. God, what a weekend. It had all seemed innocuous...meet John but spend the remainder of the weekend with Robert. That had happened but she'd fallen into an embrace with John at his house. She'd eventually pushed him away as reason took over. Reason? She had pushed him away to prevent herself from doing anything more regrettable and now, she tried to avoid thinking about John. But the more she tried not to think about him, the more she did.

Upstairs, Robert twisted and turned as he attempted to find a comfortable position in bed. Aware that he was hyper-sensitive about Laura, that feeling was now more acute than ever. She had looked simultaneously radiant and dejected when she eventually arrived home after her dinner with John Hooper. Robert had tip-toed around the subject trying to avoid sounding either reproachful or patronising; now he was none the wiser. Today, she'd alternated between being distant and polite towards him. It was puzzling.

Rachel Appleby stood in the kitchen of her house scrutinising the calendar with its details of upcoming events. She smiled at the abundance of empty spaces; her experience was that things happened without warning and the calendar would soon fill up. Tomorrow, she'd ring Elizabeth and arrange to meet her; her impression was that Elizabeth might need some friendly advice.

In a small house on the Shillingtree estate, Michael Benson pushed aside his books, stretched and yawned. In the wake of his court appearance and reprieve, he was determined to avail of this second chance. He left the room and walked downstairs where his mother watched television while ironing clothes. Michael paused on the stairs and smiled as his mother cheerfully tackled her tasks while laughing mockingly at the game show participants on the screen. He descended the rest of the stairs grateful that he could do so...unlike that creep, Simeon, who was now locked up, unable any longer to exercise his malignant influence on Michael.

As the clock ticked over to midnight, London settled down for the night. A new week was about to begin.

***

6 - MONDAY

And so it begins, thought Geoff Harris as the train juddered to a halt. He left home early to prepare his proposal involving the discreet leak of the PJH / JD scam and disposal of AV's shares in the two companies. He was sure that Mark Llewellyn, the recipient of the proposal, would approve as long as it was presented coherently with no sign of panic - Llewellyn's mind was finely tuned to detect signs of panic. The train lurched forward again and a young man, dishevelled-looking despite wearing a suit, tie draped over his shoulder, jerked awake, spilling a few drops from a can of Red Bull over himself in the process. It seemed a badge of honour among the young bucks in the City to display their hard-living existence. The young man swore as he tried to mop up the viscous liquid from his suit and received both disapproving and sympathetic looks from other passengers. As he gazed around the carriage, Geoff identified the various sub-species of office worker among his fellow travellers.

There was the office alpha type (usually male) who saw weekends as an intrusion on their preferred routine. On Mondays, they were visibly content to return to a domain where they ruled...often a situation which didn't prevail at home.

There was a smattering of young men along the lines of the Red Bull-spiller, gathered close together but not so close as to inhibit their ability to flaunt the after-effects of their hedonistic lives. When they reached the penultimate stop before disembarking the train, as if a bell had sounded, pre-work grooming was completed by yanking the tie into position and running a hand through their hair. Work ahoy, I'm ready!

More numerous were those who went to work simply because it was a job which financed their weekends or their families or their mortgage and credit card debt. A hangdog facial expression betrayed these individuals. It gladdened Geoff to see such expressions become less weary as the week wore on until Friday when a degree of animation returned.

The final group, usually seen on the earliest trains, was the one which made Geoff uneasy – the office cleaners and support staff. Geoff knew that his monthly salary probably wasn't much less than their annual remuneration and to accentuate his guilt, they seemed to accept their status with no demonstrable protest. Geoff showed courtesy to people he identified within this group and then fretted that this would be misinterpreted as patronising.

He assumed that he didn't exclusively belong to any of these groups; his persona was more a *smörgåsbord* – a touch of worker drone here, thrusting trail-blazer there with an added dash of ruthless competitor. Today, he needed more of the latter than usual.

When he arrived at Alpha House, he listed the salient points of his proposal – inform Philip Anderson about the illicit practices with the proviso that *The Chronicle* publish the details; alert AV's traders to offload the shares once the news broke; arrange for the investment in the Canadian banks which he'd identified. He typed and printed a *précis* of how he saw events unfolding without saving the file; the less evidence linking him to whatever might happen, the better. Leaving a request for a meeting with Llewellyn as early as possible, he sat back, satisfied with his efforts.

As for the evening ahead, Elizabeth was happy to support Geoff's idea and intimated that she'd put on all her charm in doing so. 'But not too much charm, Elizabeth. We don't want Philip thinking you're trying to seduce him,' Geoff said to lighten the tone. He was sure that she'd achieve the desired effect and it was down to him to get Philip on board. Michelle Holley called to say that Mark was ready to see him.

***

Eyebrows raised, Chris Williamson unlocked the door to the ante-room of the office which he shared with John Hooper. The smell of fresh coffee indicated John was already there, an irregular occurrence. When they first searched for an office to use as their base, comfort and opulence had not been prominent among the criteria and the dingy building they chose satisfied requirements such as economy and location. Situated between Euston station and Camden Town, it was well-served by public transport and the bars and restaurants they frequented when working late at night.

'Morning Hoops,' Chris said as he walked into the office where a further surprise awaited him; John wore a suit and tie rather than his normal attire of jumper and jeans. 'Wow, somebody's making an effort today. Good weekend?'

'Yes, it was.' John grimaced as he rose to move papers from Chris' desk. 'I did, however, start a new fitness regime and boy, am I paying for it.'

'And what's brought all this on, may I ask?'

'Oh, I just fancied a change, that's all,' John shrugged.

'C'mon, you'll have to do better than that. Did it go well with Laura?'

'Yes, it did go well. Laura is still very much Laura and well, what can I say? I'd love to rewind my life to a stage when I was with her. I don't think life *chez* Armitage is too rosy right now...she was wistful about bygone days on Saturday. If nothing else, at least we're friends again and she had some intriguing ideas for me.' John paused and looked straight at Chris. 'I've decided to cut loose from here, Chris. As long as you're still OK with that, I'll sell my share to Doug but you and Frank have first option and I'll accept less than whatever Doug offers.'

Chris held out his hand.

'Let's shake on that, John. I'm not sure how interested I am in doing this without you around but I don't want to rush into any hasty decisions. I'd like to make your sale to him conditional on me being in full charge for a month with a veto on anybody new coming in. I'd also like to get Ash Dharni more involved, some of the stuff he wrote for us recently has been good. After a month, I think I'll know whether or not I want to continue.'

'Sounds like we've both given it some thought then,' John said as they shook hands. 'Assuming you wouldn't want my 40%, I drafted an e-mail to Frank. I'll fire it off now.'

'I thought this might be a significant day. Fancy a drink later?'

'Definitely,' John replied as he pressed the 'send' button and repeated the process with another draft e-mail. 'I know Frank's response so I'll send one to Doug as well. Crikey, these deals can move quickly, can't they?'

'Quickest of all will be Doug. I bet he's back to you within an hour.'

'Wouldn't surprise me. No hard feelings then?'

'God, no. I owe you a lot, John. You offered me this role and it's been fun – two guys playing at being businessmen and actually succeeding. Your phone...it can't be Doug already?'

John picked up the receiver, blanched and held it away from his ear as a torrent of words tumbled down the line. He looked at Chris and they nodded in unison.

'That you, Doug? You got my e-mail then?' John drawled as a babble of noise issued from the earpiece. 'Doug, I'm putting you on the speaker phone and for Christ's sake, lower your voice. Has the whole concept of telephonic exchange passed you Americans by?'

John pressed a button on the phone keypad. A crackle of static cleared and Doug's brash Brooklyn tones were heard:

'You English...always with the understated delivery. How ya doing, guys? You there, Chris?'

'Receiving loud and clear, old boy,' Chris replied.

'Hey, enough already with the posh boy stuff, else I gotta go to the bathroom, know what I'm saying? I'll drop the Sopranos schtick but only if you guys talk normal too. Deal?'

'Thing is, Doug, that *is* your normal dialect. What's up?' John asked.

'That e-mail is music to my ears. You want to sell lock, stock and freaking barrel? Am I right?'

'Well, there is the small consideration of a price but yes, you've got the gist. Two conditions,' John said as his computer emitted a 'ping' sound indicating an incoming e-mail. He read it, mouthed 'Frank' to Chris and gave a thumbs-up sign. 'Actually, make that one condition; I've just got Frank Garfield's agreement. That one condition involves Chris taking over for a month. I'll allow him to elaborate on his reasoning and his terms.'

'No need, dude,' Doug boomed back. 'I expected that. Now let me guess...say-so over recruits or policy decisions while you work out what the hell it is you wanna do, Chris. Am I right?'

'That's pretty much it, Doug. You're easy to do business with. Where did the fearsome reputation come from?'

'Let me tell you a story, buddy. I fish, I like catching the big ones like bass and salmon. I'm happy to reel them in for however long it takes but once they're in my sights, wham-bam, the sucker's mine, end of. This deal ain't like that, we're all on the same page, no need to dawdle.'

'Very true. I guess you'll want to talk money with Hoops.'

'Doug, which one of us opens the bidding here?' John asked.

'Well, how about Wall Street value at 10am EST plus 1.5%? And no, I'm not aware of anything likely to happen between trading opening at 9:30 and 10. It just makes it more interesting. If you're nervous about it, we can impose a limit on share movements of opening price plus or minus 10%.'

John laughed and flicked a button which muted the call from his end. 'He's a player, isn't he? You're not aware of anything likely to happen in the first hour, are you?'

'No, I've just checked the WSJ, Reuters and Bloomberg sites. It all sounds kosher,' Chris replied. John unmuted his phone.

'That sounds good, Doug. So we wait 'til 10 your time and my people get in touch with your people?'

'Hey, this ain't the cricket field here. We don't stop for lunch. Maybe you and Chris are planning on a drink and some fish and chips but I got my attorney off his ass to get in here and draft everything. He's putting together 'the party referred to henceforth as' and all that shit even as we talk. Don't you two go sneaking out to the pub.'

'Doug, it's not even 9am here. That means you're in the office at 4. I hope your legal guy is rewarded for his efforts.'

A muffled shout of 'bet your goddamn ass I am' was heard.

'Good, that makes me feel better,' John continued. 'OK, let's leave it there Doug. I'll await the e-mail with draft documentation from you.'

'It'll be with you in 30 minutes. Have you got a solicitor or whatever you English call 'em with you?'

'I don't see the need, Doug. I'm sure it's all above-board. Talk to you later.' John ended the call and slumped back in his chair. Chris arched his

126

eyebrows and reached into his desk for a small bottle of brandy and two glasses which he quarter-filled, handing one to John.

'Far too early, I know, but it's not every day you make something in the region of quarter of a million during breakfast, is it? Congratulations, John,' he said as they clinked glasses.

'No, not every day. Here's to us.'

'You have to wonder why he's so feared on Wall Street, I was expecting a proper battle there.'

'Received opinion is that the gloves come off only when necessary and then they really do come off. Besides, this is small fry for him. Well, I guess I'm out of a job,' John said with a grin as he downed his brandy.

***

'Pollen. P-O-L-L-E-N. Lily Pollen...Yes...Come on, it's not that funny...No, it's nothing to do with Lily Allen...Well, I'm glad you think so...Oh go fuck yourself.'

Susan Pierce tossed her mobile phone on to the sofa and punched the nearest cushion. She'd expected to receive some ridicule about her new name but not from somebody called Davinia Hotch1ck. Davinia, Daphne Hobson to her mother, was a gossip columnist for *The Universe* and had already caught wind of the stage name which Susan intended using. It was no big deal, Susan told herself, but Davinia's reaction alerted her to the likelihood of a mocking mention in tomorrow's paper. Well, let them scoff. She'd embarked on an interesting new career and the opinions of trashy hacks like Davinia Hotch1ck were of no relevance. Her phone rang again.

'Hi Susan, Laurence here. I've just had a call from one of my fellow scribes who wanted to know if I was now managing Lily Pollen. You've made news already, well done.'

'Oh, good. I, er, had a call from that Davinia bitch on *The Universe* sneering about my new name. God, I hate her.'

'You don't belong in that world any more. Ignore her and don't get involved in a slanging match. Rise above it. I hope you didn't argue.'

'Well, apart from telling her to go fuck herself, no. She annoyed me.'

'Don't worry, she won't print that bit. The tackier the newspaper, the more puritanical they are about er, industrial language...it's their pathetic attempt at dignity. Now, you said yesterday that you don't have a record company deal at the moment so I put out a few feelers to Interstellar Records. They fit the profile you're aiming for – independent, young, decent quality roster and two clever people in charge. Natasha Clinch rang me and said that she'd like us all to meet. How does that sound?'

'Great...but aren't they a bit too, you know, hip for someone like me?'

'Open-minded is how I'd describe them, Susan. Natasha can be a diva at times but her judgement is pretty sound and Billy Carney is a good guy. As I said, they're clued-up but you're the boss.'

'And here's me looking to you for guidance. I'm happy with that, very happy. Thanks.'

'I remain your humble servant, ma'aam. Just call if you want the blue Smarties separated from the others or whatever it is you pop stars demand from us minions.'

'Haven't you heard? The blue Smarties were banned a few years ago.'

'This world we live in! I need a lie-down after hearing that. Bye,' he said and returned to his *Tolliver's Travails* blog.

> *As winter recoils from the onset of spring, a young man's fancy turns to.....what exactly? How about the prospect of a solo album from erstwhile Dolly Mix minx, Susan Pierce? An intriguing prospect as anyone who saw her smouldering performance on Duncan Moore's show will testify. Here, I must declare an interest, an absence of impartiality. It surprises me as much as anybody else that I've become the manager of the artist formerly known as Susan Pierce, she who now answers to the performing name of Lily Pollen.*
>
> *And how did this happen? The realisation that Miss Pierce has a real talent which needs exposure led to a conversation and before you know it, we're shaking hands on a partnership. A shared interest in eclectic venues, noir-ish ballads and a desire to break free of the shackles of contemporary music is wot did it. Who knows what lies ahead? Susan and your humble scribe can only guess but it'll be fun finding out and if I ever use the word 'journey' to describe it...please kill me, there and then.*
>
> *That is all.*

Laurence smiled in anticipation of the barrage of po-faced comments which were bound to follow. 'Oh, lighten up, world,' he said aloud.

***

Tom Brady glanced around at some of the less edifying specimens of humanity sharing the upper deck of the bus. Why did these people look so miserable? Granted, it was an effort to rouse oneself on a cold, damp morning but once you did, surely you just got on with it. He heard a moan, turned and saw a man yawning so expansively that his fellow passengers could hardly avoid the view which extended beyond his yellowing teeth, curled purple tongue and into the deeper recesses of his mouth.

All around were instances of people performing domestic routines in public - a man munched his way through a bowl of cornflakes; a woman produced a compact and lipstick and applied her make-up while a glance around the bus showed four people drinking coffee or tea from a thermos mug which they'd filled at home. Tom thought it comparable to a peculiar narcissism prevalent among young people: they would happily share details of their lives on social networking sites but still complain about the resultant invasions of privacy. He was glad his youth was behind him.

As the bus made hesitant progress through the traffic, Tom returned to reading *The Chronicle* and noticed an article by one of their sports writers, Joe Lawson, entitled *Maybe This Time for Rovers' Redemption Man?* Lawson was a verbose journalist but a respected one who adopted a more restrained tone than many of his peers. Today, his column included a piece about Darren Peters which Tom read with interest.

> *We have, of course, been here before: a footballer insults the intelligence of those who pay his wages as he professes his commitment to a club while simultaneously handing his agent a brief to hawk his availability to other clubs for an increased salary. Or he shows a disingenuous contempt for the fourth estate by indignantly demanding privacy when he errs while courting publicity and adulation at all other times.*
>
> *Darren Peters, Wallington Rovers' extravagantly talented midfielder, has been dragged through the media mill of late with salacious tales of serial womanising. The facile moralising which accompanied these sordid reports is made all the more reprehensible since it comes from publications which gleefully provide this unending sleaze-fest. Peters, an uncomplicated young man, has never held himself up as a paragon of virtue and it is to his credit that he didn't resort to the High Courts for the public image preservation tool de nos jours – the super-injunction. That said, the cynic may retort that there were simply too many such stories for even these gagging orders to suppress.*
>
> *On Saturday, we saw during Rovers' exciting FA Cup win and, later, on the Duncan Moore show the most compelling evidence yet that Peters may be about to enter a more mature phase of his career. His superb second-half goal demonstrated a spatial awareness and football technique which would impress the hardest taskmaster. That this outstanding piece of skill was celebrated in a muted fashion was the first of the day's indicators of the emergence of a more palatable Darren Peters.*
>
> *He followed this on prime time television with a touching nod*

towards the advantages of a stable domestic life. If we can bring ourselves to digest the sordid details of the kiss-and-tell stories about him, it is clear that the reported liaisons took place a couple of years hence. One hopes there are no more shabby tales waiting for the dispiriting collusion of tabloid journalism and opportunistic fleeting inamoratas to drag Peters through the mill again. One further hopes that his public declaration of affection for his girlfriend and daughter sets the tone for what could be the flowering of a real football talent. It's over to you, Darren.

Tom chuckled at the grandiose tone of Lawson's piece but knew it would do no harm to Peters' profile and might add some heft to his participation in the St. Ambrose's visit. He was less pleased to read an article about increased activity among dissident republicans in Northern Ireland. Due to meet Kieran Bradley later that evening, Tom knew that if he emerged from the next two days with spirits intact, it would represent a very encouraging start to the week.

At work, a note on his desk from Jan Netherby said that he'd told Mark Llewellyn about Tom's guest for the visit to St. Ambrose's and Mark would like to see him as soon as he arrived. Rueing his late arrival, he set out for Llewellyn's office, hoping Netherby wasn't in the vicinity.

***

The damp, cold, grey morning casts a sombre tone over the tree-lined street. Even at 9:30, many front windows are illuminated from inside; the wan light permeating from outside is inadequate. Laura Armitage, nose pressed against the window, gazes out into the murk. Normally first to rise, this morning she remained in bed after her husband's early departure. Now dressed and showered, she is determined to cast aside this torpor but still she loiters, thinking about John. He'd changed...the less desirable elements of both the ascetic and the brash John had, seemingly, vanished, replaced by self-deprecation and concern for others. Her suggestion that he write a book about Fraser Guthrie was sincere but she had an ulterior motive for offering to help – a desire to see more of John. That idea planted in her mind, she called him.

'John! Laura here. What's with the music? You're at work, aren't you?'

'Laura! Music to *my* ears. How are you?'

'Have you been drinking? You're animated for a Monday morning.'

'Well, we're having a celebratory snifter. I've severed links with the big bad world of business. Correction, I'm just about to.'

'Well done, you. Crikey, that was quick. I was just calling to say thanks for Saturday night. I had a really good time.'

'Me too. I was going to call you but I got sidetracked by work.'

'Meaning you didn't want to sound too pushy?'

'Yes, something along those lines. No point in my being evasive with you, is there? Nothing escapes you.'

'I wouldn't say that was true of everything,' Laura replied wistfully. 'Let's meet again soon..if you're free, that is.'

'I'd love to. I'll have a lot of spare time now. Actually, I'd like to pick your brains on something. I'm due a windfall and I did some research on where to plant it. When I worked at Foden Barnes, I dealt in esoteric derivative products with one firm in particular whose parent company, Johnston Dudley, are part of an investment portfolio at Alpha Venture managed by Geoff Harris. I dug deeper; Geoff's fund also includes the parent company of another player in that particular market. I considered ploughing my money into Geoff's portfolio but now, I think I'll put it all into Johnston Dudley. You said you're in touch with someone from AV....is that Geoff by any chance? To cut to the chase, Laura, I just wondered whether you had any advice on this.'

'I can't offer reliable advice but if you want me to call Geoff and sound him out, I can do that. I'd imagine Johnston Dudley are OK but I'm removed from all that now. I'm visiting AV tomorrow or Wednesday so I'll make a point of seeing Geoff. Shall we meet on Wednesday afternoon? The Guthrie piece will be published by then. Maybe it'll merit a celebration.'

'That sounds perfect, Laura. Somewhere other than Franco's?'

'Yes, time we broke new ground. I'll call you tomorrow and suggest a time and place, OK?'

'Look forward to it. Bye.'

Laura closed her mobile phone. John was interested too, that was clear. There was something symbolic in his departure from business and what she assumed would be his return to a higher calling. She felt giddy at being partly responsible for this and allowed her imagination to roam over where this might lead...but things never happened that quickly.

***

'God, how quickly things can happen,' Elizabeth Harris said aloud as she padded around the kitchen writing a list of ingredients required for the evening meal. A week ago, she hardly knew Philip Anderson and now she was preparing dinner for him and planning how to tell him that their fling was over. Bizarre! She didn't know Philip's taste in food so she called him.

'Philip, this is Elizabeth. Hope your weekend was good...Yes, sorry about that. I didn't have a signal for much of yesterday. I wanted to check that you're OK for this evening and to let you know there's nothing to be alarmed about...No, no, it's all Geoff's idea, there's something he wants to sound you out about...No, nothing like that...Umm, maybe later in the week...Is pasta all right this evening?...Good, I'll, sorry, we'll see you about 7:30 then...Er, I seem to have left my scarf at your house...Yes, if you could please. See you later then...Me too...Ok, bye.'

Elizabeth exhaled and sat down...this really could get messy. For all that Philip seemed like a man of the world who accepted things don't always pan out as planned, something in his tone alerted her to possible dangers. She needed to exercise subtlety in ending their affair. Oh for God's sake, it wasn't an affair. Two unpremeditated romps between consenting adults, nothing more than that...but the more she dwelled on it, the more it seemed that there was more to it than that. She picked up her coat and bag, walked to the door and left the house.

***

Amid the bustle of the open-plan office, Philip Anderson cut an incongruous figure. Around him, people tapped at keyboards, made phone calls, leafed through reams of paper and books but Philip, pensive, stared into the distance. His desk, the only traditional wooden one amid a sea of grey work-stations, was intended to confer status upon him as the senior sub-editor. Instead, it served as a magnet for harassed journalists who viewed the well-worn commodious expanse of oak as a worthy recipient of their work. Due to the respect which Philip commanded and his inability to delegate tasks, his in-tray was habitually deluged by sheets of paper festooned with yellow post-it notes containing the word URGENT in large capitals.

Today, the pile of incomplete work was as high as ever but Philip appeared serenely oblivious to it. He'd received a puzzling call from Elizabeth who sounded distant and preoccupied. There was no explanation about the dinner invitation, just a vague assurance that it was Geoff's idea as he wanted to discuss something unspecified *and* she'd been ambivalent to Philip's proposal to meet during the week. She really was a mysterious woman. His reverie was interrupted by the arrival of Quentin Shields, *The Chronicle*'s literary editor.

'Penny for them, Philip. I hope I'm not interrupting any great thought process, you look like you're far removed from here.'

'Oh, hello Quentin. Yes, sorry, miles away. Everything OK with you?'

'Yes, fine. I just wonder whether you could cast an eye over for this for me – it's a whimsical piece for the literary page on Friday. It's probably OK but, you know, another pair of eyes and all that. No real rush but today would be good, gives me time if a rewrite is needed.'

'Surely we can rely on the literary editor to get his copy right?'

'I'm probably one of the worst offenders. Appreciate this, thanks.'

132

'I saw you on TV on Saturday night, Quentin. I liked your introductory bit. Tell me, did you get a chance to speak with Susan Pierce?'

'You're not the first person to ask me that...seems like she made quite an impression. I was part of the general chit-chat afterwards but she was absent for much of it.' Quentin smiled, winked and lowered his voice conspiratorially. 'She's a feisty young lady. Doesn't stand on ceremony if she wants something. Anyway, mustn't keep you from your work.'

Philip frowned. What was Quentin hinting at? It was turning into a puzzling day.

***

The small pile of newspapers on the coffee table increased as Darren Peters, smiling, tossed another one on it. His TV appearance, on top of his display for Wallington, had been well received by the press. Darren's daily reading rarely extended beyond mass-market tabloids but today, he'd bought all the nationals to read anything pertaining to him. This included match reports of the game, front page headlines and articles in the more reputable newspapers where the words, "redemption", "maturity" and "laudable" figured prominently. The most unlikely piece was an *In praise of...Darren Peters* on *The Guardian*'s editorial page. Darren sensed this was partly provocative, intended to highlight the vilification he'd received in other newspapers but it still added to his improved public profile.

He had a free morning as players involved in games during the previous week were exempted from Monday morning training although they were expected to attend a less onerous afternoon session. Kelly and Krystal were spending the day with Kelly's sister, Lynette. Darren's foibles, no doubt, would be part of their discussion although any newspapers to hand at Lynette's house would cast him in a favourable light. He noticed his name on the front page of *The Chronicle*, a reference to Joe Lawson's article. A scheduled interview with Lawson a year previously had been a frustrating experience for both as Lawson refused to indulge Darren's attempts to add levity to the conversation. Peters' jocular quips were deemed unworthy of interest by Lawson who aborted the exercise.

The interview cast aside, they chatted off-the-record about the fleeting nature of sporting fame and Darren was touched by Lawson's concern and his repeated assertions that he should appreciate the position in which he found himself.

With this in mind, he read Lawson's article and a wave of indignation washed over him. Why were all these hacks so eager to pass moral judgement? Journalists, of all people - renowned for their double standards - now rushing to pontificate on people like Darren for doing something which, given a similar opportunity, they themselves would do. Would Joe

Lawson turn down somebody like Susan Pierce in circumstances similar to Saturday night? Of course he wouldn't.

Darren's anger abated as he re-read Lawson's article. Behind the self-righteous tone, he noted the concern and remembered their conversation a year ago. Darren's interpretation of the temporal element of his career was to make the most of any opportunity football accorded him. In ten years time, he would be an ex-footballer and girls like Susan Pierce wouldn't be so keen to do what she did on Saturday night or to hold out the prospect of more to come. He had responsibilities to Kelly and Krystal but Kelly was no wide-eyed *ingénue*. She knew of Darren's foibles and had, no doubt, factored them into the equation when she threw in her lot with him.

Krystal, however, was innocent of all this and Darren suffered a pang of guilt at mentioning her on television followed soon after by a direct betrayal of the sentiment expressed. But how was he to know that Susan would prove so willing? Cognisant that his line of thinking ignored the crux of the argument, he decided not to dwell on the matter any longer. Curiosity about Susan led him to his games room – a room with a well-stocked bar, snooker table, retro amusement arcade machines and a seated area with an enormous plasma television screen. Here, he searched on his computer for recent internet mentions of Susan Pierce and found a link to Laurence Tolliver's website. He recognised the name as that of the music writer he'd met on Saturday and was surprised to read that Tolliver was now Susan's manager.

Darren remembered the phone call from Sunday when she said somebody was with her, something work-related. Presumably, that was Tolliver sniffing around. Susan and Tolliver? Surely not? They'd only met for the first time on Saturday night; was she *that* career-minded? Mind you, Tolliver was well-connected in the music business and Susan was certainly ambitious. Tolliver was the next name in the Google search engine and Darren read testimonies to his journalism, his promotion of emerging talent...and his reputation as a Don Juan of the music press. How genuine was Tolliver's interest in Susan's career? More importantly, what lay in store for Darren himself with the spirited singer?

Too much reflection on these imponderables made his head ache: he was, as Joe Lawson wrote, an uncomplicated young man. He switched off the computer, closed his eyes and had a snooze.

***

As Mark Llewellyn invited Geoff Harris to take a seat, Tom Brady arrived and was also invited in.

'Gentlemen,' Llewellyn addressed them. 'I hope you had good weekends. Tell me your news.'

'You go first, Tom. Mine can wait,' Geoff said.

'OK, thanks. I've had a bit of luck with my trip to St. Ambrose's. Darren Peters, the footballer, is an ex-pupil and he's happy to accompany me. Peters is a bit of a firebrand so there's potential for it go awry but his agent's a wily old boy who stressed the upside from good publicity to Darren. We should get some of the shared glory as well.'

'You've handled this astutely by ensuring the local paper will just happen to be there, Tom,' Llewellyn interjected. 'It'll seem as if both Peters and AV acted selflessly, not courting publicity.'

'Neat work, Tom,' Geoff smiled. 'I didn't envy you your trip to St. Asbo's but it should work out well. The papers were falling over themselves to compliment Peters today.'

'Quite. And your news, Geoff?' Llewellyn asked as Tom stood up.

'Tom, can you hang on?' Geoff asked. 'It's something which you'll need to know about and you may have your own take on it.'

Tom sat down again as Geoff hesitantly relayed the information he'd received about Johnston Dudley and Procter Jones Henderson and the potential impact upon AV's holdings in both companies should disclosure happen before they could off-load their shares.

'The thing is, this information will come to light soon and we have to be ahead of the game. I'm meeting a guy tonight who works for *The Chronicle* and I see this as a good way of getting the news out so that we're ready to act. I've identified suitable replacements for our investment portfolios. OK to proceed, Mark?'

Llewellyn gazed into the distance. 'I think Jan Netherby should join this conversation. I'll call him.'

'Why?' Geoff asked. 'What can he add to the discussion?'

'He's senior to you within the organisation and I think our position needs careful consideration.'

Tom and Geoff exchanged puzzled looks as Netherby was summoned and arrived almost immediately, looking pleased with the uncomfortable silence. Geoff retold his story and all three turned to Llewellyn who remained silent as Geoff shifted in his chair.

'Surely, the best thing is for Geoff to prime this guy at *The Chronicle* and we pounce as soon as the news breaks,' Tom said. 'He'll let you know when that will be, Geoff?'

'That'll be a condition of giving him the gen in the first place. Mark?'

'My recommendation is to disclose this knowledge to the regulators, Geoff. I can't be seen to endorse the course of action you propose.'

'What?' Geoff said, aghast. 'We'll lose a packet on this and our investors will be screwed royally.'

'I can't instruct our traders to ditch our holdings,' Llewellyn replied, hands held out in a what-can-I-say gesture. 'That's tantamount to insider dealing. As chief executive of AV, any involvement on my part could be ruinous for the company.'

Again, silence descended on the room. Geoff leaned back, concern etched on his face. He knew Llewellyn would now be intractable, unwilling to compromise himself in front of the others. Geoff was about to leave the room when help came from an unexpected source.

'I could have a discreet word with Paul Hamilton on the trading floor,' Netherby said. 'He could be ready to act if, or when, the news breaks. I can do so even if the newspaper guy doesn't play ball.'

Geoff now realised why Llewellyn had stalled. Llewellyn guessed that Netherby would offer to liaise with AV's dealers, exonerating himself. Geoff was shocked by Llewellyn's cold calculation and Netherby's willingness to ingratiate himself with his boss. He also, guiltily, felt a surge of relief.

'I suppose we must consider all the angles, Jan. It would do no harm if you had a chat with Paul.' Llewellyn sighed with apparent reluctance. 'I think we're done here, gentlemen. I have another meeting in a few minutes. Thanks for your time.'

Tom, Jan and Geoff left the office. Outside, Tom shook his head and smiled ruefully at Geoff as the three walked back towards their respective offices. Geoff asked them to join him in his office.

'You didn't have to do that, Jan,' Geoff said. 'Can't you see that Mark's avoiding direct involvement? You're the sacrificial lamb if it goes wrong.'

'It's what a deputy does,' Jan shrugged. 'Don't think I'm naïve enough not to realise what Mark wanted one of us to do. I reckoned I'm the most senior here so it should be me.'

'It's decent of you to do so, Jan,' Tom said. 'But are you sure?'

'Yes, absolutely,' Jan said breezily. 'I'm sure this will soon blow over and we'll move on. Let me know how it goes with the journalist guy, Geoff.'

He left the office and Geoff rolled his eyes.

'Not sure if he's gone up in my estimation or dropped even further.'

'Know what you mean. We now know what a ruthless bastard Llewellyn is. He knew exactly what he was doing by calling in Jan.'

'Well, let's not get too virtuous about it, Tom. I intend using the guy from *The Chronicle* and I'm not doing it for society's benefit, am I? I guess that's how Llewellyn got where he is today.'

'Still, though. He can't expect us to swallow the "I don't approve of this" act. I feel sullied by it all.'

'And your St. Asbo's trip is for philanthropic reasons? Come on, Tom. Let's not damn others when we're both acting out of self-interest as well.'

'Let him without sin and all that, eh?'

'Indeed. Oh and well done for getting Darren Peters onside, pardon the pun. I assume Llewellyn was exacting some revenge by sending you there. Well, you've turned that one around neatly.'

'No idea what you're referring to, Geoff,' Tom said with a grin.

***

Tom left the train at Piccadilly Circus station. Weary after his day's work, the prospect of an evening with Kieran Bradley did little to lighten his spirits as he made the short walk from Piccadilly to MacQuilters. As he found on previous visits there, locating somebody in the cavernous pub involved much walking up and down stairs. Eventually, he spotted Kieran sitting uneasily on a banquette nursing a half-finished pint of Guinness.

He was struck by the change in his cousin's appearance since they'd last met. The young, athletic Kieran became a portly figure in his thirties but now there was a new version: a gaunt, haunted-looking man with a nervous, distracted air. Tom thought it suited him even less than the ruddiness of recent vintage.

'Kieran! It's good to see you again.'

Kieran stood up and shook hands with Tom, relief evident in his face.

'Tom! Thanks for meeting me. You're looking well.'

'I'm not too bad. How about you, Kieran? You look tired, must be all that travelling, I suppose.'

'I've had a rough time of late. Here, sit yourself down 'til I get you a drink. Still on the Guinness?'

'Yes. I'll get the drinks. Same again?'

When Tom returned, Kieran was frowning at his mobile phone.

'Can't get a bloody signal here,' he grumbled.

Tom checked his mobile and nodded; his was also incapacitated. They clinked their glasses together and Tom took a long draught from his pint.

'Ahhh, I needed that. A hard day today. So, how are things? Fiona and the kids OK?'

Kieran sighed and ran his hands through his thinning hair. Tom, to his shame, felt relieved - this would be about marital problems rather than anything more sinister. He noticed the tremor in Kieran's hand as he reached for his drink and, discomfited by the silence, rested his hand on Kieran's arm and looked directly at him.

'Is everything OK, Kieran? You don't seem like your normal self.'

'Jaysus, I haven't been my normal self in ages. No, Tom, everything isn't OK. In fact, it's all a bit fucked-up at the minute. In fact, you could say I'm in hiding.'

'Hiding? Why? What's happened?'

'I got into a bit of bother...and not with people you want to cross, if you know what I mean.'

Kieran sighed again, Tom thought it best to allow him to continue at his own pace. He felt remorse at his initial reaction but had little desire to become embroiled, however tangentially, in whatever trouble his cousin was involved...especially if, after all, it did include paramilitaries.

'Tom, I'm not going to ask any favours so don't worry about that.' Kieran raised his hands at Tom's pained expression. 'This is my problem and I have to deal with it myself. I wanted to meet you for a drink because you're a clever man and you might give me some good advice. If you can't, at least we'll have a few pints and a laugh.'

Tom smiled at Kieran's perceptive reading of the situation.

'You were always a sharp cookie, Kieran. So, what's up?'

The story unfolded – Kieran was involved in the drugs trade which Republican paramilitaries governed in his particular part of the province. Having established himself with a regular cut of the proceeds, he turned greedy, went beyond his remit and was now a pariah. Anxiety at the possibility of retribution had caused him to flee.

'But that can't help, can it? Surely these bastards would think nothing of doing something to Fiona or the kids? It's easy for me to say but wouldn't it be better to come clean, pay your dues and ask to be allowed to put it behind you.'

'Aye, they're a very forgiving bunch,' Kieran laughed bitterly. 'These boys have been through.... well, you know what they've been through. Putting a bullet through my kneecap, or worse, wouldn't give them any sleepless nights. Begging for mercy is not something I'm considering.'

'But you can't keep on the run forever.'

'I thought getting off my own patch was a good idea so I came over here to think without being scared every time I hear the doorbell.'

'What does Fiona make of this?'

'She's most likely relieved I'm away for a bit. Fiona's well connected, they won't touch her. Same goes for wee Aidan and Clare. I'm running, I know but I can think clearer while I'm away. Christ, what a frigging mess.'

'I don't want to sound judgemental but, yes, it is. How did you let this happen? It was never likely to be anything other than a frigging mess.'

'Ach, spare me the sermon, Tom. You know, you can be a right pompous shite at times.'

'I'll ignore that. Here, I'll get another one.' Tom ignored Kieran's protests and walked to the bar. Knowing the ruthlessness of Kieran's new enemies, Tom had to agree with his cousin that appeals to reason were futile. He ordered the drinks and noticed that his phone now had a signal.

He had three missed calls, all from Catherine. He rang her, listened solemnly and returned to his table.

'Kieran, we had a phone call at home from someone with a Northern Irish accent who asked if we'd seen or heard from you. Catherine said you were in Derry as far as she was aware and reckons she sounded convincing. I need hardly tell you that she's scared. I'll finish this drink and return home, I can't leave her like that.'

'Aye, sure. God, I'm sorry to drag you into this, Tom. Those boys will know I'm away and are just putting out feelers with people I know abroad. Let me get a phone signal and make a call. Back in a minute.'

When Kieran returned, he smiled, intending to ease Tom's mind.

'I rang a few people who said they'd been contacted too. It's just a scattergun approach to find me so don't worry. I called Fiona and she's OK. Maybe you're right, I can't keep running from these boys, can I? I'll get in touch and see how the land lies.'

'But where will you stay in the meantime?'

'Oh, I've got contacts here and I may not stay in London much more than a day or so anyway. I'll finish my pint, go for a pee and we'll be off.'

When Kieran departed to the lavatory, Tom picked up Kieran's mobile phone and checked the log. Of the three calls made in the last ten minutes, one was indeed to Fiona, one to Michael – presumably Michael Bradley - and another to somebody called Hughie. Tom jotted down Hughie's number and replaced the phone just as Kieran re-appeared.

'Right, away home with you then,' Kieran said, donning his coat. 'I'll call you when I have any more news. I didn't mean what I said earlier and I'm sorry Catherine has been dragged into this but, honest, there's nothing to worry about. You will tell her that, won't you?'

'I will,' Tom replied as they walked out into the chilly night. Kieran was headed in the opposite direction and Tom patted his shoulder.

'Look after yourself, Kieran. Bye.'

'You too, Tom.'

As Kieran departed towards Green Park tube station, Tom wondered when they'd next meet. He clutched his coat tightly around him and hurried to Piccadilly Circus station, eager to get home.

***

To a casual observer, 28, Russell Road has few discernible differences to the residences on either side. It's a neat, semi-detached Edwardian house with a small, neatly maintained front garden behind a neatly clipped hedge. Closer scrutiny indicates that the owners possess elegance and understated taste – the curtains hang better than those of their neighbours and have a luxurious, velvet sheen; the bay trees, one on either side of the front door, are leafy and healthy; the door itself is painted a lustrous, burnished red and the wood in the sash window-frames is weather beaten but sturdy. To a well-trained eye, even the exterior of this house generates a warm feeling of contentment and permanence.

Inside, nothing contradicts this. A Turner print here, a Velazquez reproduction there and a more daring, original, abstract oil painting by an unheralded artist confirms the occupants as sophisticates. On a sideboard, *The Guardian* nestles alongside the *Financial Times,* their crumpled condition proof that the contents of both have been digested. A Greenpeace calendar in the kitchen tells us we're dealing with environmentally-aware people and the view to the back garden shows well-tended fruit trees, plants and flowers.

It's a house where a contributor to a slightly left-of-centre newspaper should feel comfortable yet Philip Anderson radiates unease. This is his first visit to the house of the woman with whom he is having an affair and as he gazes around the room, he realises how little he knows about her. Was the mirror with a gold-leaf frame shaped like a ship's porthole her choice? He didn't know. Was her taste in decor traditional or modish? He didn't know. Were the stripped floors symptomatic of that taste? He didn't know. Was she the owner of the many P.D. James novels on the book shelves? He didn't know. His unease is accentuated as he is being attended to by Geoff, her husband and the man who has some undefined favour to ask of Philip. Right now, he was asking him which drink he'd prefer.

'I don't mind. I guess from Friday that you're a red wine buff so that's fine with me. Nice house, Geoff. Mine feels shabby by comparison. That'll be down to a woman's touch, I suppose.'

Philip swallowed, embarrassed by his condescending reference to Elizabeth. But why wasn't she here to add balm to the conversation? He guessed that she was playing the role of wife and hostess but it was unsettling as he waited for Geoff to unveil the real reason for the dinner.

'Here, this is one of my favourites.' Geoff handed a glass to Philip.

'Cheers, this is good,' Philip said, sipping the Margaux. He stared at a framed picture of a street in a French or Swiss town with a snow-capped mountain in the background. Geoff smiled.

'It's where we first met. On a skiing holiday eight years ago.... eight years last Wednesday, actually.'

Philip swallowed again and turned to re-examine the photograph.

'Eight years? Last Wednesday? Gosh,' he mumbled.

Elizabeth walked in and assumed an aggrieved expression when she saw the glasses of wine.

'Typical....leave me to do the work while you two enjoy yourselves.

Thanks,' she said with a smile as Geoff poured a glass of wine for her. 'Here's to good neighbours.'

'I was just telling Philip that it was eight years ago last Wednesday when we first met.'

Elizabeth blushed, took a sip of her wine and smiled demurely.

'Oh, let's not bore Philip with our history, Geoff.'

She had steeled herself for the evening with a couple of gin and tonics while cooking. Now, she sensed the return of that light-headed feeling and for a giddy second or two felt like blurting out, 'Yes and Wednesday was also the first time I slept with Philip.' If she was fated to continue hearing unwitting references from Geoff about Philip and her, she would surely one day confess, if only to end this form of psychological torture.

'The funny thing is that neither of us was aware of the date. I only remembered it the next day and Elizabeth stayed out with her friend, Rachel, that night,' Geoff said with a sheepish smile.

'Rachel,' Philip said pensively and noticed both Geoff and Elizabeth sending warning glances. God, he thought, this was turning into some sort of West End farce. He felt like blurting out, 'No, she didn't, Geoff, she was with me.' Polite conversation followed for a few minutes before Philip was ushered through to the dining room for dinner. After more amiable chat, Geoff's exaggerated casual tone alerted Philip that the main business was about to be unveiled.

'Philip, I need some advice,' Geoff said. 'Not really advice, more a proposition which could benefit us both. I've been alerted to some sharp practice between two companies, something the financial regulators should know about. I'd like to share this information with your newspaper, make it public. Of course, I'm not doing this just for society's benefit. Disclosure will benefit my firm obliquely. Are you interested in hearing more?'

Philip tilted his head and looked into the distance.

'I'm not actually a journalist but I'm near as damn it to being one and I'm sure *The Chronicle* would be interested. We'd need conclusive proof and I'd also like to know how it benefits you or your company.'

It was Elizabeth who replied.

'The documents you returned to Geoff on Friday night sparked this, Philip. Geoff read through them and realised there had been a breach of rules, further realised that it affected his company and that the financial world should be made aware. I know it's all a bit self-serving but...'

Philip smiled and held his hands up. 'Makes sense to me, thanks for offering the scoop to us. If you tell me some more, I can probably get the go-ahead tonight from a guy on our business pages.'

Geoff gave a summary of the situation to an increasingly bemused

Philip who then agreed to call *The Chronicle*'s chief business correspondent, Brian Curtis.

'Brian...I've got something which may interest you. A friend has told me about price-fixing between two major institutions....Yes, I know it's rife but...Oh, I see. Anyway, are you interested in hearing more?...Really? Probably not as good as this one though...If I said the names Procter Jone...Yes and they're the other one. That doesn't sound like a guess to me...Oh and do you intend using it? My contact has some pretty conclusive proof...I can ask him. Hold on.'

Philip turned to Geoff and asked whether he could provide documented proof early next morning. Geoff nodded.

'Roger on that one, Brian...Yes, he's reliable...That too, he's hardly doing it solely for society's benefit...Very funny. So, are others chomping at the bit too?...C'mon, don't go all mysterious on me...Ok, fair point. I'll contact you first thing. Cheers.'

'It sounds like a flier, Geoff but you'll have to act fast. It seems you're not the only person with knowledge of this.'

'Why? Who else knows about it?'

'I'm not likely to say, am I?' Philip laughed. 'You know what, there's another story here...one about banks with knowledge of dodgy dealings, said banks contact newspapers so that the story will break, all the while protecting their own interests. In fact, that would make a better story than the collusion one. Hmmm, I wonder.'

'You journalists, you'd do anything for a story,' Geoff said, laughing nervously. 'I'm glad I work in a profession where ethics still exist.'

Elizabeth smiled hesitantly at her husband's jocular comment. This wasn't turning out as she'd hoped and she now envisaged an awkward conversation with Philip. Should she say something this evening so that he didn't think she'd used their relationship to help Geoff? If the story broke to Geoff's benefit and she then ended their affair, she would feel cheap and manipulative. But if she told him now, and even that was assuming she got the opportunity to do so, Philip might take it badly and refuse to help Geoff. This was turning into a real dilemma.

***

After a miserable day of introspection, regret and guilt, Laura couldn't face being at home when Robert returned. Her sullen mood would trigger an equally surly response from her husband; it was better to disappear for a few hours and by the time she returned, maybe she'd feel more upbeat...maybe. Faced with time to fill, the obvious place for a film and music journalist to go was either a cinema or a concert but Laura's lethargy and discontent left her ill-disposed to either.

Exasperated by this irresolution, she paced the house trying to think of a satisfactory way to spend the evening. Her gaze fell on the final proof of the Fraser Guthrie article and she recalled a vague promise to Laurence Tolliver to buy him a drink should the story get published. Yes, that was it, ring Tolliver and see whether he was free. He was amusing company and she could mention John Hooper so that his name would register should John wish to speak to Tolliver. With a start, she realised that helping out John had been paramount in her thoughts. Well, so be it.

When she rang Robert and told him she might be out for the evening, the wounded silence from his side settled the issue for her. She called Tolliver and he - ever happy to spend time in the company of a like-minded soul, especially one with Laura's looks - arranged to meet her at a bar in South Kensington. Laura walked for 20 minutes before the evening chill forced her on to a bus. Tolliver's chivalrous concern when she arrived cheered her. He was happy to help should John need any introductions and he then regaled her with news of his tentative entry into the world of music management and his dealings with the Interstellar label.

'Why do you want to do this, Laurence? It's not really your field. What's good about your music writing is the outsider's perspective, you never sound like you're extolling the talents of someone you have a vested interest in. Won't you feel compromised when it comes to Susan Pierce?'

'I don't intend writing about her, just nudging her in the right direction and helping her to avoid pitfalls.'

'But why her? I thought you'd prefer some of the edgier Interstellar acts? Maybe somebody like Double Dip or Johnny Furriskey.'

'That's the whole point, nobody expects this. Besides, she has talent.'

'And the sultry image has nothing to do with it? People will recall your remark to her on TV on Saturday night - it was practically a proposition.'

'One spoken in jest. Give me credit, Laura. I'm more subtle than that.'

Laura remembered John's assumption that Tolliver had an ulterior motive for helping her. She, however, was sure that the stories about his assistance to young musicians and journalists were more pertinent than those involving his roving eye. She mentioned her husband and Tolliver listened to her effusive account of his work in the arts world.

'Methinks the lady doth protest too much,' he said.

'What do you mean?'

'Well, all the Robert-this and Robert-that sounds like it's masking something. Are things OK?'

'No, they're not,' she sighed. 'My life is currently some place south of perfect, a distance south of perfect, actually. It's still north of despair but...you know.'

'I hope you're not expecting a panacea from me,' he replied. 'I'm a disaster zone when it comes to relationships although I noticed that your mood brightened when you mentioned this John Hooper guy. Anything you'd like to add?'

Laura spoke about John, their time together, how their lives changed as a consequence and their recent meeting. Tolliver smiled knowingly.

'What? What does that smile mean?' she asked.

'I think you've pretty much declared where your interests lie.' Laura blushed as he patted her arm and smiled. 'I'm guessing you wanted to get away from home for the evening and if you want to continue talking about that, fine. If you want to leave it at that, that's OK as well.'

An hour later, they left the pub and at the tube station boarded trains headed in opposite directions. Laura felt better; the cheery conversation and anecdotes had diverted her from the turmoil in her mind. Now, if only she could introduce some of that levity to her domestic life.

Sitting in the next carriage for part of the journey was Tom Brady, glad to be heading home after an unsettling and truncated evening with Kieran Bradley. Unlike Laura, all he wanted to do was re-immerse himself in his domestic life.

***

Across London, John Hooper returned home. Happy with the day's events, he took a bottle of brandy from the drinks cabinet, poured himself a small measure, raised the glass to a photograph of his parents on the mantelpiece and polished off the contents. His deal with Doug Greenlees successfully concluded, John had instructed a broker to invest the proceeds in Johnston Dudley, an investment he felt sure would see his new-found wealth increase. He reclined contentedly on the sofa and dozed.

***

7 - TUESDAY

It was a scene of domestic contentment which would melt the heart of any onlooker. Below the huge retro-style clock which showed 7:30, a young man wearing a food-smeared t-shirt and tracksuit trousers was smiling at the toddler responsible for the mess. The toddler gurgled happily, the young man laughed and the toddler gurgled even louder. Unnoticed by either, a young woman stood a little way off leaning against a door, arms folded, observing the scene with approval. Clearly, she is the toddler's mother - they share distinct facial similarities – and is reluctant to impose herself on the happy tableau in front of her; she could derive no more pleasure were she a participant rather than an observer.

Darren Peters had assumed the role of feeding the baby to allow Kelly some extra time in bed but hearing the sounds of laughter, Kelly descended the stairs to watch. This was how she'd hoped life with Darren would evolve, the party and restaurant invites once a vital component of their lives were now of secondary importance. Darren, she knew, was guilty of infidelity and lapses in behaviour but it seemed that he'd turned a corner. Maturity came to men at different stages and Kelly often heard of the impact fatherhood could have on even the most errant philanderer. The scene which she serenely gazed upon bore testimony to this and she padded back upstairs, her eyes moist with tears of happiness.

Oblivious to their role as entertainers, Darren and Krystal continued the messy process of having breakfast with Darren peeling a banana for himself before Krystal made a lunge for the fruit. They grappled happily over it as banana mush was added to the food already smeared on his t-shirt. He glanced up at the clock and realised he would have to soon leave for that wretched visit to St. Ambrose's. Despite the inconvenience, he trusted Jack Watson's judgement and it would occupy little more than an hour or so of his morning anyway. As Wallington Rovers had a game the following night, there was a short training session scheduled that morning and Darren would be free soon after 1pm to enjoy whatever Susan Pierce had in mind for the afternoon. To confirm their tryst, he fished his mobile phone out of his tracksuit trouser pocket, glanced around to ensure Kelly hadn't suddenly appeared and sent a text to Susan.

Hiya. Will b free bout 1:30 today. U still OK? My knees r trembling. LOL. Daz

Krystal had finished her breakfast and Darren cradled her in his arms as he trotted upstairs; Kelly could take over now. He stripped himself of the soiled t-shirt and tracksuit, deposited them in a laundry basket outside their bedroom and padded towards the en-suite bathroom for a shower. He gently handed Krystal to Kelly who appraised her naked boyfriend with a smile.

'You handsome devil,' she said. 'Gonna share that buff body with me?'

'Aww, I can't, babe,' Darren groaned. 'I have to go to this bloody school thing and I'd better not be late. Time for that later, eh?'

'OK. I'll make us something special for dinner and don't give me that no sex on the night before a match rubbish. You'll have 24 hours to recover; I'll be gentle with you...maybe.'

'Promises, promises, Kel. And why would I use that excuse anyway? I'm getting a bit excited already. I'd better make this a cold shower.'

Darren disappeared into the bathroom and Kelly reclined on the bed, laughing as she cuddled Krystal. From next door came the 'ping' sound of an incoming text message. She sighed, climbed out of bed and made a mental note to change the tone on her mobile to make it distinguishable from Darren's.

***

'And you've checked with him? Not being funny, Jack, but he's not exactly Mr. Reliable, is he?'

As he walked to work, Tom Brady made a call to Jack Watson to ensure everything was going to plan. Unsettled by his encounter with Kieran Bradley, Tom was jittery and felt compelled to call Darren Peters' agent for reassurance.

'Tom, I spoke to him only 25 minutes ago. He's in top form and looking forward to revisiting the school of which he has such happy memories or to put it another way, he'll be there and let's make it as quick and painless as possible, OK?'

'Sounds good to me, Jack,' Tom laughed. 'I'll meet you in the car park.'

Assured, Tom completed his journey and walked through the revolving door into the lobby of Alpha House. He noticed Geoff Harris stepping into the elevator and quickened his pace across the lobby towards Geoff's receding figure but was accosted by a security guard.

'Good morning, Mr. Brady. Can I see your security pass, please?'

'Good morning, Simon. I take it there's been a memo stressing the need for vigilance?'

'You got it, Mr. Brady. We have to challenge everybody who enters the building and...' Simon nodded towards a security camera, 'any divergence from this er, policy might be captured.'

'Simon, I feel so much safer with you around.'

146

'Good to know that,' Simon replied with a wink. 'I hear you're off to build some bridges between us and the local community today. Valuable work that. Let me know if you need me or one of my colleagues to help out.'

'I think it would send out the wrong message if I turned up at St. Ambrose's with a security guard in tow but thanks anyway. Must go.'

Tom walked up the three flights of stairs, left his briefcase and coat in his office and called in to Geoff's office.

'Would've thought this was too early for you, Tom? What's up?'

'I've got a bit to do before my school visit. So, how did it go last night? Is Deep Throat on board?'

'Well, yes and no. The JD/PJH story seems to be circulating among the financial press. My man at *The Chronicle* is, by the way, the guy you met at the courthouse on Friday. Anyway, that's neither here nor there...'

'Hang on,' Tom interrupted. 'The guy who approached me last Friday is the guy you're using to leak the scam story? Philip something? Let me think this through for a sec, Geoff.'

'There's nothing to think about. It was me who approached Philip Anderson about this story. It's just a coincidence.'

'Hmmm, maybe,' Tom replied. 'I'm dead against coincidence though. When Anderson spoke to me, he condemned our original testimony against Michael Benson. I don't see him as a friend of AV.'

'But we retracted that statement. Philip was impressed, he said so in the pub on Friday.'

'You were drinking with him? I thought you barely knew him?'

Geoff recounted how he'd bumped into Philip and shared a few drinks with him, the incident with the file and how he formulated his plan when he'd read through the file.

'Geoff, I don't like this at all. This guy had the file so what's to stop him reading it? Maybe that's why *The Chronicle* is so clued up already.'

Geoff paused as he re-ran his conversations with Philip. Philip had said that the real story wasn't the collusion between the two firms but their rivals circling like predators, waiting for the first blow to be struck....but that was just an instinctive observation. Geoff racked his memory to dredge up anything from the previous evening which either supported or disproved that theory. He remembered thinking during dinner that Anderson knew something which he didn't but there was no point in augmenting Tom's conspiracy-fuelled imagination with this piece of speculation.

'He only had the file for a few minutes and it would take somebody with insight into derivative products to grasp anything untoward in that length of time. No, he's OK. He asked me for some proof so they can run the story so I sent a text to my source last night and he's going to send the documentation which proves the collusion, I'll pass it to Philip, he'll get Brian Curtis on the case, I'll alert Netherby and our traders will be ready to dump the shares. Job done.'

Geoff smiled disarmingly at Tom who shrugged.

'If you put it like that, Geoff but I won't be happy 'til we're shot of this whole business. I'll prepare a press statement in case it takes a nasty turn. Rumours in circulation...responsibility to our shareholders to sell the shares...purely market forces driving this action...AV condemns the collusion and regrets the taint of malpractice inflicted on the markets...in these times more than ever, transparency in dealings imperative...blah-blah-blah...'

They laughed and the mood lightened.

'I'll get either Hilary or Calvin to help prepare it but the fewer people in the loop, the better. Let me know of any developments, won't you? I'll also prepare something about the St. Asbo's visit in readiness for whatever the local paper writes about it and tweak it accordingly when I return. It'll be a press release which apparently tries to avoid any publicity. Wish me luck while I get down with the kids.'

'Break a leg, Tom. Preferably not Darren's though,' Geoff said.

***

After a tense silence with the only audible sounds those of coffee being sipped, toast being munched and cutlery clattering against crockery, Laura could stand it no longer. She slammed down her coffee mug.

'Look, I'm making you miserable and you're not a bag of laughs right now anyway so I'm going to go away for a few days. It'll give us both some space. OK?'

'But I don't want you to leave, Laura,' Robert replied in a measured tone. 'And surely you want to be around when your article is published tomorrow. If you want me to move out for a few days, I will, but I don't see why either of us should.'

'Oh stop being so bloody reasonable, Robert. If you can't see we've got some serious problems, well, it's time you woke up. I've got bigger concerns in my life right now than receiving plaudits for a piece of music journalism. And frankly, you should have too.'

'I don't know what to say. I want you here. Yes, we may have some communication issues but we can address that. You seem restless, short-tempered about anything I say or do. Tell me what the problem is, Laura.'

'You're doing it again, being reasonable. You're...'

'Well, what do you want me to do? Shout at you? Throw a punch?'

'I'd prefer that than this whole what's-the-problem-Laura crap. Look,

148

I'm fed up, fed up of being monitored and scrutinised. I feel trapped and I want to escape from that. I know it's not your fault you have a possessive streak but I just can't live with it right now. There's stuff which I hate about myself but none of them compare to how much I hate that about you.'

'I see. Well, if it's got to the stage where you hate me, we *have* reached an impasse. I don't hate you, Laura, I love you but a relationship as one-sided as the one you describe is hard to sustain.'

'Oh, for Christ's sake! Let's just leave it there, OK? I didn't say I hate you but I'm edging ever closer to saying something along those lines.'

Laura swept out of the kitchen and slammed the door behind her. Robert heard her tramp up the stairs and within minutes heard the route being reversed. The front door slammed shut. He sat at the table, stupefied, trying to digest the last few minutes and heard the front door open again. He dashed into the hallway, hoping to meet a contrite Laura. Instead, his wife brushed him aside mumbling that she forgot her car keys. Robert trudged back into the kitchen as she retrieved the keys from their hook in the hallway and departed again.

God, what a dismissive attitude! It had been the norm of late but this meltdown was new. Robert tried to rationalise the situation. OK, he was possessive but damnit, she was his wife and he expected some semblance of decorum. Running around with music hacks and ex-boyfriends had clearly turned her head and now *he* was the victim. Logic told him to ignore this, she'd come to her senses and return, full of remorse. Meanwhile, he would suffer anguish and foreboding. Selfish bitch. Fired by martyrdom and anger, he deposited the crockery in the dishwasher and manfully went to get dressed and go to work. Life goes on. But first, he'd send her a text.

So, which one are you running to? Ex-boyfriend or music hack? I expected better from you, Laura

That would give her something to think about, make her realise how silly and petulant she'd been. He didn't actually think she was with either Tolliver or Hooper but wanted her to know she'd sunk that low in his esteem.

***

Twenty yards away, Laura paused for breath and waited for the trembling in her hands to abate - she didn't want to drive the car in this state of heightened agitation. Besides, she had no idea where to go. Home to her parents' house in Suffolk would lead to questions and she might end up defending Robert; her parents had never liked him. Nor was John an option, she owed it to Robert not to do this while they attempted to resolve their differences. Besides, she would see John on Wednesday.

Where did that leave her? Asking Nick Ellis would send all the wrong signals to an unworldly young man whose knowledge of life was derived more from song lyrics, films and books than actual experience. Laurence Tolliver? No: he was at the other end of the spectrum to Nick in terms of worldliness and her request could be misinterpreted as seduction. But she had to get away. She started the car and drove for a few minutes when a click indicated an incoming text on her mobile. She swung the car into a parking space and laughed at the self-pitying tone of Robert's text. Was that the best he could manage? She opted for a curt, dismissive reply.

Way to win back a girl, Robert. Grow up

Immediately, she regretted her reply lest this dissolve into an inelegant slanging match and resolved to ignore any response from him. At least his petty, whiny text removed any vestige of doubt from her mind about her immediate destination – anywhere away from Robert would suffice. She had already made plans to meet a friend from her days at Alpha Venture, Chandra Ghosh, and rang her to confirm. Chandra, once a work colleague, remained a trusted friend and it was rare for more than a few months to pass without their meeting. Theirs was a supportive friendship; both had, at some stage, assumed the role of sounding board or adviser. Laura would first call in to see Geoff Harris. She was pleased by the prospect of helping John - a similar feeling to one she recalled from childhood when she did something she knew would please her parents. Unsure about this line of thinking, she put away her mobile, restarted the car and drove in the direction of the City.

***

Just as John occupied Laura's mind, she was in his thoughts. John knew Laura's endorsement of his decision to abandon his job so abruptly was central to his *volte-face*. It made him feel like a child basking in parental approval, an idea he found silly without being able to dispute its veracity. Ambling around his house, he felt uneasy at the idea of an entire day with no pressing engagements; all his adult life, his work revolved around mental agility and he found it difficult to allow his brain to rest.

Laura's suggestion about writing a book intrigued him but could he apply himself to the task of chronicling Guthrie's life and music? Why not? An avid devotee of American music and culture, he could contextualise Guthrie's place within this world. Snatches of ideas on how to do this flitted through his mind and he jotted them down. He wanted to read Laura's article about Guthrie and walked to the local newsagent hoping it might be on sale but was told *Rosebud* wouldn't appear until the next day. Although impatient to read it, he would wait rather than ask Laura to e-mail it to him. Tomorrow was an important day for her and he was glad that he might be a part of it. Knowing Laura, she would probably deflect the praise

150

towards Nick Ellis, yet another endearing trait of hers. Laura, Laura, Laura...never out of his mind these days.

He returned to what might become his Guthrie project and jotted down ideas, ideas which he could later expand upon. An hour and pages of gnomic notes later, he set aside his pen. Reading Laura's article would be his starting point; some of her observations or revelations might render his musings superfluous or maybe he could embellish them. He'd find out tomorrow. Meanwhile, a triple-bill of Eisenstein films was showing at the National Film Theatre - the perfect way to while away an afternoon.

***

Finger poised over the 8 button on the phone, Elizabeth paused before pressing the last digit of Rachel's number. She remembered a strange incident from the previous night. During Philip's visit, Rachel's name was mentioned and as Elizabeth flashed a warning glance in Philip's direction, she was sure she saw Geoff doing something similar. Had Rachel been a subject of discussion between Geoff and Philip on Friday? If so, why? Elizabeth had a good reason to warn Philip not to acknowledge Rachel's name but why would Geoff have any similar concerns? She cut the call to Rachel at the sound of a ringing tone and rang Philip instead.

'Hi, it's me. How are you?'

'Hi Elizabeth. I'm fine. Thanks for dinner last night. It was, er, an interesting evening. So many times I had to bite my tongue and I guess that applied to you as well.'

'Yes, it was strange. I hope you weren't too fazed by everything. I just wanted to say thanks for er, not giving anything away. Last night was something I never envisaged.'

'No, I guess not. So, do you want to meet again, preferably without hubby in tow this time?'

'Er, sure. Let's just give it a few days though. I've had a pretty bizarre last week and I...'

'It's OK, Elizabeth. It's been odd for me too. Odd...but exhilarating.'

'Yes. Philip, can I ask you a question? Last night when Geoff mentioned my friend Rachel, I wanted to warn you not to acknowledge her name. I know that was hardly necessary but I noticed that Geoff seemed to do something similar. Was there any particular reason?'

'No. I saw your warning but I didn't notice anything from Geoff. I can't er, think of any reason why he would. I don't know Rachel – well you know that – and I've only heard about her from you.'

'Must've been my imagination then. I have to go, Philip. I'll call, OK?'

'Yeah, sure. Oh, I got an e-mail from Geoff about that scam thing. I think it'll work out as you planned.'

151

'Good. Er, what do you mean by "as *you* planned"? It was Geoff's idea; I knew nothing about it until Sunday.'

'I know. I wasn't implying anything.'

'OK, I'll be in touch. Bye, Philip.'

Elizabeth wondered who had been less convincing – Philip, when he said that he didn't notice Geoff's warning glance nor was there a reason for it or her vague comments about meeting up again. Her brief dalliance with Philip had indeed been exhilarating; the frisson of danger heightened her senses and for somebody who had been monogamous ever since she met Geoff, the sex had been interesting...but she had to end the relationship. She'd re-evaluated Geoff and their marriage and he emerged favourably. Those mutinous thoughts about their future had been hedonistic post-coital reverie. She was now a wiser person, wiser and grateful for what she already had. She picked up the phone and rang Rachel's number. The familiar slightly stilted voice answered hesitantly.

'Rach, Elizabeth here.'

'Oh Elizabeth, did you call a few minutes back by any chance?'

'Yes, I er, had to answer my mobile so I cut the call. Why?'

'No why, just wondered. I've had calls recently when somebody didn't speak at the other end.'

'Rachel, if you're ever stalked, I'm sure he'll be articulate and not the sort who remains mute.'

'Er, thanks for that, not sure if it was a compliment but I'll take it as one. How's life? Is, er, your mysterious man still on the scene?'

'Yes and no. It's complicated...'

'These things always are, Elizabeth...or so I'm told.'

Their conversation continued, Elizabeth referred to Geoff a few times but Rachel maintained her usual studied indifference upon hearing his name. Elizabeth was none the wiser about whatever she'd picked up on between Geoff and Philip; maybe she had imagined it after all.

***

'Christ, it's freezing. How much longer will he be?' Tom Brady asked.

Jack Watson shrugged and clapped his hands together as the two men shivered in the February morning chill of St. Ambrose's car park.

'He should be here any minute,' Jack said, glancing at his watch. 'Hello, this must be the bloke from the local rag.'

A man holding a camera bag emerged from a dilapidated VW Golf, opened a notebook, approached them and proffered his outstretched hand.

'Tony Jeffries, *East London Recorder*. I'm guessing you're...,' a glance at the notebook, '...Tom and you're the, er, mystery guest?'

'Yes, I'm Tom Brady from Alpha Venture,' Tom said, shaking Jeffries'

152

hand. 'This is Jack Watson and he won't mind me saying that *he* isn't the main attraction, not that I am either.'

'Nice to meet you,' Jack said. 'Thanks for coming, I think you'll find it worth the effort.'

'So, you're Jack Watson? The football agent?' Jeffries smiled as Jack nodded. 'That clears up Mystery Man's identity. Is it really Darren Peters?'

'Darren Peters? Here?' Jack said, feigning surprise. 'Now that would be something.',

'If he ever turns up,' Tom sighed. 'Don't you think you should give him another call, Jack? We're due to start in less than half-an-hour and we need to see the form teacher first.'

'He'll be here,' Jack said authoritatively. 'Any minute now.'

Silence fell. St. Ambrose's was a typical inner city school with yellow signs pointing towards various buildings, walls freshly painted and devoid of any graffiti - the latter a point of pride to the school administrators. One classroom was visible where an unruly atmosphere prevailed as small groups of boys chatted, oblivious to a lone figure standing in front of a blackboard. Tom hoped that this wasn't the Year 10 class. The hush was broken by the sound of Jack's mobile phone.

***

Whistling, Darren stepped out of the shower and sensed a perceptible change in the climate. Krystal's happy gurgling and Kelly's cheery chatter had given way to a sullen silence; it was as if the February morning chill had permeated the walls of the house. Darren steeled himself for reproach but speculation on the cause was pointless. Maybe Krystal had regurgitated her breakfast over the bed or Kelly had received a text cancelling a scheduled jaunt with her friends; whatever the cause, it was unlikely to be his fault although he would still bear the brunt of her annoyance.

'Darren, come here.'

Kelly's measured tone confirmed his hunch; she had a disconcerting tendency to sound controlled when angriest and, more than once, Darren had been lulled into treating a grievance lightly due to the timbre of her voice. A warning of imminent disaster came when he saw Kelly sitting on the side of the bed, his iPhone on the bedside table, Krystal presumably in her cot next door.

'Darren, what are you doing this afternoon?' she asked...again that steady, ominous voice.

Fuck, she's seen something from Susan. Why didn't I put my phone away? This *was* serious.

'Training, you know that. Why?' he asked, affecting nonchalance.

'How about after training?' Kelly nodded towards the bedside table.

153

'Someone who refers to herself - I assume it's a her - as SP is looking forward to more than just a knee-trembler. Apparently, they'll do on Saturday nights but you'll have more time today.'

Darren gulped. Striving for a plausible tone of bewilderment and indignation, he ducked as his iPhone whizzed past his left ear and landed with a clatter on the tiled bathroom floor. He wasn't so fortunate when this was followed by the only other item to hand for Kelly – a small toy, Tufty the Squirrel, Krystal's favourite. Darren's immediate reaction was surprise that a toy squirrel could hurt so much until he realised it was Tufty's hard button nose which hit him on his right eyelid.

'Owww. Jesus, Kelly, whatcha doing? I can't see. What's wrong?'

Kelly pointed towards the bathroom.

'You'd better check your texts to find out. You've got ten minutes to get out of my sight and fuck off back to whichever tart it is this time.' She paused and clamped a hand over her mouth. 'Oh my God, it's Susan Pierce, innit? Saturday night, SP, it makes sense now and there's you saying that stuff about me and Krystal on telly and all. You're a worthless piece of shit, Darren. Half-an-hour ago, I was watching you with Krys and thinking we was going to be all right, the three of us. I should've known better. You're disgusting. You can say goodbye to your daughter but if you ain't gone in ten minutes, I'll get my brother and his mates over for a word.'

Darren sat on the bedroom floor dabbing his eye to check for blood; it was already starting to swell. He had that bloody school visit this morning and a match tomorrow night. How could he cover this up? Of more immediate importance, what could he say to Kelly? He crawled into the bathroom, picked up the phone and checked his messages. There it was...

LOL! Knee tremblers OK for Sat'day nites but we got all afternoon today. C U at 1. SP

How had he been so stupid? Leaving his phone switched on in the room next door! Susan should've known better too...although, to be fair, she had only replied to his text. Darren contemplated whether annoyance at Kelly's invasion of his privacy held any merit as a counter-attack. No, definitely not. Not since she'd mentioned her brother - Sam Spencer and his thuggish mates would take great pleasure in roughing up Darren or hinting menacingly that he should avoid Kelly to avert a roughing-up.

He considered claiming that he'd merely kissed Susan goodnight after the TV programme and calling it a knee-trembler was her way of joking about it. He might get away with that but the reference to this afternoon was damning evidence which couldn't be glossed over. No: he'd screwed up big time here, Kelly was off-limits right now. Maybe he could talk to her tomorrow or the next day though that looked a forlorn hope as well.

His mind raced ahead. He had to scrap the St. Asbo's thing, get his eye checked by the club doctor and sort out a place to stay for the night. But where? A hotel room might lead to a busybody porter telling his mates, the story would get around and reach the media. Susan Pierce? He was due there this afternoon after all and it was the least she could do after landing him in this mess although she might not wish to get involved. First things first, he had to collect some clothes and leave before Kelly acted on her warning. Then he had to concentrate on tomorrow's game. It was crucial and he couldn't miss it, black eye or not.

Five minutes later, Kelly watched as Darren descended the stairs carrying a hold-all and suit carrier. The bastard hadn't even looked in at Krystal. He stopped, clicked his fingers in a gesture of recollection and retraced his steps back to the room where Krystal slept contentedly. A minute later, as he left the room, he saw Kelly glaring in his direction and was about to speak when he was cut off.

'Don't, Darren,' she warned. 'Don't say anything, you'll just make me proper angry. Er, sorry about the shiner, I didn't actually mean to do that.'

He shrugged wearily, turned, trudged back down the stairs and left.

***

Reclining in the bath, Susan Pierce stretched out her legs, rested her feet on the tap and closed her eyes...luxury! The acceptance of Duncan Moore's invitation to appear on his show now seemed serendipitous so she allowed herself a day off from the rigours of her career. Although she wasn't ambitious to the exclusion of everything else, she had an innate talent for singing and was captivated by the alchemy of recording and performing. Tolliver's encouragement was welcome, distinguishing Susan from her erstwhile colleagues in Dolly Mix. For them, the media attention, endorsements by clothing companies and cosseted treatment would've been welcome from any arm of the entertainment world whereas Susan was in thrall to music alone.

She was still uncertain about the motives behind Tolliver's backing although her original assumption of a carnal interest had acceded to the pleasing notion that he wished to bring an untapped talent to the public's attention. Dolly Mix didn't inhabit the same hemisphere of Planet Music as Tolliver so she was a relative *ingénue* in this world and his guidance and advocacy would open doors which might otherwise remain closed.

Laurence's suggestion of playing small, intimate venues rather than the cavernous, soulless arenas where Dolly Mix performed appealed to her and the possibility of involvement with a cutting-edge record label like Interstellar was equally exciting. She imagined Billy Carney discussing the label's roster in an interview....."Yeah, it's all good; we've got Double Dip,

Benson the Butler, Duct Tapes but the act we're really proud of is Susan Pierce". Or Lily Pollen, she'd have to get used to her new moniker. The other girls in Dolly Mix scoffed at the notion of critical acclaim in preference to mass sales but Susan was uneasy with a relentless pursuit of money and fame.

So, why did she invite the self-obsessed and intellectually-bereft Darren Peters to her flat this afternoon? She recalled her strange encounter with Peters in the BBC studio. Susan considered herself neither a prude nor promiscuous but she was still amazed that she had sex with somebody she had met only an hour or two earlier. The preamble in the hospitality room after the show had seemed innocuous. Darren quizzed her about changing her image as he was attempting something similar; she politely replied that his remarks about his girlfriend and daughter were endearing; he admitted they weren't entirely spontaneous but something he'd planned in advance. Susan's flirtatious comment about his still being "a bad boy" elicited a wolfish grin as he turned the full beam of his charm on her.

Darren asked to be considered for tickets to one of her concerts and she added his number to her phone. She excused herself to visit the ladies' and with adrenalin from performing live on television coursing through her, rang him to ask if he wished to continue their conversation in a nearby room. Darren joined her immediately and any attempt at discourse was abandoned in a flurry of discarded clothing and a passionate knee-trembler, as he described it.

Guilt kicked in next morning when she saw the positive reaction to Peters' televised eulogy to domestic life but she didn't know Kelly Spencer and felt no sense of betraying the code of sisterhood. She had no intention of a prolonged affair with him; this afternoon would be an indulgence and he certainly knew how to press all the right buttons, as it were.

Her feet slid off the tap and landed with a splash in the bath. It was time to get dressed, have some breakfast and browse through a small pile of magazines and newspapers. She started with that morning's edition of *The Universe* which she leafed through until she saw a photograph of herself on Davinia Hotch1ck's page. Pleased by the eye-catching shot taken during her television appearance, her mood changed when she read the two accompanying paragraphs :

> *Susan Pierce (above left), the former vocalist for Dolly Mix, will use the performing name of Lily Pollen for her solo career - a career which, she announced, on TV on Saturday would feature material with a more, ahem, adult theme. When I asked the glamorous singer whether her name change was in any way*

connected to a famous pop star with a similar name, she denied it...in terms which do not bear repeating in a family paper.

Why has the sweet, demure Susan of Dolly Mix become raunchy Lily? Is it the company she's keeping? Rock music writer, Laurence Tolliver, is now her manager even though I'm willing to bet my last pair of Louboutins that he's never knowingly listened to a Dolly Mix song. It also begs the question as to what could possibly attract laydeez man Tolliver, 48, to the role of managing the lovely Susan/Lily, 22. Answers on a postcard, please!

Susan fumed with rage. The bitch! The insinuation that Laurence had taken on the role purely with an eye to bedding her was bordering on slanderous. Did other people think this? She stomped into the living room, picked up her laptop, found Davinia's page on *The Universe*'s website and scrolled down to the comments section. There were just a few so far...

...Phwoar! Don't blame that Tollyver geezer. Wot a stunna!!!!
...The music writer guy is hardly interested in her singing, is he? Debbie was the only one of Dolly Mix who could hold a tune.
...Saw Susan Peerce on telly Sat nite. Tolliver near enough asked for a ****. LOL!!!! **(This comment has been moderated to conform to The Universe's code of conduct)**
...So is she any good or not? That's wot we wanna know.

Susan recognised the wisdom of Laurence's advice against involving herself in any unseemly spats but it was difficult to read this innuendo without responding. She counted to 20, then she counted to 50 and then started to count to 100. She had reached 84 when her phone rang.

'Susan? Hi, it's Darren.'

'Hello. Is everything OK? You sound stressed.'

'Things have gone a bit pear-shaped indoors. Kelly saw your text and she's chucked me out.'

'Oh my God, I'm sorry. Er, does she always read your messages?'

'No, of course not. Our mobiles have the same ringtone, mine went and...anyway, that doesn't really matter. She saw your text, sparks flew and I was kicked out.'

'I really am sorry, Darren. I never thought someone else might read it. Where are you now?'

'Actually I was calling to see whether I could, you know, crash at your place for a night or maybe two. I've got a big game tomorrow night and I can't get distracted scrabbling around for a hotel.'

'Oh. Er, yeah, I mean, maybe. Is that a good idea, Darren? Don't you want to, like, talk to Kelly and try sort things out?'

'You don't know her, she's threatened to get her brother and......no, there's no point in trying to reason with her at the moment. Besides, I was looking forward to meeting you again.'

Warning bells rang in Susan's mind. His girlfriend had just thrown him out and all he was worried about was football and the next girl; his daughter and girlfriend appeared irrelevant. Such dedication to oneself was impressive but not something she wanted to be a part of.

'Me too but isn't it, you know, dangerous to risk being seen with someone else? A few newspapers are based here and you *are* high profile.'

'Yeah but wherever I am, I run that risk. I was thinking of spending the time indoors anyway, know what I mean?' he chuckled.

'Darren, I'm not being funny but I don't want to be the person Kelly holds responsible for your, er, relationship difficulties.'

'Oh, I wouldn't worry about that. Lots of other girls are equally responsible for where I am now. Er, sorry, I didn't mean to put it like that, I think you're great but if you don't want to get involved just now, that's cool. I'd like to see you again though, let's see what happens, eh?'

'Yeah, OK. I hope things get sorted or however you wish it to work out. Take care, Darren.'

Susan ended the call and laughed; his vanity and self-absorption were astounding. She sighed as she saw Davinia's article again. Ah yes, what should she do about that?

Just a few miles away, Darren closed his phone and drummed his fingers on the steering wheel. Screw her, then. He remembered his scheduled visit to the school. Oh bloody hell, more grief in store there. With a weary sigh, he rang Jack Watson.

***

Geoff Harris was pleased with his morning's work. His contact had provided details of the JD/PJH collusion which he'd given to Philip Anderson who responded half-an-hour later to say that Brian Curtis would write up the story in *The Chronicle* without attributing his source. Geoff contacted Jan Netherby and AV's dealers were now ready to off-load their holdings in the two companies in discrete tranches. Others would follow suit so the likelihood of AV alone being exposed was slight. The stock price of the companies he'd identified as portfolio replacements were stable. He checked the sale of PJH and JD stock; the volume of activity was normal, the share price fluctuating within a narrow band.

He rang Elizabeth, told her the news and said that he'd book a table for them at a Soho restaurant later in the week. She sounded both pleased and relieved. Since her court acquittal and weekend at Harry's, she'd been more like the Elizabeth he knew and loved. Also, Geoff was sure that Philip Anderson would enjoy his contribution in bringing the scam to light...and he was now a friend of theirs. Yes, this had been a successful few days.

His phone rang. It was Simon from the reception desk.

'Simon, are you calling to ask whether I still have my security pass?'

'Very amusing, Mr. Harris. There's a lady down here who wishes to see you. Laura Armitage. Shall I send her up?'

'Laura Armi...oh, Laura Holmes. Yes, please do.'

Laura arrived and walked in. It was a while since Geoff last met her and he found himself inadvertently staring at her. A colleague for years and, briefly, Elizabeth's ex-boyfriend's partner, Geoff often forgot the impression she could make. Her auburn hair was tied in a pony-tail and the combination of pale blue cardigan and knee-length skirt evoked a 1950s youthful radiance which had probably taken about two minutes to achieve.

'Laura!' Geoff exclaimed as they hugged. 'What brings you here? Meeting Chandra?'

'Yes, I'm meeting Chandra and I wanted to say hello to you too. How are you? And Elizabeth?'

'Yes, we're both fine. Busy, busy, busy – you know how it is. How about you? Robert?'

'OK.' Laura hastily looked away. Her gaze settled on his battered briefcase which she pointed to, laughing. 'I thought you could afford a new one by now, you've had that since forever.'

'Come on, you of all people – a film critic – should appreciate the...' he adopted a mock profound tone, '...the true worth of this *objet d'art,* something which resonates beyond its intrinsic value.'

'Hey, listen to you! If you ever get bored by the City, maybe you can turn your hand to writing too. Oh and I'm branching out into music these days. Are you still into all that Americana stuff?' Geoff nodded. 'You may be interested in something I've written, sorry co-written. It'll be published tomorrow in *Rosebud.*'

'Oh yeah? I'll have to buy a copy of that. Are you lunching with Chandra or can I take you out?'

'Chandra has some place in mind but thanks for the offer.'

'Ah. Girlie talk. I'll tag along and spoil it unless you promise to meet me for a drink one evening soon or come over for dinner, you and Robert. Yeah, that's an idea.'

'Er, thanks. Actually, I wanted to ask a favour. Long story but I've been in touch with John Hooper and...as I said, it's a long story but he wants to invest some money and asked me for advice. He's tracking two companies, both of which are part of your portfolio here and is unsure whether to invest in your portfolio or put all the money into Johnston Dudley. I told him I'd ask your advice. I guess JD would be a good choice?'

Geoff swallowed and stared intently at Laura.

'What? Why are you looking so startled?' she asked.

Geoff paused before replying.

'Laura, what I'm going to say probably, no, not probably....what I'm going to say contravenes City regulations on insider dealing but tell John to avoid investing any money in Johnston Dudley. He should be OK with my portfolio but it's best for him to wait a few days before doing so. And, for God's sake, don't mention my name in this.'

'Oh, OK. I won't ask anything else and I'll make sure John keeps schtum as well. Thanks for that, Geoff. I'll call him now.'

Laura's call went straight through to John's voicemail and she left a message asking him to call her back.. Geoff checked the share prices again, JD and PJH had dropped a penny or two but not enough to cause concern.

'Well, that's all very intriguing,' Laura said. 'I'm sure I'll find out more in due course but thanks.'

'You said you're back in touch with John. Is there anything you'd like to add?' Geoff asked, smiling. Laura blushed.

'Like I said, I'm just in touch with him a bit more.' She glanced at her watch. 'I have to go. Sorry to dash but Chandra will be waiting. Thanks again for the advice, on John's behalf that is.'

Laura left. Intriguing indeed, Geoff thought as the door closed. Laura valued her privacy and Geoff didn't wish to pry but he'd like to know more about this. It wasn't just prying, she was someone he cared about. He'd ask Chandra later - she'd understand his concern. Right now, he badly needed a sandwich himself. Ignoring his ringing phone, he left the office.

***

Tom looked on apprehensively as Jack answered the call.

'Darren! We were getting worried about you. Where are you?...But you said only an hour ago...How did that happen? ...What? Why?'

Jack stepped away and his voice dropped a few decibels.

'I said why did she...I can't raise my voice, I'm with people...Yes, I can hear the traffic...Can you hear me now?...What happened?...Who?...Oh Darren, you didn't really...When? Er, don't tell me, I can guess...Well, can you blame her?...I know it's not my concern but we're in a dilemma here. Can't you just pass it off as a minor injury? ...Already? Must've been quite a punch...A squirrel? Squirrel? Are you sure? ...OK, never mind that for now. Look, this is important, even just ten minutes, Darren. It'll be worth it...There's a guy here from the local paper. I'll have to fob him off too...Yeah, I know it's my job but...I'll pretend I didn't hear that...Of course that's more important but you know....Jesus, you're incorrigible ...incorrigible, er, difficult to, er, never mind. Yes, you can for a couple of nights. I'll get Magdalena to set up the spare room. At least I'll be able to keep an eye on what you're up to...OK, give me a call.'

Jack exhaled and waited a moment before rejoining Tom and Tony.

'We have a problem,' he said gravely. 'Darren's picked up an injury and needs it attended to, urgently. He won't be able to join us so we'll have to do this between the two of us, Tom.'

'Oh, that's really great,' Tom groaned. 'You said he was on his way. What happened?'

'That's not important right now. He's OK but...he just can't be here for the next hour.'

'Well, there's no point in me hanging around, is there?' sighed Tony Jeffries. 'I gave up my morning off for this and all. Anything you'd like to throw my way for the *East London Recorder*'s readership? Maybe you could elaborate on this mysterious injury?'

'It doesn't work that way, Tony, you know that. I'm sorry, there's nothing I can add. I apologise on Darren's behalf for wasting your time. You sure you don't want to get a picture of Tom addressing the pupils? Maybe something about AV's community work?'

Tony shot Jack a withering look.

'I don't think so. No offence, Tom, but that won't interest our readers.'

'None taken, Tony,' Tom said politely. 'My apologies, too, for not providing a story. Best if we put this one down to experience.' They shook hands and Tony trudged back to his car.

'So, what do we do now? Do we abandon the whole thing?' Jack asked. 'It won't have quite the same er, resonance without Darren.'

'It'll be an utter waste of time without Darren...but we can't just swan off, that'd be even worse. Let's see the headmaster and get his take.' Tom peered at Jack. 'What did happen? What's all this about a squirrel? Am I right in thinking there's a lady involved?'

'You shouldn't eavesdrop, Tom. Let's just say Darren appears to have reneged on his pledge to, as he put it on TV, "live as normal a life as possible". Mind you, normal has different connotations when it comes to Darren. You'll keep this to yourself, won't you?'

'Yeah, yeah, don't worry. Let's report to the head, shall we?'

They walked towards the Administration office and waved to Tony Jeffries as he drove away.

***

An unanswered phone in the sub-editing room of *The Chronicle* wasn't unusual. Many of its residents worked on the maxim that 'if it's important enough, they'll call back' but for Philip Anderson's phone to continue ringing with Philip present was unusual. He chewed the top of a pencil, eyes fixed on his computer screen, oblivious to the metallic tone. Sally Tresco, two desks away, scowled as she located the source of the distraction. Her efforts to coax coherence from an opaque political commentary was hampered by Philip's failure to pick up the receiver.

'Philip, do you want me to get that for you?' she asked impatiently.

He swivelled around. 'What? Oh, sorry, didn't realise it was mine.'

He answered the call, wrote down a number, replaced the receiver and resumed his scrutiny of the screen. His phone rang again....again it was unanswered. Sally exhaled, strode to his desk and picked up the phone.

'Mr. Anderson's desk,' she said sharply. 'Yes, you might well have been speaking to him seconds ago but he's a very busy man.'

Philip shrugged apologetically and took the receiver from her.

'Yes, don't worry...I know, I've been watching them myself...Well, it's your story. I think it would rest better in the paper than on-line but if Glover's going to steal your thunder, I can see why you'd want to...I do know Glover but it's a giveaway if I call him out of the blue...I could do but he's a banker, caution is his watchword and all that...I said banker, Brian, let's not get puerile...Ok, leave it with me, I'll call you back.'

'Sorry about that,' Philip said to Sally. 'It's getting a bit hectic for the boys on the money pages.'

'Not another banking scandal? Yawn, yawn. Isn't the public bored with those yet?'

'They're a new form of blood sport, Sally although I think I know who'll win in the end.'

'And who'll pick up the bill too. Here, do you have any idea what's meant by this 'big society' stuff the Tories are banging on about?'

'It's some rubbish idea which they think sounds good and allows them to weasel out of doing their job if elected. They'll drop it as soon as the obvious faults are pointed out.'

'Hmm, I think that's what this article is attempting to say but it's vague. I guess I'll just correct the grammar mistakes. God knows there's enough of those.'

Philip returned to his monitor where he tracked the share prices of Johnston Dudley and Procter Jones Henderson. His knowledge of what constituted normal levels of activity on the financial markets had grown exponentially after a short conversation with Brian Curtis earlier. It was evident from the numbers skidding across his screen that the two companies had become the subject of considerable interest during the last

30 minutes. The share prices had dropped and were now oscillating in a manner inconsistent with recent days. Curtis alerted Philip to this, adding that the two companies were attracting the interest of a journalist on another newspaper, Martin Glover. Philip offered to call Geoff Harris to see what he knew and was about to do so when his phone rang again. Sally mimicked applause when he answered it. It was Elizabeth Harris.

'Philip, are you alone?'

'Er, no. Why? What's up?'

'I want to tell you something. It's not best done over the phone but I'd prefer not to wait.'

'Can I call you back from my mobile? I just need to step outside.'

Uh-oh, this sounds ominous, he thought as he left the room. Elizabeth had cooled towards him over the last few days and sounded strained during her earlier call. But it had hardly been a normal week for her...unless she was a very different person to the one Philip believed her to be.

'Hi Elizabeth, it's me. What's up?'

'Philip, I just wanted to say I think we should end our... our affair, I suppose is the word. What I did was completely out of character for me and I'm sorry if I, God this sounds conceited, if I led you to think there was a future for us. Sorry, this is all coming out wrong. Those days last week were, as you said, exhilarating and I got swept up in it but I'm lucky enough to have a husband I love. I said some disparaging things about him but I was caught up in, you know....I went away to have a think about things and oh God, I'm babbling on. Say something, Philip.'

'Not much for me to say. It all happened very quickly, we both needed time to digest everything, I guess. I was just about to call Geoff which is quite surreal. Odd things are happening to the companies he's dealing with. Maybe you could call him and let him know.'

'And what am I supposed to say?' Elizabeth asked wearily. 'Or were you being sarcastic? I don't want this to end with bad blood, Philip. I don't want it to end, period. I hope we're friends from now on. Oh, hell, I'm not enjoying this conversation. I'd prefer to say this in person but I thought it best to let you know sooner rather than later.'

'OK, I appreciate that. I hoped for something different but life doesn't work out how we hope, I guess. I have to go, Elizabeth. Bye.'

'Bye. Philip, I'll always...oh you've gone.'

Elizabeth rested her head against the wall. That was never going to be easy, it could've been worse but still wasn't good. At least it was now behind her. She knew that her future was with Geoff; she'd flirted with an alternative future and rejected it. That was something she'd put down to experience. It was time to plan ahead with Geoff, she wanted to return to work and the idea of having children increasingly occupied her mind. One chapter ended, a new one begun.

Philip walked back to his desk, deep in thought. He wasn't surprised really and admired her candour in contacting him rather than allow things to drift. That phone call made her even more attractive in his mind; she was assertive, considerate, amusing and yes, sexually desirable. And now he had to ring her husband and talk about share prices. Funny thing, life.

***

Even better second time round, John Hooper mused as he walked towards the bar in the National Film Theatre. He corrected himself, it was more like fifth or sixth time. The screening of *Alexander Nevsky* had finished and there was a ten minute break before one of John's favourite films, *The Battleship Potemkin,* started. He took out his phone and returned it to his jacket pocket without switching it on. He preferred to sit and think about the film; besides, he wasn't expecting any calls.

God, what it must be to direct a film like that: historical document, visual epic and even a rattling good story. His proposed book about a rock musician didn't have the same cachet but it was, at least, a start. John gazed around a foyer adorned by Russian agitprop posters and Rodchenko constructivist prints as he finished his espresso and strolled back to the auditorium. Habits die hard so he switched on his mobile phone and listened to Laura's message. When he rang her, the call went to her voicemail so he left a message and walked back into the small theatre just as the lights were dimmed. An hour of cinematic bliss awaited him.

***

'Hello. My name is Tom Brady and this is Jack Watson. For the last twelve years, I've worked for Alpha Venture. We're located about 15 minutes walk from here and we're committed to bridging the gap between the banking world and the more important world around us. I'd like to thank Mr. Murtagh for...oh, he's just left. Anyway, I'm pleased to have an opportunity to talk to you about, er, the role of financial institutions in the community, our desire to help that community and to answer any questions you might have. Does that sound OK?'

Tom was conscious of two things – complete indifference among the thirty or so teenagers in front of him and a sense of vulnerability since Murtagh's departure. Then again, the teacher's presence wasn't particularly reassuring. At first welcoming, Murtagh became apathetic bordering on hostile once they'd left the headmaster's office and his caustic address to his class ratcheted up their collective indifference a few notches.

'This is Mr. Brady who wishes to speak to you about the valuable role which banks perform, to answer questions and, maybe, even accept your praise for his part in performing this valuable role. I'm sure you'll have questions and rather than inhibit that important exchange of views, I'll leave you with Mr. Brady. I'd like to add that Mr. Brady is giving up some of his valuable working hours to do this. Please bear that in mind.'

Kevin Murtagh left the room, happy with the opportunity to smoke a couple of cigarettes and read the paper rather than deal with this notorious Year 10 class, his least favourite collection of pupils in the school. Brady struck him from the outset as supercilious and Watson was clearly there under sufferance. Kevin wondered whether they'd ever been likely to receive a visit from Darren Peters. Almost definitely yes, Brady and Watson wouldn't risk antagonising the local newspaper by requesting their attendance. Still, it was a shoddy effort on their part and he was content to leave them to face the incessant sneering of the Year 10 class. He'd keep an eye on proceedings from afar as the window of what was grandiosely termed the Staff Common Room – a drab, poorly furnished room reeking of over-boiled vegetables from the school kitchen located directly below - afforded a direct view of the Year 10 classroom.

The school headmaster, a relentlessly upbeat man called Trevor Skinner, had been upset by Peters' no-show. Kevin thought Skinner possessed amazing fortitude in view of the thankless position which he held. He could normally be relied upon to "see the positives" in even the most dismal situation. News that St. Ambrose's disciplinary record was the worst in the borough's schools was lauded by Skinner as "the yardstick by which we track progress going forward". Skinner's vocabulary contained countless examples of corporate gobbledygook and he'd anticipated meeting the banker as an opportunity to indulge himself. With the added bonus of Darren Peters' involvement and the related press coverage, the headmaster's customary optimism scaled new heights over the last couple of days.

When the taciturn Brady arrived and broke the news of Peters' absence, even Skinner couldn't disguise his disappointment. Kevin left him sitting disconsolately in his office, for once unable to locate a single positive from the morning's events. Moved by this, Kevin wanted to involve himself in making the visit something other than a fractious stand-off between the Year 10 thugs and their guests. A few minutes, however, of Brady's hauteur, Watson's indifference and the pupils' oafishness stripped him of these laudable intentions and he fled the classroom.

Now, Tom stood in front of the class while Jack Watson lingered in a corner of the room smiling hesitantly. Tom, isolated, silently cursed the idiot footballer who'd left him in this mess. There was no response from the class to his opening preamble.

'OK, I work in a finance house or a bank as we're more generically, er as we're normally referred to. You might have a pre-conceived, er you might have some idea of what a company like Alpha Venture does. You've maybe seen movies set in banks featuring lots of men wearing striped shirts and red braces staring at screens and shouting excitedly. Yes?'

A pale boy with a floppy fringe had raised his hand.

'Er, can you please say your name when you ask questions,' Tom pleaded.

'Sir, my name is Jacob. I just want to...'

'Jacob, no need to call me sir,' Tom said affably. 'This should be an informal chat. Call me Tom.'

'Mr. Tom, sir,' Jacob said to a chorus of sniggers. 'Why is they excited? Are they watching porn on the screen?' Jacob swivelled round to his friends, exchanging a high five with one.

'Of course not,' Tom said. 'They're not watching pornography at work.'

Jack Watson grimaced and retreated further into the corner as a muscular boy with a corn-row hairstyle raised his hand.

'Is you one of the geezers in a striped shirt and braces, Tom? Oh and my name is Dennis.'

'As I was about to say, you may have an idea of bankers, er, you may have an idea of people who work in banks from those movies but there are many different jobs in banks, only a few of which are as exciting as being one of the guys in braces working on the trading floor.'

A sincere-looking boy raised his hand. Wearing a neatly pressed shirt and carefully knotted tie topped off by a trim centre-parted hairstyle, he struck an incongruous figure sartorially and in terms of demeanour.

'Do you ever wear braces and a striped shirt, Tom?' the boy asked. 'I think Tom would look lovely in a striped shirt and braces.'

A chorus of 'yeah, lovely' rang out and a wolf-whistle was followed by laughter and cheers. Tom strived to appear nonplussed and waited for the hubbub to fade before continuing.

'Finished? There are lots of important roles in a bank which don't have the same er, prestige as working on the trading floor and I guess mine falls into that category. I work on the communications side for Alpha Venture, we keep the public and media informed on what the company is doing.' The sincere-looking boy raised his hand again. 'Yes? You didn't tell me your name last time; I prefer to address people by name.'

'Wayne,' the boy answered. 'Tom, why haven't you got one of the good positions after twelve years there? Are you no good at your job?'

Wayne retained a polite, inquiring expression as he waited for a reply. Tom, although he admired the boy's *sang-froid* and reluctance to play to an audience, realised he had to wrestle back control before the class became unruly.

'OK,' he said assertively. 'We can have a chat and a few laughs but I have got a message for you. You boys are the future of this area and we want to be a part of this. Pupils from here have been with us on work experience.' An Asian boy raised his hand. 'Yes?'

'My name is Amit. Your company employed someone from here last summer, yeah?'

Tom hesitated. The boy presumably knew Michael Benson whose account of his time at AV probably wasn't favourable.

'Er, I can't remember his name but, yes, a St. Ambrose's pupil spent a few months with us last summer.'

A whoop came from a menacing boy with blond cropped hair. 'That was Michael Benson. He said you was too posh to even speak to him. He hated it, said you tried to nail him for nicking a watch which he didn't.'

'We retracted that accusation which I believe helped Michael get out of trouble with the law,' Tom replied, flustered by the hostility. 'Maybe you, you'd like to check with him. Er, I didn't get your name.'

'Jackson,' the boy replied. 'So, you did know who Amit was talking about, yeah? Why did you lie?'

'I didn't lie. I only remembered Michael's name when you mentioned it...but now, you're making accusations, Jackson. I met Michael last week, he was grateful to us for offering him a testimony.'

'You offered him your testicles?' Jackson shouted. 'There's a law against that, Tom. You should be reported.'

The class cheered, Tom feigned indifference. Hostile as this was, it was also becoming tedious.

'OK, does anybody have anything of relevance to ask?' he said.

'Who's the bloke in the corner?' Jacob asked. 'Is he your boyfriend?'

Jack Watson smirked self-consciously as Dennis raised his hand.

'My dad says bankers are to blame for him losing his job. What do you say to that?'

'Well, I'm sorry he thinks that, Dennis. What does, er, what was your dad's job?' Tom asked. Jackson interrupted before Dennis could reply.

'His old man's a dealer and he don't wear red braces and a striped shirt, know what I mean?'

Dennis swivelled round to Jackson who tensed confrontationally.

'You scumbag, Jackson,' Dennis spat out. 'Anyway, you'd know about dealings, your mum still giving quickies for twenty quid round the back of the Royal Oak after closing time?'

The air became charged within the classroom. Jackson and Dennis appeared to be the alpha males in the classroom and, already, some of the other pupils were egging on one or the other. Others seemed discomforted by the confrontation.

'You Shillingtree piece of shit,' Jackson responded.

Tom sensed this was an opportune time to wrestle back control. 'Look, let's show some respect for each other. One of the things I've learned in my job is that we can overcome whatever background differences exist and work together. You guys should do so too.'

The tension eased and Tom invited further questions.

'How much do you get paid, Tom?' asked a weasel-faced boy.

'I don't think that's any concern of yours.'

'Oh but it is,' the weasel-faced boy responded. 'We want to know if it's worth spending twelve years doing something that ain't interesting.'

'I never said it was uninteresting. I just said my job isn't as glamorous as some of the others.'

'If you're embarrassed about your small salary, we understand.' It was the sincere, concerned voice again from Wayne. 'Look, we'll have a whip-around for poor old Tom here. I'll start with this.'

Wayne held out a 20p coin which was augmented by small denomination coins from other boys.

'Thanks,' Tom said, smiling. 'There may be enough to buy myself a drink when I leave here.'

'So you've got a drink problem, Tom,' said Wayne. 'Hardly surprising since you've got a crap job and you're badly paid after all those years.'

A cheer arose and Tom held up his hands in supplication as the whoops and laughter grew louder. The door opened, Mr. Murtagh walked in and the noise died.

'Seems like everybody's getting along well here,' the teacher said.

Inevitably, it was Wayne who spoke up. 'Tom has been telling us about his drink problem and his low self-esteem, sir. It's very moving.'

Murtagh looked towards Tom, surprise registered on his face, awaiting an explanation. Tom smiled ruefully and shook his head.

'I'd call that a pretty imaginative interpretation of our conversation. Perhaps if your students were more familiar with the concept of discipline, they might learn something from visitors rather than cause disruption at every opportunity.'

The class, sensing a disagreement between Tom and their teacher, looked on with renewed interest when Murtagh duly took the bait.

'If your alleged guest had actually turned up, the reception might be better but expecting bankers to honour promises is a forlorn hope.'

'I'm here out of a sense of community spirit. You could contribute if you channelled the energy of these boys more productively. They might even aspire to qualifications other than an ASBO before they've left school.'

'Hark at the banker moralising,' Murtagh scoffed. Tom glared back. The class started a chant of 'fight, fight' before Jack Watson moved from his position in the corner and stood between the two.

'I think it's best if we called a halt here, Tom,' he advised. Tom nodded and turned to the class.

'Er, thanks for your attention. Bear in mind what I said about working together and I hope you make the most of whatever opportunities come your way. Hopefully, you'll find the right mentors to encourage you. Goodbye.'

He attempted a nonchalant exit from the room but his jacket caught on the corner of a desk and he stumbled into Jack who helped him regain his balance. Tom rushed out, hearing Wayne's measured voice as he left.

'Pissed, clearly pissed. Poor guy's got a bad drink problem. We mustn't laugh.' The words were greeted by a renewed flurry of derisory laughter.

***

The rain, threatened all morning, finally arrived. People scurried for shelter under shop awnings and in doorways and Geoff was marooned in a café as the rain drummed against the window. Tired of waiting for it to ease, he sprinted back to Alpha House clutching a sandwich and collided with Chandra Ghosh as she closed a dripping umbrella in the foyer.

'Oops, sorry Chandra,' he gasped and nodded towards the door. 'Where did that come from?'

'Geoff, this is February in England. Rain isn't entirely unexpected.'

'I suppose. Catching up with Laura?'

'Yes. She said she dropped in to say hello to you.'

'She did. How is she? She seemed a bit distracted.'

Chandra sighed as they walked upstairs to their floor. She explained that Laura was having some problems but, Laura being Laura, was making light of them. Aware that Laura wouldn't object to Geoff knowing, Chandra alluded to John's reappearance. She left it at that and they parted. Geoff noticed a dishevelled Tom Brady emerging from a lift.

'You too?' Geoff asked. 'I got caught in that downpour as well. How was your morning?'

'I got caught in the rain and that was only after being caught in a shit storm of juvenile malevolence,' Tom snorted.

'Why? Surely they didn't turn on Darren Peters.'

'The bastard didn't even turn up - some bimbo or other by the sounds of it - and then it got progressively worse. I need to sit down and recover. Everything OK with your journalist friend?'

'So far, so good. Catch you later.'

As Geoff reached his office, he heard Jan Netherby greet Tom and invite himself in. Poor Tom, he'd have to explain to that creep whatever misfortune had occurred. The digital display on Geoff's phone indicated four missed calls, two of them from Philip Anderson. Geoff's computer terminal flickered back to life and he was shocked to see the share prices of both Johnston Dudley and Procter Jones Henderson falling steadily. He rang Philip who, tetchily, mentioned his unanswered calls.

Geoff remembered the phone ringing when he left the office earlier and cursed the rain for delaying his return. He was told by Philip that at least one other newspaper was ready to break the story. If this happened before Brian Curtis could do the same, *The Chronicle* might change their story to one on companies waiting to sell shares, waiting in an attempt to legitimise their actions even though they were aware of the scam.

Geoff clutched his desk: this was a nightmare scenario. He said that he saw this as a betrayal of trust on Philip's part.

'Oh, it's not me, Geoff. Brian reached that conclusion without any help from me but the whole thing stinks, if you ask me.'

'It's called business and the idea of a newspaper acting holier-than-thou is laughable.'

'It's called journalism, it's what we do. I'm sorry but it's Brian's story.'

'But surely you...' Geoff paused as he remembered what Tom said about Darren Peters. 'Philip, say I put you on to a juicy story, could you persuade Brian Curtis to change his angle on this?'

'God, you're a veritable Reuters. What is it, another City scandal?'

'No, it's football related. Give me a minute and I'll get back to you.'

Geoff saw that the share prices had stabilised slightly but were still considerably lower than the morning opening price. If AV bailed out now, they would still show a profit on their dealings but if prices continued to fall, this profit would erode and eventually turn into a loss. Geoff didn't relish the ignominy of presiding over an investment portfolio turned bad, especially when he'd known it could happen.

If AV broke cover and sold large amounts of stock, it could isolate them, even more so if Brian Curtis wrote about the rumours circulating around the City. If they gave *The Chronicle* something about Darren Peters, it could delay or quash Curtis' story...surely a card worth playing. Geoff rushed over to Tom's office. For once, Netherby's presence was welcome.

'Jan, just the man I wanted to see,' Geoff said, hating himself to the core for doing so. He mentioned the falling share prices and, in another act of self-abasement, deferentially asked Netherby what they should do. Jan nodded sagely and said that he'd make a couple of calls.

'Paul...No, it's Jan Netherby...Yes, we may need to get the ball rolling...I don't need to, I have his mandate...Yes, it's a risk. Ideally, we'd do so just ahead of the avalanche but that's hard to control...Fine, but if they drop any further, call me immediately. Thanks. Bye.'

'I won't need to make the second call, no reason to get Mark involved. I'll return to my desk, keep an eye on things and call Paul when needs be. Call me if you have any concerns.' Jan left.

'OK, problem here, Tom,' Geoff said. 'If Brian Curtis is beaten to the pricing scam story, he's likely to write something about other firms' knowledge of it. However, my man at *The Chronicle* may be able to spike this story if we give him details of Peters' latest scrape. Tell me more.'

'Hold on, Geoff. I told Peters' agent that I wouldn't divulge this. Besides, I don't know the full story. There was something about a squirrel but I can't imagine what that meant.'

'A squirrel? Jesus Christ, what depravity is Peters involved in now?'

'I don't know but we can't do anything with this. We can't, Geoff,' he emphasised as Geoff stayed silent. 'Put it out of your mind. We're doing enough silly things without...no, I'm not even going to talk about it. Not happening, OK?'

'OK,' Geoff replied reluctantly. 'A squirrel though. That has to be quite a story. You know what? You were probably lucky Peters didn't show today; we may not wish to be associated with him after all. So, how bad was it?'

'Well, apart from being humiliated by smart-arse 14 year olds, goaded to the brink of a punch-up with their smarmy teacher and falling arse over tit as I tried to make a dignified exit, it was fine.'

'Oh dear,' Geoff smiled sympathetically. There was a knock on the door and Hilary St. Vincent, Tom's assistant, sheepishly walked in.

'Oh, excuse me, Geoff. Tom, I need to have a word with you.'

Geoff stood up. 'Hi Hilary, I was just leaving anyway. Fancy a drink after work, Tom?'

'Yes. I could use one right now but maybe Hilary has some good news.'

Hilary, pale-skinned and blonde-haired, blushed. Geoff winced as he left the office...it didn't look like this would be good news. He had just sat down in his own office when he heard Tom's anguished cry. No: Hilary's news definitely hadn't been good.

***

As he left the car park at St. Ambrose's, Tony Jeffries reflected on a wasted morning and a lost opportunity for a lie-in. All his life, he'd wanted to be a journalist and took the advice of his Media Studies tutor to accept whatever jobs he could get on trade magazines. A series of such postings later, he became the Chief Reporter on the *East London Recorder*.

An ability to think quickly and Olympian reserves of perseverance garnered Tony a reputation on the ELR as the man who never turned down a job. He was jokingly known around the office as Jordan Jeffries – a reference to the ubiquitous celebrity who never found the barrier of dignity set too low if it resulted in publicity. Tony, himself, used the soubriquet self-deprecatingly, hoping to convey the impression that he viewed it as amusing rather than close to the truth.

If he was honest, he would happily compromise his principles in exchange for the break which he needed to make his name but any such Faustian pact was yet to manifest itself. He played back the last 30 minutes in his mind and regretfully concluded that he might have been tantalisingly close to that break. It was clear that Peters was the bait Alpha Venture wished to use to get some favourable press; big bank with questionable ethics sends reluctant employee on token visit to notorious local school didn't have quite the same cachet without Peters' involvement. With Peters on board, it was a good story; local boy made good pitches up at his alma mater, big bank involves itself in the community, local paper gets the scoop...and then the bugger didn't even turn up.

There had to be a good reason for the no-show although the agent was clearly hacked off with Peters. He seemed a bit furtive too, lowering his voice, but snatches of the call were still audible - something about a punch and "can you blame her" and a squirrel. A squirrel? Peters had a reputation for shagging anything that moved but a squirrel? Bizarre.

There must be something of interest here. *Can you blame her? Can you blame her?* A punch and now he's injured, Peters threw a punch at a girl? Maybe. Some misfortunate girl he ditched had punched him? More likely. What else did Watson say? Think, think. Yes, something about setting up the spare room. Peters' missus had kicked him out and he wanted to crash at Watson's? There'd been a row, a hell of a row by the sound of it. There's a story here if only I can get a handle on it.

Tony stopped at a café, ordered tea and a sandwich. He was convinced that here was a chance to get his name known. Peters was in trouble, fact. There was a woman involved, fact. There'd been a punch-up, fact. Peters was barred from home, probably fact. Tony looked around him, the clientele in the café were gruff, manual labourers who'd put in the equivalent of a day's work already and were now refuelling with sausages, bacon, beans and chips ahead of another session. These blokes did their work and got on with it and he should do so too...no more reliance on others to hand him that one job which vaulted him over the barrier towards a more prestigious future. It was time to show initiative and do it himself. He hatched an improbable plan.

Tony was familiar with the outer reaches of East London where prosperous suburbs rubbed up against parts of Essex populated by self-made men, proud of their faux-Georgian houses in pleasant villages, the sort of places where extravagantly-paid footballers lived...the sort of place where Darren Peters lived. Tony knew Peters' house as he passed close by when he drove to his parents' house in the Essex countryside. In the nearby village, a florist with prohibitive prices had rescued him on occasions when he'd forgotten to buy flowers for his mother. It was a shop he used as a last resort only; £25 for a bunch of flowers which could be purchased for a fraction of that elsewhere had been a costly reminder to prepare better for these family visits.

Tony left the café, returned to his car and drove east through Stratford, through Romford, through Brentwood. This was the life! Here he was...a journalist, nose to the ground, following a lead and tracking down a story which would be discussed tomorrow in pubs and cafés and at bus stops. He reached the village where Darren Peters lived and visited the expensive florist. Three minutes later, £40 lighter, he emerged clutching an elaborate bouquet of flowers. Sorry Mum, he thought guiltily as he realised he would never spend that much on flowers for his mother.

He drove past Peters' house and parked close by. On the small card he'd also purchased from the florists (£1.99! You could buy five of them anywhere else for a quid), he wrote:

KELLY
PLEASE FORGIVE ME.....TRULY, TRULY SORRY
DARREN xxxxx

Affixing it to the red-tinted cellophane wrapper with sellotape which he carried in his car, he stepped from the car, walked to the large iron gates which barred entrance to Darren Peters' residence and rang the bell. About 20 seconds elapsed before a woman's voice tonelessly answered "Yes".

'Hello, this is Flowers Express. I have a delivery for...' short pause for authenticity, '...Kelly Spencer.'

'Yeah, that's me. Leave them at the gate, please. I'm busy.'

'I'm sorry but they have to be signed for. I'll come to the door if you buzz me in.'

'Oh, hell. My little girl is awake, I'll have to get her. OK, come in, I'll be there in a minute.'

This was promising: he could gush about the toddler, pretend to belatedly recognise Kelly, add that he was a Wallington Rovers fan and see whether that elicited a response. Waiting at the front door, Tony took in the expensive sports cars and jeep, the side gate leading to a swimming pool and what looked like a small gymnasium. Peters' residence was as he expected, clear proof that the owner's ostentatious devil on one shoulder had permanently banished the angel with taste from the other shoulder.

He noticed – joy of joys – a huge framed photograph of Darren scoring a goal for England which was visible through the full-length glass panel to the side of the oak front door. This could be his opening gambit once he'd handed over the flowers. After a short wait, Kelly Spencer, cradling a small child, answered the door, both of them puffy-eyed and grumpy. Kelly was a tall woman with a curvaceous figure and a tan which was equally the result of expensive winter breaks and hours under a tanning machine. Her surly demeanour didn't appeal to Tony who had no qualms about his act of subterfuge.

'Hello, sorry for the inconvenience but it's mandatory that the flowers are signed for. Oh my, what a cute little girl. Hello, had a nice sleep then, have we?' Tony gurgled, waggling his fingers in front of Krystal. Noting Kelly's frown, he handed over a sheet of paper and a mock-receipt replete with his hand-written curlicues...consistent with Tony's idea of an expensive florist's invoice. Kelly ignored the sheet, plucked the card from the cellophane, glanced at it and snorted.

'I don't want these. Can you return them to the sender? With a message telling him to stick them where the sun don't shine?'

'I'm sorry,' Tony grimaced apologetically, 'but I need a signature to confirm delivery and I don't think I can er, carry out your request to return them with that message.' He was pleased to see Kelly's pained smile.

'No, I don't suppose you can. OK, where do I sign?'

'Just there,' Tony pointed to a dotted line on the sheet and looked past Kelly's shoulder as she scrawled her signature. 'Wow, great photo of Darren Peters. Hang on...Kelly Spencer, aren't you Darren's girlfriend? Oh my God, I'm delivering flowers to Darren Peters' house. Sorry, it's just that I'm a Wallington Rovers season-ticket holder and Dazzle is my hero.'

'Well, he ain't mine at the moment,' she said wearily.

'Oh, sorry to hear that. None of my business. Er, give him my best when you see him. Sorry, probably not the right thing to say.'

'Not your fault, mate,' Kelly said sweetly. 'If you're a Rovers' season-ticket holder, you'll see the cheating scumbag before I do. Anyway, mustn't keep blabbing here. Thanks for the delivery.'

'No problem. I, er, hope things work out. Cheers.'

The door closed and Tony attempted to look disconsolate as he walked to the gate where he pretended not to understand the gate mechanism. He might be able to return to the house, ask Kelly to open the gate and she

174

might even say something else damning about Darren. An elaborate show of searching for the release button later, he was glad he did so when the front door opened...she had been watching him.

'I'll buzz you out from here,' she called. 'Er, I'd prefer if you kept that little rant to yourself. I've just been for a kip and I'm not really with it.' A smile was beamed towards Tony and did she really wiggle those statuesque breasts just for his benefit?

'Of course,' he replied bashfully as the gates opened.

***

In the foyer of the National Film Theatre, a small knot of people, all male, milled around wearing beatific smiles after *The Battleship Potemkin* screening. John Hooper slunk away from them. There were few things he enjoyed more than the company of like-minded people but there were few things he enjoyed less than obsessives who treated every conversation as an exercise in one-upmanship...an Eisenstein retrospective attracted lots of these types. Even a casual glance around the foyer during the break before the next film, *October: Ten Days That Shook The World*, identified five men whose eyes darted around in the hope of engaging someone in conversation. A conversation, no doubt, with a frame-by-frame analysis of the Odessa Steps scene from *The Battleship Potemkin*. John strode to the exit to avoid the geeks, breathe some fresh air and return Laura's call.

Rarely had slate-grey skies and isolation seemed so welcome as now. He walked through the building's side entrance to the deserted concrete forecourt. If he ever ran a cinema, it would include a geek-free zone where words such as "seminal", "ground-breaking" or "iconoclastic" were banned. Mind you, that would probably mean his own expulsion...he'd think that one through again. His mobile showed that Laura had rang. He called her.

'John, I've been trying to reach you for ages. Where are you?'

'NFT.'

'Ah, that explains it. I spoke to Geoff and his advice on Johnston Dudley is to keep clear of them.'

'Problem there, Laura. I ploughed most of my money into them yesterday. How serious is this?'

'Oh shit, Geoff was pretty definite about it. I can call him and see whether you should get out immediately.'

'Could you? Obviously, I'd do it but you're, er, closer to him than me.'

'Sure, I'll get back to you in a minute. Stay right there.'

John felt uneasy. It was one thing being blasé about money earned from something he treated as a bit of a joke but another thing entirely to lose it through market speculation. He drummed his fingers on a window ledge as he waited for Laura's call which soon came.

'John, get shot of them, pronto. If you bought them yesterday, they're already worth less but will be worth a whole lot less very soon. Geoff said to sell immediately and for Christ's sake, don't allude to his telling you this.'

'Ah. Good old cover-your-arse City advice then.'

'Oh for Christ's sake, John...Geoff's gone out on a limb to even tell you this. Don't be so bloody churlish.'

'Sorry, that wasn't what I meant. I meant...oh, never mind. Look, I'll call you later on your home number. You were never one for leaving your mobile on at night, I recall. Thanks for the advice, thanks to Geoff too.'

'Er, if you want to call me later, best ring my mobile. I doubt I'll be at home. Now, get off the phone and salvage your money. Bye.'

The connection was cut before he could reply. The share business sounded serious, he'd forego the film this time. It was already gone three o'clock and the markets would wind down in an hour or so. John called his broker, conveyed his instructions to sell the shares as soon as possible and strolled along the South Bank, oblivious to the drizzle. His mind drifted from money to romance and even to the brutal suppression of mutiny in Tsarist Russia. Daylight was starting to fade when his phone rang. It was Edward Chatterick, his broker, who was unsure about his ability to sell all the shares before the markets closed.

'It's difficult to find a buyer for Johnston Dudley stock; I've had to trawl around a bit. Some news is breaking and nobody wants to touch them. They're currently trading down 14p on yesterday so that's about 10% knocked off your investment already, I'm afraid. Strikes me you're doing the right thing though before they go even lower. What prompted you to sell them so quickly? Have you been following the markets today?'

'Just my intuition, Ed,' John wearily replied. 'The same intuition which made me buy the sodding things yesterday. No, I was advised to get rid of them by somebody who knows about these things.'

'I didn't hear that, John.'

'I said I was...oh, I get you. Well, I wish you hadn't heard it from me earlier. 10%, you say and likely to get worse. Bollocks, that'll eat into my survival fund a bit.'

'OK, I'll crack on with flogging these as best I can. Oops, just dropped another penny. Catch you later.'

John vehemently kicked at some leaves. What a bizarre week...he'd quit his job, reconnected with an ex-girlfriend, considered a new career, acquired a huge sum of money and now helplessly watched that sum of money become less huge. Bizarre indeed but it wasn't helping matters moping around here. He hailed a cab and went home.

***

Sally Tresco whistled in surprise as she stared at her computer screen.

'Oh my God,' she intoned and beckoned to Philip Anderson. 'Have you seen this? That guy really is unbelievable.'

Philip leaned across the desk to view a newspaper website with the headline *DAZZLE FRAZZLED*.

'Darren Peters again, I take it. What's he done now?'

'See for yourself. Go to the *East London Recorder*'s website.'

'*East London Recorder*? Hardly Reuters, are they?'

'Well, they've got a hell of a scoop with this one.'

The *East London Recorder*'s website showed an *EXCLUSIVE!* banner above a story under the by-line of their reporter, Tony Jeffries.

> *Darren Peters, Wallington Rovers' star midfielder, has been dismissed from home by his girlfriend, Kelly Spencer, and is struggling to overcome an injury ahead of tomorrow's Champions League clash with German giants, Bayern Munich.*
>
> *Peters, who eulogised his domestic life with Kelly and their young daughter on television on Saturday night, was labelled a "cheating scumbag" by Kelly, his partner since 2006. Details about the identity of the latest in a string of Peters' love interests remain sketchy but the episode has led to his eviction from the couple's £2.2m house in Essex.*
>
> *Peters refused to comment on the subject and his agent, Jack Watson, remained equally tight-lipped while admitting that Peters received an eye injury today which casts a doubt on his involvement in the Bayern game.*
>
> *Peters was recently named as the participant in three affairs, all of which occurred since meeting Kelly Spencer and two of which were conducted simultaneously. Sources close to the couple say that he had been told by a furious Kelly that any more transgressions would end their relationship. It remains to be seen whether his latest alleged affair actually does this.*

The rest of the article was padded out with biographical details about Darren Peters and the recent stories about his intricate love life.

'Bloody hell, how did a local rag get a scoop like that? And why didn't this Jeffries' guy flog the story to a tabloid? He must be the only loyal local hack around,' Philip said to Sally.

'What a bastard Peters is! I saw that programme on TV and felt a lump in my throat when he came out with the stuff about the girlfriend and kiddie. God, she must be livid, I certainly would be.'

Philip's phone rang. It was Geoff - he didn't have a story after all and asked whether the insider information story was due for publication.

'I don't honestly know. There's a lot happening right now and the scam story might be buried under other stuff. Nervous?'

'No. I, er, we've done nothing illicit other than contact you....which would make you complicit too.'

'The share prices are still on the slide. Have you sold yours yet?'

'And why should I tell you that?' Geoff laughed to modify the intent.

'Indeed. So, I'm a journalist again, no longer a friendly neighbour?'

'Well, you sound like one asking whether the stock's been sold. Look, I've no truck with whatever you publish and I'm pleased to have made your acquaintance. I hope that continues.'

'Fair enough, same here. Anyway, must get on. Bye.'

Philip, aware of Sally's attention, adopted a nonchalant air and resumed their conversation.

'Can't help wondering how Jeffries got the story, he must have some decent connections.'

'Or indecent,' Sally said. 'Kelly Spencer's a topless model...not quite a paragon of virtue, is she?'

Philip shrugged. He harboured a never-to-be-voiced hankering for girls like Kelly Spencer. You wouldn't discuss books or world affairs with her but you'd probably find other means of amusement.

***

Geoff muttered "enough" and dialled Jan Netherby's extension. 'Jan, Geoff here. They're still sliding. We should dump the shares.'

'I've been thinking along those lines too. There'll be a mass sale of the stock so we'll hardly be identified as the originators.'

'Agreed. I'll be happier when they're off our books and replaced.'

'OK, I'll call you back when the deed is done.'

Geoff didn't enjoy his involvement in the duplicity but felt he had no choice. He also hoped Tom Brady's tormented wail wasn't due to anything too serious. He saw that Johnston Dudley's price had dipped further and called Laura.

'Geoff here. Did our friend, er get the message and act upon it.'

'Geoff, what on earth are you talking about?'

'I'm thinking about bygone days, Laura. Remember the French Alps and all that started there?' He paused. 'Sorry, I'm not making sense. I'm just ringing to see if Mr. H followed my, er, advice.'

'OK, you make sense. Yes, the eagle has landed or whatever code words are appropriate. He's aware of your advice, er, he's aware of whatever he's aware of.'

'That makes perfect sense, Laura. I have to go. Talk soon.'

The phone rang again as he replaced it.

'Done deal, Geoff,' said Jan Netherby. 'It's over to you now to replenish the portfolio.'

Geoff punched the air and sent an instruction to the dealers to buy the stock he'd identified. His attention was caught by a *Breaking News* caption on the BBC's website with a link to the ELR's Darren Peters story. He grimaced as he read it...they really had been lucky not to get involved with Peters. He'd let Tom know, it might cheer him up. Before he could do so, a harassed-looking Tom Brady strode into his office.

'Geoff, it's all going tits-up. I wrote a draft press release before the St. Asbo's visit and Hilary inadvertently sent it out to our usual contacts. It was something I would've amended before release but it's now out there referring to the successful school visit and Darren Peters' involvement in it. We'll look like complete idiots when the papers receive it.'

'Ah. Have you seen the latest news on Peters? He's on the front pages again. I thought he was someone we shouldn't get involved with.'

'Why, what's happened?'

Geoff nodded to the screen and Tom, ashen-faced, read it.

'Oh Jesus, that's the guy who was there this morning – Tony Jeffries. Geoff, we're really fucked. After this, Hilary's e-mail sounds really sinister. It'll read as if Peters had it off with a teenager with our explicit approval. I'm paraphrasing but that's how it'll read.'

'What? What are you on about?'

'Come to my office, I'll show you what's gone out to the newspapers.'

Geoff followed Tom back to his office and Tom retrieved the e-mail which Hilary had mistakenly sent to a distribution list of the business desks of national newspapers and finance publications.

'There. I can't believe this. I wrote it before the St. Asbo's visit with the intention of making any required tweaks later. I assumed Darren would (a) turn up (b) get involved in a kick-around with a few school kids and (c) it would be written up in the *East London Recorder*.'

> *Alpha Venture would like to add our own message to the* East London Recorder's *Darren Peters story. We were pleased to act as facilitators allowing Darren to meet some of the young people of the area. Despite his well-deserved success, Darren has clearly not forgotten his roots and it was a pleasure to watch him displaying his charm and talents with a 14-year-old who will never forget the experience. Both participants emerged happy and breathless after Darren's virtuoso display of "keepy-uppy".*

We would like to extend our thanks to the staff of St. Ambrose's school for allowing Darren and an Alpha Venture representative the use of their premises to engage with the local community and to the East London Recorder *for recording the event for posterity. No doubt, their photographs will become sought-after mementos of the occasion.*

'I'm sorry but there is a funny side to this,' Geoff laughed.

'You may think so but link it with Jeffries' piece and it makes us sound sleazy.'

'But nobody will see it like that, Tom. Come on, you were there when Peters was getting it on with a 14-year-old and the local paper photographed it? How could someone believe that?'

'I suppose,' Tom shrugged. 'But we still look incompetent. I'd better send out a disclaimer before some smartass links the two pieces.'

'Good idea. I'll leave you to it. Ah, here's Hilary.'

Hilary St. Vincent walked in, contrition oozing from every pore.

'Tom, I am so, so sorry about this. I've just seen the ELR piece. I don't know what to say.'

'Nobody's blaming you, Hilary. It was an innocent error. Now, can you help me draft a clarification e-mail for the same recipients?'

Hilary nodded gratefully. Geoff smiled, acknowledging how Tom had defused the situation and allowed Hilary to atone for the error. Geoff returned to his desk and saw two more headlines.

The first read *UK Banks in Price Collusion Scam*. Well, that didn't take long, he thought, frowning as he realised it wasn't Brian Curtis who wrote the story. The second heading was *Darren Peters Infidelity Row Mystery* with a sub-heading *UK finance house's bizarre hint at Peters' involvement with 14-y-o*. Geoff returned to Tom's office to see a furious Tom on the phone, Hilary slumped over the desk, head in her hands.

'Well, what do you think? Of course, it's a mistake....We're sending out an e-mail to explain...Oh, for Christ's sake, grow up...Yes, we look pretty silly but right now, I'd prefer to be in our shoes than Darren's....No, you can't quote me on that...No, I'm not passing judgement. I don't even know what Jeffries' story is about...Look, just wait a few minutes, you'll receive a revised statement...Oh and please explain to any of your colleagues who might pounce on this story that it's all bollocks, OK?...Yes, you'll have it as soon as I get off the phone. Bye.'

'That doesn't sound good, Tom?' Geoff asked.

'At least the media aren't printing anything until they've checked with me,' Tom replied. 'Ah. That look tells me otherwise.'

'The BBC of all places,' Geoff said. 'Ignore them, finish your press release. You can argue the toss with the media bods afterwards. They should confirm a story before haring off to get mocking comments in print. It'll be evident to anyone with a brain that you're not implicating Peters.'

Tom nodded, turned to Hilary and clutched her elbow.

'You heard that, Hilary. Geoff's right, let's finish this e-mail. Then we won't need to talk to these people.'

Geoff left and saw Mark Llewellyn striding down the corridor. Geoff hoped he might deflect Llewellyn by saying that Tom was busy.

'What the hell is going on, Geoff? I'm getting calls about us acting as go-betweens in some sordid liaison between that footballer guy and a teenager and more calls asking for a comment about the Johnston Dudley / PJH scam. I thought you guys were on top of all this.'

***

So this is how it happens, Tony Jeffries thought. You get a hunch, follow it, use your initiative, the planets align, you breach the cordon, you're through and the world offers up its worldly goods to you. When he returned to his car after leaving Kelly Spencer's house, he transcribed their conversation lest he misremember any of it and then drove to the ELR's office at breakneck speed, mentally composing the article which he'd write. The editor's approval was a formality; never before had the ELR scooped the nation's press with a story of national interest – their usual fare of arguments at council meetings, crime figures or house price increases were of little interest to anybody outside the borough.

Tony's only lament was that his first foray into mass public consciousness should result from door-stepping a sexually incontinent footballer's girlfriend rather than something more cerebral...still, whatever it took. He was pleased with his resourcefulness in constructing the story from an overheard scrap of Jack Watson's phone call. He rang Watson and received a bland quote confirming Peters' injury; Watson's exasperated, defensive tone was that of somebody at the end of his tether with Peters. Tony also nursed a modicum of guilt over duping Kelly Spencer, a hiatus which lasted about five seconds before he dismissed such guilt as unworthy of investigative journalism's harsh realities.

Investigative journalism! For so long, his holy grail. The story wouldn't win a Pulitzer Prize or rank alongside the work of Bernstein and Woodward but so what? It could open doors to a real career in journalism. Steve Dillon, ELR editor, a cowed man in his early-50s who'd long since abandoned such aspirations was delighted with Tony's efforts. He insisted that the cost of the flowers be reimbursed as expenses and chuckled happily when Tony brandished the ersatz receipt signed by Kelly Spencer.

Tony took the unprecedented step of posting the article on the ELR's website. The newspaper clung to the idea that the printed media was the only important one and their website was haphazardly maintained; most of its hits were for links to local services and planning applications. The Darren Peters' posting changed this and eminent news' websites soon posted links to Jeffries' story. He was inundated by calls asking variously for further details, his sources, Kelly Spencer's address and other more prurient requests about the model.

Tony's colleagues were bemused by the newspaper's sudden shift in fortune and happily acceded to queries from national newspapers and TV stations for information. They asked for a name-check for their proffered quotes which, in many cases, were too bland or unenlightening or both to merit inclusion in the subsequent report.

Meanwhile, Tony revelled in the maelstrom and when the media seized on Tom Brady's false press release, the interest intensified. Briefly, he was thrown by the inference of complicity in degenerate goings-on until a chastened Tom Brady called him to apologise. Brady asked whether the scoop had its origins in Watson's phone call and whistled in admiration. He complimented Tony on his ingenuity and assured him that the recipients of his erroneous communiqué had been contacted. Tony smiled; even a rogue e-mail had unwittingly raised his profile. The one dissenting voice had been Kelly Spencer whose call came shortly after his report appeared.

'This is Kelly Spencer. Are you the bloke who posed as delivery man for a florist today?'

'Er, I'm not sure I know what you're talking about.'

'Yes, you do. I recognise the voice. I hope you're pleased with yourself, you sleazy creep. If you so much as misquote a single word of mine, my lawyers will sue the crap out of you.'

Happy that Kelly had verified his story, Tony didn't reply as she ranted about the press. He belatedly switched on a recorder but she had exhausted her vitriol or, more likely, decided to reserve what remained for her errant partner...that conversation would be an interesting one.

By 6 o'clock, he felt the need to celebrate the upturn in his fortunes and went to a nearby pub along with anybody who was still at the office. Birthdays, marriages and newly-arrived babies aside, the ELR staff rarely had cause for celebration; that this impromptu gathering resulted from the paper's elevation into public consciousness was an added bonus. Steve Dillon recognised the significance of the occasion, placed his credit card behind the bar and the spirit of Dionysius was duly honoured. Wednesday promised to be a slow day at the *East London Recorder*.

***

Near where Tony and his colleagues celebrated, the unidentified person who was the subject of feverish speculation across the internet and Twitter gulped as she watched the breaking news strapline on her television. *Darren Peters injured after expulsion from home over affair with mystery woman* scrolled across the screen every 30 seconds. It was hardly an affair – a solitary knee-trembler to use Darren's charming phrase - but that, she conceded, was beside the point.

Peters was sufficiently high profile to alert the media's most exhaustive bloodhounds. Sooner rather than later, they would identify the unnamed woman. As far as Susan knew, Kelly Spencer was the only person who could identify her as Peters' "mystery woman". Even though Kelly had little to gain from Susan's name becoming public, it was unnerving waiting for the story of her involvement to emerge. Davinia Hotch1ck, a friend of Kelly's, would surely learn of Susan's involvement. Susan needed some advice or solace and, unwisely, sought it from Darren.

'Darren, Susan here. Are you OK?'

'Yeah, thanks. The doctor checked my eye and I should be OK for tomorrow night. I got some stick from the lads and I'll get more during the game but, sod it, I'm used to that.'

'You know that a story is circulating about you and a mystery woman.'

'Yeah, some journalist went snooping round my gaff today. Kelly wasn't quite with it and fell for a stunt he pulled pretending to deliver flowers. She said a few things about me.'

'So that's how it leaked. Are you still *persona non grata* with Kelly?'

'You what? Still in the doghouse you mean? Not even in the doghouse, girl, that's closer to home than I'm allowed right now.'

'Have you been er, asked about the identity of the mystery woman?'

'Nah, just some banter from the lads. I ain't taking any calls. My focus is on tomorrow's game so I won't pay any attention to all that palaver,' was Darren's breezy reply.

Susan frowned. She wasn't getting through here. Peters was either so self-centred that he was immune to the consequences of his actions on others or he simply didn't care. A shudder of revulsion coursed through her, her earlier grudging admiration for so cavalier a spirit banished.

'And what will you say when you're asked?' She paused, her tone was hectoring and she might need Darren as an ally at some stage so she added in a gentler voice. 'I'm just preparing you for all the, er, palaver to follow.'

'No problem there. Depending on who it is, a smile or a scowl will do.'

'And Kelly?'

'Well, she knows of course,' Darren replied, puzzled. 'It was you sent the text that set her off.'

'No, I mean what happens with her now?'

'Up to her, innit? I'll give her a few days to cool down and then see.'

This really was pointless. Susan finished the call. She had no further wish for association with Darren. In a moment of contrition, she pondered contacting Kelly to express remorse for her part in the whole affair. Would that achieve anything? Probably not, but what harm could it do? She dialled Darren's home number. The call was answered promptly.

'This is Susan Pierce. I'm probably the last person you want to hear from right now but I just....'

'Too bloody right, you are. Sure it ain't Darren you're looking for?'

'No, I wanted to say sorry for my er, part in er, whatever may have....'

'You keep clear of me and Darren, right? I can cause problems for you, don't you forget that.'

'Look, I rang to say sorry but I'm not going to be threatened by....'

'Well, just fuck off then,' Kelly snapped and ended the call.

Good God, she's as bad as him, thought Susan. She decided to watch a film, needing something to occupy her mind other than Darren or Kelly.

***

'And then he's like oh my God, you have got to be joking and I'm like no, I'm way serious. And he's just standing there, literally standing there going oh my God.'

'Oh my God, what did you say then?'

'Well, I'm like so, what now and he's like I don't know what to say so I'm like well go ahead and say it and he's like this is doing my head in and I'm like it's time somebody did.'

'Oh my God, you didn't?'

'Yeah and I like walked away, literally walked away. I haven't called him since.'

'And this is like two hours ago and you haven't called him?'

'No but I might if he doesn't call soon. I mean, he's probably like thinking about things now and you know, maybe I should call him. Two hours is a long time.'

'Maybe you should. He's probably literally about to call you and....'

Laura rose from her seat, abandoning her half-eaten blueberry muffin rather than endure another second of the conversation at the adjacent table. She didn't assume all conversations from bygone eras were peppered with witticisms and dazzling *aperçus* on important topics but articulate discourse really was becoming obsolete. Apart from the content, the volume at which banalities were exchanged precluded any attempt to seek refuge in one's own thoughts. The two protagonists in the café sat yards away from Laura but were audible to almost everyone there.

In Borough High Street, the street lights were making an impact as dusk approached on a grey, damp February afternoon. Had she been over-hasty in storming out of the house earlier? What she would do with herself that evening was no nearer resolution and she longed for her living room...curtains drawn, central heating spreading its warmth but that also meant Robert's oppressive silences and an evening of stifling, simmering tension. Anything was preferable to that.

When she reached her car, she craved the abandoned blueberry muffin. Chandra was on a rigidly-observed diet and Laura had restricted herself to sharing a salad in a gesture of empathy. The detour to the café was an attempt to redress this until the shrieking girls caused her to flee. A sign for a Premier Inn tempted her...no: a hotel room was too grim. Chandra had offered a room at her house but the meagre lunch was enough to persuade her against accepting. She wanted to share wine, food and laughter with whoever her host or hostess might be; right now, Chandra was an unlikely candidate for the first two of those.

Laura stared blankly at the figures scurrying past her car and ran through the list of contacts on her phone. She reached J, sighed, closed her eyes and called John. He answered and asked if everything was OK with her, with Robert, with both of them.

'What do you think, John?' she replied sharply. 'Sorry, I don't know. I need a break from home and I've enjoyed talking and being with you. I wanted to ask whether I could stay at your place tonight. If it's an imposition, don't worry, honest.'

'No, no, Christ no, that's not an imposition at all, quite the opposite. I'd be glad to help out. Really, I would.'

She began the short journey north-west through central London, the slow-moving traffic giving her time to think. She'd called John for a number of complicated reasons...and a perfectly simple one: her life was at a critical juncture and she was increasingly certain he had a role to play in it. She ran two scenarios through her mind; one where the recent easy companionship dissolved into embarrassed silence as she realised this was a mistake; the other where John's counselling resulted in an evening of laughter and meaningful glances leading to...enough! There was little to be gained from speculation. Whatever happened would happen.

She parked close by his house, left her bag in the car for the moment and smiled bashfully when John opened the door. He ushered her in to the living room, nodded at the hands-free phone and, with a sweep of his arm, indicated that she help herself to whatever food or drink she favoured. As her gaze settled on a wine rack in the kitchen, he pointed to a corkscrew nearby. A voice penetrated the stillness as the phone crackled into life.

'Still there, John?'

'Yep, just answering the door, Ed. So, tell me.'

'You want the good news or the bad news?'

'I'm guessing, er, hoping you flogged the remainder and that counts as good news? OK, how bad is the bad news?'

'Could've been worse. I found a buyer with a different view to the rest of the market, rest of the world even and I sold them at an average of £1.23 so that's about a fifty grand loss. I have to factor in my fees but I'll halve those incurred today.'

'No, you can't do that, Ed. You spent a lot of time on this. Fifty grand, eh? Not bad for one day. To think that I was lauded at Foden Barnes for having, what was it somebody once said, a natural aptitude for trading.'

John nodded as Laura handed him a glass of red wine. He sipped his wine, smiled and motioned to her to sit down but she stood in the doorway of the room, reluctant to encroach.

'You want to hear the really galling bit, John? Say you'd invested your money yesterday morning in Monochromus, this evening you'd be sitting on a paper profit of about 20k.'

'Thanks for that, Ed, you've cheered me up no end. Seems like Doug's opinion is really valued on Wall Street.' John cupped his hand over the phone and spoke to Laura. 'Doug's the guy who bought from me yesterday.'

'Sure sounds like it. If there's nothing else, I'll leave it there. Sorry you got your fingers burned, you know where I am if you want to try again. The money will be in your account tomorrow.'

'Thanks, Ed. I think I'll wait a while before I get back on this particular bicycle again. Bye.'

John closed his eyes, shook his head rapidly and stood.

'Laura! Just the person I want to see right now...not sure about the circumstances, though. Where's your drink?'

She inclined her head towards the kitchen.

'OK, kitchen it is then,' John said. 'Now, tell me what's happened.'

**

'Tom, emotions are running high here. I'm going to leave now and I'd like you to think about what you've just said. I hope you'll wish to retract it, I really do. I'll be in my office.' Cheeks flushed, Mark Llewellyn pushed back his chair and left Tom's office. Tom stared at the ceiling as Geoff, Hilary and Calvin ruefully looked from one to the other.

'Tom, are you OK?' Hilary asked, concern evident in her clipped South African accent.

'That, Hilary, is known as clearing the air. I'm fed up with that pompous blowhard and I'm obviously not his favourite either. Maybe I should clear my desk; he's not getting an apology and I'm sure as hell not resigning, so he can fire me if he's up to it.'

'But you can't let that happen,' Geoff said, aghast. 'If we can't talk you around, at least call Catherine and discuss it with her.'

'There's nothing to discuss, Geoff. Catherine doesn't like him either and she'll agree with me...'

'But you're throwing away what you've done here. All because Llewellyn knows how to rile you and you're too stubborn to back down. I'm sure Hilary and Calvin would be at a loss, were you to leave.'

'This was my fault,' Hilary said. 'I won't let you carry the can for me.'

'Thanks, Hilary but this goes way beyond the Darren e-mail. It's to do with how that spineless prick avoids responsibility if there's a chance anything will rebound on him. He's allowed Netherby to risk his career and he'll do the same to Geoff if anything untoward results from the JD scam.'

Geoff shrugged, tacitly agreeing with Tom. Earlier, Llewellyn and Geoff had arrived as Tom and his team sent out a retraction e-mail. Llewellyn asked Tom to explain how he'd "buggered up the school visit".

'Buggered up? That's harsh, Mark. I was let down by Darren Peters, left to face a bunch of feral delinquents and then an innocent mistake was pounced on by the media. Right now, we're sending out a retraction. Yes, it's unfortunate but there's no material damage done.'

'Someone in charge of communications should know the rudiments of communication better than that and...' Llewellyn turned to Hilary and Calvin, '...ensure that they're adhered to.'

Tom bristled and glared at Llewellyn. 'And someone in charge of an organisation should demonstrate leadership and take responsibility for decisions instead of relying on yes-men to do their dirty work.'

'What do you mean by that, Tom?' Llewellyn returned the stare.

'You know what I'm referring to. Do I have to spell out the lengths you go to cover yourself instead of having the balls to issue your own directives? You forced Jan into giving the order to offload the stock and you'll deflect blame to Geoff if anything goes wrong with that.'

'I didn't force Jan to do anything.' Llewellyn turned to Geoff. 'Have I made any assertions that you're culpable for whatever Tom is referring to?'

'Oh no,' Tom hissed. 'You don't actually instruct someone to take risks but through inference and insinuation, you get the message across. You know what you are, Mark, you're...'

'Tom, don't...' Geoff interrupted but was hushed by Tom.

'It's all right, Geoff,' Tom resumed. 'It's time Mark actually answered for himself for once instead of letting other people do so.' At this point, Llewellyn gave Tom his ultimatum and left the office.

'So what will you do now, Tom?' Hilary asked. 'I don't know the full story here but I certainly don't want to see you leave over something you'll later regret.' Calvin nodded enthusiastically in agreement.

'I'm touched by that, I really am, but I'm not sure I can continue here if me and Llewellyn are openly hostile towards each other. As to what I'll do right now, I'll carry on with what I'm doing. If he wants to fire me, so be it. If not, I'll just see how it pans out. Anyway, thanks to each of you for your support.' He held up his hands in supplication. 'Ball's out of my court now and I'm not going to crawl over the fence to ask for it back.'

All three spoke at once and Tom grinned.

'Look, let's meet in the Jailers Arms at 6, OK? If you'll excuse me, I need to call Catherine.'

This time, all three nodded and left the office.

***

Brian Curtis filed his report, switched to his e-mail account and sent a message to Philip Anderson: *'Done. Fun starts now. Brian'*. He put on his coat and told his colleagues he'd be in the nearby Thomas à Becket pub, if needed. As he arrived there, he received a call from a sub-editor confirming that the article would be published unchanged.

The Thomas à Becket pub, located close to *The Chronicle*'s offices on Clerkenwell Road, served as a place to air grievances, return favours, execute favours, conduct ostensibly clandestine meetings and affairs even though the choice of venue severely reduced the clandestine component of such assignations. It played host to some of the more dedicated drinkers at *The Chronicle* and Brian was surprised to see Philip Anderson in conversation with one such individual, Christian Kirby, chief environment correspondent. Kirby's commitment to the green cause, according to the joke around the office, extended to his visage most nights by closing time at the Thomas à Becket. Brian slalomed his way through the throng towards Philip and reached the bar just as Kirby drained his glass.

'Philip, Christian. What can I get you?'

'I'm off, Brian. Thanks anyway,' Christian said. 'Cheers, Philip.'

'Bit early for him to leave,' Brian said as he slotted into the place vacated by Kirby. 'I didn't expect to find you here. Shouldn't you be at work defending your friend's honour?'

'My friend's honour? What do you mean?'

'Your mate at Alpha Venture...isn't it him who released an account of something which never occurred and then sent a message threatening plagues of lice, frogs, boils and press releases should anyone refer to it?'

'The Darren Peters story? No, he's not the guy I know there but I did briefly meet their media guy last week. A long story, too boring to relate.'

188

'You *are* well connected there,' Curtis said teasingly. 'Anything you wish to declare? I'd hate to see you in danger of being compromised.'

'No, nothing to declare. So, what happened with your article?'

'Glover beat me to the scam story and he didn't even have the quality of evidence you sent me...but getting in first was all that mattered and I dithered too long. I ended up writing a piece about vultures circling.'

Philip frowned.

'What's with the faces, Philip? You're a journalist. Don't let friendship sway your judgement.'

'First, I'm not a journalist and second, it's more complicated than you think.'

'Is there a lady involved, perchance? Aha, there is...that look is a giveaway. Come on, tell Uncle Brian about it.'

'There's nothing to tell, Brian.' Philip looked down at the bar counter.

'"There's nothing to tell, Brian," he said, suddenly developing an interest in examining a beer mat,' Brian replied, relishing Philip's discomfort. 'Now shall I turn investigative hack and really grill you?'

'There's nothing to tell. Nothing, *nada*, *rien*, zip, zilch, nothing. OK?'

'Protecting your sources, that's admirable. Cheers.' Brian supped his pint. 'Christ, I needed that. It's been a hell of a day.'

'So, did you go in all guns blazing? Name any names?' Philip asked.

'Philip, you'd never make an actor. I don't know why you're so concerned but no doubt you have your reasons. No, I didn't give them both barrels – them being the City as a collective, before you ask. I just referred to pre-warned vultures circling. I decided not to use your information as evidence of how the collusion was common knowledge. It would seem like I was trying to steal back Glover's glory.'

'No, Brian, it would've emphasised how you faffed around on the scam story and got beaten to it by Glover. Look, let's forget the cut-and-thrust. I just want a relaxing drink and a chat before heading off home. OK?'

'Cool. Me too.'

***

Laurence Tolliver sat in what he referred to as his music room, a term which could be applied to most rooms in his house. He refilled his coffee mug and set about listening to the CDs sent by record companies in the hope of eliciting a review. Some he would pass on to a local Oxfam shop - best to allow somebody who might appreciate them to buy them cheaply and generate a few quid for charity into the bargain.

He selected three new albums - Double Dip, Laura Marling and Gorillaz. Double Dip was the *nom-de-plume* of Jim Thorneycroft, not one of Laurence's likes. Thorneycroft, a former pupil at the prestigious

Westminster School, wrote songs about inner-city turmoil which he sang in a confrontational, guttural voice entirely at odds with his natural clipped, patrician tone. This will be 38 minutes and 18 seconds of my life I'll never get back, Laurence sighed as he loaded the CD into his stereo. Nine minutes and 24 seconds later, he yanked it back out of the machine and placed it in the Oxfam pile...another album destined never to be reviewed by Laurence Tolliver.

He was sure that Thorneycroft's record label bosses at Interstellar - Natasha Clinch and Billy Carney – didn't really rate Thorneycroft but his records sold well. The Laura Marling album promised better, the opening track had just begun when his phone rang. It was Susan Pierce.

'You don't happen to know that Davinia woman who writes the gossip column for *The Universe*?'

'Not personally, no. Didn't you have a run-in with her yesterday?'

'Yes and another one just now. She's found out something about me which I'd prefer didn't reach the papers. Did you know she made snide comments about you in her column today too?'

'No...and I'm not interested anyway. So, what's she got on you?'

'Er, I'd prefer not to say.'

'So you hoped I'd have a word with her about something which you don't want to tell me about. I'm not sure how that works, Susan.'

'It's man-related. The wrong man, as it turns out.'

'Ah. It usually is. So, is this affair current or something from the past?'

'It's not an affair, just a...er, it isn't something I'm proud of or want widely known. As you're my manager, I guess I should tell you.'

'No need to unless it's relevant. How serious, or embarrassing, is the story she has on you?'

'It's embarrassing enough.'

'My advice is that if the story is going to get out, it's best that it does so under your terms and if the story isn't likely to break, forget about it. Which is most likely?'

'The former,' Susan sighed. 'Davinia has it in for me right now and I think she found out about this from someone who will be referred to as "the wronged party". So you think I should say something?'

'I can't think anything until I know more. Care to enlighten me?'

***

'Get that fucking microphone away from me, you...'

'Darren, this is live. I apologise for any offensive language, we'll return to the studio...more on this breaking story later. Peter.' The radio reporter made a slashing gesture to his sound technician and turned back to Darren Peters. 'That won't help your case, Darren. It's going out live'.

'Don't you have other stories to cover? Earthquakes, wars and stuff?' Peters hissed.

'Don't underestimate your newsworthiness. Now, can't we have a more civil chat for our listeners'.

'Get the fuck away from me or I'll set security on you.'

'I'll take that as a no-comment,' the reporter drawled. 'A harassed Darren Peters refused to comment on speculation about his domestic life. Sporting a bruised eye, allegedly the result of an altercation with his girlfriend, Peters blah-blah-blah. Is that how you want it to go out?'

'Just fuck off, I'm saying nothing.' Peters replied, waving dismissively at the reporter. His mobile rang and Jack Watson told him that he had been heard swearing on Radio 5. He swore again.

***

The Jailers Arms, despite its doleful name, was a popular pub among office workers from the abundant catchment area surrounding it. It had a boisterous clientele and the sombre group seated in a corner - Geoff, Hilary and Calvin - were incompatible with the prevalent bustle and hubbub. They awaited Tom Brady's arrival, speaking in muted tones.

'So this Deborah left and Llewellyn never alluded to Tom's press release?' Hilary asked. She laughed, lifting the gloom. 'Trust Tom to do something like that...he's fun to work with.'

'True but it may yet be his downfall. He's too clever at times,' Geoff said. 'Ah, speak of the devil.'

Tom strode through the bar, glanced at the table as he assessed the drinks situation and deemed it time for another round, ignoring the eager, quizzical looks from his colleagues. Drinks bought, Tom told them that Llewellyn had packed up early and departed.

'So one-nil to him if his aim is to keep me guessing. Mind you, I've had so many bloody calls from gloating hacks that I've not had time to think. That particular media storm has quelled but another one's brewing. Brian Curtis from *The Chronicle* rang, asking whether we wished to comment on the lack of surprise about the scam story and if this was pertinent to the stock prices plunging today. Doesn't your pal work with Curtis, Geoff?'

'Yes, he does. Well, he can hardly point a finger at us, everybody else dumped their shares too,' Geoff said and laughed ruefully. 'There's always someone worse off though. I know a guy who invested a huge chunk of his own money in Johnston Dudley yesterday. Poor guy must have lost a packet *and* he used to be a derivatives trader.'

'Well, here's to there always being someone worse off than any of us,' Tom said, raising his glass. A television screen in the corner of the bar showed footage of Darren Peters scowling at a man with a microphone.

'As you say, there's always someone worse off,' Calvin said, nodding towards the screen. 'Now, he's *really* having a rough day.'

Tom's phone rang and he rolled his eyes anticipating another query about the Peters' fiasco. Instead, it was Michael Bradley who asked him whether he'd seen his brother, Kieran.

'I met him last night for a drink. We left just after he called you.'

'He didn't call me last night, Tom. What makes you think he did?'

'He made a few calls while I was with him and I checked the recipients on his phone. One was to Fiona, one to you and another to someone called Hugh, sorry, Hughie.'

'Yes, Fiona heard from him last night but neither of us can reach him since and this Hughie guy isn't exactly the best company for Kieran....but I definitely didn't get a call. Why are you so sure he did?'

'When I checked his calls, I saw Michael listed among them.'

'Oh fuck. Kieran always calls me Mikey and he has one particular contact in London called Michael and this guy is, well, he's bad news. What made you check Kieran's calls?'

'Catherine got a call at home from someone asking if we'd seen him. I told him this and he was all apologies. He made his calls and said ours was nothing to worry about so I just checked who he'd called. He sounded like he was going to return home and face...well, whatever.'

'I can understand your checking his calls. Did he tap you for money?'

'No. He seemed worried but sort of *blasé* at the same time.'

'He's away in the head, that boy,' snorted Michael. 'He crossed paths with an offshoot of the Provos, tried to take in excess of what they deemed to be his fair share of drugs money. He's also dabbling in drugs himself and those feckers take a dim view of one of their own doing drugs instead of other healthy pursuits like intimidation, murder and thievery.'

'You've changed your tune a bit about the freedom fighters, Michael, if you don't mind me saying.'

'Ach, we all grow up eventually, Tom. Well, most of us, anyway....my wee brother's an exception. I've tried talking some sense into him but when he's on the smack, he thinks he's invincible. This Michael Doherty, I assume it's him who Kieran rang last night, is a real low-life, so he is.'

'I got Hughie's number if it's any use. Do you know where this Doherty guy lives?'

'Hughie's number, aye, I'll have that. Doherty lives around your neck of the woods, I have the address here. 36, Brompton Avenue, Clapham. Do you know the area?'

'Yes, it's a pretty upmarket place for the sort of guy you've described.'

'I said he's a scumbag, I didn't say he's an impoverished scumbag.'

'OK. So, what's the best thing to do? Shall I swing by Doherty's house and see if Kieran's there?'

'We're talking about a grade-A bastard here, Tom. He won't invite you in for tea and a wee chat and give the latest on Kieran, even if he is there.'

'Well, what can I do to help then?'

'Just Hughie's number will be fine. Thanks for the offer to help. I'll get Kieran out of this and I'll let you know when I track him down. OK?'

Tom provided Hughie's number and ended the call.

'Conclusive proof that there's always someone worse off than you,' he said to his colleagues. 'A hot-head cousin of mine is in a bit of a jam; that was his brother. Anyway, I need another drink.'

After a while, Tom left. He felt light-headed at the end of a bewildering day...his future at work was uncertain and Llewellyn could, if he wished, make life difficult for Tom. Although Tom relished a battle, he wasn't sure he had the appetite for this particular one.

The phone call from Michael was unsettling and Tom wanted to help Kieran in whatever way he could. Maybe he could glean something from a detour to the house in Brompton Avenue. Fired by alcohol-fuelled bravado, it seemed the right thing to do. Besides, it was only five minutes away from his local tube station. Without any real idea as to what he would do, he arrived at Brompton Avenue where the parked cars - BMWs, Range Rovers, Audis – bore testimony to the wealth of the inhabitants.

No. 36 was a well-maintained house with a leafy rosemary bush to the left of the door where a sign politely requested that no junk-mail be posted through the letter-box. The house was brightly-lit and, such was the prevailing sense of ordinariness, Tom felt undaunted when he rang the bell and assumed an insouciant look as he waited on the doorstep.

Footsteps approached and the spy-hole in the front door darkened. After a brief pause, the door was opened by a tall man in his late twenties, his lank black hair complementing a Ramones t-shirt, torn jeans and trainers. A blast of heat escaped into the chilly night and the man shivered in response to the outside exposure. He exuded a sense that although his evening had been disrupted, he was willing to help and said 'hello' in a Northern Irish accent. Tom assumed his strongest rural Cavan accent.

'The name's Tom. Is Kieran Bradley in at the minute?'

The man's impassive expression changed to one of puzzlement.

'Kieran Bradley? Wrong house, no one here by that name'.

'But I was given this address,' Tom replied, checking the number on the door. 'Yeah, number 36.'

'Well, I can check if anybody of that name is known here but I doubt it. You're from the North, aren't you? What's your name again?'

'Tom.'

'Tom...?'

'Tom,' Tom repeated, determined not to be cowed. The door closed to without shutting and he heard voices from inside. Pretending to tie a shoe lace, he stumbled into the door which swung open. Tom saw two figures recede into a doorway as the tall man advanced aggressively.

'What the hell do you think you're doing, pal?'

'Sorry, I lost my balance. Had a few, you know how it is.'

'Well, you should be more careful. No one knows of a Kieran Bradley, best if you check the address again. Mind how you go.'

The door was slammed shut on Tom. If only he'd got a better glimpse of the two people in the hallway. He'd tried, at least, but it was now time to go home. He reached the corner of the road when he heard a door close behind him. In the murky light, he could see a figure on the pavement looking towards him. It wasn't the man he had spoken to and Tom's instincts told him this individual was cut from a nastier piece of cloth then the Ramones' clone. It had been a bad day but there was nothing to gain from hanging around here. Yes, it was definitely time to go home.

***

'And that's how it is and here I am. Sure you're OK with me staying?' Laura asked tentatively.

On the table, plates bearing pizza crusts nestled alongside an empty salad bowl, two empty wine bottles and a cafetiere of coffee. Laura knew what the answer would be but still had to ask. She'd been candid when she spoke of her doubts about Robert but careful not to condemn her husband outright. She wanted John's advice and - she guiltily acknowledged - his disapproval of Robert, however he chose to express it.

Then, she felt bad for trying to engineer what might be the end of her marriage. How had it all come to this? Were they beyond retrieval? Did she even want to continue with Robert? Not a question she was ready to answer at this juncture. Why was she at her ex-boyfriend's house? A man she'd left six years ago because she'd grown to dislike him and someone who now seemed to have transmogrified into the person she'd hoped he would become all those years back. Oh John, why now? Why not then?

'No problem. I er, set up the spare room when you called. It's not Claridges' but you know....'

'Now he tells me,' she mock-sighed. 'Still, needs must. I'll get my things from the car. John, I really appreciate this, I appreciate you listening to me, I appreciate your concern, I appreciate...Oh John, don't you sometimes wish you could roll back the years and, and...'

The tears came as she rushed into the hallway and out to her car.

Christ, she really is on the verge of ending it with Robert, John thought. He pondered on the correct response when she returned; empathy, yes...but not in a take-advantage-of-the-situation sense; rapprochement, no; bewilderment; no. He was amazed that she seemed to want to return to him as much as he wanted the same of her. The front door closed. Sheepishly, Laura walked back into the room clutching a bag.

'Sorry about that. I'm all over the place at the moment. I really...'

'You really appreciate this...Laura, you've said it already. Look, I've done little more than listen and offer some clichéd advice. You go to bed, darling and we'll...er, when I said darling, I, er, meant...'

'Darling? Perhaps you meant darling?' Laura suggested, smiling. 'Can I call you darling as well?'

'Laura, you go to bed. We've had too much wine and you know...'

'Yes, you're right. I'll say something inappropriate soon and...I'll just shut up and toddle off to bed. Goodnight, John and thank you for er, everything. I really...'

Her voice trailed off and she wiggled her fingers, walked towards the door and ascended the stairs. Seconds later, she returned and poked her head around the door.

'Er, I don't know which room to go to.'

***

8 - WEDNESDAY

'Bastard, he really is a bastard. There he is on telly, all pious and reformed and all the while, he's got yet another woman on the go.'

'I know. Pretty poor show, isn't it?'

'Didn't he say that all those stories about him were in the past and he was a changed man? Doesn't sound like it to me.'

'I know. He shouldn't say that and then carry on as normal.'

'It's the little girl I feel sorry for. What sort of a father will she have?'

'I know. Not a good example at all.'

'Feel sorry for his girlfriend, too. No surprise she took a swing at him.'

'I know. You can hardly blame her, I suppose.'

'Mind you, she's no angel herself, is she? A topless model, hardly innocence personified.'

'I know. She must know that whole world pretty well.'

'Still doesn't deserve that, though. What an utter bastard.'

Howard Simpson's emphasis on "utter" indicated this was his final judgement on Darren Peters allowing Philip Anderson to return to reading *The Chronicle* while he had tea and toast at the café. He read Brian Curtis' article under the heading *After You, No, After You – Etiquette in the City*. A cumbersome heading was Philip's first thought, not one he'd use. The article spoke of firms circling like vultures, waiting for news to break about the pricing scam, the rush to sell shares in those firms and concluded:

> *The financial regulators may find it interesting to check the precise timing of large sales of Johnston Dudley and Procter Jones Henderson stock and find many of these sales were very adjacent to the scam story breaking. It beggars belief that so many firms were able to react so speedily without prior knowledge. Of course, such an occurrence would not be unique but one can only feel unease at the brinkmanship displayed here. The feeding frenzy (or, more accurately, its bulimic counterpart) sparked when news of the scam broke saw share prices dipping even lower than would be the case in a market less primed for the news. As is often the case, it will be the smaller investors who bear the brunt of this rather than large corporates.*
>
> *At a time of public scepticism over the antics of so many financial organisations, transparency in share dealing is essential*

if the credibility of the City is to remain unimpaired. It would be informative to hear details of strategies employed by the firms involved in the deluge of shares sold between 3:15 and 4pm yesterday. It would also be a surprise if any of those firms broke the City's code of omerta.

That should set a few minds thinking, Philip thought. Geoff Harris won't be thrilled to read it although Brian could've really stoked it up had he alluded to firms asking newspapers to break the Johnston / Procter story. Geoff probably wouldn't see it that way though.

***

'The bastard, the bloody bastard,' spluttered Geoff Harris as he read Brian Curtis' article in *The Chronicle*. Elizabeth put down *The Guardian* which she was reading and looked at Geoff quizzically.

'Bastard. You send a story their way, they dither over it, someone scoops them...so they try to turn it around against you,' he moaned. 'Brian Curtis has written a wink-wink-nudge-nudge piece in *The Chronicle* hinting at insider trading. Philip wasn't much use to me there, was he?'

'Can I see it?'

Geoff passed the newspaper to her and she read the article.

'It could've been worse,' she said. 'Curtis knew the scam story was being hawked around but hasn't alluded to that. Maybe Philip did you a favour and got Curtis to modify his piece.'

Geoff re-read Curtis' column.

'You could be right but it's a call to arms for the regulators. If they snoop around too much, they could cause trouble.'

'That's the chance you took though so nothing much has changed.'

'Hey, whose side are you on?'

'The side of justice...as always, darling,' Elizabeth replied with a smile. 'Now, shouldn't you be on your way? I hope it goes OK for Tom today. Today's *Guardian* has a gloating dig at his problems yesterday although that's hardly surprising. Something like that is a godsend to the press.'

'OK, I'll be off. Anything planned today?'

'Oxfam first and, as I said last night, I have a few calls to make.'

Geoff frowned. It had turned into a lengthy discussion in the Jailers Arms and he arrived home the worse for wear. Now, he struggled to remember what Elizabeth had told him.

'Oh yeah. Which call will you make first?' he asked.

'The one I mentioned last night, Geoff.' Elizabeth smiled. 'Thought so, you were pretty gone when you got home. I want to return to teaching...at least, I think I do. We'll talk about it tonight.'

Geoff left for work and, en route to the bus stop, called into the newsagent to buy a copy of *Rosebud*. Passing Simpson's café, he saw Philip Anderson sitting at a window table reading a newspaper. Perhaps Elizabeth was right; Curtis certainly had enough information to write something more incendiary. Geoff boarded his bus, flicked through the magazine and saw that the cover story - *Sowing Seeds: the strange tale of Fraser Guthrie's 'lost year'* - was written, or co-written by Laura.

***

'Bastard, the smarmy bastard,' was Tom Brady's reaction as he read *The Guardian* diary column which described the press release faux pas.

> *The Diary notes with dismay more problems for our friends in the City. Mega-roller Alpha Venture (not the mega mega-roller which the tax-payer bailed in 2008 but the mega-roller who made a killing on that bail-out; do keep up) yesterday became an early contender for PR gaffe of the year subsequent to the Darren Peters scoop in the East London Recorder. The ELR's hardly startling news that the anti-monogamist footballer's wandering eye had resulted in his falling foul of Kelly Spencer, his demure belle, gave rise to only one question... who was it with this time?*
>
> *Within minutes of the ELR's story breaking, AV issued a press release alluding to their role in helping Peters display "his unique charm and talents with a 14-y-o" as alluded to in the ELR. Bizarrely, they claimed to have facilitated Peters' "virtuoso display of keepy-uppy" and assured us that both participants "emerged happy and breathless" afterwards.*
>
> *The Diary prides itself on its urbane, broad-minded outlook but this was too much. Hoping for an innocent explanation – the Diary disdains the voguish trend to heap opprobrium on our City friends - we contacted the droll, highly-regarded communications guru at AV, Tom Brady, and received a terse reply that this had, indeed, been a mistake. Whew!*
>
> *Given Brady's reluctance to elaborate further, the devil on our left shoulder suggests that a carefully stage-managed PR exercise involving Peters was cancelled at short notice due to some domestic unpleasantness. The angel on our right shoulder abhors the suggestion that AV prepared their press release in advance to claim some of the resulting kudos. The Diary maintains a balanced view...we merely see a regrettable break in communication within said communications guru's team. Schoolboy error, Tom.*

Tom couldn't help smiling at this laconic ridiculing, one he would relish an opportunity to reply to were it not for his certainty that this was precisely what the writer wanted. Besides, AV's creed was to maintain a low profile where possible and Mark Llewellyn's reaction to more adverse publicity didn't bear thinking about...best to take this one on the chin.

He had enough to occupy his mind already. He had been on the verge of modifying his stance and apologising to Llewellyn for his comments but the chief executive's early departure put paid to that idea. Overnight, Tom's view solidified into defiance of his boss who, he felt, had been unfairly harsh on Tom and his team. Pleased with the restoration of his customary self-assurance, he strode into Alpha House.

An e-mail awaited him from Mark Llewellyn requesting his presence at a meeting in the board room at 9am. The list of invitees included Geoff and other department heads. Another e-mail sent to all staff requested their attendance at a meeting in the auditorium, the building's biggest assembly room, scheduled for 10:30. Most likely, this was a response to the previous day's events and a reminder to staff of the need for vigilance in compliance with regulations. Tom knew that Llewellyn would find it hard to resist making a reference to Tom's problems with the press. Again, best to take it on the chin, he thought...this time with less conviction as he bristled at the prospect of a public humiliation for him and his team, however oblique or restrained it might be.

***

'Bastards,' Kieran Bradley mumbled through what seemed to be a mouth containing fewer teeth than normal. He noticed his bloodied shirt as he ran his tongue around the inside of his mouth....yes, a front tooth missing. His head pounded as he pieced together the last 12 hours which started with a few drinks with a friend of his, Hughie MacDonald.

MacDonald combined occasional labouring jobs with a less legitimate but better remunerated role dealing drugs and was Kieran's favoured procurer of drugs during his sojourns to London. Before he left MacDonald at 8pm for a scheduled visit to Michael Doherty, Kieran scored some methadone. They arranged to meet again the next day when Hughie would place his wider range of pharmaceutics at Kieran's disposal.

Michael Doherty was another *émigré* from Northern Ireland. His genial disposition masked a volatile and ruthless character who fraternised with diverse influential groups, from paramilitaries to politicians to community groups, careful to be either conspicuous or discreet depending upon the circumstances. Although Kieran was wary of Doherty's propensity to switch allegiances when it suited, he also knew Doherty exercised influence which could be brought to bear in easing his return home without fear of retribution.

Doherty's house in one of Clapham's smarter roads was known to Kieran who had spent a night there previously. He was welcomed by Doherty, especially when he proffered a bottle of whiskey, and the host poured two glasses from the bottle as they chatted about their current status. Doherty, by eight years Kieran's junior, was doing well - something he modestly attributed to providence and good fortune. Kieran complimented Doherty on this and asked whether he could exert some influence to help him through his current difficulties.

'Ye know me, Kieran. I'm always happy to help a pal whenever I can. Now, what sort of trouble have you got yourself mixed up in?'

Kieran outlined the problem, earnestly sounding repentant and voiced his intention to hitherto distance himself from any undesirable lines of work in which he had been involved.

'That's admirable of you, Kieran but I'm never one to sit in judgement of others. We all need to make a living as best we can and there isn't always the opportunity to do work which benefits others.' Doherty paused, giving Kieran a chance to contemplate Doherty's own unstinting community work. 'Now, does anyone know that you're in London or in this house, even? I mean any of the boys who want a wee word with you.'

'No, they don't. They know I've left the North...my cousin here in London got a call yesterday but I'm guessing that was more of a shot-in-the-dark than one based on any better information.'

'Guessing can be hazardous, I prefer to take the element of guesswork out of my dealings. Now, I've acquired some credence with certain of the gentlemen you refer to, so I have. I'd be happy to chat with them and try smooth things over but there is, of course, the matter of what the legal boys refer to as a *quid pro quo*. I'm wondering what you can offer there.'

'Oh, I can stump up some money for you, Michael....'

'Kieran, Kieran,' Doherty interrupted. 'I'd merely act as intermediary and I wouldn't dream of accepting payment. I may request some small favour in return at some stage but I'm thinking more along the lines of what you can offer the gentlemen you've crossed.'

The air of feigned indifference was reinforced by Doherty topping up Kieran's glass. As Kieran tried to think of an appropriate gesture or offering, the door bell rang. Doherty looked puzzled, walked towards the hallway, tapped on the door to an adjoining room and called 'Raymond.' A tall young man, scruffily-dressed, emerged and followed Doherty to the hallway. Seconds later, Doherty returned, leaving Raymond to attend to the visitor. Kieran was astonished to hear his name mentioned and saw the accusatory look as Doherty glared at him. Kieran shrugged and rose to his feet, recognising Tom Brady's voice. He was grabbed roughly by Doherty before he could walk to the front door. Raymond returned.

'Says his name's Tom, looking for Kieran Bradley', Raymond whispered. 'That's you, isn't it? What are you play....' Raymond was interrupted as the front door swung open and Tom Brady stumbled through. Kieran was yanked back into the room by Doherty as Raymond slammed the front door shut on Tom. Shoved into an armchair where Raymond stood menacingly over him, Kieran shivered as Doherty's mouth twisted into a rictus of confrontation.

'You said nobody knew you were here, ye wee shite. Who was that?'

'He's my cousin, the boy I mentioned earlier.'

'And why's he here? Why did you give him my address?'

'I didn't. I have no idea where he got it from or why he's here.'

'And you expect me to believe that? Jaysus, wise up, man. Now, you've got 60 seconds to give me some answers or I may have to find ways of loosening your tongue a bit.'

Kieran couldn't provide any answers and wasn't allowed to ring Tom. He was bundled into a car and, after a short drive, arrived at the house where he'd now woken up. Still unable to provide Doherty with satisfactory answers, he was dragged into an unfurnished basement and roughed up by two thugs while Raymond stood by, palpably discomforted by the violence. Before long, Kieran slipped out of consciousness. Now, a searing pain shot through his body as he stood up and noticed a camera positioned high on the wall. He slid down into a sitting position again.

***

'A bastard, that really is a bastard of a shiner you got there, Daz. Hope she was worth it, mate.'

Darren winced as Bob Gray, Wallington Rovers' physiotherapist, pressed an exploratory finger against the area just above his right eyebrow.

'Ouch, yes, it bloody hurt that time.'

Darren's eye had swollen overnight and Gray examined it as a precaution ahead of the game that evening. Darren's night at Jack Watson's house had seen him treated with equal parts disdain and fascination by Watson's German wife, Magdalena. Younger than Watson, Magdalena was disdainful of Darren's preference for a reality TV show as his evening's viewing but cast an approving eye over his toned physique and stylish blue suit. Frank and forthright, she alarmed Jack by declaring Darren 'very handsome, lacking intellectually but maybe he has other charms'. Christ, I've taken this monster in under my roof and now have to keep an eye on my missus as well, he thought.

Jack was relieved to escort Darren from the house and drive him to Rovers' training ground to have his bruised eye checked. The newspaper review on the car radio mentioned the headlines generated by what was termed 'Shinergate'. Jack switched off the radio as Darren gingerly probed his eye. When they arrived, Darren was whisked away to see the doctor.

'I'll be OK for tonight though, Bob, won't I? It's not as if heading is part of my game.'

'I'll give you a tentative all-clear although you might like to wear some sort of protective mask or plaster...whatever's permitted. It must've been a hell of a punch though.'

Darren remained silent as Bob dabbed on more ointment and then allowed him to leave. Darren rejoined Jack who sat in the canteen using his lap-top. Jack looked up inquiringly.

'I'll be OK but I may have to wear a mask or a plaster. That'll act like a bleedin' target for some of their blokes. Shifty lot, those Germans.'

'Not an opinion I'd voice out loud, Darren.' He held out his lap-top. 'Did you know about this?'

Darren stared at the screen and shook his head, both in resignation and denial. The headline on *The Universe*'s website read – *Black Eye, Pierce: Dolly Mix singer the cause of Dazzle's shiner.*'

***

'Bitch! I really hate that meddling bitch,' fumed Susan Pierce as she read Davinia Hotchick's page on *The Universe*'s website. Laurence Tolliver read it over her shoulder, unable to suppress a smile at the "Black Eye, Pierce" pun. They were in an office at Interstellar Records waiting to meet Billy Carney and Natasha Clinch.

'Hate to say it, Susan but I did warn you.'

Susan sighed and nodded. On Tuesday night, Susan told Laurence that she'd been asked by Davinia Hotchick whether she wished to comment on her relationship with Darren Peters - something she declined to do. His advice was to phrase her reply to say she was not involved in any such relationship. Susan knew that Kelly Spencer, a friend of Davinia, had to be the gossip writer's source - based on what Susan hesitantly described as "certain precise details". Laurence told her, if pressed any further, to say that she met Darren at the TV show and only intended seeing him again to fulfil a promise to provide tickets for a future concert. If Susan adhered to this script, she shouldn't see any adverse publicity.

Susan, however, fell for Davinia's line of questioning and managed to inadvertently confirm the liaison. Her appeal to Davinia's better instincts to let the story go was met with contempt at which point, Susan launched into a tirade of name-calling which Davinia assured her was being recorded. Davinia waited until morning before posting the story on-line. Susan and Darren were cast as smitten lovers, leaving a distraught Kelly Spencer with no option other than to evict Darren from their home.

'I've bodged this up, haven't I?' Susan said sheepishly.

'I'm afraid you have but it's done...best thing now is to move on and there's no better place to do it than at a record label where you're removed from manufactured reality TV and tatty gossip columns. You'll find the people here aren't remotely interested in that rubbish.'

Susan switched off the computer as Clinch and Carney arrived to lead her to one of the studios. Susan ran through her new songs as Billy and Natasha nodded approvingly. She was further pleased by their apparent disinterest in her extra-curricular activities when she explained that she was the subject of unwanted media attention.

'Whatever,' Natasha replied. 'So long as you don't frighten the horses and there are no children or Tories involved.'

It was agreed that Interstellar would draft a contract for Susan; a standard one album deal with an extension option. Elated by this, Susan and Laurence left the studio and decided that a celebratory lunch was in order. As they were signing out at the reception desk in the lobby, Double Dip - Jim Thorneycroft - came bounding through the doors. Dressed in a D/D-emblazoned sweatshirt, outsize jeans and white trainers, his cropped hair failed to add a desired air of menace to his polite demeanour. He spoke into a headpiece attached to his mobile phone.

'Got that, yeah? Sweet, mate. Let's hook up later, yeah? Stay safe'.

He paused and performed an exaggerated double-take when he saw Laurence and Susan walking away from the reception desk. He stood to attention with his hand raised to his forehead in a clumsy approximation of a salute and called to the man sitting at the reception desk.

'Yo, Harry, look who's here. It's the lady in the news, the home-wrecking Dolly Mix babe.' He turned to Susan. 'Hey, respect is due. I love that whole meet and get-to-it-there-and-then thing you got goin' on, yeah? Man, we so need that at Interstellar. Tell me you're joining the crew here, yeah? Aw, don't be like that,' he said as Susan dashed out of the lobby.

'They won't all react like him, Susan,' Laurence said when he caught her up. 'He's just an idiot.'

'I've lost my appetite,' Susan mumbled, her lip trembling. She hailed a taxi but changed her mind when the driver's face lit up in recognition. 'See, this is what lies ahead for me. Look over there, two more staring at me.'

She pointed to two teenage boys, dressed almost identically in fur-trimmed parkas and jeans. They nudged each other and giggled as they approached Laurence and Susan.

'I don't believe this,' Susan mumbled. 'If they start on about Darren, I'll...'

'Excuse me,' the taller one said. Laurence and Susan looked towards him, Susan glowering. 'Sorry but we just wanted to say hello, Mr. Tolliver. We love your music writing. Are you writing something on Interstellar?'

'I can't say right now,' Laurence replied. 'But I'm here for a good reason which you'll hear a lot more about.'

'Wow,' uttered the second boy. 'Thanks, Mr. Tolliver. We'll keep our ears to the ground.'

Content with this, the boys walked away, their conversation still audible to Laurence and Susan.

'Me neither, mate, no idea. Maybe she's a photographer or his assistant. Not bad-looking though.'

'Yeah, she's OK. She'd do,' was the indifferent response.

Laurence had to look away from Susan to hide the grin on his face.

***

'Bastard.'

'Bitch.'

'Stupid bastard.'

'Silly bitch.'

'Stupid, badly-dressed bastard.'

'Silly, inaccurate bitch.'

'Hey, that was uncalled for. OK, you win.'

Laura affectionately punched John's arm. They sat at the table in John's kitchen, reprising an old routine of theirs which involved trading insults. It was a game which baffled their friends but was indicative of happy times for John and Laura. John had bought a copy of *Rosebud* and read the Fraser Guthrie article before Laura emerged from her bed in the second bedroom. He enjoyed the account of Guthrie's spell as a gardener although he felt it would benefit from a less reverential approach. He didn't say this to Laura but pointed out a minor factual error concerning the backing vocalist on one particular album track. This prompted her to begin their verbal sparring with John winning by dint of the most topical insult.

'Well done, me. Did you sleep OK?'

'I did. Do you really think it's good?' Laura nodded to the magazine.

'Yes, I do. There are bits I'd do differently but there's a lot of stuff there which never occurred to me. The story will be devoured by anyone with an interest in Guthrie. You do realise that some geeky men will pester you for the woman's address.'

'She wasn't all that bothered about that. She seemed more concerned about her neighbours and Fraser's then girlfriend being the object of

204

interest from those same people. Otherwise, she would've been happy to see her name disclosed and photographs of her garden included.'

'And she's a Guthrie fan? You don't really say that in the piece.'

'Yes, she was...still is. Again, we excluded that bit of detail in the interest of preserving her anonymity.'

'You know, this will change some people's view of Guthrie's er, genius. Had I known *A Good Education* was so lyrically whimsical, I might not have revered it as much.'

'But it doesn't make you dislike him or it, does it? I'd hate to be the agent behind something like that.'

'No, it doesn't but I'll now rethink some other assumptions I've made.'

'Oh dear God, you're going to spend the next few days reappraising *Blood on the Tracks*, *Unknown Pleasures* and dozens of other albums. What have I done?' she mock-wailed, rocking back and forth. John laughed and reached out, steadying her motion. She looked up and smiled.

'Surely we can find better things to do than that, Laura? It's good to spend time with you again. Do you have anything planned for today?'

'Nope, nothing really. Is there anything you'd like to do which involves not doing very much?'

'Now, that's what's known as a leading question.'

Laura smiled again. A brief silence was broken by the shrill staccato sound of her mobile phone. She glanced at the screen and frowned.

'Sorry, John, I have to take this,' she said as she left the room.

***

Just before 9am, Tom, Geoff and their colleagues made their way to the boardroom. Conversation was muted as people laughed without conviction and futilely speculated on the reason for their summons. The chatter died as Mark Llewellyn appeared outside, opened the door and paused when Michelle Holley said something to him.

'Ask her to wait in my office; I'll be with her as soon as I can. Thanks,' he said to Michelle smiling wanly at the apprehensive faces as he walked towards the seat left vacant for him. The oval-shaped table in Alpha Venture's boardroom could be seen as indicative of a democratic organisation. Not for us a rectangular table with its implicit assumption of one person sitting at the head of table, it seemed to say...we're equal here, we sit as one.

The more prosaic truth was that Ernest Fulborough, the first president of what was now Alpha Venture (the original name of Blackfriars Finance was changed on the recommendation of a consultancy firm in 1980) was a devotee of rugby union and tried to incorporate rugby-related images wherever possible. To him, the table shape evoked a rugby ball and the chairs with their H-shaped backs were goalposts. Fulborough, long dead, could look around the room now and see familiarity; the table, the chairs and the group of men – there were no women among Mark Llewellyn's direct reports – all soberly dressed in either black or blue suits.

'Thank you for getting here at short notice. I won't take up much of your time, there's a meeting for all staff at 10:30 and I need to see some of you individually ahead of that,' Llewellyn began.

Around the table, the eleven men present listened and watched, wordless and motionless. They registered the emphasis he placed on the word "individually" and watched to see whether his gaze dwelled on anybody. Llewellyn paused, choosing his words carefully.

'I'm sorry to say that I have to step away from Alpha Venture for an unspecified period. Over the last year, I've developed health problems and my attempt to overcome them has been unsuccessful. The medical advice was for me to take sick leave but I've been reluctant to do so during such a turbulent time. My condition is one where I should avoid stress and it was my opinion that through selective delegation, it would be possible to do so. However, it's become evident to me that this approach,' and here Llewellyn's gaze lingered on Tom, 'would only aggravate my condition...as well as not being in the best interests of Alpha Venture.

'I shall hand over the stewardship of AV on a temporary basis to Jan here.' He gestured to Jan Netherby. 'I will, of course, be available to provide any advice or assistance required and I know I can call on each of you to assist Jan. To ensure that we still function effectively and to further help Jan, a role has been offered to one of our former colleagues. I'm pleased to announce that Deborah Jarvis will return to work on specific tasks which I'll elaborate upon later this morning.

'Most of you have worked with Deborah and she will provide the continuity and experience which we now require. Since she left, she's held a senior role at First Imperial Bank until recently. Her knowledge of the banking world is something we'll all benefit from and I know I can rely on you to provide the support which her demanding role requires.'

'This hasn't been an easy decision to make and even though I hope to return here soon, I would like to express my sincere gratitude for the support extended to me. I said I'd keep this brief and if anybody has any concerns or issues which they wish to air, I encourage you to do so now or contact Michelle and arrange an appointment with me.'

Llewellyn paused, granting an opportunity for others to speak. The room remained silent so he ended the meeting having added that Jan would convene them again after the staff meeting. Llewellyn asked Tom to remain behind as the others left.

'Mark, I had no idea,' Tom said contritely. 'I'm really sorry to hear about this. How serious is it?'

'Heart-related, Tom. I first experienced discomfort last spring and it's been more pronounced recently. I've been kidding myself and it's a relief to come clean about it. The medics say some relaxation away from the workplace should do the trick whereas had I remained here, the situation could become serious. That might still happen but I'm removing the main source of the problem, so to speak.'

'I'm sorry for my outburst yesterday. I'm sure you'll appreciate what I said was said in ignorance of...er, what I'm really trying to say...'

'Forget about it, Tom,' Llewellyn interrupted. 'We've all been under stress. The reason I want to see you is to let you know I appreciate the difficulties you've had with the media...and not just yesterday either. We work in a brutal environment and I want to help ease your workload. The first role I've asked Deborah to perform is to oversee the Communications team. She spent her time at First Imperial resolving their media problems and can do something similar here by working with the media, freeing you up to concentrate on existing work.'

Tom inhaled. Deborah bloody Jarvis was his new boss! She'd risen through the ranks at AV through a dogged work ethic rather than initiative and now Llewellyn had given her a job where initiative was a prerequisite. It would also, no doubt, allow her to humiliate Tom routinely. Boy, would she enjoy doing that. Tom's press release mocking her and Mark was really being avenged and the sympathy Tom felt for Llewellyn evaporated.

'You want me to report to Deborah and she'll report to Jan? What about Hilary and Calvin?

'Why, they'll report to you as normal. No change there. Do you have a problem with this arrangement, Tom?'

'I think you already know the answer to that. Of course, I'll continue to the best of my capabilities...as always'.

'I'd expect nothing less, Tom. If you want to see Deborah, she's in my office. I'll announce her role during the 10:30 meeting. OK, anything else?'

Tom shook his head, stood and left. As the door closed behind him, he caught a fleeting glimpse of Llewellyn's serene expression and fought the urge to return and punch him. Had Llewellyn gloated or been triumphant, Tom would've borne his humiliation better but his boss' calm equanimity was hard to bear. Passing Llewellyn's office, he decided to get it over with and knocked on the door. Deborah looked younger than he remembered, probably the result of expensive grooming and a tanned complexion. Five years Tom's junior, she had always been guarded in his presence but the shift in power now allowed her to be more expansive.

'Tom, it's good to see you. You look well,' she said. They shook hands causing a clatter of jewellery as her silver bracelets jingled together. 'Take a seat, Mark's allowed me to use his office this morning. Poor Mark, it's such a shame he's being forced to take this step but he'll benefit from it. I've tried to persuade him to do so for some time.'

'Good to see you too, Deborah. So, you and Mark have kept in touch since you left?' He might as well get this out of the way too. There was no point in allowing any lingering resentment to remain.

'Yes, we have. I'm er, about to move in with Mark. I can ensure he sticks to the medical advice.'

This was deteriorating further. Tom now saw Llewellyn as a puppeteer in control of his career; here a tug to remind him that he couldn't do x, there a nudge to force him to do y.

'Oops, I forget what a private person Mark is. I'm sure he'll tell you guys soon but please keep that one to yourself for now. I guess he told you how he sees things panning out in his absence. We feel AV would benefit from a more touchy-feely approach to the press. Your methods, successful as they've been, need modification in the current climate. The press are out to get us, we can no longer be dismissive of them. I saw at First Imperial how different the media's perception was when our overtures towards them were collaborative. That's how I want it here too. How does that sound?'

'You're the boss. I won't form an opinion until I see how it pans out but one thing I insist upon is that Hilary and Calvin remain firmly in the loop. We work closely together.'

'Absolutely. Is there anything else?'

Tom swallowed. 'I hope you'll accept an apology for that press release business two years ago, Deborah. It was unprofessional of me.'

'Tom, I have no idea what you're referring to,' she said with a smile. Tom's morning of humiliation was showing no signs of deceleration.

***

Kieran shivered. A combination of the basement's moist, cold air and his inadequate clothing (sweat-streaked shirt, thin jumper) left him ill-prepared for a spell of confinement. The harsh lighting increased his discomfort but, at least, provided some semblance of heat. His jacket lay in a corner of the room and he gratefully put it on, noticing that his mobile phone was missing but the small wrap of methadone was intact. Kieran's first thought was that it could ease the pain coursing through him but the closed-circuit camera was a deterrent. Some of Doherty's wealth was an indirect result of narcotics dealing but he was virulently anti-drugs among his acquaintances. The last few hours had seen a definite downturn in this particular friendship and Kieran had no wish to inflame the situation.

The worst part of that situation was ignorance of events elsewhere. Had Doherty contacted the hoodlums who wished to make an example of Kieran for his effrontery? Why had Tom visited Doherty's house? How did he even know of Doherty's existence? Mikey was the likeliest source of Doherty's address...Tom, concerned about Kieran, had contacted Mikey. Yes, that must be it but Mikey detested Doherty *and* knew the kind of person he was; he wouldn't ask Tom to visit the house in Clapham. Clapham? That was where Tom lived, was that relevant?

Footsteps descended the stairs to the basement and Kieran squirmed. To his relief, it was Raymond who told him to come upstairs. Kieran gingerly climbed the steps and was amazed to see a woman, of an age with Raymond, bustling around the kitchen, happily singing along to the radio as she cooked sausages and bacon in a large frying pan.

'Ach, ye poor mon. Ye must be starving,' she said in a Belfast accent. 'Sit yerself down, I'll put the kettle on. Raymond says you'd like some breakfast. Sure it's the only cure for a hangover and you look like you've got a bad one, so you do. Oh, I'm Monica. I didn't catch your name.'

Raymond's presence was enough to persuade Kieran that he should adhere to this, admittedly plausible, story and having introduced himself, he moaned about not doing this again in a hurry.

'That's what you all say,' she laughed. 'Pound to a penny you'll be back swallying pints tonight. Right, I'll be off. Raymond, look after your guest here. Nice to meet you, Kieran. Mind how you go.'

'What's going on? Why am I now being treated like a welcomed guest?' Kieran asked as Monica departed. Despite the circumstances, he couldn't prevent himself from laughing.

'Mr. Doherty's orders,' was Raymond's terse reply. Kieran smiled, he was now just a nuisance to Raymond who gracelessly shoved a plate with sausages and rashers in front of him. Kieran politely asked for some brown sauce which Raymond sullenly provided.

'Don't you want some tea, Raymond?' Kieran asked. A curt shake of the head indicated that Raymond didn't. 'Not one for conversation, are you Raymond?'

'Why don't you shut up, eat your breakfast and we can get out of here,' Raymond scowled.

'We're away on a wee jolly then?' Kieran realised he shouldn't push Raymond too far and raised a hand in supplication. 'OK, I'll finish this up'.

Raymond's scowl disappeared as he sat down at the table. Kieran sensed an ease in the tension.

'Nice grub this. Who's Monica? She sure cooks a decent breakfast.'

'I refer you back to my previous answer.'

'Good one, you'll make a stand-up comic yet, son.' Kieran chuckled and finished the last piece of sausage. 'Right, that's me done. What now?'

Raymond shrugged.

'And what does that mean? Do I just leave here?'

'Mr. Doherty said he'd be in touch. I think he'll tell me to let you go.'

'Decent of him,' Kieran said sarcastically. 'What's your role here? Hope you don't mind me saying but you don't strike me as a hired thug'.

'It's not just us two here in the house. All I have to do is shout out for help and you'll see what happens'.

Kieran said that he needed to use the toilet. Raymond went to the foot of the stairs and shouted, 'It's all right, he's just using the loo.'

The scraping sound of a chair being moved was heard in the room above them as Kieran slowly made his way upstairs towards the bathroom. An upstairs door opened and a man's face protruded. Kieran nodded, the face remained impassive. Downstairs, the phone rang and Raymond was talking as Kieran walked back into the kitchen.

'Yes, I can...Oh yes, he is. Hang on.' Raymond cupped his hand over the phone and handed it to Kieran. 'The boss wants a word with ye.'

'Kieran, Michael Doherty here. Look, I had a chat with the gentlemen back in Derry. An inconclusive chat. I interceded on your part and said you'd gotten a going over on account of my suspicions. That perked them up a bit so I've done you a favour, so to speak. You may want to speak to them before returning.' Kieran didn't respond. 'Kieran, you still there?'

'Yeah. I'm not sure about this, Michael. I had seven bells knocked out of me last night for no good reason so I'd expect a man of your standing to go the extra mile on my account.'

Raymond nodded admiringly. Kieran had even surprised himself by challenging Doherty.

'I hear what you're saying but you did come to me for help. I'm sorry about the misinterpretation but them's the breaks. I'm not sure I can do any more for you.'

Sensing defensiveness from Doherty, Kieran grew bolder.

'That's a shame. When I return home, I'll do my best not to spread the word that you had me beaten up for nothing and then let me down as a negotiator but I can't guarantee that I won't.'

This time, Raymond smiled in Kieran's direction.

'You just be careful what you say, Kieran. I've gone out on a limb already. Now, put me back on to Raymond.' Kieran maintained a hurt expression as he handed the phone back to Raymond.

'Yeah, OK...What? No, I haven't...I doubt if they have either...I can get some when I drive him there...OK, bye.'

'I'd buy a lottery ticket this evening if I was you,' Raymond grinned as he replaced the phone. 'The boss has instructed me to give you a lift to a tube station, so he has, and to slip you a few quid as well...quite a few quid, in fact. Believe me, that doesn't often happen. Now, are you ready to go?'

'Ready when you are. Can I have my mobile phone back?'

'Oh, yeah. It's in the hallway, Mr. Doherty had to check it, you see.'

'Oh, sure but it's a shame he didn't let me call my cousin. The whole thing could've been explained without any of the nastiness.'

Raymond shrugged as he held the door open for Kieran. Outside, a smartly-dressed woman in her late-50s passed by and nodded to Raymond.

'Morning, Mrs. Hudson, chilly one today,' Raymond said politely and was greeted warmly in return. Kieran smiled; what an odd neighbourhood this was - gentility and brutality in co-existence.

***

Elizabeth put down the phone. She hadn't seen that one coming – Tom Brady had been demoted and would now answer to the woman he'd once mocked in a press release. Knowing Tom as she did, Elizabeth realised that this was effectively a directive to either kow-tow or leave. Would Geoff feel isolated if Tom left? Yes, they were friends. Would Geoff consider leaving in some misplaced gesture of solidarity? No, he had a survival instinct which would see him through whatever occurred at AV. Poor Tom....he could be annoyingly smug and supercilious at times but he didn't deserve this treatment.

Elizabeth spent two half-days each week as a volunteer in a charity bookshop and her Wednesday shift was due to start soon. She saw her leopard-print scarf hanging in the hallway, smiled ruefully, put it on and left the house. Outside, she was greeted by Donald the cat.

'Come on Donald, say something,' she said, stroking his chin. Donald emitted one of his customary quacking sounds. Elizabeth laughed and tickled his ear. 'Sorry, Donald, I can't stay all day,' she said and walked away. Donald looked at her, mildly disappointed, and then moved away to pursue somebody else.

Elizabeth priced books at the shop, enjoying the immersion in a world of books and conversation. For the last hour of her shift, she took over till duty from another volunteer, Melissa. Towards the end of the hour, a teenage boy arrived and began sifting through the DVD rack. He seemed familiar but she couldn't place him. Tall and muscular, aware of being watched, he smiled shyly at Elizabeth. Who was he? An ex-pupil of hers? Possibly. The boy walked over towards the till.

'Mrs. Harris? You're Geoff Harris' wife, aren't you? I'm Michael Benson. We met when I was working for Mr. Harris.'

Ah, that was it...the young boy who seemed overwhelmed by Alpha Venture. She remembered him as a pleasant, affable youth.

'Michael! Of course I remember you. I've been trying to place you since you came in. How are you?'

'I'm good. Your husband did me a favour last week, can you thank him for me?'

'Geoff? Geoff did you a favour? How?'

'Well, I got into trouble and he wrote a letter which helped me out.'

'I'm glad he could help. Are you still at St. Ambrose's?'

'Yes, but I want to move. It ain't a good school and I'd like one where I might achieve something'.

Elizabeth was struck by his sincerity and desire for self-improvement and her plan to resume teaching came to mind. She looked at her watch, only five minutes remained before her scheduled departure.

'Michael, are you free for a while? You see, I'm thinking of returning to teaching and I'd like to hear your take on a few things.'

'Yeah, cool,' Michael replied. 'I'll hang on here, OK?'

Elizabeth finished her work and offered Michael the choice of a café or a bar. He opted for a bar; 'I'll get served with you,' his rationale. She chose one of Islington's ubiquitous gastropubs and noted his new-found swagger as they walked in. God, I hope he's not getting the wrong idea, she thought. Her unease intensified when the barman glanced towards Michael.

'Not underage, is he?'

'What? Of course not,' Elizabeth said indignantly.

'I was referring to serving alcohol,' the barman leered. Elizabeth glared back and asked for a menu. She chose a sandwich and gave Michael the menu hoping he'd select something other than the hamburger option.

'Burger and chips, please, Mrs. Harris'.

Oh well. She affected an experimental accent as she ordered Michael's food and the barman grinned, asking how she liked her burger. 'Cooked,' she snapped. She sat with Michael and talked about his school and his aspirations. Michael explained how his employment prospects were hindered by the St. Ambrose association.

'To be honest,' he said, 'I had a chance at your old man's place last year, er, I mean at Mr. Harris's company, but I blew it. I thought people was taking the piss out of me but I now realise that wasn't it. It ain't easy for someone like me to fit in at a place like that.'

Elizabeth cajoled him into considering other schools in the area. She explained that the school where she had taught – St. Mark's – tried to take on pupils from what she delicately referred to as 'problem schools'.

'I want to return to teaching but I may try a different place this time.'

212

'I can't see you at St. Ambrose's, Mrs. Harris. I'd like to but it won't happen. Why do you want to teach again? Surely you don't need the dosh?'

'There's more to life than money, Michael. Besides, I enjoyed teaching. I was good at it and I miss the involvement.'

Michael shrugged, searched his wallet and peered at a business card.

'Hey, do you know someone called Philip Anderson?'

Elizabeth coughed and attempted nonchalance.

'I've got a neighbour by that name, yes. Why do you ask?'

'I said I was in a bit of trouble last week. It was a court case and he was one of the jurors. Your name came up when I spoke with him. He seemed to know you.'

'Why did my name come up?'

'Through your husband. This Anderson guy asked me about him and I said I'd met you at your husband's office. He acted like he knew you,' Michael smiled knowingly.

'We're neighbours,' Elizabeth said with emphasis. Eager to change the subject and to help Michael, she asked him whether he'd like her to put a word in for him at St. Mark's.

'Dunno,' Michael shrugged. 'Not sure there's much point, I'd have a lot of catching up to do.

'Which subjects are you most interested in?'

'History, English and Art, I suppose.'

'Well, I taught English and History and a friend of mine is an expert on art history. I'd be happy to give you some tuition if you wish. It would get me back into teaching and might benefit you.'

Michael seemed unconvinced - something Elizabeth attributed to a lack of familiarity with such offers - but her enthusiasm was infectious and he warmed to the idea. She mentioned that Alpha Venture would be looking for young people to work on a placement during the summer.

'I think they'd like to offer a role to someone from your school again. You've already been there, you know the score. Geoff liked you but thought you were overawed. Don't take this the wrong way but maybe you were too aware of your own background? Is that a fair comment?'

'Maybe. As I said, it ain't easy for someone like me in a place like that.'

'I wasn't being critical, Michael. Shall I ask Geoff whether he could find a slot for you there?'

'Fuck yeah, sorry, I mean yes, please Mrs. Harris. I'd be different this time, I'd like to learn and stuff.'

Elizabeth smiled and clinked her wine glass against Michael's beer.

'Let's see what I can do, then.'

***

Contented, convivial domesticity would best describe the scene; Laura read a newspaper, John sat at his computer, Laura glanced at John and smiled indulgently, John was oblivious. It was as if the years had been rewound. Robert rang her earlier saying her mother had sent flowers congratulating her on the *Rosebud* article, as had Laurence Tolliver and Fraser Guthrie whose card read *'These are hardly perennials but neither am I.'*

Robert heard the background music, asked where she was and was told she was at a friend's house. This was met by a disgruntled sigh. She felt no need to elaborate further and the call petered out. She then rang her mother to thank her for the flowers and an awkward moment ensued when Mrs. Holmes asked which flowers had been sent. She crossed her fingers and guessed crocuses.

'Oh, I asked for irises. I've had doubts about that new florist in town and this confirms it. I won't use them again,' Mrs. Holmes sighed.

There would always be collateral casualties in these situations, Laura reflected. She resolved to buy the most expensive bouquet possible from the florist on her next visit to her parents and absolved herself of blame. It was Robert's fault. Everything was Robert's fault...except the things which weren't, of course. Well, that cleared everything up neatly.

John emitted a snort of surprise and looked up. 'Hey, I didn't know your friend, Tolliver, is managing one of the bimbos from Dolly Mix, the one who's having an affair with Darren Peters.'

'I met Laurence the other night and he told me about Susan Pierce. I was surprised too,' Laura shrugged. 'He reckons she's talented...and before you speculate on any ulterior motives on his part, there aren't.'

'Yes, you said something along those lines the other night. It seems Tolliver, Susan Pierce and Peters had never met before Saturday night and now she's being managed by one and having a fling with the other. Lady knows how to get her way, I'll grant her that...and quickly.'

Laura was seized by a desire to be alone, maybe not alone but doing something neutral, something devoid of nuance, something which couldn't be misconstrued or mused over. Last night, the possibilities seemed endless as she spoke openly about herself and her dilemma while John listened and gave impartial advice. Now, listlessness overwhelmed her. Maybe she wanted some grandiloquent gesture from John rather than cosy domesticity. Could she articulate this without alarming John or making him feel trapped, without maybe evoking the scenario she herself had fled from at home yesterday? Unsettled by her own mood swings, she told John that she wanted to go for a walk.

'OK, just give me a minute, I'll be with you,' John replied, eyes still fixed on the computer screen.

'Er, I'd prefer to go by myself, just to clear my head. Is that OK?'

'Umm, sure, fine.' He turned and met her gaze. 'Is everything OK?'

'Well, you know. Everything feels a bit odd just now. I'm sorry about all this, it's not really fair on you...but bear with me, please.'

'Of course. Look, you do as you wish while you're here, Laura. That was implicit when you rang me yesterday and it hasn't changed. OK?'

'Thanks. I mean that. I won't be long.'

With that, she was gone, leaving John staring at the door. In truth, John was also pleased to be alone for a short time. It had been a tense few days...ending the partnership with Chris Williamson, selling his shares, the subsequent losses, acting as counsellor to Laura and, all the while, conscious of re-igniting their relationship. Yes, he wanted Laura back but was reluctant to see her involved in a prolonged dispute with Robert although one was hardly likely without the other. Life was complicated.

Laura, too, was happy for some solitude - she didn't wish to intrude on John or to talk endlessly about herself and her problems and she was unsure how to proceed with John. It was best to go for a walk...where she would probably just brood on these subjects. Life was complicated.

***

The crowd gathered in the auditorium hushed as Mark Llewellyn walked to the podium and exchanged a few words with people sitting in the front rows. Tom Brady sat back and tried to assess Llewellyn from a fresh perspective. He looked frailer than usual but also at ease, clearly glad to have taken the decision he was about to announce to AV's staff. Tom had relayed the salient points from his earlier meetings to Hilary and Calvin and emphasised that their roles shouldn't change although he couldn't second-guess Deborah Jarvis's intentions for the department.

He turned and nodded to Geoff in the row behind. There hadn't been sufficient time to tell Geoff about his talks with Mark and Deborah. He guessed that Geoff would be angry on Tom's behalf but there wasn't much either of them could do. After years in this environment, Tom knew how people adapted swiftly to changing circumstances - practical considerations tended to outweigh any indignation felt at hearing unwelcome news. He also knew he should apply this maxim to himself.

After a few preliminaries about recent events in the markets, the need for increased vigilance and some generic complimentary words about the staff's contribution to Alpha Venture's increased profits, Llewellyn moved on to more personal matters.

'I want to share with you a difficult decision which I have made. For health reasons, I will take a sabbatical from my position as Chief Executive - a brief sabbatical, I hope, but I'm unable to be more precise about the duration for now. In my absence, Jan Netherby will assume responsibility for the organisation. Many of you will be aware of Jan's increased involvement in work which had hitherto been mine. I am confident that the stewardship of Alpha Venture is in the best possible hands and I know I can rely on you to provide Jan with the support I've received.

'I will be available if any advice or help is needed. To assist Jan make a seamless transition to his new post, I'm pleased to welcome back one of our former colleagues, Deborah Jarvis. Deborah will report directly to Jan on specific tasks, the first of which will be in the Communications department. The media focus on the financial world is increasingly hostile and invasive and Deborah, as head of Communications, will ease the workload for Tom Brady and his team, allowing them to maintain their habitual high standards.'

Tom, conscious of heads turning, strived to retain a neutral expression. He heard an intake of breath from Geoff and noticed wry smiles around the auditorium. Llewellyn fielded a few perfunctory queries and ended the meeting. Tom returned to his floor, aware of people who would normally be eager to hear his take on Llewellyn's departure but now walked past without speaking to him.

So, was this how it worked? Did the feral nature of office politics mean he was now perceived as less potent than an hour previously? Was he to be accorded pariah status? Someone to avoid lest his diminished status prove contagious? Would he adopt the same approach in similar circumstances? Did he really want to remain at AV should events unfold along these lines?

'Tom.' It was Geoff. 'I didn't see that coming, I can tell you. Deborah Jarvis.' Geoff shook his head, apparently still trying to digest the news.

'Well, I'm sure I'll benefit from Deborah's extensive knowledge of dealing with the media and the outside world,' Tom answered with exaggerated sincerity. 'I hope my role won't involve actually getting into bed with reporters to ensure that I maintain a good working relationship but if it does, I'll have expert advice on tap from my new boss'.

Geoff looked at Tom warily.

'Give it time before jumping to conclusions, Tom. Llewellyn wouldn't make a choice which could jeopardise the company. You know that.'

'*Et tu, Brute*? Jesus! I thought *you* would see this for what it is.'

'All I can say, Tom, is that if you take such an entrenched view of everything that happens here, you'll end up marginalised and embittered. It isn't all about you, you know. Look, I don't want to take sides but you should rise above that mentality.'

'Whatever,' Tom shrugged as he arrived at his office. 'I'll drop by later to see whether you want tea or coffee when I go to get Deborah's order.'

Tom flopped into the chair and rubbed his eyes. Geoff's point was valid but surely he didn't expect Tom to be immediately acquiescent with the new structure. Tom called Calvin and Hilary to his office to discuss current projects. Yes, it was business as normal in Tom Brady's world – that was the dignified approach to take. When they arrived a few minutes later, he gave what he saw as an even-handed, impartial assessment of Deborah and asked them to allow her time to settle in to her new role.

'Oh, that shouldn't be a problem, Tom,' Hilary said cheerfully. 'She dropped in to see Calvin and me just now. She seems really nice, down-to-earth. I can see her fitting in well. I joined after she left so I didn't know her but Calvin's been here longer. You thought she came across better than you'd remembered, didn't you, Calv?'

Calvin nodded but averted his eyes from Tom who realised that he was in danger of losing these two allies unless he acted magnanimously.

'Good,' he said, rubbing his hands together. 'Let's crack on then, OK?'

***

The blue Ford Escort slowed, then halted alongside the pavement outside a branch of HSBC. Raymond McNulty hopped out and extracted money from the cash machine. He added the notes to a larger wad already in an envelope in his coat pocket and returned to the car.

'Here,' he said, handing Kieran the envelope. 'Mr. Doherty said you were to have this.' Kieran thumbed through the £50 notes which amounted to more than £2,000.

'Well, that's something, I suppose,' Kieran said. 'Tell me, what exactly is your involvement with Doherty? You really, really don't seem the type.'

'Mr. Doherty helped me out a while back or, at least, gave me a chance to get myself away from a bad scene. I'm just helping him out in return.'

'I suppose Monica has a similar tale to tell, eh?'

'You could say that, yeah. Now, which station do you want?' Raymond asked, easing the car out into the road.

'Oh anywhere will do. Stockwell's near here, isn't it?'

'Yeah. That's odd.' Raymond checked his rear mirror. 'The jeep behind us pulled over when I did and has now started again. I'm going to stop at the next free space to see what happens.'

Raymond indicated and veered into a vacant slot. As the jeep passed, a leather-jacketed man in the passenger seat glanced disinterestedly at them. The jeep turned left at the next corner.

'Coincidence, I guess. Did you recognise yon boy?' Raymond asked.

'No. Look, here's OK for me. The station is just on the left and I might drop in to a bar for a wee drink. Don't suppose you fancy one, do you?'

Raymond shook his head and bade an apologetic farewell to Kieran

217

whose sunny disposition masked his physical discomfort, the contents of the envelope seemingly adequate compensation. He would visit a bar and then return to the seedy hotel for a much-needed shower and change of clothes. Steeled by a new sense of purpose, he'd meet Hughie McDonald later as planned but refrain from buying any drugs and, then, make a few calls to his contacts back home to see how the land lay. Maybe Doherty had inadvertently given him a way out of this impasse after all.

Kieran fished his mobile out of his coat pocket and rang Tom Brady's work number. He wanted to know the reason for Tom's visit to Doherty's house and also wished to make Tom aware this had been the catalyst for his roughing up. With this implanted in Tom's mind, it would help should Kieran have cause to ask a favour in the future.

The phone was unanswered. Kieran's attempt to leave a message was interrupted when two men stepped in front of him as he walked towards the pub. Kieran recognised one as the man in the passenger seat of the jeep, sensed trouble, ended his call in mid-sentence and turned to run. However, the lingering effects of the previous evening thwarted him and he was roughly grabbed by one of the men.

'You're Kieran Bradley, aren't ya?' the burly man in a long leather coat asked him. The accent was Irish, Southern rather than Northern. The man and his equally thickset sidekick glared at Kieran. It was pointless to deny his identity so Kieran nodded and asked who they were. The men laughed mockingly as they bundled Kieran into the jeep which had attracted Raymond's attention and warned him not to try any funny stuff.

'Oh I won't, don't worry. Care to tell me what this is about?'

There was no response as the vehicle veered away from the main roads and entered a street devoid of pedestrians which ended in a small cluster of pre-fabricated buildings, presumably once offices, now abandoned. Kieran twitched in his seat, eyes darting around anxiously hoping to see somebody else in this sinister-looking neighbourhood. The bravado which coursed through him earlier was now spent, his captors' stern silence adding to his anxiety. The jeep stopped outside the last of the buildings, Kieran was ordered out and told to wait in the low-roofed building.

The small building had once been an office – evident from cork notice-boards on the wall and a small kitchenette at one end of the room - but now, abandoned, devoid of furniture and musty-smelling, it was redolent of menace. Kieran, perched awkwardly on a rusty chair, wondered why his mobile wasn't confiscated until he noticed there was no signal. His stomach churned as he pondered the significance of this. Soon, a car arrived and the dilapidated office's door was flung open. As a squat figure was silhouetted in the doorway, Kieran heard a chuckle and then a familiar voice.

'Kieran Bradley, what about ye? Been avoiding me, haven't you?'

Kieran gulped, the squat man swaggering towards him was Danny Gallagher, flanked by the two thuggish men. Gallagher was known as an "enforcer" in Derry's Republican circles. Although the peace process and decommissioning of arms had brought about a cessation of terrorism in Ulster, a shadowy cabal of hard-liners clung to the belief that their efforts on behalf of Irish freedom merited them an exalted rank in certain circles.

Gallagher, believed to have perpetrated a number of atrocities during the 1990s, was one such individual. It was he who decreed that Kieran had over-stepped the mark in his dealings when he infringed upon Gallagher's territory. Known to be reluctant to venture far from his own patch lest he find himself out of his depth in somebody else's, Kieran surmised that Gallagher's trip to London to see him didn't augur well. Fiona, Kieran's wife, had family connections in Republican paramilitary circles and he'd assumed this granted him some latitude should anything untoward arise. Now, he wasn't so sure.

'Danny,' Kieran said cheerfully, rising from his chair before Gallagher ushered him to sit down again. Gallagher dragged over a chair for himself but remained standing when he saw its decrepit condition. 'I was going to give you a call this evening to talk things over. I was, honest.'

'Ach, I'm sure you were, Kieran, but I can't be sitting around waiting so I thought it best to have a chat face-to-face. Well, I did once I knew where you were. Yon Doherty gave me a call last night gassing on about social responsibility and there being a time for discourse. I never heard such shite in my life...away with the frigging fairies, that boy.'

Kieran chuckled companionably. 'He can be hard work, right enough.'

Gallagher's stare intensified. 'Then why did you run to him instead of contacting me? You knew I wanted to see you.'

'I don't know why, Danny. I panicked, I'd gone too far. I wanted to think it over for a wee while and hoped Doherty could act as a go-between.'

'I wonder about you, Kieran. People think you hide behind Fiona and now you're hiding behind Doherty. It's not what we want in our people....'

'What do you mean about Fiona?' Kieran interrupted, Gallagher's insinuation emboldening him.

'Ach, you know how people are, Kieran. She's a grand girl is Fiona; you were a lucky boy to catch her eye. I hope you don't mind me saying but better men than you tried and weren't so fortunate. I hear she might be more receptive to such approaches these days but I'm sure you have your own take on that....'

'What are you talking about, Danny? Fiona wouldn't get involved with any of your henchmen and you've got a fucking nerve to suggest it.'

'Oh, have I now? I don't like being spoken to like that, Bradley...not by a gobshite like you anyway. Now, I came here with an open mind but I don't like what I see or hear. Your brother is a better man than you, he may have abandoned the cause but he stands up for his principles and he'd never mess around with drugs. I'm sorry but folks won't be happy if I just gave you a wee slap on the wrist and told you to behave yourself.'

Kieran looked around wildly as the words registered and Gallagher's men moved towards him.

'What are you doing, Danny? Look, I said I'm sorry. I'll make it up to you, whatever it takes. I got a beating already last night and I've got wee Aidan and Clare to look after...'

Gallagher gave a barely perceptible nod to the man in the leather coat. Kieran saw it, jumped from his chair and ran, zig-zagging crazily across the room before he felt a searing pain as everything went black.

***

A curt nod was Darren Peters' response to Larry Downing's question.

'Thought as much, Daz. You're a trooper, mate, take more than a black eye and a story in the paper about a slapper to keep you away from a crack at this lot, eh?' Larry said and clapped Darren on the back. 'Not that I condone your er, whatever it is you've done this time. It's about football here, son, let the papers say what they want. Not that you shouldn't take note sometimes, you're setting an example to young kids but the best example you can set is to bang in a goal or two tonight, eh?'

'Boss, you're basically saying score goals and nothing else matters.'

'Yeah, I mean no, no, that's not what I'm saying. It was different in my day, son. You didn't have all them reporters snooping into your life. Not that I was up to anything too naughty and, you know, you should be looking after your missus and kid. You shouldn't be out with pop stars and girls from the telly. Not that I'd blame you, you're a young man and you're given the sort of opportunities any bloke would consider. Tell you what, I wouldn't mind...er, look Darren, just keep your nose clean, son, OK?'

'And score a couple of goals tonight, eh?'

'That more than anything else, son. Now you're sure your eye is OK?'

'Never better, boss. Well, it has been but nothing to worry about'.

'T'riffic.' Larry smiled and turned away. He saw Bob Gray, the club's physiotherapist, and gestured back to Darren. 'Smashing fella, Darren, heart as big as a lion, he has. A black eye won't stop him tonight, not that I approve of him getting a black eye but, you know, always two sides to every story. Smashing fella, t'riffic.'

'Er, yeah, Larry,' mumbled Bob in response.

Darren had a few hours to kill before the team assembled for the game, a European Champions League second-leg against Bayern Munich, the German champions. Munich won the first-leg 1-0 and Rovers faced a difficult, yet achievable, task to qualify for the next round. Darren moped around the stadium and looked at his watch again...2 o'clock.

It would be a long afternoon. Susan Pierce's apartment was nearby but he'd probably blown his chances there. Of course, he could act indignant that Susan had given that tart from *The Universe* all she needed to put together a story about them. Yes, that was an idea – probably best to show restraint if she allowed him to go to her place but, at least, he could do the groundwork to ensure she was still an option. He rang Susan.

'Hey, it's Darren. How you doing?'

'Awful. That bloody Davinia! Sorry but she duped me into confirming what Kelly told her about us. I shouldn't have fallen for it but...'

'Hang on a sec, did you say Kelly told her?'

'Well, Davinia had pretty er, precise details of what um, occurred between us and she didn't get that from either of us. You said Kelly saw my text, she's a friend of Davinia...so it had to be Kelly.'

'Stupid cow. Why did she do that? What was she thinking?'

'Presumably she was very angry, Darren.'

'Yeah but still. Besides, it was her who fell for that newspaper guy snooping around yesterday. You'd think she was trying to get rid of me.'

Not for the first time, Susan was amazed by Darren's self-centred view on everything and his abundant reserve of self-confidence. What it must be to possess such unshakable assurance in oneself even if – especially if - it's based on nothing other than football talent.

'Perish the thought, Darren. Anyway, you called?'

'Oh yeah, I did. I'm just kicking around here, nothing to do for a few hours. I wondered whether I could drop by. I don't enjoy the hours of waiting that you get before an evening kick-off and since your place is nearby...What? What's so funny?'

'You're something else, Darren, you really are. No, I don't think you should drop by for a few hours though it's charming of you to think of me.'

'Oh, OK. I just thought, no, forget it. Watching the game tonight?'

'I didn't intend to but I'll see. What time does it start?'

'7:45. Wish me luck. I'll be the one with a black eye, Pierce,' he giggled.

'Er, yeah, good luck. Hope you win and I'm glad you appreciate Davinia's headlines. Bye.'

Darren set aside his phone, shaking his head. So serious, that girl...she needs to chill. Oh well, maybe worth a call another day. Maybe he should call Kelly and give her a piece of his mind? No. He would just get angry...it was best to concentrate on the game.

Susan set aside her phone, shaking her head. Five years in the music business and she'd yet to meet an ego of this magnitude; it *was* impressive.

***

After a few minutes with no phone calls, the *East London Recorder* office reverted to a normal, sedate pace allowing its occupants to tackle their normal, sedate tasks. For many of the staff, working for a newspaper was much like any other office job. The buzz of activity during the last 24 hours had been an amusing novelty – they'd chuckled at the sidebar articles in the morning newspapers about the small, local publication which scooped the nationals - but as daily routines and, more worryingly, lunch breaks were disrupted by incessant calls, the mood changed.

Unrest festered and Tony Jeffries faced hostility as the agent behind the disruption. Jeffries fielded as many calls as possible, placating some of his colleagues but that compromise was threatened when editor, Steve Dillon, began to allocate some of Tony's duties to other members of staff.

'Look, can't you see he's busy?' Steve pleaded. 'He's talking to somebody from *The Times* right now. It'll only take a few minutes to phone around and see whether there's any interesting cases in the local courts. We have to look after our usual stories as well, you know.'

'Tell bloody Jordan there to get his finger out then,' was Ted Cohen's resentful reply as he donned his jacket. Cigarette breaks punctuated Ted's day and he still felt aggrieved by what he termed discrimination since smoking had been outlawed in the office. 'I need a cigarette before I can turn my mind to anything else.'

Tony finished his call and saw that the prevailing mood was not in his favour. 'OK, that's all the calls I'm taking for now,' he announced loudly. 'Stuff to be getting on with. Are you OK, Steve?'

'You couldn't dial around the courts and see if there's anything afoot?' the editor asked, deferentially. 'I'd get one of the others to do it but...'

'No problem, boss,' Tony replied, gazing around the near empty office. 'Feeding time, I guess.'

'They haven't all got your work ethic, Tony,' Steve said wistfully.

'Different strokes for different folks. Once I've rang around, I was thinking of trying another angle on Darren Peters, maybe give him the chance to respond. What do you think?'

'A dog with a bone, huh? You think there's more mileage in it?'

'Could be worth a try, Rovers are playing tonight and there was something on the TV just now about Peters arriving at the stadium for a check-up before he's given the go-ahead. I may wander over there; we're always accredited for home games although we're probably not their favourite at the moment, certainly not Darren's favourite anyway.'

Steve grinned and tapped Tony gently on the shoulder.

'You won't be here much longer if you get another scoop is what I'm thinking. OK, go for it, mate.'

Tony made his phone calls and drove the short distance to Wallington Rovers' stadium. The club liked to portray the image of being proud of their roots in London's East End even though they were owned by a consortium of Dubai oil magnates. To endorse the club-as-part-of-the-community profile, local newspapers were welcome albeit with subtle hints that favourable coverage was anticipated in exchange for the hospitality.

The Darren story jeopardised the ELR's place in this cosy arrangement and Tony thought it advisable to appear at the stadium as soon as possible to smooth over any difficulties and maybe have a conversation with Peters into the bargain. He sauntered to the media centre door and smiled when he saw Bill Smith was the security guard on duty. Bill, a kindly man in his sixties, usually ensured that ELR representatives were well looked after at the stadium. He waved cheerily when he saw Tony.

'TJ! You OK, son?'

'Yeah, I'm good, Bill. You?'

'Mustn't grumble. Hope you're not causing more trouble for our boy wonder?'

'Oh, I'm just a humble hack, Bill, seeking out the truth and keeping the punters informed. Am I still welcome here?' Tony asked.

'Probably more than ever with some of us. Great footballer and a nice bloke when he wants to be but he sometimes acts as if he owns the place.'

'No one player is bigger than the club, eh?' Tony replied using a stock football cliché...one which Bill evidently didn't subscribe to.

'Well, certain players are more important than others and Dazzle's one of those players. No, the theory is he'll play out of his skin to prove a point. Here, is it true you posed as a delivery man to get a quote from his missus?'

'Some role-playing was used, yes.'

'A word to the wise, TJ. Don't ruffle Kelly Spencer's feathers too much. Her brother is a nasty bit of work and she's not above using him to put the frighteners on anyone who puts her nose out of joint.'

'Cheers, I'll bear that in mind, Bill. Anything happening here today? I hoped to get a word or two in advance of the game or the skinny on Darren's fitness. Sounds like he'll be playing?'

'It'll take more than a black eye and a tabloid story to keep him out of this one. I was in Germany for the first leg and he was like a caged tiger on the flight home, itching to get another crack at them. I can't give you free access today. Everyone has to go through the press office and they'll be reluctant to let you near Darren. Is that why you're here early?'

'Can't get much past you, Bill,' Tony laughed. 'Yes, I hoped to have a few words with the man himself, get the ELR onside with him again.'

'More than my job's worth to let you through. Sorry, mate, I have to play this one by the book.'

'No problem, Bill.' Tony patted the security man's shoulder and walked back to his car as it was too early to wait around for kick-off. He saw Jack Watson in the car park. Since Watson was unlikely to answer any of his calls, talking to him represented Tony's best chance to make contact. He approached the agent and asked to speak to Darren.

'Run that past me again. You want him to...what exactly?'

'Comment on recent stories, give his side, mention the abandoned school visit yesterday, whatever...engage with the local readership.'

'I don't think you're high on the list of people Darren wishes to engage with right now but I'll put it to him.'

'Thanks. Like I said, it gives us a chance to hear his side of things.'

Jack smiled. Darren's side of things was probably best kept to himself but he made the call, saying a reporter was looking for a few words.

'Why? What's in it for me? Who is it anyway?'

'It's the guy who door-stepped Kelly yesterday. No, wait, he wants a different angle, your side of the story or however you want to put it'.

'Nah, not interested. He got his story by hassling Kelly and I can't forgive him for that, last thing the girl needed...although, hang on, I've got an idea. I *will* speak to him. I'll see you in a few minutes.'

A sense of trepidation crossed Jack's mind. Darren's "ideas" didn't have a good track record - even some of those sanctioned by Jack himself. However cleverly conceived, the idea was always at the mercy of Darren's unpredictable and dissolute lifestyle – the St. Ambrose fiasco being just the latest example. He told Tony that Darren would meet him in a short while, once he'd arranged a suitable venue.

***

Having walked for 30 minutes, Laura decided to return to John's house. She turned a corner and found herself in Lincoln's Inn Fields outside Sir John Soane's Museum. John's house was relatively close to the museum so it wasn't an unlikely occurrence but it added to the sense of providence which occupied her during the walk. The museum, much loved by John, contained a cornucopia of artefacts, curios and paintings.

Laura had accompanied him there but it was some time since her last visit. As she entered the elegant townhouse which housed the museum, she was transported back to her first visit. John was enthralled by two sets of William Hogarth's paintings in the museum - the *Rake's Progress* and the *Election Entertainment*. He explained the nuances and coding implicit in the paintings and she understood their appeal to someone besotted by cinema and literature. *The Rake's Progress*, John's favourite, depicted a young man's descent from entitlement and wealth, ending his days the subject of public ridicule in an asylum. Hogarth's mastery of narrative painting came from capturing significant moments in his subject's life and Laura tried to visualise how Hogarth would interpret her "progress".

The first scene would show the Holmes family departing an American clapboard house, 'England' emblazoned on their luggage, parents smiling, daughter too young to register what was occurring as relatives waved goodbye. Scene 2 would depict Laura, wearing a graduation gown and mortarboard, strolling across the quad of her Cambridge university, a red-bricked seat of learning in the background. In one hand, an employment contract protrudes from an open envelope while her other hand holds a glass of champagne. She looks happy, eager to embrace what lies ahead.

Next, we'd see her sitting at a desk in a high-tech office, peering at rows of green numbers on a computer screen while a man wearing a pin-striped suit stands nearby gazing approvingly at her, holding a newspaper with the headline *AV profits up...again.*

Scene 4 would show Laura sitting opposite John at a table in a bar with snow-topped mountains in the distance, a key with no. 14 in her jeans pocket, no. 43 in his, both of them laughing as their eyes linger on each other; alongside them another couple, her with key no. 43 on the table in front of her, him with key no. 6 visible in the back pocket of his jeans.

Scene 5 would see Laura and John sitting at a table, him reading the *Financial Times* while she scans *Sight & Sound*. Portents of discontent are visible - a scattered pile of DVDs hint at an argument and an invitation to a National Film Theatre screening addressed to John, torn in two.

Scene 6 would depict Laura and Robert departing a hotel after their wedding, looking happy as the guests, many of a decidedly bohemian bent, wave to them. Laura's parents are seen smiling but their smiles have a rueful edge, Robert clearly not their choice for her.

She could then only speculate on the next scene...Laura and Robert proudly watching a toddler crawl on the floor in their house? Or Laura at John's house with a removal lorry outside? She looked again at the Hogarth paintings, searching for clues but the callousness, avarice and debauchery depicted therein was something she hoped never to be privy to.

Marrying Robert, she was now convinced, had been a mistake. She wanted a way out, one which involved John. He was a different person to the one she'd left six years earlier – more considerate, mature and with a more rounded view on life. He seemed eager to reunite with her but would his ardour withstand a prolonged divorce? Earlier, she'd wanted some significant gesture from John but, on reflection, why shouldn't it come from her?

As she left the room containing the Hogarth paintings, she glimpsed the scene in the *Rake's Progress* series with the marriage of the eponymous rake, Tom Rakewell, to a one-eyed heiress while Sarah, the girl he'd repeatedly rejected, tried in vain to prevent the marriage. Tom's motive for marriage was to help offset debts incurred from his profligate life.

John had lost a lot of money over the previous couple of days, should she see this as a warning? Chiding herself for this line of thought, she left the museum with a fresh resolve; her progress revolved around John, not Robert. The mistakes which she and John had made would serve them well if they faced a future together whereas her relationship with Robert was beyond repair. She hailed a taxi and returned to John's house.

John was reading comments posted on a Fraser Guthrie website forum when the doorbell rang. He padded towards the door, recognised Laura's silhouette and wondered why she hadn't used the key he'd given her. Politeness, presumably. He opened the door to a flushed-faced Laura.

'You should use your key,' he said with a smile.

'Sorry. I hope I'm not interrupting anything.' She smiled coquettishly and flopped into an armchair as he nodded towards the computer.

'I've been on the Guthrie website. You've certainly sparked off a debate…a few comments along the lines of women being suited to writing on gardening, a few who've hunted down your journalism and are amazed you write authoritatively about cinema, politics and music. Poor Nick gets some flak, basically for having views other than that of the person posting. There's a thread on the address of the garden. One guy thinks it's in the same road as his mum's house and he's going there to check. There really are some sorry cases out there. Anyway, where did you go?'

'Oh, I just wandered around. I was at the John Soane's museum and wondered how Hogarth would depict my life. I guess you could call it progress. Sorry,' Laura added as John groaned.

'But what would Hogarth call such a series? He did *A Harlot's Progress* but you don't really fall into that category.'

'I'll take that as a compliment. Wasn't the girl in *A Harlot's Progress* called Moll Hackabout? How about calling mine *A Hack's Progress*?'

'Good one. It tracks the life of Laura Writealot as she wends her way through the labyrinth of journalism. So, tell me what happens to Laura.'

'She has her ups and downs but I didn't see the later scenes. I'm not really sure what happens.'

'I think I know. We need to go upstairs to find out.'

***

Tom stifled a yawn and jiggled his right foot to ease a tingling sensation. Ennui set in during Jan Netherby's meeting with his new hierarchy and Tom realised he'd spent a full minute trying to remember the correct term for the sensation of one's foot falling asleep. What was that word? Para-something? He felt isolated, his presence here hardly necessary with Deborah speaking for the communications team. Jan was questioned deferentially and his excruciating attempts at humour were greeted by approving nods. Tom grimaced when someone addressed him as Ned.

'I'd prefer Jan from now on. Ned doesn't strike the right tone for acting CEO of Alpha Venture,' Netherby replied.

Geoff flashed Tom a sympathetic smile and Tom regretted his earlier sarcasm; he had no wish to distance himself from Geoff. Again, he tried to remember that word. Immediately after Netherby's meeting, Tom had to attend another with Deborah, Hilary and Calvin and sighed when Hilary enthused over Deborah's "vision, going forward, on how we should interface with our external contacts in a more collaborative partnership". To Tom, it was all style (and not even much of that) and no substance.

Geoff's warning about being marginalised was already becoming fact as he longed to escape this litany of managerial mumbo-jumbo, buzzwords and platitudes. It came to him...paraesthesia. That was the word he was trying to remember. He surreptitiously checked it on his Blackberry and saw "numbness" as one of the definitions. How apt.

The meetings finally over, Tom wearily returned to his office and listened to his voicemail messages. One had a backdrop of whooshing sounds, somebody calling while on the move.

'Tom, are ye there?...You're not. Listen, give me a call when you get a chance. I got in trouble last night when you turned up out of the blue at Michael Doherty's house. What were you doing there? Anyway, give me a...oh fuck, him again....'

Kieran's call ended abruptly. Tom played the other messages in the vain hope of another call from Kieran. So, Kieran had been at Doherty's house after all and he'd suffered as a result of Tom's attempted intervention. Not badly, Tom hoped, but it seemed that Kieran was now in fresh trouble. Doherty? Worse? Tom called him but could only leave a message. Five minutes later, a call came from Kieran's number.

'Hello, is that Tom?'

Tom didn't recognise the tentative voice. 'Yes. Who is this?'

'Detective Sergeant McCulloch. What's your connection to the man you just called?'

'I'm his cousin. What's happened? Where's Kieran?'

'Can you describe Kieran to me, please?'

Tom did so. After a pause, McCulloch said that a man answering Tom's description had been shot and rushed to hospital where his condition was giving cause for concern. Tom was asked whether he knew of any reason for the shooting and replied that Kieran had a tendency to rub people up the wrong way but he didn't think he was in danger of being shot. Cognisant that his defensiveness wasn't helping Kieran, Tom told the detective about his cousin's call. They agreed to meet.

Tom excused himself from work - a domestic issue to deal with – and took the underground to Stockwell, then a cab to the police station located between there and Clapham. He was met by McCulloch and ushered into an empty room. McCulloch, a softly-spoken Londoner, was a wiry man with a tendency to avert his eyes from his addressee before suddenly fixing them with an intense stare.....this, presumably, the undoing of many suspects when interviewed by the detective.

Kieran had been found in an office on a disused industrial estate nearby. A security guard on another part of the estate heard a shot followed by a car's hasty departure. He quickly located the building where Kieran, bleeding heavily, was unconscious with two bullet wounds in his shoulder. The guard's alertness had saved Kieran.

Tom relayed what he knew about Kieran's visit to London, vaguely mentioning the circles in which Kieran moved. McCulloch filled in the blanks for himself and contacted his counterparts in Belfast for more information. He called Fiona and allowed Tom to assure her that Kieran was being attended to. McCulloch asked Tom what he knew of Michael Doherty and Tom described his visit to Doherty's house in detail.

'Doherty's known to us, not necessarily as somebody who'd carry out a shooting but he exists along what could be called...,' a wry smile, '....the margins of legality. So, your cousin was there last night; seems like your visit was to his detriment.'

Tom swallowed.

'I'm not blaming you for that and I doubt Mr. Bradley would either, I'm just stating what seems to have occurred. I guess Doherty is the man I need to see now. It shouldn't be hard to find him.' McCulloch smiled at Tom's puzzled expression. 'Of course, you don't know him, do you? Let's just say he likes to make himself available to anyone who may be of use to him. That includes the police although maybe he won't be so eager to see us this time. Do you know Mr. Bradley's wife well? She didn't sound too perturbed by the news that her husband had been shot.'

'Fiona's a firebrand and I guess you could say that she's not very forthcoming to the forces of law and order.'

'Would you like to elaborate on that?' McCulloch fixed Tom with his steely gaze. 'It may be of help to Kieran. Am I right in thinking he's mixed up in something dodgy?'

'He has been in the past.' Tom returned McCulloch's stare. 'Fiona is well connected by all accounts and, as I said, she's quite a feisty person.'

'OK, I get the picture. He had over two grand in cash in his jacket. Do you know anything about that?'

Tom didn't and the detective gestured to Kieran's mobile on his desk.

'I'll hang on to this phone. Mr. Bradley won't need it just yet by the sound of things and it may help us find whoever shot him. I don't think he or they intended to kill – either that or they're a pretty lousy shot, he was in an enclosed area and unarmed. Hopefully, I'll know more soon. You can visit him but when he comes around, I'll want to talk to him. One last thing, are you close to Mr. Bradley?'

'Not particularly. We make promises to meet more often but it never happens. He is family but we've had our differences over the years. Why?'

'Just wondering. OK, I have your number if there's anything else.' McCulloch paused. 'Do *you* have anything else?'

'I was curious as to why you rang and immediately identified yourself. Mine was probably the last number he called....surely I was a suspect.'

'True, would've been slack on my part were you involved but I ran a check on your number...an office number which Mr. Bradley rang not long before the shooting and also a distance away. You were hardly likely to be the gunman.' McCulloch smiled. 'I also looked up your name and job and Mr. Google led me to conclude that you've got issues of your own at the moment and would probably be happy to help me. I'm sorry it was your cousin who was shot and I hope he comes through all this.'

Tom picked up his coat and left the room – truly, there was no escape from humiliation for him today. Outside, he rang Fiona and was struck by what McCulloch had picked up from her tone, albeit a tone which now contained genuine concern. She was booked on the next flight to London, her sister would look after the two children and no, she didn't need a place to stay. Tom told her of his unwitting involvement in Kieran's problems.

'Doherty! Jesus, Kieran will never learn,' she snorted. 'Had I known he'd contact that bastard, I wouldn't have let him leave. Is he OK, Tom? I'm not sure yon copper was giving me the whole story.'

'Well, he wants to speak with Kieran which is encouraging - he must expect him to come around soon. Did you ring the hospital?'

'Yes. Under observation, serious condition...that sort of stuff but they sounded positive-ish too.'

'That's good. Er, do you have any idea who did this?'

'I've got an idea right enough. Kieran's made himself enough enemies but I didn't think it'd come to this. He's been...he's been dabbling in drugs and, you know, I'm not sure it's done him much good.'

Tom bit his lip, resisting the urge to ask whether Fiona expected otherwise. He made some conciliatory noises, said he'd visit Kieran and ended the call. It occurred to Tom that Michael Bradley could be of more use to the detective than Fiona. He retraced his steps, gave McCulloch a number for Michael and left the police station. "All this", as McCulloch had put it, placed Tom's tribulations at work into perspective and he recalled the pub conversation with his colleagues and their mantra - there was always someone worse off than you. How very true.

***

Testosterone was almost tangible in the air as 18 men performed various rituals governed by superstition, habit and nerves. Victor Obeyi, tall, African, eyes closed, hands clasped together, swayed trance-like. Gio Antonelli, a swarthy olive-skinned Italian, balanced a football on his left index finger, spun it clock-wise, then anti-clockwise, two rotations in each direction. Vassily Cherenko, a pallid Serbian, plucked nervously at his scraggly beard, repeatedly checking the clock on the wall. Noël Rotane, the serene Frenchman, sat with legs splayed as he stared at a door jamb yards away, a smile playing on his lips. Dave MacKinnon, an imposing Londoner with cropped hair bounced a football repeatedly against the whitewashed wall, rocking back and forth on the soles of his feet...and then there was Darren Peters, laughing at a text message and relaying it to the Wallington Rovers players sitting either side of him.

'Get it?' he asked Paul Nevin. *'Good luck Daz, turn 'em into sour Krauts.* Sauerkraut's a German sausage, innit? He's funny, my mate Gary, wicked sense of humour, clever bloke, you and him would get on.'

'Er, yeah. Sauerkraut isn't a sausage, by the way. It's a, oh, never mind...' Nevin's voice trailed off.

'Here, speaking of sausages,' interjected Ashley Murdoch, the giant goalkeeper who even Darren viewed as vulgar. 'Who you gonna play hide-the-sausage with next, Daz? Going to work through the rest of them Dolly Mix birds, eh? You're a boy, Daz.'

'Leave it out, Ash. I've already got a girlfriend. Me and Kelly are solid.'

'You what? So why the black eye? A love bite is one thing but I ain't ever heard of a love shiner.'

'Just leave it, all right?' Darren said sternly.

'Only a bit of banter, is all.' Murdoch mumbled as he concentrated on his own pre-match ritual – reading tabloid newspapers. Darren smiled and nudged MacKinnon who wagged a finger in warning to Murdoch. Murdoch glanced at Darren with concern.

230

'Had you there, Ash,' Darren guffawed. 'Don't worry, mate, I've not gone soft in the head over all that newspaper palaver. Ah, here's the boss.'

Larry Downing, wearing a generously-cut blue suit, bounced into the dressing-room, a vapour of after-shave trailing in his wake. He clapped his hands urgently.

'All right, lads, this is it, the big one. You hardly need any words from me tonight. A big European night, get in there! Let's see some passion, let's see some fight. We're Wallington and these foreigners, they don't like it up 'em. No disrespect, Noël, Vassily, Bratislav, Juan, umm, Victor, Andreas, Olaf, Gio, er, Ivan, Jean-Paul, Sean, Dimitri, Christian, Felipe...' Downing scanned his squad, the native British-born forming a very small minority.

'No disrespect but foreign teams can wilt when they come up against the best English sides. We have the crowd behind us, roaring us on, worth a goal to us they are. Get in their faces, show 'em what we're about, get stuck in. OK?' he yelled, slamming a clenched right fist into the palm of his left hand and wincing as an out-sized ring jagged the flesh. 'But don't forget they're German, they ain't like other foreigners, they're strong, controlled. We have to be clever, keep our focus, slow it down, draw them out.'

Downing lowered his voice. 'Yeah, we have to be clever, patient, focused. And then...' A smack of his left fist into the palm of his right hand as his voice soared again. 'And then, we hit them, hit them hard, get in their faces. We bloody do 'em. Got that? You're smashing lads, t'riffic, now go out there and do it. Get in!'

'You heard what the gaffer said,' Dave MacKinnon roared, chest thrust forward. 'Passion, fight, hit them hard, focus, clever...and that.'

The players scrambled to their feet and filed out into a wide corridor which led to the pitch. Darren stopped and muttered, 'Oh bloody hell.'

'What's up, Darren?' asked a concerned Paul Nevin.

'I left a journalist bloke, him who wrote the story about Kelly, while I answered a call and forgot to return. He's probably been stuck in the kit-room for the last hour, the door locks from the outside.'

'Tell Bill Smith. He knows all those guys and everyone likes old Bill.'

'Good idea. Serves him right for stitching up Kelly anyway but I'd better not give him a reason to write something nasty about me.'

'Especially since you give journalists so little ammunition, Darren,' Paul replied with a grin.

Darren quickly tracked down Bill Smith, asked him to release Tony Jeffries, get Jeffries a seat in the directors' box, a few drinks and promise him an interview after the game.

***

The rain persisted as Geoff rushed along Russell Road, broken spokes in his umbrella rendering it ineffective. Donald the cat sat forlornly under a tree which barely kept him dry. His strangulated croak alerted Geoff who stroked the cat's chin. A few friendly words were enough to fortify Donald for the next stage of his vigil.

'You're welcome to come to our place, Donald. Poor puss, not a nice evening to be out, is it?' Geoff said as he heard footsteps approaching.

'You do realise that he'll never answer you,' drawled Philip Anderson, slowing to a halt. 'Poor old Donald, it's not a good evening to be out.'

'That's what I said to him. Good day? Better than mine, probably.'

'Ah.' Philip swallowed. 'Was there fallout from that shares business?'

'Oh that died down, to be honest. Other issues came to the fore.'

'Er, sorry about Brian writing something other than was intended. I hope there aren't any repercussions for you.'

'I don't think there will be but thanks for your concern. I don't blame him for writing that article and, to be honest, he was pretty restrained. He had enough material to really put us through the mill.'

'Honour among thieves, eh? Had Brian penned something really damning about AV, he would've needed my help and I like to think I wouldn't have given it. But who knows? I'm only human. Must get myself inside. Say thanks to Elizabeth from me, that meal was lovely. I'll invite you two for something to eat soon...or as soon as I learn how to cook.'

'We'll look forward to it. She enjoys visiting houses she hasn't been to, always on the look-out for ideas. Have a good evening.'

'You too,' Philip said as Geoff completed the short walk to his house. Philip scratched Donald's ear and was rewarded with a guttural quack.

'I think this is an act, Donald,' Philip said as he stroked the cat's glossy coat. 'You worked out that cats don't make the noises you do and it gets you attention, you clever boy.'

Philip stepped away and opened the gate which led to his small front garden just as Howard Simpson also arrived at his house. 'Nasty evening, Philip,' Howard said cheerfully. 'Forecast said it would get worse too.'

Philip unlocked his front door, walked through to his living room and stretched out on the sofa. He felt a wave of melancholy as he viewed his current circumstances and thought enviously of Geoff going home to Elizabeth and Howard joining Geraldine. His married friends often made jocular remarks about envying Philip his perceived freedom but it was a freedom imposed upon him rather than one which he chose. His mind returned to that bizarre evening with Elizabeth and his fanciful speculation on a future for them. Elizabeth had alluded to future trysts being more meaningful than a snatched few hours together. Did she really mean it? Perhaps, after all, it had only been a few days of hedonism for her.

232

Oh well, it had been fun while it, briefly, lasted. Had he really expected more? Probably not but she'd interested him more than any woman he'd met for some time. He thought of the story about Darren Peters and Susan Pierce. It seemed Peters just hit on her after the TV show and she was his. That was a world removed from Philip's. Journalists were viewed as in cahoots with celebrities but Philip rarely experienced that. Then again, did he really crave inclusion in a circle of self-obsessed ego-maniacs? If it led to closer contact with women such as Susan Pierce...probably yes.

***

Since speaking to Michael Benson, Elizabeth had phoned her old school, St. Mark's, to ask about opportunities. The response was positive and she knew her old job was there for her if she wished. She told Geoff when he arrived home and, pleased by her restored enthusiasm, he said he would pull a few strings to get Michael an intern job at AV.

All of this coalesced in her mind and, despite her behaviour over the last week, she felt virtuous. The court case, itself the result of a gnawing discontent, led to her involvement with Philip which, in turn, allowed her to put her life into perspective. She was energised and Geoff's reaction to her news sealed it in her mind that whatever crisis she had undergone last week, it had been overcome. Geoff had played a significant role simply by not pressuring her and she wanted to acknowledge this without revealing too much of her recent thoughts and actions.

'Geoff, I'm sorry if I've been a bit weird or remote. It's just that I've had a lot on my mind but things are clearer now. You've been patient and I really appreciate that. I know you've had a lot to worry about at work and I haven't been much help there.'

'Nonsense, that was of my own making. Besides, you played the hostess to perfection the other night even if that didn't quite have the end product I wanted. I'm glad you want to return to teaching. You seemed happy in that role and you'll be a success at it again.'

'We'll see. What's the latest with Tom?'

'God knows. He had a day from hell. I went to see him this evening but he'd left early due to a domestic problem. In the pub last night, he got a call about a cousin who's in some sort of trouble. He doesn't talk much about his background but some of his relatives sound like real nutters. I'll ring and see if he's OK. We had a disagreement today, I don't want it to fester.'

'Yes, do that. Dinner will be ready very soon. Best to call him now.'

Tom's mobile was unanswered so Geoff dialled his home number where a worried-sounding Catherine explained that Tom was visiting his cousin in hospital. She outlined the circumstances and Geoff asked whether there was anything he could do.

'No, I'll let him know you called. He'll appreciate your concern, Geoff. The last couple of days haven't been easy for him.'

'True but he doesn't always make life easy for himself.'

'Well, that's Tom, I don't really want him to change. He thinks a lot of you, Geoff. Thanks for calling.'

Geoff gave a neutral answer, ended the call, and rang Tom's mobile again. Now at the hospital and waiting to see his cousin, Tom sounded apprehensive but glad of Geoff's concern during their exchange.

'This smells good,' Geoff said as Elizabeth placed a casserole dish on the table. 'You've become Superwoman...working for charity, fighting the inadequacies of state education and cooking a dinner like this. Impressive.'

'It was the house speciality in the restaurant we went to on that skiing holiday years ago – *poulet à la savoyarde*. Remember it?'

'Yes, I remember it and you cook it as well as any French chef,' Geoff smiled, nuzzling the back of Elizabeth's neck as he passed her.

'Food first,' Elizabeth said with a smile as Geoff picked up a bottle of red wine and uncorked it. 'Not trying to kill the moment but shall we watch the football on TV tonight? I'd like to see what that Darren Peters guy is like since he's been such a thorn in Tom's side.'

'How unlikely. Us watching football. OK, let's do that.'

***

John padded downstairs, barefoot, took the last three steps in one bound, filled the kettle and lit the gas hob. The lavatory flushed upstairs and he heard Laura as she walked around collecting clothes she'd haphazardly discarded earlier. He felt exhilarated and light-headed as he dropped teabags into two mugs. Just like old times, he thought. No, it was better than that, he appreciated Laura more now. He picked up the copy of *Rosebud* and leafed through it, missing Laura's light footfall as she descended the stairs. She smiled indulgently at John.

'A seminal piece of journalism which you couldn't wait to read again...am I right?' she asked.

'Yeah, something like that.' John allowed the magazine to fall open. He had been reading an article other than hers. 'Yours is OK as well.'

'A prophet hath no honour in his, or her, own country...it's so true,' she mock-sighed, affecting a wounded look.

'Or in her own kitchen, even.'

'Her *own* kitchen? Whatever are you suggesting, Mr. Hooper?'

'Oh, you know, a slip of the tongue,' he answered. The conversation returned to Laura's article but the elephant in the room was becoming ever more elephantine and was, by now, waving its trunk around.

'You said you thought it was too deferential, yes?' Laura asked.

'Well, the circumstances behind Guthrie's album are probably as interesting as the album itself but I guess you didn't have carte blanche to elaborate on that. Not criticising, just making a point.'

'Point taken. Er, that slip of the tongue a minute ago: did you really mean what you said or, I don't know, did you mean something else?'

'There's nothing I'd like more than being back with you, Laura. I really mean that and I wouldn't say it unless I thought you were thinking along the same lines but I guess you have more, er, baggage than me, so to speak.'

'"There's nothing I'd like more"…I so hoped you'd say something like that. Baggage, schmaggage. I don't wish ill on Robert but it's not working out and it isn't going to change. Meeting you again has really brought that home to me. He may not make it easy for me to sever things, may even cut up awkward. That doesn't really bother me but I wanted to tell you now rather than you discover later that I'm not worth the hassle.'

John nodded, extended his hand towards her left hand and gently squeezed her unadorned fourth finger.

'You're worth whatever hassle it takes, Laura.'

She rubbed her right eye, her voice faltered and she coughed to clear her throat. 'This time, we'll get it right,' she said.

'However you want to do this is fine by me and whatever you want me to do as part of it, ditto,' A mischievous smile flitted across John's face. 'OK, first test for you. Fancy watching football on TV tonight? That Darren Peters guy is playing and I'm curious enough about him to watch it.'

'Sure. Watching football on telly together, eh? I never envisaged that.'

'Life's full of surprises,' John smiled. 'God, this is like being back on that skiing holiday again; we've gone full circle, Laura.'

'We should have that dish they always served in the resort restaurant for dinner tonight. What was it? Chicken *à la Savoy,* something like that.'

'Something like that, yeah. We could invite Geoff and Elizabeth over so they can exchange doe-eyed glances as well.'

'One for another night, methinks. A takeaway is fine for me.'

***

Raymond McNulty first noticed the two men lurking furtively when he returned from buying groceries at the local shop. Having dropped Kieran Bradley close to a tube station, he spent the next two hours sending his CV to agencies and e-mailing former colleagues. Raymond's IT career was interrupted in 2007 when his devotion to a hectic nocturnal lifestyle cost him a job which he'd enjoyed.

There followed a period of depression and insularity which culminated in a descent into petty crime, paranoia and accommodation in a fetid squat. It was there that Michael Doherty encountered him and, touched by the young man's helplessness and their shared Northern Irish background, offered Raymond a chance to make some money, a place to stay and gradually weaned him back towards a more normal life.

Raymond's technology skills helped Doherty and his pragmatism allowed him to overlook the less savoury aspects of Doherty's business dealings. Now mentally robust enough to return to a conventional job, he was elated by the response to his e-mails having already received two interview invitations. He was grateful for Doherty's help but knew altruism had little to do with it. It was, now, time to strike out on his own again.

He savoured the levity, the sense of a weight lifted from his shoulders although this was compromised by the two men dressed in nondescript clothes, clutching magazines and making calls on their mobiles. He walked towards them for a closer look, they walked away but returned minutes later. Unsettled by this so soon after he thought he'd been followed in his car, he watched through an upstairs window as one of the men pointed towards the house next door and then his. A tall, narrow, wrought-iron gate led to the side-entrance of the house next door and he was astonished to see the two men approach and peer through it.

Were these the most inept burglars in existence? Raymond loudly opened the window and the men scurried away again. Soon they returned and displayed an interest in a street light. Were they electricians of a very nervous disposition? No, they were up to something more covert. Again, they walked away, again they returned, this time wearing yellow high-visibility jackets. Were they trying to look like maintenance men? And why the interest in these two houses? Raymond rang Doherty who shared his concerns and said that he'd be there within half-an-hour.

Raymond returned to the window but the men had vanished and when he walked up and down the road, there was no sign of them. Concerned for his neighbours, the Hudsons, he decided to check their safety. Mrs. Hudson, a lecturer, was often at home while her husband worked in the West End. She answered the door distractedly although her face softened when she saw Raymond.

'Hi, Mrs. Hudson. I just wanted to see if you're OK. Two men were hanging around earlier, so they were. They were looking at your house.'

She sighed and nodded. 'Thanks, Raymond, but it's nothing to worry about. My garden has a link to a rock musician and a magazine article published today alluded to this without actually giving the address. Somebody who read the article seems to have identified the garden and a few people trekked over here in the hope of seeing it for themselves.'

'Oh, I see. Who's the musician?'

'An American called Fraser Guthrie. Have you heard of him?'

'Yeah. I like Guthrie, he's a bit like Bruce Springsteen or what Springsteen could've been had he any talent or song-writing ability.'

'I like that,' she said, laughing. 'Anyway, a few Guthrie fans have tried to see the garden. The first one asked me directly and I refused. Since then, I've had a guy wanting to read a meter and two claiming to be electricians checking a fault. I told them to clear off and if you get any similar requests, I suggest you do the same. I expect they'll give up soon enough.'

'That explains it. Thanks, I'll do as you say if anyone turns up at my door. Mind how you go.'

Raymond returned home, whistling a guitar riff from one of Guthrie's songs, happy with the explanation for the men's presence. He walked to an upstairs room which overlooked the Hudson's garden and tried to gauge the connection with Fraser Guthrie. No answers were evident in the gloomy light. Michael Doherty arrived and was pleased when Raymond relayed Mrs. Hudson's tale and even more pleased when Raymond confirmed that he'd taken Kieran to a tube station.

The doorbell rang and Raymond greeted two casually dressed men; one a wiry figure, the other heftier, both with serious expressions.

'Yes?' Raymond asked as he tried to guess which guise these two would try after the failure of the meter-reader and electrician ruses.

'I'm Detective Sergeant McCulloch, this is D.S. Norton and.....'

'Detectives! You jokers are priceless. Away to fuck, the pair of you!'

Raymond slammed the door on the startled pair. They looked at each other in disbelief as Norton called through to the station for back-up. He was told a car was close by and would be with them soon.

'Very odd, we hadn't even asked about Doherty. You're sure that's his car?' Norton asked as he nodded towards a Volvo parked nearby.

'Yep, that's definitely his car. He spends a lot of time here although it's not his main residence, uses it as an office, apparently. Ah, back-up's here already. Right, let's find out what Doherty's up to.' The police car halted and two officers joined McCulloch and Norton.

'We want to talk to a Michael Doherty,' McCulloch briefed the new arrivals. 'A non-local, name of Kieran Bradley was shot earlier today and is in hospital. We have reliable information that he was at Doherty's home last night. Bradley's no saint, has history with Doherty and either left or escaped from Doherty's house. Bradley met someone he didn't wish to see – this we know from a call made to his cousin – and was shot close to Stockwell. From what we know of Doherty, it doesn't sound like something he'd do but we can't be sure. I want to see what he knows and whether someone can vouch for his whereabouts today. Got that? Good. Now, one of you wait outside in case anything untoward happens.'

The door was opened by Michael Doherty who confirmed his identity and allowed the police inside. Doherty was surprised by the news of Kieran and provided an account of Kieran's visit and overnight stay at the house, omitting the less savoury aspects of the evening. Raymond verified that Kieran had been driven to Stockwell tube station earlier that morning and he hadn't seen or heard from him since. McCulloch noticed Raymond's nervous confirmation of this and turned his unflinching gaze on him as he asked why he'd slammed the door shut earlier.

'Is there something you're hiding, Raymond?' the detective asked and hushed Doherty when he tried to intervene. 'I asked Raymond, not you.'

'No, I've nothing to hide. N-nothing,' Raymond stuttered.

'Maybe you'd like a solicitor, Raymond. Of course, we'd have to take you to the station first.'

'I did nothing. I thought youse were pretending to be coppers.'

'Can you tell me where you were early this afternoon, Raymond?'

'Look, leave him alone,' Doherty said. 'You're pressuring him.'

McCulloch swung around to Doherty. 'OK, so how about you provide me with your whereabouts this afternoon then?'

'Oh, that's easy. I attended meetings and was in company all the time. I can give you the names of people who'll confirm that and the lady next door can vouch for Raymond's presence here.'

'Yes, that's right,' shouted Raymond. 'She'll also tell you why I doubted you when you said you were police.'

McCulloch's mobile phone rang and he nodded to Norton when he saw the caller ID. 'The constable at the hospital,' he said quietly.

'DS McCulloch here...He's not what? Sorry, bad line...Oh, I see. Not likely, you say...Hmm...Who?...Oh, of course. Tom is his name, by the way...I see...Yes, that's not good at all. OK, thanks, let me know if anything changes...Sure, bye.'

McCulloch nodded gravely to Norton's questioning gaze and saw the concern on the faces of Doherty and Raymond.

'That was about Kieran, wasn't it?' Doherty asked. 'Is he OK?'

***

Susan stared at her reflection in the mirror and sighed. Too much make-up...maybe she wasn't cut out for a life lived in the public eye. Having featured in the media glare for a few years, she should be accustomed to it but this was different – being the recipient of ridicule and reproach wasn't pleasant. Someone like Darren appeared oblivious to it but she had no desire to morph into a female Darren Peters.

She was grateful to Debbie Cavendish who'd called her and insisted that they meet for a drink. Debbie was a member of Dolly Mix, the one

Susan was closest to or, more accurately, least distant from. Debbie had seen Susan's press coverage and wished to show solidarity although her choice of venue – the Bang-Bang Club, a Soho bar regularly frequented by journalists and paparazzi – may not have been the wisest choice. Her reasoning, however, convinced Susan.

'So what are you going to do? Sulk at home and give in to the likes of Davinia or walk tall and show them you couldn't care less?'

Swayed by this logic, Susan agreed and opted for a bold approach. She swept her hair up, put on bright red lipstick and a figure-hugging dress and then thought she should maybe tone it down a bit. No, to hell with it, she'd cut a swath through the crowd and not worry about the reaction.

The harsh sound of the buzzer indicated that her taxi had arrived so she picked up her coat and bag and left the apartment. In the cab, Susan expected some remark from her driver but his conversation concerned the weather. She relaxed until he switched on the radio where a sardonic commentator was previewing the evening's football.

'And, of course, eyes will be focused on Wallington's main creative source although how focused his own eyes will be after recent events is unsure. The teams are doing their pre-match warm-up out on the pitch and I can see the purple bruising around Darren Peters' right eye.'

'What's the mood like among the Rovers' crowd, Alan?' the studio presenter asked. 'Towards Peters, that is.'

'I think they're behind him, Simon. He's a hero around here and I can't see too many of the Rovers' faithful having issues with him spending quality time with Susan...'

'I'll just stop you there, Alan. We'll be back in time for the kick-off.'

Susan saw the driver's smile reflected in the rear-view mirror.

'Had a good day, love?' he asked.

Susan frowned and gave a non-committal answer. The driver took the hint and the remainder of the journey passed in silence. Taxis queued outside The Bang-Bang Club - testimony to its popularity - as Susan swept past the doorman whose curt nod and polite "Good evening, Miss Pierce, it's good to see you again," put her at ease.

The Bang-Bang Club, spread across four floors in one of Soho's quieter streets, had been through many incarnations before settling in its current niche as a place to be seen for London's young glitterati. The ground floor was, theoretically, open to anybody although one's presence there was deemed the death-knell to one's social aspirations.

Entry to the other floors was subject to subtle gradations requiring approval from doormen with a practiced eye for celebrity recognition. If in doubt, a discreet referral to the arbitration of a small cabal of the bar's inner circle decided whether admittance was granted. To be turned away was a mortal blow to the egos of minor celebrities and many refrained from attending lest this fate befall them. The *décor* throughout was subdued apart from the opulent third floor where a theme of decadence meant it was known as the Bordello Room.

One area where the Bang-Bang Club considered itself unique was in the deference shown to clientele by its staff. The door men, or butlers in the parlance of the club, were expected to speak in the style of servants to the gentry of bygone years. It was deemed an endearing eccentricity of the club and never ceased to amuse those among its clientele who hailed from what such gentry would view as the wrong side of the tracks. Susan took the lift to the second floor and was greeted by a courteous half-bow from a young man whose frame was barely contained by a tuxedo.

'Good evening, Miss Pierce. Miss Cavendish awaits you. I do hope you have a pleasant evening.'

As Susan's eyes adjusted to the muted lights, she saw Debbie wave enthusiastically from the far side of the horseshoe-shaped bar.

'Susan, my God, look at you!' Debbie exclaimed. 'You look amazing. I love the dress, it's so you.'

'Good to see you, Debbie. You look well too,' Susan said, grateful for the dim lighting which modified the glare from Debbie's luminous pink shirt. Debbie, petite, effervescent and prone to gushing in a shrill voice about whatever was under discussion, had been Susan's friend since their schooldays. Her more ill-advised liaisons were often the subject of tearful late-night phone calls but, on this occasion, it seemed that Debbie would be the advisor as she ordered drinks and rested a hand on Susan's arm.

'So, how bad has it been?' Debbie asked, wide-eyed.

'I won't pretend not to know what you're talking about but, you know, you just have to rise above speculation.....even when it's, er, not *just* speculation.'

'You go, girl!' Debbie punched the air. 'But you've got so much going on...TV on Saturday, a new manager and a new name too. Like, wow!'

'I've had a rethink on the name. I'm not so sure. It was something me and Laurence Tolliver conjured up over a few drinks but I think I'll drop it.'

'Laurence, he's got a reputation, hasn't he?' Debbie lowered her voice. 'What's he like? Has he, you know, tried anything?'

'Oh, Laurence is a gentleman and a good manager. He's enthusiastic, fun and has great ideas. We discuss music and art and politics, everything. He's opened my eyes to a whole new world.'

'Wow,' Debbie said with less conviction. 'Good for you. And Darren? What's happening there?'

'It was a one-off, shouldn't have happened. OK, he's good-looking and has a roguish charm but I'm not into footballers, that shallow world. I'm beyond that. Hey, enough about me, tell me what you're up to.'

'I split with Josh from BoyzBoyzBoyz, not so much split as haven't seen him again after a couple of nights. Thing is, people see me as the bubbly girl, up for anything, but that's not really me. I'm deeper than that.'

'Of course,' Susan replied, her turn to sound doubtful. 'So we're both overcoming people's ideas about us. We're the ones laughing, huh?'

'Yeah, go us! Uh-oh, look who's arrived.'

They glanced towards the bar where the barman welcomed Daphne Hobson, or Davinia Hotchick, and discreetly nodded towards the corner where Debbie and Susan sat. A smile crept across Davinia's face as the barman prepared her drink and said something which made her throw her head back and laugh. Susan downed her drink and strode to the bar.

'Susan, don't do any...' Debbie's voice trailed off.

The barman turned to Susan who performed a showy double-take when she saw Davinia at the bar. Susan was beaten to the opening salvo.

'Susan, can I get you a drink? Bygones and all that.'

'What? From *you*? I didn't realise they served arsenic here.'

'Come on, Susan, we're both in the entertainment business. You need me as much as I do you.'

'Bollocks I do,' Susan snorted. 'I'm a creative musician, you're a sleazy, tittle-tattle, tabloid hack.'

Debbie, sensing confrontation as the chatter around the room died, walked briskly towards Susan.

'You're up there with Patti Smith, Kate Bush or Joni Mitchell among the great female singer-songwriters, I agree but they tend not to hang out with people like Darren Peters,' Davinia sneered. 'It's good, though, to see that you're not taking the media attention sitting down. Then again, I hear you like taking it standing up.'

'You smarmy bitch,' Susan snarled and threw her vodka and tonic at Davinia. In the shocked silence, Susan politely turned to the barman. 'Can I have another V&T, please and whatever Miss Hobson would like.'

The barman hesitated as Debbie reached the bar. 'Susan, what the hell are you doing?' she implored. 'Let's go before things get even worse.'

'Why? I'd like to have a chat with Davinia here, allow her to justify herself. Don't worry, Debbie, I won't do anything silly.'

'Probably too late for that,' Davinia drawled. 'I respect your right to free and open discussion but you shouldn't throw a drink at a newspaper columnist unless you have a real grievance...which I don't think you have, a real grievance, that is.'

Davinia's valedictory toss of her head was too much for Susan who picked up the nearest drink to hand – Debbie's glass of Bailey's.

'Susan, don't, don't!' Debbie's lunge towards Susan distracted her and the drink's trajectory reached Debbie instead.

'Oh God, I'm sorry Debbie.' Susan noticed the disapproving looks, the flashes from camera phones and the young, svelte woman wearing a Bang-Bang Club t-shirt walking towards her.

'I'm sorry, Miss Pierce, but I have to ask you to leave,' the woman said quietly and turned to Davinia who smiled at Susan's discomfort. 'Can we offer any facilities to you, Miss Hotch..., er, Miss Hobson?'

'I just need wi-fi connectivity, thanks. Reluctant as I am to do so, I'm afraid it's incumbent upon me to refer to this incident in my next column.' Davinia shrugged in an I-have-no-choice gesture.

'Oh, spare me that crap. I'm sorry I even wasted a drink on you. I'm sure you'll write another story about me but isn't that a sorry way to make a living?' Susan looked over Debbie's shoulder and raised her voice. 'You can go back to your drinks now, everybody. Nothing to see here, let's all...'

'Susan, pack it in, you're making it worse for yourself,' Debbie whispered fiercely as she dabbed away the thick, creamy liqueur from her face. Susan struggled to avoid laughing at the bizarre spectacle, conscious that doing so would result in more photographs being taken. She meekly allowed Debbie to steer her to the exit where a doorman opened the lift.

'I trust this unfortunate incident didn't detract from your evening at the Bang-Bang Club, Miss Pierce, Miss Cavendish,' he said in an unctuous tone, escorting them to the main door as the lift arrived at the ground floor. 'Good evening, we hope you return soon.'

***

A ripple of applause died, the band left the stage and most of the crowd retreated or returned to the bar. Roadies cleared the stage as a small knot of people, a significant portion of Squirrel Nutkin's entire fan base, engaged in animated conversation. Almost everyone else present, Laurence Tolliver included, attempted to erase Squirrel Nutkin from their memory.

'Dearie me, that was dreadful,' he sighed to his friend Dominic Tate as they stood at the bar. 'You don't suppose there's a record company out there actually encouraging them, do you?'

'Your new buddies at Interstellar won't be snapping up Squirrel Nutkin, then? I guess the warning was there in that twee band name.'

'Fancy being a record label A&R man, leaving here now to catch another Squirrel Nutkin at some other venue.' Laurence shook his head in sympathy with the plight of any such person.

'It's not all glamour in the music business, is it?' Dominic mused. 'Tell me, how are you finding it? You never did explain what possessed you to try it from the sharp end.'

Dominic was a long-standing friend of Laurence who sometimes availed of the opportunity to be Laurence's "+1" on guest lists. Theirs was a friendship with the unlikely twist that Dominic's wife, Cressida, had once been Mrs. Tolliver. After a protracted break-up and a wrangle over custody of their son, Patrick, the desire to provide Patrick with a stable upbringing brought a cessation of hostilities. So much so that it was now the custom for Cressida, Patrick, Dominic, Laurence and whoever was Laurence's partner at the time to spend Christmas Day together...a very modern, very nuclear family as Laurence described it.

'It's interesting. I've always had my own theories about music moguls and it's partly to test these that I'm doing it. Susan has a good voice and her music taste is infinitely better than you'd expect from somebody who was part of that awful Dolly Mix group,' Laurence said.

'Her looks had nothing to do with it, I suppose?'

'She's certainly not unattractive, I'll grant you that...although her latest consort makes one question her judgement. Mind you, a middle-aged music hack with receding hair and a modest income may not have the wherewithal to compete with a young, athletic, millionaire footballer. Were she to view me favourably, I daresay I'd succumb...she's a sweet girl, eager to learn and she talks about art and the like with enthusiasm but not much knowledge. I don't suppose you'd see her as the type to have a Gary Hume original hanging in her apartment?'

'You're kidding! Good God, how did that happen? By the way, why were you at her flat? Anything to declare, old boy?'

'A song-writing workshop, you could call it. She frowned, chewed her pencil, looked endearing and wrote lines which need some work, a lot of work...but it's a start.'

'Say no more, Laurence, I get the picture,' Dominic looked towards the stage where the road crew tuned guitars and sellotaped set lists to the floor. 'What are the next lot like?'

'Lacanian Theory? Better than Squirrel Nutkin, it goes without saying. Let's just say that Jacques Lacan contributed more to linguistics than these chaps. I reviewed their debut album last year and they took umbrage with my use of Lacan's ideas to analyse their lyrics. I think they possibly missed the irony and may not, after all, be scholars of psychoanalysis. Not that there's any reason why they should be but if you choose a name like that, you should at least grasp the rudiments of its derivation.'

'If Lacan's theories can't be condensed to 140 words on Twitter, it's beyond today's youth. God, we sound like grumpy old men.'

'Being a grumpy old man is something I aspire to. Let's fortify ourselves with more alcohol, I think we'll need it. Same again?'

'Yes, please. I have to visit the loo, back in a minute.' Dominic walked towards the public bar, the better to avoid a queue. As he returned, he watched the TV screen for a few moments and rejoined Laurence. 'It looks like your protégé's most recent squeeze is having a pretty bad night.'

***

'One Kelly Spencer, there is only one Kelly Spencer, one Kelly Spencer,' sung to the tune of *Guantanamera* in Teutonic accents rang around Wallington Rovers' stadium. It startled Darren Peters as he tried to control a pass from Rovers' midfielder, Sean Hayes. The momentary hesitation caused him to miss the opportunity and most of the crowd groaned while the Bayern Munich fans cheered mockingly. Peters gestured his disapproval by extending his middle finger to them; their raucous cheers increased. Darren turned and caught a disapproving glare from Dave MacKinnon who jabbed an index finger against his temple.

'Focus, Daz, focus,' he yelled.

'Yeah, they're taking the piss, though. Singing in English and all,' Peters shouted back as Michael Schulz, the Munich captain, jogged past.

'I think the words may not mean much to you in German, my friend,' Schulz said amiably. 'It's just our famous German sense of humour.'

'Do one, Kraut,' Darren snarled. There was a pause as a player received treatment for an injury. After a frustrating evening for Wallington, it was still 0-0. Time was running out and at least one goal was needed for Rovers to stay in the competition. During the lull in play, the Munich fans started an improvised song, this time in German, which included Peters' name. Darren saw a Munich player smile as he heard it.

'Andy!' he called out to Andreas Klein, Rovers' German-born centre-forward. 'What are they singing about now?'

'They're, er, questioning your manhood because you get a black eye from a lady, something like that. Darren, ignore it, concentrate.'

The Wallington Rovers' fans picked up the taunting chants about Darren and retorted with "Two world wars and one World Cup". The German fans sarcastically applauded the rendition of this clichéd response and replied with "Three World Cups and a stable economy" in English. Paul Nevin, positioned close to Darren, nodded approvingly.

'Good one. Come on, Daz, we're off again. Get your game face on.'

But Darren was distracted, he was susceptible to ridicule. Aware that he was being mocked in two different languages, he wanted to lash out in response. Play restarted, the ball was passed to Michael Schulz who Darren pursued and brought crashing to the turf with a crude tackle.

'Daz, you idiot, you took the bait,' Paul Nevin yelled as Darren protested his innocence to the referee.

'I went for the ball, ref. I just mistimed it is all. Aww, you can't book me for that,' he groaned as the referee waved a yellow card and motioned him away. Darren fumed and tried to clear his head of the turbulence coursing through it. He heard a fresh taunt from the Bavarian supporters and this time, he ignored it. He needed to stay out of the action for a minute to regain his composure but was denied this respite.

Play resumed. The free-kick was cleared and Noël Rotane reached the ball before his marker. Gesturing to Darren to start running, Rotane took a few steps forward and his precise pass bisected two back-tracking Munich players. The ball skidded along the wet pitch and then slowed about 15 yards ahead of Darren as he sprinted towards it, flicked it past the last defender and steadied himself as the goalkeeper advanced towards him. Darren shimmied, the goalkeeper dived despairingly and Darren was past him, the unguarded goal yawning invitingly in front of him. In a moment of hubris, he was already considering his goal celebration as he nonchalantly side-footed the ball towards the net.

Darren turned away as a guttural roar cut through the damp night air but froze when he heard gasps and swivelled around to see Johnny Siebers, Munich's speedy Dutch full-back, slide towards the ball and flick it away with his left foot just before it rolled over the line into the net. Darren stood, head in hands and heard screams of abuse from the crowd.

He turned to Rotane, held his hands up in contrition and glanced at Larry Downing who stood with his head thrown back, arms raised towards the skies. Darren, eyes downcast, jogged back to his position, his mind a blank. He looked at the huge screen positioned in a corner of the stadium and saw the seconds ticking away...7:14, 7:13, 7:12. Rovers had less than ten minutes to get the two goals they needed. His peripheral vision saw a fist waved in his direction from the crowd. Christ, it wasn't his fault alone, others had missed chances too. Right, he'd show the ungrateful plebs.

Pumping his arms, he yelled encouragement towards his team-mates and sought a chance to get involved. It soon came as he raced a Munich player towards the ball, lunged at it and almost in slow-motion, realised his foot would slam into his opponent's shin rather than the ball. The referee had little option but to caution him again and send him off. Darren slumped back on the wet turf, too angry with himself to plead for clemency. He rose to his feet and his vision almost blurred as he saw the yellow card being raised, immediately followed by a red one. Wearily, he trudged away, contempt and derision raining down from the stands.

**

In an echoing hospital corridor, another figure trudged along wearily. Tom Brady, pale-faced and stunned, tried to convince himself he wasn't to blame for Kieran Bradley's death. He'd merely tried to help his cousin by visiting Doherty's house; since then, Kieran had left there and even rang Tom. Surely, that wasn't the action of someone who held Tom culpable for whatever had befallen him and it wasn't as if Tom had held the gun which shot Kieran.

Kieran hadn't recovered; a blood clot coagulated with such rapidity that the surgeons were powerless to save him. He was now dead and a sombre hospital orderly ushered people away from the operating theatre. Fiona was en route to the hospital on the underground unaware of the news which awaited her.

Tom decided that the best thing to do was to wait in the lobby to greet her when she arrived. It was preferable she hear the news from him rather than hospital staff. Before he reached the lobby, he called Catherine and relayed the news in a wracked voice. He declined her offer to collect him from the hospital on the basis that the girls needed her at home. Catherine emphasised that he wasn't to blame. He knew she was right but his mind wasn't working rationally.

'Why did I go to that bastard's house? Why?' he wailed.

'Out of concern for Kieran. None of this is your fault, we know that.'

Catherine continued talking in a reassuring voice but Tom barely heard. He just wanted the anger and guilt to dissipate. Tom had learned vital lessons over the last few days. His vanity and pride had been pricked badly but what did that matter against Kieran Bradley lying dead? Or against his own wife and daughters at home waiting his return, his wife spooked by a phone call, a phone call possibly from Kieran's killers? He must revalue what was really important in life and not obsess over slights and, frankly, inconsequential power struggles. It was time for a change.

He ended the call and walked through to the lobby to start his vigil. Glad that people were bustling around the marble hall, he latched on to a conversation between two orderlies, struggling to understand it.

'Open goal, the flash git screwed it up and then he goes and gets sent off. I don't like him, never have. A show-off, can't be relied upon.'

'Don't suppose he's all that bothered anyway. Paid a fortune, chasing women all the time and acting like a prat. Tosser.'

Tom looked up as the door revolved but it was a young couple visiting a patient. The wait for Fiona was excruciating, if only he could do something. Should he call her? No, that wouldn't help. Another arrival. A young man, familiar looking to Tom, walked in hesitantly, shooting darting glances in all directions. He walked to the reception desk and spoke in a low voice to an attendant who checked a list and leaned forward, patting the young man's arm. The visitor reeled back and mumbled a response in a Northern Irish accent. It was then that Tom recognised the visitor – the Ramones' fan from Michael Doherty's house.

He jumped to his feet and rushed after Raymond McNulty just as Fiona Bradley pushed her way through the revolving door into the lobby.

'Fiona,' Tom said quietly and she turned towards him.

'Tom! What are you doing down here? How's Kieran? Where can I find him?' The flurry of questions eased as she took in Tom's pale complexion. 'Tom, is he OK? Tom, Tom, say something.'

Tom held Fiona's arm and steered her away towards the nearest corridor. As he did so, he passed by a television screen where, amid a scrum of people, an irate-looking Darren Peters was gesticulating and pointing towards a man wearing a suit.

***

The cause of Darren's anger was Tony Jeffries. Jack Watson had promised Tony an interview with Darren after the game as recompense for his confinement. Jeffries insisted that Peters honour this although Jack argued that Darren wouldn't be in the mood having watched the remaining minutes of the game on a television set in the dressing room. The rest of the team returned and within minutes, accusations over where the blame lay for Rovers' failure were voiced. Darren showed remorse for his lack of self-control but refused to accept sole responsibility and stormed out, almost colliding with Jeffries and Watson. A camera crew waiting to speak to Larry Downing was on hand to capture the scene as Darren ranted semi-coherently at the bemused Jeffries.

'Yeah. Hounding Kelly and all, you've got a nerve you have. You're getting nothing from me, not a word, mate. Following me around, what are you after, eh? I ain't talking to someone like you,' Darren yelled at Jeffries as Watson and club officials tried to restrain him. 'Let me go, I want to talk to him face-to-face and tell him I ain't saying a word to him.'

In the departure lounge at Birmingham Airport, Danny Gallagher watched the chaos on a large flat-screen television as he waited to board a flight to Belfast. Michael Doherty's call had provided an address for Kieran Bradley which was passed to two henchmen in London. Danny took the first flight to Birmingham, attended two meetings and drove to London with an associate. When one of the henchmen fired the shots at Kieran Bradley, the three fled the scene and Danny returned to Birmingham to meet other people who would confirm his presence should an alibi be required. Gallagher felt at ease, regretting only the fact that Bradley hadn't been finished off – the three had panicked when the silencer malfunctioned

– but he was certain that Bradley, if he survived, wouldn't name his assailer for fear of repercussions. In any case, witnesses could corroborate that he'd been in Birmingham. Gallagher leaned forward and commented on Peters' behaviour to the man next to him. The announcement to board the Belfast flight was made over the tannoy.

At King's College Hospital, Greg McCulloch stood awkwardly a few yards away from a sobbing Fiona Bradley as she clung to Tom Brady. The detective, on hearing of Kieran Bradley's worsening condition, rushed to the hospital in the hope that he might be able to speak to the wounded man. By the time he got there, Bradley had lost his survival battle and McCulloch now watched the stunned couple in front of him. Eager not to intrude on their grief, he glanced up at a muted television screen which showed a group of men pointing and gesticulating while a shocked presenter watched open-mouthed.

Dot Benson leaned on the banister and called upstairs to Michael who was in his bedroom looking out of the window at the rain-slicked streets of the Shillingtree Estate. He heard his mother and knew she was surprised he had not watched the football on television, instead opting to spend two hours studying. Now, finished for the evening, he turned to walk down the stairs of their cramped house. Dot smiled benignly at her son, ruffled his hair and asked him to join her for some tea and biscuits. Michael nodded his acceptance and draped himself over the armchair in the living room. He switched the TV to the station showing the evening's football and watched in amazement as an enraged Darren Peters flailed his arms wildly at a placid, besuited man a few feet away.

The lights dimmed and a cheer rose from the rapidly filling floor of the small venue but Laurence Tolliver and Dominic Tate were transfixed by the images on the television screen where Darren Peters shook himself free of the three men who attempted to placate him and lunged in the direction of an astonished man a few feet away. The attempted punch missed its intended target and Darren's fist hit the wall of the corridor. The view of Peters was replaced by one of a ceiling as the TV cameraman took evasive action. Laurence and Dominic shook their heads in disbelief before turning to the room where Lacanian Theory bounded on to the stage.

Debbie and Susan ran into a bar a short distance away from the Bang-Bang Club with the dual purpose of evading the rain and resuming their conversation. Susan insisted there was little point in dwelling on the altercation with the gossip columnist: instead, they should salvage something from the evening. One half of the bar was crowded with a predominantly male clientele watching football on a large television screen. The two women were pleased as it afforded them a choice of seating and having selected a banquette, Susan walked to the bar to get drinks. A collective cry of surprise from the television viewers made Susan crane her neck to see the source of the commotion. To her amazement, she watched as Darren Peters swung a punch at somebody who was off-camera and then the picture dizzily swung around before resettling on an image of Peters being restrained by two men and a policeman. At least that will keep *me* off the front pages tomorrow, she thought.

Fifty yards away, in the reception area of the Bang-Bang Club, Davinia Hotchick grinned as she peered at a television and saw Darren Peters escorted by a policeman away from a group of bewildered men. Davinia had two photos, surreptitiously snapped, on her mobile phone of Susan Pierce being escorted out of the Bang-Bang Club. Now, it seemed that her most recent lover was enduring a not dissimilar fate. Davinia left the club and hailed a taxi to *The Universe*'s offices. The front page of tomorrow's paper could be rejigged to show images of the two secret lovers being separately led away from the scenes of their disgrace. Perfect!

Robert Armitage stared at his mobile phone willing it to ring. The kitchen of the Armitage house was cold, something which suited his mood or, at least, matched it. His finger had hovered over the "call" button of his mobile phone on three separate occasions but each time, a sense of pride prevented him from calling Laura. No, it wasn't pride. It was the dread of being told by his wife that she had no wish to speak with him. He wanted her to ring and, at least, tell him where she was. He considered doing something drastic such as driving around to Tolliver's house to confront him. Surely that's where she was, music had been playing in the background when he spoke to Laura earlier. But such a confrontation would just make him seem ridiculous and leave Laura even further estranged. He switched on the TV as a distraction and watched the odd spectacle of that footballer who was constantly in the news arguing vehemently with a policeman.

As Robert sat disconsolately in the kitchen of Laura's house, miles away Laura lounged on a sofa, her head resting on John's shoulder as she dozed. John, unwilling to disrupt her, remained stationary as he watched television. Laura had drifted off to sleep during the football and John savoured the loose strands of her hair as they tickled his nose. It itched but it itched pleasantly and he'd entered a reverie of his own when the excited voice of the football commentator caught his attention. Darren Peters had been sent off during the televised game and now appeared to be in some sort of meltdown as he confronted a policeman live on television. John nudged Laura awake, she wouldn't want to miss seeing this – it was better than football any day.

At 28, Russell Road, Elizabeth Harris switched off the television and slowly shook her head. So this was the sort of person held up as a role model for young people. OK, Peters came from humble origins, had presumably worked hard to hone his football talents and was now rewarded by a huge salary and the adulation of thousands but what a depressing spectacle it made to see him ranting at a journalist and a policeman. Geoff chuckled at the sight which confirmed many of his opinions about modern day footballers but Elizabeth was appalled. She was, now, even more determined to return to teaching; she could encourage loftier ambitions in young minds than a desire to be a sportsman. She smiled at Geoff. Maybe she could instil such ideas in the mind of a child of their own one day.

Just down the road, Philip Anderson gazed out of a window as the rain swept across his view of Russell Road. Television images were reflected in the window from the set behind him where Darren Peters had calmed sufficiently to leave the corridor accompanied by a policeman and a discussion was taking place in a studio between two animated football pundits. Philip ignored the screen as he watched puddles form in the street outside. The weathermen were right and rain was falling all over London and beyond. It was falling at Wallington Rovers' stadium as evidenced by the backdrop beyond the studio window where it glistened, illuminated by floodlights. It was falling outside King's College Hospital where a distraught woman was helped into a police car by an apologetic detective who said that he just needed to speak to her for a few minutes. Beyond London, it was falling at Birmingham Airport as the late-night flight to Belfast taxied down the runway. Philip turned away and drew the curtain to further insulate the house against the chilly dampness as the rain turned to sleet.

ABOUT THE AUTHOR

Andrew Byrne was born in Wexford, Ireland in 1963. He attended University College Dublin, moved to London in the mid-1980s, spent more than 20 years working in banking and doesn't believe that he was in any way responsible for the problems which have befallen that profession. He now lives in North London with his wife. *Some Place South of Perfect* is his first novel.

Printed in Great Britain
by Amazon.co.uk, Ltd.,
Marston Gate.